CURSED

A Novel

Avenol Franco

Cursed is a work of fiction. The people, events and locales that figure
in the narrative, people, names, characters, places and incidents are
the product of the author imagination or are used fictitiously.

2018 - CURSED – Published by La Finca Films/Books
Copyright 2008 by Avenol Franco
All rights reserved.
Published in the United States by La Finca
Library of Congress Cataloging- in – Publication Data
2019905650
Franco, Avenol
CURSED: a novel / Avenol Franco

ISBN (Print): 978-1-54397-084-5
ISBN (eBook): 978-1-54397-085-2

Printed in the United States of America

Isn't there anything in your life worth
losing everything for?
Watch me.....
Alex!

E – Books by Author
The Report Card
Casanova 'downsized'
Romancing Isadora

Screenplays
ESCAPE – A thriller
TO CATCH THE WOLF – A thriller
BORDER CONFLICT – A comedy
TRIUMVIRATE – A Romantic- Drama

Play/Sitcom
THE LAND OF OPPORTUNITY

TO MY SON – NOLIN

And

DULCINEA

TABLE OF CONTENTS

EL BRUJO

"Alex?"

"Hey Roberta!"

"I met a Brujo yesterday and he talked about you."

"What were you doing with a Brujo?" I asked her.

"I have been waiting for the proper time to call you, but I couldn't wait any longer. When are you coming to Miami again?"

"Soon, in a week or so. Why?"

"You won't believe what happened."

"Ok. Tell me."

"I had a fascinating encounter with a Brujo yesterday afternoon. I visited him with my friend Evelyn; you don't know her; she's a gringo like me. She has been consulting this man, for a year or two, trying to establish a connection with her dead husband. You know, one of those séance sessions. I know it is silly but I'm not the one to tell her that."

"Did he tell you anything you didn't already know?"

"Wait! Let me finish. Evelyn was the one looking for advice. But inexplicably, right in the middle of the session, your name came up out of nowhere."

"How could that be?" I said somewhat amused by the revelation. "You won't believe this, but this Brujo pointed his finger at me and said 'your friend is in trouble. He's going to lose everything and needs help.' I looked at him and asked myself, who the hell is this guy to talk about my friends?

Nevertheless, I asked him what friend he was talking about. That is when he said your full name. Faust! Alejandro? I was transfixed."

"Roberta my dear, you met this Brujo in the afternoon and dreamed of him saying my name during a nightmare last night."

"No sir. I not only heard him say your name, but Evelyn did too. She couldn't believe it either. He not only mentioned your name but said you're going to lose everything. That's an ominous warning. Then he asked me if I had anything on me that was yours, a gift of some sort you had given me. I said yes. You know I use the Parker pen you gave me. Remember? You broke up with someone and you gave me the pen she had given you.... remember?"

"Yes, I do."

"Well, I looked at Evelyn and she said, 'of course, give it to him.' He held it for ten seconds, believe me, ten seconds and said, 'Yes, it is him.' I couldn't believe it."

"Just like that?" I asked her.

"Just like that. What kind of powers does this man have to make that kind of connection, I don't know. Then he went on and told us that a man whose name he didn't remember, but to me sounded a lot like André, had visited and asked him to do a job on somebody; you know, one of those Santeria curses. He said he explained to André — I'm sure it was him — that he needed a different kind of a Santeria priest. He called Brujos priests."

"You mean there are specialists in brujeria as there are in medicine?" I said laughing.

"Don't laugh! The man was serious. He told us he had arranged a session for André to meet a Babalao who, he explained to us, is the one who does that kind of job.... you know. They call it a job. He didn't say much more, but added that the curse could be reversed and asked me to tell you. When are you coming to Miami again?"

"As a matter of fact I have a flight scheduled for Monday, a week from today."

"Great," Roberta said. "I'll set up an appointment for Tuesday next week."

"Roberta, you haven't asked me if I want to see this Brujo." "Are you crazy? You must see him. The chance of something like this happening is one in a billion. You must see this Brujo even if I have to drag you. Call me the minute you get in!

The week went by in no time. Monday came and my plane landed in Miami at noon, a friend picked me up and drove me to my condo in Key Biscayne. My apartment at the beach was convenient and very appealing. I turned the key and found myself in another kind of environment with all the comforts of a full house; as if I had never left it two weeks ago. I called my office in Miami and let them know I was in town and immediately after I dialed Roberta, got no answer but left her a message on her machine; "I'm yours. Call me when you can." She did minutes later and said we had an appointment next day at 2 p.m. sharp. "Would you like lunch first?" I asked her. She declined. "It is important to be there on time," she insisted. We agreed to meet half way and continue to the Brujo's place in Little Havana.

My life at the Key was generally relaxed and free of social constraints. I'd walk the beach, go to the office by nine, took care of business, ate lunch with clients and played a game of tennis whenever I could swing it. My evenings were not much different; I usually dined by myself, read a book, went to a restaurant with a friend or saw a movie I had missed in New York. Had anyone asked me, I'd have said that I had it all.

But, that was my life at a glance; behind the facade it was a different story. What had been a relatively easy sprint to the top inexplicably began to falter a year or so ago. Chance and circumstance played foul with many of my ambitious plans; my time was wasted by ridiculous delays and my life consumed by an endless number of economic and personal roadblocks. Somehow, I didn't know where my life had taken a detour and I found myself now in a real swamp.

Was the idea of seeing el Brujo a good one? I don't know. I don't believe in God to begin with, but then again, why not? I had always toyed with the occult. Card readers, astrologers, gypsies were people I would seek out occasionally, especially during trips when sometimes — together with a companion — we'd look for the romantic message the Tarot cards would deliver. Were the messages always positive or fulfilling? Perhaps not. But life continued and I fought every step of the way not to be derailed no matter what.

Now, I'm back at the Key for my hands-on fortnight at the creative side of my business and I have the afternoon all to myself. I opened the French doors to my terrace. It was warm, the Atlantic was calm — as if taking a rest — and the sky was bluer than the ocean. *Let's walk the beach,* my alter-ego insisted and I couldn't resist.

My building was the last standing structure before a mile and a half long state park. The walk was a real treat; the ocean on one side and a lush tropical forest on the other, all the way down to a serene — out of service — lighthouse, that I called 'El Farito,' at the very end of the Key. The beach was mostly peaceful, perhaps a flock of pelicans having an all-you-can-eat kind of feast or seagulls roaming the shore, but no visible humans anywhere during the week. I'd walk to the lighthouse, sit on the rocks, meditate and try to find a reasonable explanation to the labyrinth I found myself in. Sometimes, out of pure frustration, I'd share my worries with the lighthouse — not that she ever answered, though — but somehow I thought we had a connection; come to think of it, we both were solitary entities. But whether she heard me or not, after my daily tread, I'd go back to my routine; another espresso, a warm shower and a drive to my office in a renovated section of downtown Miami.

At noon Roberta met me in a parking lot of a tapas bar that we frequented. She squeezed into my car, we kissed and she immediately said. "We have enough time to get to his place. I'll do the introduction and step out if you don't want me to listen."

"I don't mind if you stay."

"Are you sure?" she demanded. "This fellow knows your most intimate secrets."

"I doubt that, but why burden you with my problems? I'll ask him and we'll decide."

We drove into the Little Havana section of Miami. This neighborhood was a mixture of the original Cuban refugees — that arrived back in the sixties — and new groups of illegal South American immigrants seeking a better future in the "promised land." The house in question was a large, elegant colonial that still retained the charm of earlier years. There were three old cars parked in the driveway. We parked ours by the curb, crossed the portal and walked to the entrance. Roberta pushed the door open and we entered a large living room where two women were seated talking to each other.

A few minutes passed before an elderly lady came through a narrow hall escorted by a young black man dressed with in a purple tunic. The young man turned to Roberta, and with a smile, approached us extending his hands in a sign of friendship. He led us back through the same narrow hall to a door adorned with dried corncobs and Easter palm leaves. Roberta and I went in while the fellow gently closed the door behind us.

The room was large and rather dark, even if it was only two in the afternoon. The windows were covered with heavy red curtains and two large saint statues stood directly across from a thin, old, black man sitting in a throne-like armchair behind a large antique desk. One of the saints was Santa Barbara and the other San Lazaro of the Crutches, not the Catholic saint of the same name. There were two more altars with burning candles and a number of small glasses of water in front of the deities. A large, noisy, old air-conditioning unit in one of the windows kept the room cool, even though the distraction and the noise were intolerable.

The Brujo extended his hand, shook Roberta's first and then mine; his was cold and bony. He invited us to sit right in front of him, all along looking into my eyes. Roberta immediately broke the ice and told the man I was her friend, the one he mentioned ten days ago. The Brujo said; "he's the one alright." He then slowly faced me and asked if I had any questions. Roberta promptly reminded him we were there to hear about André and the job. She also told him we wanted to know if there were any remedies to reverse a malefic job, but he chose not to answer and instead addressed me.

"I hope you're ready to listen, are you?" the Brujo asked me.

"Of course," I responded.

"Most of what I have to disclose is delicate, perhaps embarrassing. Do you object to your friend being present?"

"Not at all," I responded and told him Roberta was a trusted friend. I said, I had been intrigued since she mentioned her meeting him and that I considered, if anybody could dispel the mystery, he seemed to be the right person to do so. The Brujo assented and, pointing to the two saints behind us, said the deities had to be invoked before going into any serious discussion."

"Please, do what you must" I responded, and he immediately lifted a cup full of water, toasted the two saints and began a prayer I couldn't understand.

The prayer finished, the Brujo told us that a man, he didn't remember his name, had come to see him for a consultation about a year ago and during the session had disclosed he wanted a job done on somebody. The Brujo said he had asked him "what it was all about." And that the man had responded; "he had serious problems with a partner. That he had suffered irreparable harm. That the partner had not kept his word and that all the promises he had originally made to him evaporated overnight." The Brujo continued, "That he knew his partner had in mind, all along, to dump him the minute the business took off. That he, his partner, conspired with all the other employees under his tutelage, to undermine his authority, make his life impossible and eventually dispose of him. That his muse had abandoned him. That he had lost his touch with his art and his fashions had lost the styles that had made them appealing for a long time."

As the Brujo spoke I could visualize André elaborating his conspiracy theories, talking about my planning his demise with the same vehemence as he had described them to me during our turbulent association. I knew the man was a psychopath a few months after he started working for us but, by then, it was too late. Then I chose the path of least resistance, some kind of gradual accommodation that would give me time to either get him to change his behavior or provide me enough ammunition to remove him with the minimum amount of disruption to our business.

NATIVIDAD

The time was the late nineties, beginning of the new century. My wife Maxine, had a longtime friend, named Cheche, who was a great couturier playing second fiddle — and the real inspiration — to a well-known, male designer in New York. Besides being close friends, Cheche, Maxine and I often mingled at social gatherings and industry related shows where, inevitably, her anonymity and behind the scenes confinement were a hot topic of conversation and moral outrage among her friends.

It was one fateful night — during one of those heated exchanges — when we decided to correct the score and help our friend gain the recognition she deserved. Right then and there, with her consent, we began a serious effort to organize a haute-couture venture with her at the helm.

The time was right. I had successfully completed the sale and transfer of a media company to its new owners, and the idea of having a designer's line — the ambience and the aura at the top level, if not the sweatshop aspect of it at the bottom — was one that appealed to me. Maxine, for a change, was also enthusiastic about her friend having a breakthrough of sorts and one idea, together with another, gave us the impetus to begin negotiating with our friend and her counsel.

While the negotiations with Cheche's lawyers were difficult and painstaking, our friend trembled at the possibility of going out on a limb; of failing under the pressure of competition and the long agonizing early years of any start-up enterprise. In a matter of weeks it was apparent to me that, even if she was a great designer, she wasn't prepared to carry on with the complexity any such volatile enterprise would entail. A week or so before the papers were to be signed, she let us know her boss had learned of our negotiations and had made her a counter offer and she said she regretfully accepted it.

Once bitten by the glamour bug, with a corporation and lines of credit approved, the idea of going ahead with the original plan was quite alive in my brain. I immediately began to reassess all my options and took a quick inventory of all my previous contacts in the business. Among my notes, I found another person who could take Cheche's place; a female designer from Barcelona, Spain. Her name was Natividad Entrialgo, a thirty something woman already established as one of a select group of couturiers in that nation. I had been introduced to Natividad briefly during one of her sojourns to Fashion Week in New York. I had also met her, and her live-in boyfriend, on another of my Barcelona trips when I took them both to dinner. During that dinner, even if we were each accompanied at the time, we took an instant liking to each other and, all through the night, we kept an animated conversation over the heads of our two companions. Such was my enchantment with Natividad that, upon landing in New York, I immediately mailed her a short note proposing meeting again. She wrote back suggesting whoever crossed the Atlantic first should let the other know in advance in order to facilitate the encounter.

A week or two after reassessing all my options, I telephoned Natividad in Barcelona. After the regular chitchat, I mentioned my stillborn fashion project and my interest in discussing it with her. She said she had no plans to visit the States for another six months. I told her that I was planning to visit Madrid in two weeks and I might take the opportunity to make a stopover in Barcelona if she was willing to meet me. "I will be waiting," she responded and asked me to call and let her know a week before my arrival.

Natividad was an intriguing woman. She had a degree in classics from the Salamanca University, the most prestigious institution in Spain. Right after her graduation, she became an apprentice of Salamandra, an old Spanish couturier of worldwide renown. Besides her recognized talent, she was also an engaging woman. She could talk of world affairs as well as recite you a Neruda poem during the course of a conversation. Her refinement was also impeccable, something she had demonstrated during our extended dinner in Barcelona and the subsequent visit to her apartment, a jewel of a place, full of antiques and works of art from different periods and parts of the world. She was about five-five, dark, with black eyes and very thin; a figure that — with her exquisite attire — made her look like a model straight out of Vogue. A most enticing woman, Natividad.

It took me a month to cross the Atlantic and land in Madrid. My visits to Spain were frequent and no matter whether coming or going, I'd stop there, meet friends and enjoy everything the city has to offer. I'd always stay at my favorite hotel, 'The Palace,' in a corner mini-suite, overlooking the artful Fountain of Neptune.

My call to Natividad went unanswered, but I left a message on her machine. That night, at about 2 am, I got a return call from her. She had been out and assumed I would still be up. After the regular pleasantries, we tactfully inquired about each other's evening and wished each other good night and sweet dreams. Before I hung up, I announced my Friday arrival in Barcelona and she said she'd make sure she had the weekend free to talk.

Friday afternoon I arrived in Barcelona and went directly to my hotel. The Ritz was my regular destination and I always enjoyed one of the superior rooms on the top floor with an ample terrace overlooking the city. I placed a call to Natividad's atelier and she answered welcoming me to her town and reciting a series of activities she had programmed for the weekend. I suggested a cocktail at my hotel and she promptly agreed.

As Natividad entered the bar, I stayed put with my drink in hand, watching the crowd at the counter turn their heads and follow her all the way to my corner. She had a dark tan and was dressed in black, with her hair resting on her shoulders. She looked great and, if the stares of the people at the bar were a sign of her appeal, she was a complete success. What a specimen of a woman!

I rushed to embrace and kiss her on both cheeks. We moved back to my table and I signaled the waiter to take her order. She asked for a "fino" and I said to make it two. "Two finos, por favor."

After a few amenities, the conversation quickly turned to her private life. I asked if she was still seeing the brute I saw her with in New York and she dismissed it laughingly, saying it was in the past. That she was so busy with her couture she hadn't had a serious relationship since she divorced her husband of ten years, four years ago, something new to me.

"Did you decide on a restaurant?" I asked her, having the last sip of my sherry.

"Yes, my favorite; a small tavern en El Barrio Gotico, behind the Cathedral. The mariscos are great."

Natividad suggested walking and we made our way through a number of narrow streets to El Barrio Gotico; a thirteenth, fourteenth century neighborhood, now home to a community of writers and artists; something very much like our old Village section in New York.

We arrived at an old baroque style kind of building on a narrow street. The porter welcomed us as we entered a cozy salon full of people. A young woman was playing the cello, a flock of waiters was busy tending tables and the room was buzzing with a million animated conversations. The maître d' approached, kissed Natividad and led us to her favorite table close to a fireplace.

The waiters surrounded us, with a selection of ham and cheeses, mineral water and a basket of different kinds of bread. The sommelier greeted Natividad, asked me if I had a special kind of drink in mind or if I would settle for the lady's regular aperitif. Intrigued, I said I'd go along with her taste and he promptly reappeared with a twenty year old port. "It is superb," he assured us and poured a couple of glasses.

I liked Nati's flair. She was classy and self-assured; a combination that made her very appealing to me. I never knew if it was just because I was a latent feminist — who admired strong women — or just a simply lazy fellow who preferred someone else to take over if she was doing the kind of things I'd have done otherwise. We toasted each other with our fine port and began an animated conversation that lasted through the first and second courses of a wonderful meal.

Even if it was true I liked Natividad as a woman, I had not crossed the Atlantic just to get laid. I politely turned the conversation to business and began describing how far we had gone to complete our negotiations and how cleverly her designer-boss outmaneuvered us. She smiled and said "don't blame him, I'd have done the same." "After all that effort," I continued, "we found ourselves empty handed." She smiled and said I shouldn't complain. "It wasn't meant to be, that simple" and she went ahead and mentioned her own failed effort with a designer in Florida. "But putting everything aside," she continued, "if we were to discuss doing business," she conceded, "we'd have to change hats and sit down with my team and that would take some time."

"I agreed," I said and asked her about the weekend.

"We're going out of town, if you don't object."

"Me? Never!" I responded.

"A bit of business and some sightseeing. I must stop at Figueres first to meet a print designer. I assume you've been to Figueres," she said, waiting for a positive response.

"In two different occasions. Both to visit Dali's museum. I also love La Costa Brava, though."

"He might be of interest to you too. But I don't want you to compete with me. Is that understood?"

"Come on, woman. I am not even in the business yet. Just introduce me, say this is so and so, my new stud imported from America," I said laughing.

"As if he was going to believe me," she said jokingly. "He's gay, you know. He might be interested in your services, after all."

The drive to the hotel was short. At the entrance, while the doorman held the car door open, she told me to be ready by ten sharp, to pack a change of clothing and my tooth brush. I said, "Yes ma'am" and after a few words and a tasty good night kiss we said good night and she took off.

It was a clear morning in Barcelona. I called room service and they delivered breakfast and the morning papers. By ten, I was sitting in the lobby finishing my paper and having another espresso. Minutes later, a bellboy informed me a lady was waiting at the hotel's entrance. I grabbed my bag and ran out to meet Nati. After a few pleasantries about the previous night, weather, etc. we took off.

"Are we taking the scenic route by the coast or the expressway to France?" I asked her casually.

"Better to get to Figueres fast," she responded, "meet this fellow, have lunch and then drive down to the coast. You've been to Cadaques, haven't you?" She asked me.

I said "yes, a few times."

I had discovered Cadaques driving along the coast from Barcelona to the border of France some years ago, when the expressway was still a dream. Even if my first experience on those dangerous roads had been taxing, the beauty of the scenery was out of this world; a hundred and some miles of narrow roads, mountains and precipices, with dozens of small coves. Add to that a brief encounter with a dear friend and you have the rudiments of an everlasting memory, something I wouldn't mind doing again.

The expressway to Figueres was relatively empty. Other than trucks and buses, automobiles were few, considering it was Saturday morning. Natividad drove fast and in about an hour and twenty minutes, we were at Figueres' gates. Nati drove directly to this designer's studio on the outskirts of the city, a half a mile or so from Dali's surrealist museum. A few turns later, a shortcut, and we stopped at a sort of small compound at the end of a tree-lined street. The house, if petite, had been built chateau style. There was another structure, supposedly the studio, in the same style, attached to the main building by a covered corridor. Nati blew her horn twice and a medium built fellow, with hair to his shoulders, in shirt sleeves and sandals, came to the door to welcome us. Nati embraced him with affection and introduced me as a future business associate. "Carlos," he said his name was. "I'm Alex," I replied shaking his effeminate extended hand.

After a few pleasantries and a brief stop in the center of his living room to show us his latest acquisition — an abstract painting of an up-and-coming Catalan artist — he led us through a long corridor to his studio. Another gay man asked us if we would like a cocktail. Carlos asked for a fino and Nati and I seconded his request.

The studio was a much larger structure than it looked from the road. There were several sky lights and three of the four walls were made of glass overlooking a surrounding garden. Two or three long tables dispersed throughout the room and a large, glass and metal desk where Carlos mused his designs. In a corner there was a long, flexible hanger where a hundred or more printed fabrics hung. All together the room was full of light and color, a most enticing atmosphere for such a creative endeavor.

Nati took me to the hanger and showed me some of her friend's creations. I was really impressed and told him. We walked then to another corner of the room where his assistant had deposited the three dry Sherries we had requested. We toasted each other and Carlos went to his work table to look for the last batch of drawings he had created for Nati's new collection.

"Here they are," Carlos said, giving Nati three sheets of long paper full of color and precise drawings.

Nati took and compared them with her own drawings, a few patterns she had sent him ahead of time.

"I think they are marvelous," Nati said passing me his designs together with her own drawings.

I took both samples and looked at them in detail. Being a jack of all trades and having dealt with Cheche — my aborted in-house designer — I had developed an acute interest in patterns and designs.

"What mills do you deal with?" I asked him.

"Well, it all depends. The expensive stuff, the exclusive designs I do for Nati and other couturier houses here and in Paris, are done in Italy, in the Milan-Florence region. The trade stuff, I mean cheap, that I don't sign, is done mostly in Portugal, around Porto. I don't know if you are familiar with Portugal. You know, in the Northern part."

"I know Porto well," I said reassuring him.

"Could I take the samples with me?" Nati asked him.

"Of course. They are for you," Carlos responded. "Are you going back to Barcelona?" he asked her with some curiosity.

"No, no!" Nati said. "After lunch I'm driving him to Cadaques. Alex loves Cadaques."

"I'd have gone with you had I not committed to a dinner with friends tonight."

"What a pity," I said thanking my lucky stars he was busy; "Perhaps some other time. If everything develops as it should, I'm pretty sure we're going to see each other frequently; I hope."

BEAUTIFUL CADAQUES

The road to Cadaques was narrow, picturesque and descending all the way to the coast. While admiring the scenery, Nati and I carried on an animated conversation about the overrated restaurant, the mediocre lunch we shared and a place or two in Cadaques that would make us forget the unpleasant experience. She added she had been associated with Carlos for more than seven years. Then she went into the gossip realm of their relationship. She confided he had an Aids scare recently. And that he had been there for her on more than one occasion when she had experienced one or two difficult situations in her life. I asked her if they were frequent and, with a laugh, she ignored my comment.

Cadaques appeared in front of us with the Mediterranean Sea in the background. A quaint, postcard, fishing village with whitewashed buildings around a cove no more than a mile and a half long. The church tower was the tallest and most conspicuous structure in town, and a small plaza, with trees and an outdoor café facing the sea, gave the village a romantic character and a spot for its people to congregate and shoot the breeze.

"Do we have reservations anywhere in town?" I asked Nati.

"Yes, I reserved two rooms at the Quijote, a pleasant walk from midtown."

"Two rooms?" I asked her with an air of reproach.

"Yes, two. What did you expect?" she said coquettishly.

"Well, I like to save money and I hate to sleep alone. I'm afraid of the dark..."

"They are next to each other. You can yell and I'll call the night guard," she concluded with infectious laughter.

The hotel was on the outskirts of town, on a hill overlooking the village down below and the Mediterranean farther down. The building was an unpretentious, modern, Moorish style structure, four floors high with nice size balconies for each room. The doorman promptly took care of our bags.

As Nati had said, we were assigned adjacent rooms. Mine was a large, well-appointed one with a beautiful view of the town and the sea. A sucker for unobstructed views, I checked the balcony out and found myself enchanted with the scenery. The ambiance was charming and I began looking forward to an overnight stay, perhaps with a mixture of business and romance. A most desirable situation, considering I was in my dreamy Cadaques.

The telephone rang and it was Nati. She suggested we take a nap and meet at half past seven for cocktails and tapas; the works. She had selected a restaurant she was sure I was going to like. "Fantastic," I responded, and we hung up.

I went to my bag and got my Ingmar Bergman book of screenplays. I could never rest my head on a pillow without something to read, no matter how tired or somnolent I was. Having reread The Seventh Seal, the first of his movies I ever saw, I began to read Wild Strawberries again. The story of an old man who watches his life and death paraded in front of him. Bergman's fascination with death was also my own. First the knight playing chess with death, trying to delay the inevitable, and then Professor Borg watching his cadaver in an open casket fallen from an ancient hearse. Heavy stuff, indeed. I passed out almost at the beginning.

That evening, Nati and I decided to walk to the restaurant. I loved Cadaques; the narrow streets, the flowers on balconies and adorned windows. I'd have come by myself had Nati not thought of it first. The restaurant was a typical fish eatery; another one. I was bored with fish and shellfish and I was craving a bloody, dripping piece of red beef to sink my teeth into. Nati decided the menu and we ended up having more of the same, 'camarones al ajillo,' shrimp cooked in olive oil with plenty of garlic, bread and a bottle of wine. Espresso afterwards and we were ready to walk the rest of the way to the little plaza in the center of town across the road from the lapping water.

The place was crowded. We waited a few minutes and ended up with a table under a beautiful, wide old tree.

"Love this place, don't you?" I asked Natividad.

"I come here quite often," she responded.

"Why?" I asked her.

"I don't know. It is so simple. Away from the daily routine; the people I know. A fishing town; a kind of simple life. I like that. We're surrounded by people yet we are alone. I haven't been too happy lately. Lately . . . that's wishful thinking. The last three years have been tough! A very trying period. Thank God for business. Otherwise, I'd have killed myself."

"Romance?" I asked her. "The last time I saw you in New York you seemed happy. The fellow you were with seemed very attentive and you looked contented."

"We split the minute we got back. Coming off the plane we went our separate ways," she said disgusted.

"Look, I don't want to bring back bad memories."

"Perhaps I need that more than I'm willing to admit," she said firmly. "Thrash it out. Bring it into the open." She stopped for a moment and continued with a sad expression on her face. "That was my second foolish adventure with a married man; another two years of my life. Men seldom leave their wives, you know."

I didn't say anything, but looked at her inquisitively as she probably rehashed in her head everything about the affair.

"Foolish of me."

"Human relations," I said. "A difficult topic. Make me happy. A tough proposition."

"It isn't so simple. I was willing to work at it and I proved it. I held up for more than a year knowing that it was a lost cause. He came into my life like a breeze. We all need a break, especially a woman like me who has built her life around a business career since I was nineteen. It's true, I derive a lot of satisfaction and self-esteem from my creations and, why not, my public image. But I wasn't whole. Inside me I yearned for a relationship, a family, a child. In four years I'll be forty, you know."

"You could have fooled me," I said sincerely.

She smiled briefly and added. "You're a hypocrite. Talk about you."

"Me? What about me?" I asked her back.

"Are you happy?" she asked me, looking into my eyes.

"I don't know. I carry on with my life. I guess I could complain about the same things you do. Not much outside of business. I was glad when you accepted my invitation to talk and even more when you suggested this sojourn outside Barcelona. I enjoy successful women. You're engaging. You seem to know what you want and I'm pretty sure it is only a matter of time before you find it."

"You're talking about me, Alex. My question was about you. Are you happy?"

"Yes, I am!" I said with conviction. "I have a home, family, business. But I dread to confess, I'm not monogamous. I get bored easily. I need change, challenge. I've been very fortunate though. I don't have a person looking over my shoulder all the time. It wouldn't have lasted otherwise. Obviously I'm not a Casanova, but I've been fortunate to encounter exceptional women at certain times in my life. Women who perhaps, and I say perhaps, saw life the way I do. They really helped me."

"Don't fool yourself. Women don't see life the same way men do. We don't want to make you run the minute we talk about our needs."

"Men are weak; I am. A daring brain is irresistible to me; you possess intellect and beauty."

Nati smiled and looked at me. "I guess Cadaques affects you in the wrong way."

"I'm feeling great," I told her, reaching for her hand over the table. "I seldom feel this way and I'm grateful to you."

She smiled and held my hand with both her own. She opened it and looked at my palm. "A long life, I see," she said. "Has anyone ever read your palm?"

"A few times," I responded.

"Were the predictions accurate?"

"Some have come true. Some are still possible. No fortuneteller predicted this encounter, though, and here we are. Who knows?"

"It might be time to ask for a refund?" she said with a coquettish smile.

"Fortuneteller or no fortuneteller, I love it."

Nati looked at her watch. "It is two thirty already," she said. "Shall we go?"

"You don't mind walking back, do you?" I asked her.

"Not at all," she said showing me her low heels. "The night is beautiful."

I signaled the waiter to bring the check. We had been talking about us for more than two hours. She shared a few secrets. A couple of romantic setbacks in a life full of professional successes; 'can't have it all,' we both agreed. Still I couldn't ascertain if her confessions were motivated by a simple need to unload or if she was looking for a way to establish an emotional bridge. It was obvious she felt frustrated, lonely and vulnerable but — even when I felt her pain and was immensely attracted to her — I saw her, above all, as a possible business partner. A difficult decision to make when business and romance interact with one another.

We began our walk back to the hotel. Wanting to reassure her, make her see that we all have experienced difficult situations in our lives, I offered some tidbits about my own. Nothing specific; I never talk about specifics. Nati smiled and asked questions, prodding me for details. She wanted to know more. If I continued seeing that person; how the affair ended.

As we began our walk, I reached for Nati's hand; it was cold. And I said to her, "manos frias amor de un dia. Manos calientes amor de siempre."

"Never heard that saying," she said interested. "Did you make that up?"

"Cold hands love for one day. Warm hands love forever, I wish I had." I repeated the story I told every woman I ever found to have cold hands. That I was a college student, writing a paper, went to a museum and met a female curator. It had been raining, I was dripping wet and my hands were cold. We shook hands, she holding mine between hers told me 'your hands are cold' and proceeded to tell me the saying. The place was empty, one thing led to another and we ended up being lovers.

"What a beautiful story. How did it end?" Nati asked me.

"After that evening I went away and never saw her again."

"How sad! The prediction turned out to be true," she said.

"This might be a good opportunity to test the theory once again."

Nati stopped right on the spot and turned to me. "Are you implying that I am cold, frigid or something? You don't know me."

"No! Come on! I said you had cold hands, that's all. There is nothing wrong with that. It is a cool night after all and it is only a saying."

We resumed our walk, holding hands as before. We laughed and looked at each other amorously at every step of the way. Anyone looking at us would have concluded we were two people in love. And at that moment, at least I was.

"I don't know about you, but I feel great," I said stopping to take a pink carnation from a pot, on a window sill, and gave it to her. Nati took it, smelled it and threw her arms around my neck. She rested her back against the building's facade and I pressed my body against her. We kissed tenderly at first and embraced passionately as I caressed her hair, kissed her neck pulling her tightly against me. In my fantasies I had dreamed of an opportunity like this and the topography and the ambiance — I'm sure — contributed to it. Two thirty in the morning, narrow, empty, dimly lighted cobblestone streets. Flowers hanging from balconies, and every window at street level, Jesus Christ, if you couldn't romance a woman in those conditions you're either dead or a complete fool Alex, I said to myself.

We continued our walk with my arm around her shoulders. Somehow we had taken a different path going back to the hotel and we found ourselves across from a small park with beautiful trees and thick bushes. Nati pulled me instinctively into the park. We rushed as if we were trying to hide from a crowd intent on watching us. It was childish, but an enticing prelude to love making. We dropped behind a number of high bushes in a dark, isolated area of the park. We kissed and I lowered myself, unbuttoning her blouse, anxiously kissing her breasts, her still covered belly, trying to raise her skirt. She was wearing black undies with a garter-belt holding her stockings. That portion of her uncovered thigh looked scrumptiously ambrosial to me.

"Come inside me. Come inside me now," Nati insisted as she assisted me undoing my belt and lowering my pants.

And I pushed myself in and she reacted with a sigh full of pleasure.

"Oh, my God! Oh my God! Hard Alex. Hard!" she insisted.

I tried to kiss her as a way of covering her mouth, but she continued as if we were alone in the world and not surrounded by houses with people sleeping in them. I felt the same uncontrollable urge to cry my pleasure. I felt like her master as I stroked her again and again, a built up crescendo of moans, cries, all kinds of muted sounds, until she yelled the unmistakable successive sounds of a wild, uncontrollable orgasm.

The lights went up in a few homes and a few windows opened. "Pigs! Get a room. Go back to the jungle where you belong, you filthy, dirty dogs," an old man yelled. "This is a decent neighborhood. I'm calling the police!" a visibly disturbed older woman cried out loud from another window.

Nati and I shook with uncontrollable laughter. We felt perhaps like Adam and Eve after committing their first sin. A real irony; two grownups, with beautiful rooms in one of the most luxurious hotels in town, risking everything for an opportune tryst. A veritable reminder of the apple and paradise lost.

Holding back our laughter, we promptly tidied up before one of those outraged neighbors could really call the cops. Bending, getting as close to the ground as possible — going through the dark areas of the park — we quickly gained the opposite street and walked quickly behind parked cars, putting as much ground between us and the scandalized residents as we could.

"That was something, wasn't it?" I said as we entered her suite.

Nati put her arms around my neck and kissed me passionately.

"Would you like some grass? I'm going to have some," Nati said and she went looking in her bag. "I love grass before sex."

It was eleven when I woke up. It had been a cool night and Nati, covered with a light blanket, was still sleeping on top of me. She was deliciously warm and affectionate as she worked my thigh between her legs, pressing against me, kissing first my shoulder, then my chest and finally my lips.

"Hey," I whispered in her ear.

"Hi," she responded. "What a wonderful surprise to wake up in your arms."

"You went out right after we finished our first installment," I responded as if reproaching her.

"I'm sorry. I hope I didn't disappoint you," she said amorously. "It's my turn to be in control now. Would you like that?"

"I'd love it."

"Don't move," she said as she sinuously made her way to the bathroom, returning in no time, throwing herself on top of me. She kissed me sweetly at first and then went down on me caressing with her lips my chest, my trembling belly, my thighs, until she took it in her mouth and sucked it amorously. She was good and I told her so. "Talk to me," she demanded. "I like it when you talk to me." And I did, and I told her how she made me feel, again and again, until she jumped on top of me and had one of the most erotic, wild rides, that I had ever experienced, finally collapsing, incapable of prolonging her ecstasy a moment longer.

Pressed for time, we decided for a late lunch on our terrace. Promptly after, we collected our things and hit the road back to Barcelona. The expressway was packed and the closer we got, the heavier the traffic became. Fortunately we felt good and amorous and had plenty of time to talk about each other. The pleasantries eventually turned to business and she used the opportunity to talk about her financial backer and partner, Julian Zamora — an older man — friend of the family. According to her, the old man was considered part of the family long before she was born and seemed to have been in love with her mother all his life. If single and straight, he had been her father's business associate and a close friend. Now that her father is dead, he escorts her mother as if they were reckless teenagers. Zamora was about sixty-five, the same age her mother was. She suggested that I meet him before I went back to the US and I readily agreed.

"I always thought mixing business and romance was a bad idea," Nati continued.

"There is a saying," I responded; "'you shouldn't eat where you pee or something dirtier; 'shit' where you eat.'"

"It is true. I don't want you to have the wrong impression," Nati said. "I might be a great lay, as you said. But I'm a tough business woman. I'll always defend my business and my interests above everything else. You are aware of that, aren't you?"

"I understand. I never expected it to be otherwise."

"Now, you remember I told you about André, don't you?"

"Yes, the designer you have in Florida. Is that his name? André is Andrés in Spanish; it adds a bit of cache, though. You said he's Cuban, didn't you?"

"Yes. But that's his professional name. I like the guy," Nati continued. "He came to work with me for six months. He has his own label in several chain stores. Cheap stuff. Don't tell him I said that," she said squeezing my arm. "He's gay, a great bullshitter and knows the market inside out besides having contacts at all levels. Especially with one or two of the big stores; Mays, I think, and another one I don't remember. But we need a larger representation. A bigger showroom. You can't sell high-priced stuff from a shitty place. You know what I mean. He said he had a backer but it didn't work out. Perhaps he never did and he lied to me. Anyway, whatever deal you and I do, I'd like André to be part of it. I don't mean he has to be your partner, but perhaps a manager, something. This is not a condition; only a suggestion. I wouldn't like to dump him if I don't have to."

"I'll talk to him. I need a person with that kind of experience anyway."

"Good," she said. "Would you like to meet Julian at the office tomorrow?"

"No. I'd prefer to have dinner, the three of us, before I start to talk business with him."

"Something like you did with me," Nati said smiling.

"Don't fool yourself, Natividad Entrialgo. You're good at everything you do. You're a panther dear, between the sheets; both in and out of them."

"Pick you up at nine thirty?"

"Why don't you come for a cocktail at six? You haven't seen my terrace yet!"

ZAMORA – NATI'S PARTNER

Julian Zamora had been at the restaurant waiting when we arrived a half hour or so late. He stood up, shook my hand and then kissed Nati on both cheeks. He called the waiter and asked us what we wanted to drink. He was a distinguished gentleman, about sixty-five or so, perhaps older but well kept. He was dressed in a dark suit, gold cuff links, blue tie and shining black shoes. I always looked at my companion's or new acquaintance's shoes. They tell you as much about their personalities as a long, expensive psychoanalytic profile. He was a numbers cruncher, I quickly concluded — and a difficult nut to crack — my opposite I'd say.

Natividad initiated the conversation introducing me in personal terms. Zamora looked at me often, as if trying to verify everything Nati was saying. At one point she mentioned I played tennis and he hurried to say, "Perhaps we could play before you return to the US." I said I'd gladly play next time we met; that I was flying back to New York the following morning. We settled for a match whenever we met again on either side of the Atlantic.

"Natividad tells me you have a communications business and fashion is something new you want to explore," Zamora said.

"Well, I don't know if explore is the right word," I said, piqued by his remark.

"No, Julian," Nati interrupted. "I said he wanted to get into the business and that he had made great inroads already."

"I'm sorry. I didn't mean any disrespect. It is obvious you want to get into the business even if it is altogether new for you."

"Well. It isn't exactly like that but the point is I am interested in representing Nati in the US and that's why we are having dinner now," I said, a bit troubled with the old man's intransigent behavior.

"Alejandro, I hope you understand us," Zamora said. "You and I are business people. Nati is an artist, a designer, a brilliant one at that, but she knows very little about the financial side of the business. Still it is her business, but she has three backers. She made a hasty decision with this fellow, André, in Florida, who offered us a lot of things, none of which have come to pass. Now she is introducing you and I'm pretty sure she has discovered a few qualities in you that perhaps make you an ideal partner but, from my angle, I have to look at other qualifications."

Sensing an underlying sort of hostility in the old man's rhetoric, I used the opportunity to try to put him at ease. "Well, why don't you ask your questions and I'll try to answer. Anyway, Ben Lonetto, my numbers guy, will gladly provide you with all the financial information you might require. You have my word," I said, and he seemed to be satisfied.

As the dinner progressed, I started to worry about my future relationship with the prick. Obviously, he backed Nati one hundred percent, but he was also looking to recover André's balance and said so in so many words. *'What?'* my alter-ego interrupted. *'Tell the fucker goodbye, now. Fuck him!'* Listening to my always reliable other-yo, I mustered all the aplomb I had left and told Zamora, "If that is a condition, I might as well walk out before dinner is served."

Nati jumped up immediately and told the old man, "That proposition is out of line. André's debt has never been mentioned in previous conversations." The old man apologized.

By night's end things had changed considerably. The food had been good, if predictable. Tired of seafood, I ate my default entree; rack of lamb. Nati had Chilean sea bass and Zamora devoured what is called a "mariscada," all kinds of seafood, crustaceans you had to open with your hands. It was also a good thing the old man could write the dinner off as a business expense because his demeanor changed at the same rate his wine consumption increased. He became a jovial and amusing entertainer. Three bottles of the extremely expensive Vega Cicilia wine were consumed and he was so happy he even gave me a hug, when we said goodbye.

Nati drove me back to my hotel and excused herself with an early appointment she said she had. "I'll be seeing you in Miami soon," she reminded me. "And don't forget André. He could be very helpful getting started," she repeated. We kissed and she took off.

NEW YORK, NEW YORK

My plane left for New York at one sharp and eight hours and some minutes later we were landing in Kennedy. Maxine was waiting. Driving home I recounted the essentials of my trip. Next step was to see André in Florida, I said, giving her an idea of who he was and his involvement with the designer in Barcelona. Heavy lifting with Zamora would have to take place before the deal was concluded; tough guy, that old man, I told her, as we entered our driveway at home.

Early the following morning I began contacting everyone I knew who could give me some insights about this famous André of Florida. The news was mixed. A forty something, tough gay activist with a longtime companion. Unstable. Knows his stuff. Had been in business for twenty years working on his own and for different designers; fired twice and now representing Nati's shop in Florida and pushing his own label on the side. Difficult man to handle was the establishment's consensus.

A meeting with André was arranged. I gave him three options: a restaurant, my office in Miami or my apartment in Key Biscayne. He chose the latter. He liked the ocean, he said, and preferred an informal setting. The following Tuesday afternoon André arrived on time, I met him in the lobby of my building and together we walked out to a pergola overlooking the ocean. I offered an overall idea of what I needed to accomplish, the possibility of his being our general manager and asked him to sell himself.

André began talking about Nati in glowing terms and said she could become a power house in the international world of fashion. He then went on to enumerate a number of jobs, successes and some failures in his background, but omitted mentioning being fired as well as the reasons on each occasion. I said that if we finally decided to give him the job, I'd still have my secretary handling all my personal matters as well as the financial aspects of the operation. He didn't react. He said he'd like us to support his moderate priced label. I asked him if that was a condition and he quickly said that it wasn't. Next on the agenda was for me to visit his operation. He had been working from a small warehouse but confessed to having problems keeping up with the rent.

Thursday morning I drove to a dilapidated small warehouse in a seedy area in Miami proper where he was waiting with three other employees who tried to look busy. The place was neat and much better than my first impression from the outside. We walked to a small, poorly lighted office and after closing the door, he showed me several catalogs he said were a compendium of his most successful apparel lines, although not necessarily the ones he was most proud of. I asked him who handled his financial books and he gave me his accountant's business card. I mentioned Ben Lonetto, my VP and numbers man, would be contacting his accountant, we shook hands and I walked out.

On our side, Ben had been in contact with Zamora in Barcelona and a considerable amount of financial information had been exchanged between them. He told me Zamora's main concern was an open letter of credit from an accredited bank, preferably one with Spanish representation. He originally demanded five million dollars but after a call or two to Nati, I got the prick to come down to three million. A meeting between Ben and Zamora was also arranged. The old man wanted to visit us, but I insisted Ben go to Spain first and Zamora reluctantly agreed.

Two months from my visit to Spain and my meeting with Natividad, the deal was completed. Negotiations with the representatives for the other two labels were finished and ready to roll. In a subsequent conversation with

André I informed him we were in no position to support his private label, but offered him the general manager's job. He asked for a two-year contract and a five percent bonus. We counter offered with a one year contract with incentives for performance and he grudgingly accepted.

Another floor in the building we already occupied was duly refurbished and — four weeks later — our fashion group was a full-fledged operation. Maxine decided to stay in New York and forego the inauguration, but Natividad and Zamora came from Spain and stayed a week. The media response was a real coup, an international fashion magazine gave us a two-page color reportage. Two TV stations covered the atelier's blessing. The Herald gave us half a page in the financial section and a printed interview in the style magazine. The spread featured Nati and I discussing her fashion style and expanding horizons in Europe and now America, with Miami becoming an alternate fashion center to New York. A good send off for a business if there ever was one.

Before Nati returned to Spain, I suggested a weekend at a convenient hideaway on Florida's Gulf Coast. The Keewaydin was at Key Island, just off the tip of Naples, with a seven-mile pristine beach, magnificent sunsets, a hundred or more species of birds, accessible only by launch with no TV or telephones to speak of. Paradise! After three days of beach combing and two beautiful nights of love making on the beach under the stars, far from the maddening crowd, our penchant for each other was lustily rekindled.

Sunday night we returned to Miami and Nati spent the night at my apartment at the Key. She loved my place and pledged, if everything went as well as planned, she'd buy one in the same building. On Monday evening I took her to the airport for her return to Spain. It was a sad and tender farewell as most of them are, at least for me. We wished each other the best of luck and committed to keep seeing each other as often as we could. A last embrace, a mushy kiss and off she was. Altogether a spectacular week.

I returned home alone, but with a renewed sense of purpose. I thought of my luck, the uncharted turns my life often take, and wondered how long this new adventure would last, if it did. Feeling hungry, I prepared a filet-mignon and, with a bottle of wine, I sat on my terrace to ruminate.

Even if I had no religious beliefs left in my life, somehow I was certain most things, if not all, develop with its beginning and its end already set; as if with a genetic code. A law of nature I thought, perhaps a product of the Big Bang. But one thing I knew, we build our lives as children build sand castles on the beach. Being a beach walker, I marvel at them moving toy buckets of sand a few feet, watching their sand piles washed away by the sea and starting all over again, as if it was the most natural thing. Being older is no different. We don't move sand, but we move dreams. We create or try to create a world of our own, sometimes small, sometimes big, and gravitate around it. I wondered about my life, the routes taken, the future ones to come. I never felt at ease belonging to one single place; perhaps to no one single person. I needed to feel free, my stay brief. The minute I got to any of my places I was ready to take off again and go to the next one, whether my home in New York, my three hundred acre retreat in the Adirondack Mountains or my condo at the beach, here in Key Biscayne. An enchanted life I had created for myself and I wanted it never to end.

Time passed and our fashion group grew beyond all expectations. In a relative short time, we had secured retail space in the flagship stores of the four largest retail chains in the nation; a success and a paradox nevertheless. While our own labels were doing great and Nati's luxury line was a smashing success — her garments, because of contractual negotiations — were marketed with a very low profit margin. A temporary arrangement that worked to the detriment of our own bottom line.

The more we grew the bigger the conflicts with André. Beyond all the quirks peculiar to his nature, it seemed he had grown resentful at the growth of our lesser lines. He thought, and he told everyone whether they wanted to hear it or not, that his line could have done as well and probably even better than the ones we chose to represent over his. As the days passed he grew despondent and abusive with the employees until one day he threatened my assistant physically, forcing her to run out of the office in tears.

That afternoon Josefina called my office in New York and told Roberta about the incident; a retinue of abuses the staff had suffered for the last two months. "They are ready to quit if André stays," Roberta told me, "we had better do something fast." The dye was cast; I had no choice but to confront and fire André, my unstable Lilliputian masqueraded in emperor's clothes.

The following morning promptly at eight I called André; he was already at his desk. After a brief exchange, he showed no signs of remorse only vindictiveness toward the group. Relieved he had not pleaded for a new opportunity, I asked him to remove all his personal belongings and to drop his keys on Josefina's desk. He complained and demanded a face to face meeting. "There is nothing to talk about," I responded. "I sincerely regret not acting sooner." In fact he and I had discussed his conduct at least twice before and there was no point in rehashing the same arguments all over again. "You'll be receiving your severance pay as well as your performance bonus in less than a week," I told him.

"Go to hell," he yelled and threw down the phone.

ANDRÉ GONE & ADMONITION

It took us two weeks to reshuffle our management structure. Francine Gardiner — our New York rep — was promoted to General Manager and a new person was hired to take her place. Francine was an experienced, able salesperson, with an encyclopedic knowledge of the industry and good contacts at the main department store chains.

Francine's appointment was a welcome relief to the harassed staff and she promptly developed a close synergy with our young designers. In less than two months we were getting ready for the spring season; another nine months away. Designs were sketched and the samples mailed to Porto, home of our fabric-supplier and contracted manufacturer.

As our enthusiasm evolved so did our financial worries. The bigger our success, the larger our economic commitment to support Nati's label growth. True, her name and the quality of her brand were our passport to many large chains and high class boutiques but by the same token, the return on the money was less than adequate; almost unacceptable, business wise.

Two more years and some into the business, Zamora's demands became taxing and absurd. He wanted a higher rate of growth in the following quarter even if he knew we had already saturated the higher end of the North American market, including Canada. He also imposed a number of price increases that made Nati's line pricier than many famous French and Italian couturiers in the market. It was a crazy policy that none of us could understand and immediately suspected.

Ben, Francine and I discussed the new Zamora's demands and decided to postpone any decision until we had some clarification from Spain. That same day Nati called.

"I'm going to Florence for fashion week," she said. "We must get together! We need to talk."

I used the opportunity to ask Nati about Zamora's plans, but she refused to engage in a long conversation and insisted I meet her in Italy; "I'll tell you all about it," she responded.

Ten days later I landed at Leonardo's Milan airport and rented a car to get to Florence. It was a dark and drizzly day in Northern Italy, but against my better judgment and the car rental office manager's advice, I insisted on making my way to Florence — a relatively short haul over the hills — while a raging ice storm was in progress. Needless to say, I got to Florence ten hours later — after skidding off the road — and waiting for a tow truck for more than three.

My encounter with Nati was as charged by the passion we felt for each other, as for my need to find out more about Zamora's new scheme. Natividad refused to entertain any questions and instead pulled me into her bedroom, disrobed and pushed me onto the bed, falling on top of me, in a renewed display of passion and intensity, reminiscent of many we had experienced before.

The lovemaking was brief. Nati confided her need to get away from Florence. Away from the same faces and people she often runs into on this kind of occasions. She also complained to be under enormous stress, in need of advice. I had no advice to give, but pulled her against me and asked her to calm down. She quit talking, closed her eyes and went to sleep while I held her tightly against me. I succumbed moments later, tired from my own overnight flight and torturous drive from Milan.

The bells of 'Il Duomo' woke us up still in each other's arms. We kissed, rolled over in bed and each took our turn at the bath. I felt good and rested. Nati returned and I was struck by the signs of stress in her face. I had observed them in Barcelona, two months before, but she dismissed it blaming the pressures of putting together several lines of apparel a year. This time she looked worn out, worried, and I asked her. What is it?

"We'll talk at the lake, not now," and she insisted that we leave as soon as we could.

It was a glorious morning in Florence. I felt a bit of nostalgia having to leave it as soon as I got in. But now it was a matter of driving north and getting to Como quickly and the farther we drove away from Florence the happier Nati became. She seemed more relaxed, finding music on the radio, laughing, and making fun of the most inconsequential things.

The Villa d'Este hotel was fully booked; I should have known, it happened to me once before. However, not having made a reservation paid off grandly. I was directed to the Grand Hotel Tremezzo, right in the middle of the lake, a boat ride across from the quaint town of Bellagio.

We promptly found ourselves in another enchanted mini-suite, with a great balcony, overlooking the lake and Bellagio in the distance. I grabbed Nati and together, as if one person, with my chin resting on her shoulder, stepped out onto the balcony. That moment, as in many others in my life, I wanted to thank someone for my luck, but didn't know who. Either chance, fortune or fate, one or all three. Who knows? They were my deities and I thanked them all.

That night we had dinner at the hotel restaurant, in a beautiful long, open-air terrace facing the lake. The sky was black with millions of brilliant stars. Nati was quiet, not eating much and not talkative; something other than her usual self. As we were ending our dinner, watching her lost in her thoughts, I decided to ask her what her broodiness was all about.

"What is it? Can you tell me?" I asked her.

"I am at a crossroad," she responded with no preambles. "I'm being forced to make a series of decisions; in my personal life, my business affairs, and none of them are easy."

"Ok, can I be of any help?"

"I want to have a child, Alex. Time is passing and I have no serious relationship of any kind in my life. Believe it or not, you're the closest person to my heart. I know you belong to someone else even if you play the field as if you were not tied to anyone. This is no melodrama believe me. I'd hate that. I'm alone, fending for myself. I have no one to share my things with. I've been thinking. I want to have a child of my own before it's too late"

"Are you trying now? As we speak?" I asked her with some concern.

"Yes!"

I sat back in my chair and took a long look at the lake. A number of thoughts rushed through my brain; self-preservation, one of them. I couldn't get involved in a situation not of my own making, against my better judgment. A long time commitment that a child represents was another. I knew, given time, I could amass a number of reasons why I shouldn't be the one to assist her. Even if I liked Nati a lot I couldn't do it, even if I wanted to. But how to tell her, here, tonight, without hurting her feelings.

"You're not mad at me, are you?" she said with teary eyes.

"No, I'm not. But I think we should think about it together."

"I know it is unfair to put you in this kind of situation. But I'm desperate. Believe me. There is something else going on at the same time. You haven't heard yet, but it is only a matter of days."

"Okay. Just calm down we will handle everything together. Go ahead, be frank with me," I said. "I'm here to help you and I will!"

"Zamora is selling our company and there is nothing I can do about it."

"Hmm!" was all I could utter. If the first news had been troublesome, the second was devastating. At least the pregnancy was not a fait accompli. Even in the worst scenario there was always the possibility of doing something about it. But the selling of the corporation was something else. That could have immediate repercussions; their business represented almost fifty percent of my revenues.

"No wonder you seemed so troubled. I had been wondering all along what was eating you," I told Nati stretching my hands over the table and holding hers tightly. "Don't say anything else. Let's go for a ride on the lake and we'll talk," I said, holding back my impatience and curiosity.

We walked down to the lake, a few meters to the pier and took the next vaporetto to Bellagio. I wanted Natividad to feel at ease so we could talk about everything that worried her and I could have a peek, perhaps a preview, of the next big worry in my life.

The vaporetto began its lazy crossing to the other side of the lake. It was a breezy, beautiful night at Como. Gigantic mountains surrounded the lake and the lights of a dozen scattered towns enlivened the hills. I pulled

Natividad to the boat's bow and stood at the rail, facing Bellagio reluctantly coming closer and closer to us. No matter how many times I had done this crossing, I never tired of it. The whole exercise was me, and even if the earth was shaking under my feet — my business and future were about to collapse — I loved that moment and no one, not the devil, God, fate or even Zamora, could take it away from me.

Nati leaned on the rail and I rested behind her. I kissed her neck and she turned her head like a lioness looking at her mate.

"Now that we are leaning on the rail and can't fall, I'm ready to handle everything you mentioned before."

"Do you want to ruin this moment?" she asked me. "We'll talk tomorrow, before we go our separate ways?"

"You're right!" I told her. Little did she know that all my highs and lows have taken place in moments like this in which I thought I was on top of the world when in fact I was touching bottom with my feet.

"You are not mad at me, are you?"

"No. I'm flattered that someone would consider having a child with me. You reminded me of Bernard Shaw. Isadora Duncan wrote him note saying, 'Mr. Shaw, I would like you to father my son."

"Did she really?" Nati asked me.

"Isadora was a free spirit and she ended her note, 'could you imagine our son with your brain and my body'?'"

"Did he answer?"

"Of course. He wrote back: 'Madam, could you imagine our son with your brain and my body?' I'm paraphrasing, of course."

Nati laughed and immediately riposted hitting my chest with both fists. "We have good brains and good bodies. Our son would also, regardless of whose brain it was."

"Oh Nati," I said hugging her tightly. "That's the kind of offer that also reminds me of all my own limitations."

"I know it is unfair. Perhaps I shouldn't have said anything and just go ahead and, if providence so desired, have the baby and never tell you. But I also thought of sharing the dream, of knowing that someone wanted to have a baby with me. I love you Alex, I really do! I don't mind if you don't."

My eyes got wet. I felt an immense sadness, as if I were God and for a moment I could grant someone a wish, a bit of happiness, even if briefly.

"I love you too," I said and I embraced and kissed her deeply.

Nati cried inconsolably and our tears mixed, running down our cheeks. I couldn't honestly say that I loved her, but at that moment I did, and I told her. She was the kind of person I could live my life with as many other couples do. She was someone I felt comfortable with — that I could talk to, share experiences with — if, at this stage in my life, I still was capable of doing so. But, for how long?

Bellagio was lit and beautiful as we approached it. I thought a walk by the lakeside and a quiet espresso would do us good and that's what we did. We walked around the restaurants and cafes until we finally found an outdoor terrace right next to the water. We ordered several espressos and took until the last vaporetto to Tremezzo to consume them. We spoke of everything except her cherished ambition, as if we wanted to forget, she even mentioned it.

We returned to our hotel close to one thirty in the morning. We spoke little during the trip back. We went directly to our room and sat on the balcony as any other ten year married couple would, away from each other, and each lost in deep thought. Realizing what we had done instinctively, I moved my chair next to hers and took Nati's hand. Nati looked at me, smiled and gave me a sweet kiss. Moments later we moved into the room and went through the motions of a passionate encounter, although in reality it was a tame exercise intended mostly as mutual reassurance rather than one of our genuine acts of real passion.

Nati woke up early, but moved silently not to disturb me. Subconsciously aware, that she wanted to go to mass, I rolled out of bed, kissed her briefly and headed for the shower. The bellboy came for our bags and we walked down to the terrace for breakfast, our last look at the lake and those majestic mountains — our dreamy backdrop — to an emotionally packed weekend.

We hit the road again and in a few minutes we were in the town of Ospedaletto. Nati had read of this beautiful, Romanesque church of La Maddalena — with a peculiar tower — we couldn't miss. We stopped at the quaint little church and heard mass by a fiery old Franciscan priest whose homily was devoted to the sanctity of matrimony. He not only blessed married couples, but was mercilessly critical of modern ones' tendencies to live in sin and have children outside of the holy vows of matrimony. Natividad and I looked and smiled at each other. By the end of the service we staged a strategic retreat, discreetly beating the priest to the door of the church where he began shaking hands with his mostly elderly flock.

The mass over, we began our short drive to Milan's airport. Nati's demeanor had changed considerably and she had become ostensibly broody, as if she was dealing with her inner self. I kept quiet letting her handle whatever was eating her, but it wasn't long before she began a sort of soliloquy, enumerating a number of her concerns, among them a few issues related to my own future. I was astounded, incredulous, as if I was listening to Zarathustra himself, divulging my future with the certitude of its inevitability.

"You know Zamora owns a venture capital company. They invest and then sell," she said. "Well this big French conglomerate offered him three hundred million dollars for our corporation. One hundred million dollars up-front and two hundred more over the next five years. What he's selling is me, my name, my label. Fifteen years of sweat and tears, and the next twenty, if I live that long. Without me there is nothing. It is true I stand to make fifty million dollars up-front. And two million dollars a year plus incentives. When this is finally signed in a week or two, I'll be a millionaire; a slave millionaire. If I forsake the company in the first ten years, I'll be sued for the money. Wouldn't get my name or label back and not be able to do business related to anything in fashion, retail, styles, not even a fashion magazine. The conglomerate is "The Alsace Partners," she continued. "They own retail stores all over Europe and have a minority interest in your Bloomingdale and Nordstrom chains in the US. They also own a brewery and a film production company in Germany, a magazine publishing company, a luggage manufacturer, eight television stations in France, Italy and Spain. To tell you the truth, I don't know why these people are interested in buying us. Even if I stand to make a fortune, I won't have any freedom. I'll be a corporate puppet, trotting all over the globe selling soap, powder, lingerie, furniture with my name on it."

I kept quiet as she spoke. I knew she was sincere. I also knew there was very little she could do. So much for free will. Nevertheless, I asked her.

"Is there anything you can do?"

"What?" she responded. "Zamora owns me now. His company invested thirty million dollars ten years ago. Perhaps forty or fifty all together now, if you count operating expenses. Now he stands to make two hundred million. Not bad!"

"Do you have a lawyer?" I asked.

"Of course. He was the first one to advise me to sell. He also said I could refuse to go along, but that would mean going out of business. That's no option," Nati said emphatically. "He is also philosophical; 'even if everything goes down the drain,' he says, 'you're a multimillionaire.'"

"It's true!" I said acknowledging the obvious.

"So here I am. Going through the most critical phase of my life. With no one to turn to other than you."

There I was, driving to Milan, with my beautiful lover and business partner — contemplating the unraveling of the next phase of my life — as if I was having an-out-of-body experience. As much as I wanted to say something, I couldn't. I was sitting next to the possible mother of my unwanted child and perhaps one of the defendants of a future lawsuit. I looked at the road ahead of me, astounded at my luck.

We got to the Milan airport less than two hours before Nati's departure. We returned the car, were driven back to the terminal and together walked to her gate. Nati was distraught and hung from my shoulder. I, in turn, behaved like a stoic character in an epic novel, trying to reassure her and not displaying the angst starting to consume me.

We hugged; she cried, we kissed and reminded each other of our mutual love for the other. Nati walked through the gate, turned back, threw me another kiss, and disappeared. Some passengers were startled, a woman or two became emotional. They couldn't imagine what was going on, but it was obvious; we both were in pain.

My Al-Italia to New York was half empty. I sat in my aisle seat, with no one next to me. "I requested a Cuba Libre," and a rum and coke was promptly served. I was confounded with my luck. I knew it was all the product of chance and if there was anyone to blame, perhaps me. But I had never suffered a one-two punch like this in my life. A child? At my age? I'm forty-six and counting. If there was damage, it was already done and there was nothing I could do. That was the negative. Are there any positives? If there was no alternative, a little girl. *Are you crazy? You're losing it. That's unthinkable*, my alter ego insisted.

Then my thoughts turned to Zamora, the prick. Three hundred million. Jesus! No wonder he was sitting on me. 'We have to do better, sell more, and add an extra million before September'. Son of a bitch. The better my end looked, the better he looked. '*Alex, dummy,*' my alter-ego interrupted me again. *Don't tell me I didn't alert you. He is a venture capitalist. He's going to do what is natural to him; sell, make his money and run. This is a new ball game for us; we're fucked, out on the street. If they are Bloomies investors they're in, don't need us. You're an intermediary; toast! We should begin looking for a very good lawyer.*'

BANKERS GO FOR THE JUGULAR

We landed in New York and Maxine was at Kennedy airport waiting for me. Driving home I told her the whole story about the conglomerate and their investments in Bloomingdales and other stores in the United States. Maxine was a cautious woman with the tendency — or perhaps the ability — to foresee the worst possible scenarios. I wasn't naturally inclined to hear negative assessments, but as a policy, I always listened. Maxine repeated, almost verbatim, my internal arguments with my ego. A wise woman, no doubt, and an even better Monday morning quarterback.

If the news I brought with me was disquieting, the news at the office was upsetting. I handled a call from my banker in Miami, who apprised me in confidence of André's visit to the bank's president. According to my banker, André told the president that he knew there was a brake-up in the works and that I would probably lose Natividad's representation. My banker knew the Alsace's name and their international scope. Obviously my friend was not giving me only a tip, but a sort of warning. Our ten million dollar line of credit was exhausted and before I left for Spain, I had confided in him our intention to renegotiate it.

That afternoon I asked Ben to call Zamora to inquire about the rumors circulating in the industry; to complain about not being informed and to try to find out everything he could about the deal, the conglomerate and their intentions. Ben did and Zamora told him he was in the process of sending us a letter with all the details. That their closing was in a week. He told Ben these people had no preconceived plans and, as a matter of fact, they had reassured him they did not intend to take over the representation of their lines in the foreseeable future.

My alter-ego was right; we're fucked! 'No preconceived plans,' 'not taking over . . . in the foreseeable future,' prick. Those were code words for 'I'll tell you when it happens.' What do I do now? Just wait?

We got the letter from Zamora two days later. He didn't explain much. He gave us the name of the executive who would handle our side of the business and suggested we call him for more details in a week's time, a few days after the deal was signed. That same afternoon I got a call from Natividad in which she commiserated with me. She wasn't happy she said. She wished we could be together soon and offered to do everything in her power — whatever she might still have — to help me through the transition.

A day or two after the Alsace's deal was completed, I got a call from Phillipe Sands, VP Foreign Markets. The French was extremely cordial. He said to be planning a trip to the US and South America and that he'd love to spend a full day with me and Ben in Miami. He also offered not to have any dramatic changes in the offing and used the opportunity to invite me to Paris, all expenses paid, after his visit in the coming weeks.

My first priority then was to address my relationship with the bank and, after a hastily arranged flight to Miami, first thing Monday morning, I showed up promptly at the bank. After the regular pleasantries, the VP in charge of my account, informed me he had arranged for the two of us to meet the bank's president. He said "you should know, he is very concerned with the Alsace's takeover and wants to discuss a few options with you." Together we walked directly to the president's office and sat in front of a big table, with a magical window behind it, overlooking the Miami skyline and the seaport in the distance.

After a rather offish greeting the fellow asked me point blank what was going on with our business. I mentioned we were doing very well, but we were also experiencing delays collecting our account receivables. The economy, the cut of the hemlines, new prints and styles were a number of factors that affected the industry. Nevertheless, I told him, I was confident it would only be a matter of time before everything would be back to normal. As I spoke, I could see this fellow's impatience with my pitch and asked myself why was I wasting my time giving him such a report. After all, those details were of no interest to an outsider whose only concern was collecting the interest on his loans.

"And how is the conglomerate's takeover going to affect us?" The president asked me.

"There is nothing to worry about. We not only have a contract but I just had a telephone conversation with the Foreign Markets VP and he reassured me they contemplate no changes. The man even invited me to visit him in Paris," I said trying to give the president the rosiest spin I could.

"But you only have a year left on your contract, don't you?"

"Yes! We do."

"So? What's the story? Did the Frenchman tell you what their intentions are?"

"We have a clause, you know, like an automatic rollover. It's just a mechanical thing."

"There is a possibility of a renegotiation. At least it is contemplated on the contract," the president said.

"Well, technically speaking you're right. That possibility exists."

"I'm not trying to give you a hard time but we have to cover our ass. But you're high up there on your line of credit. You also owe money to another bank. We discussed your request for another three million. Thirteen million in total. Frankly I'm not very happy about it, but your friend here insisted," he said pointing to my banker. "We'll increase your line another two million. Will that help you?"

"Well, it is not what I want but I guess I could compromise," I said feeling relieved.

"But there is a catch," the President said. "We need more collateral."

"You have everything I've got already."

"Not exactly. You have a leisure property in upstate New York, don't you?"

"You're talking about my retreat. La Finca."

"Yes! Your retreat. You have it listed in your assets with a value of a million."

"Look, you already have almost fifteen million in account receivables and another five to seven million with my apartment in Key Biscayne, my home in New York and my factory building."

"If we are risking ten or twelve million in your business, don't you think it is fair we are first in line in case of a collapse?"

The president had a point! But La Finca? I could part with everything but my retreat. My head was boiling. *'Don't say anything else and get the hell out of here, fast!'* my ego advised me. *'Let's regroup. Tell him you will give an answer in a day or two. Play it cool. You're not the only one in trouble. He is too! Tell the fucker goodbye. Now!* My alter ego insisted.

"Ok. I'll get back to you tomorrow or the day after," was all I could say before we shook hands and I walked out of his office and their building as fast as I could.

Monsieur Sands, the Alsace's VP, arrived on schedule and I met him promptly at the Hyatt Regency in Coral Gables. Nice chap Sands. Very affectionate, easy going and extremely clever. I took him to visit our offices and took a spin by our atelier where I had my troops dressed up and on their best behavior for the occasion. We spent the afternoon together and met him for dinner again at night after a brief break to refresh and change his attire. I asked the Frenchman if he had a particular restaurant or cuisine in mind and he said he would enjoy a good Cuban place. He raved about a small joint he frequented in Paris run by a Cuban couple. The French turned out to be a fan of black beans and white rice, as well as pork and fried plantains. He said he wouldn't care for a fancy place, but the real thing. Sands was in his early fifties and spoke English, Spanish, Italian and German fluently. He studied at the Sorbonne and was married with two children, a boy and a girl. Right after dinner, I took him back to his hotel; 'I'm tired, he said,' and we agreed to get together promptly the following morning.

Ben and I arrived at his hotel at eight thirty sharp. Sands was enjoying a large glass of orange juice although he had not ordered any breakfast yet. I introduced Ben to him and, right after ordering a continental breakfast, he began questioning us about the development of our business, our financial viability and future plans. He added he was also a member of Bloomingdale's and Nordstrom Boards of Directors. When breakfast was over, he asked us to drive him to the closest Bloomingdale store, and we did. He immediately went to our designer's corner and counted the samples we had on display.

"We need to do better," Sands said. "Do you have any special plan for the boutiques?"

"We do Bijan's already. Brandels is tough. They want us to pay for the space."

"Well, if we are going to try to expand our lines we have to take some risks, don't we?" Sands asked me.

I drove him to the airport to take his flight to Brazil. Three days after his departure I decided to call Natividad. I thought it would be a good idea to compare notes with her. Natividad wasn't available, her secretary told me. She had been indisposed on and off for more than a week now, but she would definitely relay the message. That afternoon I locked my office door and, with a lot of concern and anticipation, I did call Nati at her apartment. Her maid answered and said she was in bed but if it was important she would wake her up. I said who I was. After that the maid put me on hold and, a minute or two later, Natividad came on.

"Oh, my love. How wonderful to hear your voice again," she said.

"It's great to hear you too! I understand you're not feeling too hot these days. . ."

"I'm feeling terrible, but I'm very happy."

"Oh?" was all I said, thinking my worst fears were being confirmed.

"I wish you were here. With me, now! I have good news but I wasn't sure how to share it with you. Can't you take a short trip? A few days, a weekend perhaps?"

"How does four weeks sound to you?"

"It's music to my ears, but I don't know if I can wait that long to tell you the good news?"

"Well, if it makes you happy why don't you share it with me now?" I said, preparing myself for the worst.

"Alex, I'm pregnant," she said with some hesitation. "We are going to have a baby!"

"Have you been to the doctor?" I asked hesitantly.

"Yesterday," she answered. "I'm six weeks into it already."

My head was bursting. I went back to our time in Florence and Como and counted the days as quickly as I could while looking for something to say. Yes, this is three weeks and a few days after the take-over. She said then the transaction would be completed in a week or ten days and it actually took two weeks, so she was right. Six weeks is right.

"I'm happy for you," I said flatly, thinking more of my deteriorating situation than my luck impregnating her.

"I understand, you think this is a capricious thing. Something of my own doing and I'm forcing you to play a role against your will."

"No, no, please. Do not misunderstand me. I want the best for you and I'm willing to do anything I can. But remember I am an old man."

"You are forty-one, Alex. You're in your prime," she said emphatically. "I knew you were going to be upset by the news, but it is our child. A child conceived out of love in an ideal place under beautiful circumstances. And I want you to come soon. I want to be with you. I love you Alex. I love you."

"I love you too," I said and after a few more torturous moments and reassurances we hung up.

That was my conversation with Natividad ten days ago. The last of a number of disastrous events since we became lovers at Cadaques almost three years ago. Since then I met André, completed the deal with Zamora, introduced her fashion line in the US, fired André, my financial situation became strained, her company was sold and now I was going to become a father. What a ride. That's why when Roberta mentioned the curse, the conversation with this fellow, my curiosity made me wonder. Was it possible? Well, regardless if I believe it or not, since I fired André I have suffered a number of setbacks. I've gotten entangled in a web with no apparent clean exit. My curiosity turned into urgency. And now I'm hearing there might be a reason for all this; surreal and Kafkaesque as it may seem.

EL BRUJO REDUX

"Sir," I asked the Brujo, "Is there a way I can meet the Babalao André used to do the job on me?"

"Has your life changed in the last year or so?" the Haitian asked me. "You can be frank with me."

"Definitely! I can see a clear trend, both personal and in my business. I don't know if it is the result of a curse, my astrological star, or chance simply playing its tricks."

"You could lift the curse or maleficio," the Brujo said. "But it won't be easy. I couldn't help you even if I wanted to. But I could introduce you to a Babalao. He's the only one with power to heal or to punish. You know about Babalaos, don't you?"

"Well, I've heard of them."

"There are only two or three in Miami that I'd trust."

"I'd prefer to meet the one who did the job."

"That might be impossible," the Brujo answered.

"I'm obviously confused. I need to have an idea of what this is all about. How it works? What happened in my case?" I asked the Brujo with some concern and a great deal of curiosity.

"It is all about Orishas, what you'd call saints. You know about Yoruba, don't you?"

"I know it is a West African religion," I answered.

"And about the Orishas," he said, pointing to the two life size saints behind us.

"Yes, I know they're deities. I know the African slaves substituted their deities for Catholic saints. That much I know."

"The Babalao — a priest in other words — chooses the saint according to the kind of work he's doing. Those two behind you are 'Chango,' which you know as 'Santa Barbara' and 'Babalu-aye,' that is 'San Lazarus of the Crutches.'"

"Yes I'm familiar, but only know them by their Christian names."

"You know, Olorun, or the man from heaven, is what you call God. You don't speak to him directly. You speak to him through the Orishas, the secondary deities."

"So which of the deities, or Orishas as you call them, were used in my case?"

"I don't remember if it was one or more, but if you want to understand what's happening to you, you have to give me time. I'll try to explain how the whole thing works. Do you want me to tell you or is the consultation over?"

"No, please, take your time," I said, realizing my haste could jeopardize the purpose of my visit.

"I already mentioned this fellow, what's his name?" the Brujo asked me.

"André," I responded.

"André came to see me. I told him I wasn't the right person to do the job, I took him to see Ramon. He was the most prestigious Babalao in the entire US. He used to be flown to California to consult Hollywood celebrities. They would send their jets to fly him over. Ramon was Cuban, famous long before he escaped to the US when Castro tried to wipe out all religions in the early nineteen sixties. He died, by the way, a month ago. He was kind of old, eighty-seven, eighty-eight; strong as a bull and his mind sharp as razor. Heart attacks don't respect holiness."

"Can I interrupt you just for a minute?" I asked the Brujo.

"I anticipate your question," he responded. "He would have been the ideal person to reverse the curse, but he's gone. He is dead. I could recommend another Babalao who is taking his place in the community. Was I correct about your question?" the fellow asked me.

"Yes! That's what I wanted to know. Go on please."

"During the first consultation your man André explained his situation in detail. No Babalao would do a job unless he was really convinced the person had been done wrong. He'd never use his powers for a frivolous cause. André, I remember clearly, was very persuasive; his story compelling. We spent close to three hours with Ramon and at the end of the session, it was agreed a remedy to his malaise was justified. Your man was asked if he had any kind of maleficio, a curse, in mind and he answered he wanted it to be a slow one. Something comparable to what he had suffered while working for you. What about body effects? Ramon asked him. He said he wanted you to conserve your wits but everything else should be part of the job, including family, relatives, anyone who feels any kind of affection for you. I remember it clearly, the Brujo said, André wanted to see you crawling, begging to keep afloat but be consumed slowly by the forces around you. I've seldom seen such a vindictive person, this André," the Brujo observed and then continued. "He went on insisting in preserving your brain intact so you could fully appreciate the extent of your misfortune. Then he added something else about his lover suffering and eventually dying of Aids while his conflict with you was red hot. He added if anything, he wanted you to pay for that too."

I was dumbfounded; didn't know what to say or how to react to such a recipe of misfortunes and ill inspired deeds. I took a look at Roberta and she extended her hand in a sign of support. If all these things were possible, I was in for a rough ride. Fortunately my intellect prevented me from taking those threats at face value just because this fellow says so. Even if it's true, I'd heard of those jobs being done all the time, I really doubted they'd ever cause the damage they pursue. By the same token, I was fascinated by the intricacies of the Santeria world. To think that in this day and age human beings are still toiling with the unknown, believing in the powers of deities to perform miraculous deeds was incredible but fed my curiosity even more.

"Please, go on," I urged the good fellow to continue.

"At the end of the session they agreed to go on with the job and reached an agreement on fees due Ramon for his services."

"How much does a thing like this cost?" Roberta asked him.

"Usually five thousand dollars. But I think your man claimed poverty and Ramon came down to four. These things are not cheap and they take time to prepare," the fellow said. "Ramon said it would take most of a day starting at seven in the morning. Then he asked your man . . ."

"André," I said interrupting him.

"He asked André if he had a private garden or a backyard. He said yes and they scheduled the job in three weeks' time. He gave André a long list of things he needed but said he was able to procure them, probably easier than André could. Among them; a young goat, about 20 pounds or so. A French cock, a small amount of a Jewish cemetery's ground, human bones and Guinea pepper. André would have to provide a large pot, not to cook the goat, of course, because that would be done separately. He said he'd bring a butcher to prepare the goat for what he called, 'a goat feast,' at the end of the ceremony in the afternoon. He asked André to invite his friends for the feast, but not to tell them what the whole thing was about."

Jesus Christ, I could never have imagined all those things were necessary to screw somebody out of his future. Jewish cemetery ground, whoever heard of that? Human bones? A goat? Well at least they could eat the goat. And four thousand dollars. That's a profitable profession. Four grand for a half day's job. Jesus!

"I helped Ramon the day of the ceremony. We got together early, about seven thirty. I arrived first and Ramon right after me. The butcher came minutes later with the goat and a beautiful French cock, with his legs and spurs covered by feathers. We opened up a six-foot table that would serve as an altar. Ramon brought with him all kinds of stainless-steel pots, a thin long knife and I helped him with a box full of many other artifacts. At about eight thirty Ramon was ready to begin and he quickly changed his attire to a long gown and a pillbox kind of hat. Have you ever been to one of these ceremonies?" he asked us.

"Never!" Roberta and I responded.

"We tied the goat's paws and placed it on top of the table. The poor thing bellowed as if he knew his luck had run out. Ramon insisted on not suppressing it, saying it was necessary for the offering. André had provided Ramon with a little book, a pocket appointment book, I think, that at one time he said had belonged to you. Ramon asked us to hold hands and recited a long prayer in Yoruba. Then he took André's hand, and holding an awl, sort of a thin skewer, punctured the goat's heart. The idea was not to kill it instantly but to let it bleed to death, slowly. Ramon had placed a pan under the table and once the blood ceased dripping it was removed and placed on another table. Then the butcher skillfully sawed the goat's skull in two and let Ramon and André remove the brain from the animal's carcass."

Roberta and I were mesmerized listening to the re-enactment. Neither one could believe and even less understand how killing one or more animals could impact another person's life and bring about the desired effects on the targeted victim.

"Next, Ramon removed his left shoe and sock," the Brujo continued, "took the French cock and locked its head between his two large toes and grabbing the animal by its legs — with a strong jolt — decapitated the cock whose head and blood fell into an empty pan."

Roberta horrified jumped on her seat and covered her eyes as if not wanting to watch the execution.

"Ramon cleaned his foot," the Brujo continued as if he hadn't noticed Roberta's dismay, "and placed the new pan next to the first one. He took André by the hand and walked to the table where the two pans laid next to each other and raised his arms to heaven. Ramon then began to pray in the Yoruba language, asked André to take the small pan with the cock's offering and pour it into the one with the goat's blood. He then asked André to drop the goat's brain and lift the pan to heaven as he recited a new prayer, also in Yoruba, while André held the pan high above his head. Afterwards they dropped a fistful of Jewish cemetery ground, a fistful of crunched bones, sprinkled it with Guinea pepper and added a page of the appointment book. Next, Ramon signaled André to put the pan on a small gas stove and light the fire.

"What happened to the rest of the goat? Did you eat it?" Roberta asked him.

"While the ceremony proceeded," the Brujo answered, "the butcher skinned the goat, seasoned its flesh and put it to cook in a small Vietnamese oven, designed just for the occasion. In the afternoon we had the feast!"

"Was it good?" Roberta asked again.

"Delicious! But I haven't finished, or do you want me to stop?"

"No, no. How can I miss them cooking me alive," I said, with a mix of satire and concern.

"When the offering was boiling and the brain fully cooked, Ramon took it down and covered it with a gold trimmed black cloth. Afterwards he asked André to hold it over his head and repeat after him another prayer, this time addressed to 'Eshu,' the God of Vengeance. — The equivalent of Satan in the Catholic religion. Your name was mentioned three times and the offering was left outdoors to rot for several days. Ramon said he'd return in five days to complete the offering. By two in the afternoon a bunch of André's friends began to arrive. He had invited about twenty, but by three o'clock, the group was close to forty. Most of the attendees were gay and pretty soon they were all dancing which each other. I left at five and the party was going strong."

"You mean, unbeknown to them the group was celebrating my future demise?" I asked the Brujo.

"André, Ramon and I were the only ones who knew what the goat was all about."

"I had heard a goat's sacrifice was a way of thanking the deities for favors granted," I told the Brujo.

"Yes. But Ramon said he had improvised it. In your case the goat represented you. Your heart was made to die a slow death. Your brain to cook under the pressure of long-lasting disputes, personal dramas, relatives' devastating illnesses, never-ending disagreements, shrinking businesses, unresolved litigations, culminating all in a devastating defeat."

"Have you ever seen something like this work in the past?" I asked the Brujo.

"Frankly, this is the first time I witnessed this kind of job done the way it was performed. Will it or is it working? I don't know. You'd know better than anybody else. Now, pay attention to what I'm going to tell you. Your situation is different; you know about the curse and could do something about it, if you decide to. Now, have I seen these kind of jobs reversed? Yes, I have. Ramon had the ability to do so. Unfortunately, he is no longer among us."

"What can Alex do to reverse the curse?" Roberta asked the Brujo.

"I mentioned two other Babalaos still active in Miami. None as good as Ramon was, but you never know. Think about it. If you decide to do something, I'm here to help you," the Brujo concluded.

The conversation sounded ominous; the details scary. It was like learning of a threat and having to live the rest of your life waiting for it to happen. Now, if he was a seer, maybe he could see in my future; the results of André's revenge. A kind of second opinion about the power of the curse bestowed upon me.

Roberta asked him for his fees. He looked at his watch and said three and a half hours. It is alright. Three hours at a hundred and fifty each, four hundred and fifty dollars. I was shocked. There is money in Santeria. I asked if I could write a check. He responded a check is alright, a credit card even better. But we settled for a check.

We shook hands and he walked us to the door.

"Should I be concerned?" I asked him while we shook hands again.

"Yes, you should. You have a strong mind, but there are powerful forces aligned against you. That much I can see. If I were you I wouldn't wait for the deluge to begin if you want to have a say in your future life."

"Thanks a lot," Roberta said.

"We will be in touch," I added and together we walked to our car.

PARIS – THE ALSACE - CHLOE

"Guys," I said, addressing all our sales representatives via a telephone hook-up. "I just wanted to address the group together to congratulate each and every one of you for a job well done. Ben is going to give us a briefing of last month's sales and the extent of our market's penetration. So far a spectacular month with record sales and product placement in all our different lines. At the higher end, Natividad's line also had a spectacular month. But we can't rest! Thanks again for a marvelous effort. I will leave you with Ben and then Francine.

That was me giving a pep-talk to my sales force. Indeed it had been our best month since we started the business. Now it was a matter of delivering the goods and getting paid for it.

Later on that afternoon, I called Natividad at home, in Barcelona. I had followed her pregnancy closely and a week or so ago, she mentioned she had experienced some spotting, but nothing serious. Nevertheless the doctor had asked her to rest as much as she could. Today she said she continued to experience some but not as often as before. I mentioned my trip to Paris to meet the Alsace's Chairman, her boss. Sands had invited me and was paying my stay. I told her I had taken advantage of the trip to schedule a stopover in Barcelona on my way back to New York. The news made her euphoric. She repeated a few times how much she'd have loved to spend time in Paris with me. We finished the conversation as we started it, professing our love for each other; we said goodbye and hung up.

I arrived in Paris ten days later and went directly to The Rafael Hotel, near l'Etoile. Having done the crossing many times, I got used to the last flight from New York — as if I was going to bed at home — waking up a few hours later in Paris. A quick shower and I was ready to hit Paris running. The city was as beautiful as ever and the weather was perfect; twenty one degrees Celsius and no humidity whatsoever.

A few hours at the Louvre, a short lunch at an outdoor café and I returned to my hotel for a recharging nap. An awakening hot shower, a pair of slacks, a turtle neck, my leather jacket and I was ready for the Left Bank; a brisk walk through Saint-Germain-des-Pres, a cocktail, dinner at Brasserie Lipp, a cognac at the bar and back to my hotel for a good rest before my big day at the conglomerate headquarters the following morning.

I got to the "Alsace" headquarters promptly at eleven. Sands was waiting for me at his spacious, exquisitely decorated office. A few pleasantries and we plunged into a small mountain of numbers and projections. Immediately after revising the last charts, I reminded Sands, how important for me was to return to New York with a signed contract. Sands appeared very sympathetic to my concerns but pleaded for time. He said there was an extensive reorganization going on throughout the conglomerate and our franchise was something very important for the Chairman's future plans. Having heard some unfavorable rumors in the industry, I asked Sands about the Chairman's standing with his board. Sands smiled, but in the same breath he said, "The Chairman wasn't completely understood and many of his critics were naysayers who resented a French Harvard educated CEO with a global reach. Nevertheless," he added, "he was confident the man would be proven right in the end."

Still not completely satisfied with his assurances, I gently pressed Sands yet again to accelerate the negotiations. Sands politely begged for time and asked me not to bring the issue to the Chairman's attention; "no one is ready to discuss the contract and it wouldn't sit well with him." Having said that, he graciously led me through the building, showing me the beautiful art hanging from the walls, the tastefully decorated executive offices and a number of large conference rooms until we got to the Chairman's quarters. A few more minutes of idle chit-chat at the Chairman' antechambers office, Chloe, his female personal assistant ushered us into the biggest and most luxurious quarters I had ever seen in my entire life.

The Chairman was elegantly dressed in a sharply tailored, Armani like, blue suit with an aquamarine tie. He stepped around his desk and greeted me effusively.

"Jean Francois Tessier," he said. "But call me Jean, please."

We shook hands and he asked us to sit on the couch, ordered some refreshments and, in a well-rehearsed pep-talk, talked about the progress they had made, their global reach and ultimately thanked me for all I was doing for their products in the US. He mentioned Sands being an integral part of the conglomerate's future and assured me they had plans for America's markets and hoped I'd be somehow associated with them. He mentioned he was visiting New York in a week or two and that perhaps we could squeeze in lunch and if not, a cocktail. Then his assistant came into the room and reminded him of his luncheon appointment, we shook hands again and that was that.

Right after the lightning visit with the Chairman and still trying to figure out a reason for their invitation to come to Paris, Sands and I went to a restaurant for lunch and spent another hour talking about wine, women, chance and the future. He asked me how long I was going to be around and I said I'd probably be heading home the next day. He said it was a pity because he was having an intimate dinner for a few friends on Saturday. He mentioned Chloe, the Chairman's attractive assistant, was coming.

"I introduced you to her this morning," he said. "She's attractive, intelligent and single."

"Intriguing," I responded.

"With her we are nine for dinner," Sands continued. "Her date couldn't make it and I don't want her to skip the occasion. You would be the tenth rounding off the group. What do you think?"

I said I had plans. That I'd have to cancel flights, make some calls.

"I could ask her to pick you up," he said.

I asked Sands if I could call him if I decided to stay. He said of course and we left it at that.

56

Having the rest of the afternoon and the evening all to myself, I decided to take another leisurely stroll through Paris. I was a sucker for La Plaza Vendome and its surroundings since I was a kid and saw "Rififi" in the movies. Once at Vendome I decided to go for a cocktail at the Ritz. I had been thinking about Sands' dinner invitation and the more I thought about it, the more I was convinced I shouldn't miss it. The idea of meeting Chloe — a potential inside channel to the Chairman — intrigued me tremendously. After all, she was the Chairman's personal assistant. If anybody, she'd know what was going on. I didn't expect her to divulge all the secrets, but a tidbit here and there could help me figure out her boss's intentions. She was also a good looking woman — alone in Paris of all places — I could use some cheering up. Halfway through my whisky, I asked the bartender for the closest telephone and he directed me to one at the end of the counter; Hemingway's Corner, as it was known. I called Sands at his office and he promptly answered the phone. He said he was delighted I could make it and that the corporation would cover any additional expenses. He'd call Chloe and, if she agreed, would give her my number at the hotel. Fantastic I said; finished my drink and returned to my hotel.

That night I mixed with the artists in Montmartre and — not happy with any of their paintings, but delighted by the atmosphere — decided to stay and have dinner somewhere around the square. I settled for a charming, open air brasserie, a few steps, as you walk away from the piazza. An exceptional gifted, floating musician was playing a large, rather old bass; his music? A sorrowful seventeenth century piece you'd not hear anywhere in today's world. I loved the cello, so the bass was an easy substitute in a night full of doubts but promising exchanges. Sometime after ordering my meal, I asked the captain in my tortured French 'Le telephone, s'il vous plait,' and he directed me to one right in front of the restrooms. Yes! I had two messages at my hotel; one from Natividad in Barcelona and another one from Chloe, with a number for me to call. Nati would have to wait and I went ahead and dialed Chloe.

"Oui," she answered. "It's me, Alejandro," I said, and she quickly greeted me in English. I was as gracious as I could be talking about our brief encounter at noon time and added I'd be delighted to escort her to Philippe's on

Saturday if she so desired. She said "she'd also be delighted to pick me up," and suggested six in the evening; "that would give us an hour to get to his house," she said, "and be there at seven, for cocktails." I mentioned I had two more days in Paris before Saturday, that I was alone and even if I knew the city relatively well, there was nothing like a local to find those charming places that escape even the most inquisitive foreigner's eyes. She laughed and said she'd love to be my chaperone, but she was quitting work around ten every night. Nevertheless, she suggested meeting earlier on Saturday and have coffee or a cocktail anywhere in the city. "Of course," I immediately said and asked her to come to my hotel. She agreed and that was how my date with Chloe was arranged.

Thursday morning I placed a call to Natividad in Barcelona. The maid answered the phone and told me not to believe anything Nati said. She had been losing blood every day and her family was very concerned, the old woman repeated. Nati got on the phone and asked me if I had arrived. I excused myself, blaming Sands and the Chairman. I mentioned there was a general meeting on Saturday morning and a dinner later that night and they had insisted I stay. "It was important for me to create a bond with these people," I told her. "I'll be with you Sunday morning." She didn't want to hear about it. There were no excuses, she said. "You don't care what happens to me or our baby," she complained. "Tell me how you're doing?" I demanded. Nati only answered she was alright, holding on, but that she didn't have any support; she was alone, by herself, and it was very difficult. "What about your mother?" I asked. She responded she didn't want her around. "She's vindictive," she said. "She insists on reminding me that God punishes in peculiar ways." Do not pay attention to her, I suggested. "I'll be there Sunday morning, I promise," I repeated again and again before I hung up.

Chloe arrived at The Rafael promptly at five in the afternoon and excused herself for not coming earlier. "I normally work half days on Saturdays. The Chairman is so busy," she said, "Believe it or not, I take work home every night."

I looked at her closely as she spoke. Chloe was elegantly dressed which made me give up any idea of a leisurely stroll in the city. I praised her attire and told her I had hoped for a more relaxed afternoon. She apologized again and added the dress was one of Nati's designs. "Why don't we have a cocktail at the bar?" I suggested. And we sat at a cozy corner, in a comfortable love-seat — with a Martini and a dry sherry in hand — to talk about business, life and the beautiful city Paris was.

"Your boss seems to be a slave master," I said, wishing for some sort of personal response.

"Far from that," she answered with a smile. "He is a busy man with a head full of projects. I feed off the energy around him."

"How long have you been working for him?"

"We came together when he was made Alsace's President four years ago. I was his assistant at a venture capital company he owned. The man is a maverick. He was made Chairman and CEO two years ago. There are quite a few magazine stories if you want to know more about him.

"I read two recent articles, one in Fortune and the other at The Wall St. Journal. They all celebrate his meteoric career but are astonished at the diversity of his acquisitions. A credit card company, magazines, television stations, now fashion companies. Does he know what he is doing? Is there more on the way?"

"Wait and see," she said with a picaresque smile. "But should we talk about business?"

"No! Please, that's the last thing I want to talk about. But, before we change subjects; does he have plans for the US?"

"I'm not at liberty to say. But, for him, the US is the Promised Land. He's a Harvard graduate."

"Any time soon?" I insisted.

"He has to consolidate what we have acquired so far but he'll be ready for bigger and better things in a year or two; perhaps sooner."

I was astonished; first André, then Zamora and now the Alsace. What could come next? I asked myself. Nevertheless, I laid back in the sofa, toasted Chloe again and took a large sip of my fino. Even if one side of me was having a cozy interlude with this intriguing woman, my alter ego couldn't stop wondering about our luck, our future and what kind of business we had gotten in.

Brushing aside my puzzlement I focused on Chloe. She was good looking, early forties, easy going, unpretentious and quick to laugh; she was contagious. I knew she was a divorcee because Sands had told me, so as interested as I was about business, I began to dig into her personality and her past.

"Working late every day is not very conducive to having a life of your own, is it?" I asked her.

"I'm very fortunate, I enjoy a lot of the perks my boss can't. Opera, the philharmonic, theater, you name it, we have them all."

"Do you go by yourself?"

"Most of the time I invite friends. On Thursday I took Phillipe with me to see Claudio Abbado in a concert."

"You told me you were working late."

"I'm sorry. I had just met you. I wasn't going to start explaining why I couldn't go out with you. You understand that, don't you?"

"Of course," I responded. "Is Phillipe a frequent companion?" I asked her, suspecting a close relationship between them.

She looked at me as if she had been taken aback by my question. "No, not necessarily," she responded. "But we work closely."

"He seems to be a nice man," I said. "Did the three of you come together from the old company?"

"Yes we did. We have been working together for more than ten years now. Talking about connections. Have you heard that Natividad is having a baby?" she asked me.

"Yes!"

"I like her very much. She was here last month and we got together two or three times. She's having a child by herself. She's so brave. She isn't married nor does she have a steady boyfriend."

"Yeah, I heard that too," I said swallowing hard.

"Brave woman. She told me she had met this wonderful man and fell in love with him. It was something impossible, she said, but never explained why. But she decided, if she was to conceive out of matrimony, he'd be the one. I told her, 'in your situation, I'd have done the same.'"

"Did she give you any hints of who he was?"

"No! But she raved about him."

"Do you have a family?" I asked her trying to change the subject.

"A daughter. Sixteen years old; and my mother, aunts, you know. My father died in an accident five years ago," she said looking at her watch. "Oh my. It is almost six already. We should go."

It took us almost twenty minutes to get to a road out of Paris, and another twenty five, at close to eighty miles per hour, to arrive at a beautifully walled community on the outskirts of Paris. Sand's villa was a large Mediterranean style structure set among beautiful old trees. The property seemed to be worth millions. There were three other cars parked on the driveway and a Mercedes sedan and a Land Rover in the open garage.

Sands greeted us affectionately at the door and immediately led us to an inviting family room, with large glass walls, tastefully decorated with abstract art and comfortable furniture. He led us to the garden, showed us the large pool, a cabana and the white wrought iron furniture with beautiful cushions. Back inside, there was a bar in a corner of the room where three couples and a good looking woman were having drinks while conducting an animated conversation. Sands introduced me first to his wife Marie and then to the three other couples whose names I didn't register. They were all in their forties and early fifties. One guy was a banker, another one a lawyer and one of the women worked for the education ministry; she didn't mention in what capacity. An interesting group, leisurely yet elegantly attired all drinking whisky.

Chloe knew the couples well and after serving ourselves a drink the conversation turned to my visit, my business and my life in the Big Apple. Remarkably the group was well informed about my doings in Paris and were curious about my life in the US. They knew of my residence in New York and my place in Key Biscayne, where a couple of them had visited three months ago. Another drink or two and the conversation changed to politics and Monica Lewinsky. Sands immediately interrupted me and said that should be the après dinner topic for the night, so we continued chit-chatting about New York, Woody Allen, the theater and other generalities.

Dinner was served in the spacious dining room also with large French doors opening to the garden. A round table with simple candelabra dominated the space. Place mats for each one and two types of wine glasses; one for champagne and another for red. A maid served the champagne as soon as we took our seats and Sands made a gracious toast for happiness and the future. A large tray with all kinds of vegetables was passed around and immediately after, we were invited to the carving table where a leg of lamb was being apportioned by a male steward. The maid came around again and served a wonderful 1985 claret. Sands asked me to make the toast and I complied with my habitual one; raising my glass I said, "For all the good things in life and time to enjoy them," and everybody said amen.

Dinner continued for more than an hour and a half and after a delicious "tart-tartan," regular coffee for some and espresso for Chloe and me, we moved to the garden and, sitting under a gorgeous tree, we had more drinks and began a conversation about the US and the Monica Lewinsky affair. Strangely enough the group was very much attuned to the same issues being discussed in the States. The majority agreed it was too much to conduct such a salacious affair right next to the Oval Office. Some wondered why the Senate acquitted him and the impact in the coming elections when a second Bush aspired to become the new President of the United States.

After a few rounds of an excellent cognac, we entered the cultural realm and the fascination with Hollywood movies. The general consensus was the mindless blockbusters, the monopoly of screens with one single picture and the rampant escapism influencing the minds of future generations. Woody Allen was the exception to their ire against the American cinema although one or two complained about his constant reference to all things Jewish. But they also loved some of the better known American actors, Pacino, DeNiro, Streep, etc. Their French New Wave was also discussed and we all concluded that Goddard had become senile. I mentioned my youthful fascination with The Lovers, by Malle, and of course my long love affair with Jeanne Moreau. Chloe said she liked Bunuel for his cerebral eroticism, something I readily agreed with and I mentioned my icon, Ingmar Bergman, who the majority professed to revere.

A most pleasant evening, I concluded, driving back to Paris. Chloe had confessed being a bit woozy and had asked me to drive. She sat next to me although I had suggested her taking a nap in the back seat. After all it was a forty minute drive, but she refused.

"Did you have a good time? She asked me.

"A most enchanting evening," I responded.

"They are a great group. We get together at least once a month and have dinner at each other homes."

"Do you usually come alone?" I asked her.

"No, I have what you could call a boyfriend. I don't know if, at our age, we can still call them that," she said laughing.

"Does he work with you?"

"No, he owns a chain of shoe stores."

"How did the two of you meet?"

"I needed a pair of walking shoes, went by his store one day and saw a perfect pair. He was collecting the take for the day, we started talking. We met again walking one Saturday morning, had breakfast and have been together now for four years."

"That's a good story," I said with curiosity. "Do you have a lot of things in common?" I asked her with some delicacy.

"The fact that he sells shoes doesn't mean he's a moron," she responded quickly.

"I didn't mean any disrespect. You seem to be a high caliber woman," I said apologetically.

"He's a Sorbonne graduate; physics, but he hates it. He covered this weekend for his manager, who had the week off."

"I was lucky then. Otherwise Phillipe wouldn't have asked me to bring you along," I told Chloe.

"Oui. A pure coincidence, perhaps chance, as you would say."

"You know what I considered remarkable about tonight's dinner?" I said, puzzled by the omission. "We didn't exchange a word about work, your company, the Chairman or sports all night long. Back home work, illnesses and sports are the main topics of conversation."

"Here too. But our group is different. We are tired of each other's problems already."

As we got closer to Paris, I extended my arm and squeezing Chloe's hand softly told her, "I want you to know I had a great time. I'm not only talking about dinner. I'm talking about meeting you. Since the moment we got together for drinks at the bar, I felt as if I had known you all my life. You know what I mean?"

"I felt the same way," she responded.

"Well, what I mean is that I'd love to continue our friendship, if we can call it that, regardless of our business relationship."

"Absolutely!" she promptly responded. "You've got my home number already. Call me anytime. Just remember, I work six and sometimes seven days a week."

We got back to the hotel rather quickly. I got out of the car and Chloe walked around to the driver's side. I waited to kiss her goodbye, but she threw her arms around my neck and kissed me tenderly on my mouth. At that moment I felt aroused, wanting to take her upstairs, but somehow I resisted. I felt it was a little too soon to get intimate with her, if that was what she wanted. A wrong move could jeopardize an inside channel. A source of information directly connected to the Chairman.

"Au revoir" I said.

"Au revoir," she responded and drove away.

END OF THE AFFAIR

My plane landed at 11:10 am, Barcelona time; forty minutes late. I promptly took a taxi straight to Nati's apartment. It was a miserable, rainy day. The temperature hovered around fifty and the streets were desolate. The driver said it had been raining nonstop for the last three days. I wanted to surprise Nati and, with some anticipation, I entered her building and asked the doorman to announce my arrival. The porter seemed troubled when I mentioned Natividad and after requesting my name said, he thought she wasn't in. Nevertheless, he dutifully dialed the apartment. "Angelina," I heard him say, "Hay un senor aqui preguntando por la senora Natividad. Que le digo? There was a brief pause and he immediately said; "Ok, Ok, le dire que suba." The doorman told me: "Go ahead, Don Fausto. Ninth floor. There are two apartments per floor, I guess you know that. The one on the left."

Apprehensive by the exchange, I took the elevator up and found Evangelina, the maid waiting for me at the door. She was a bit agitated as she ushered me in.

"Senor Fausto, la senorita Natividad esta en el hospital," she said with tears in her eyes.

"Desde cuándo?" Since when? I asked her.

"Anoche a las diez."

"Anoche?" Last night? I asked her again.

"Tuvo una hemorragia y el doctor se la llevo para el hospital."

"Bleeding? How bad?" I asked her.

"Toda la cama llena de sangre. Estaba muy debil, la pobrecita, casi no podía abrir los ojos."

The bed full of blood, she told me, not able to contain her tears. She was very weak and could not keep her eyes open, she continued.

"What hospital is she in?"

Evangelina gave me the hospital's address and said she'd call the car service. I hugged her briefly and took the elevator down to wait for the car. Going down the elevator I felt as if I were being lowered to the bottom of the Inferno. Each floor was like one of Dante's circles encrusted with questions begging to be answered. Even if I was a convinced atheist, I couldn't help but ponder questions a believer would ask his God to explain. His lack of mercy, if he had any. Why do these things happen? Why her? Why not let her have her wish? A child of her own was all she wanted.

While my brain debated an answer to these questions my logical make-up reassured me — as if I needed reassurance — of the nonexistence of a super-being as such. At least not the one they had taught me, and still do, in Catholic and mostly Christian schools. "There," I'd confront my friends. "That's your God working. If I had your faith I'd be up in arms demanding a more merciful resolution of all our problems." Knowing better, my alter-ego quickly switched to our own side of the equation. All along, I had a tough time reconciling my situation. If I felt partly responsible for Nati's condition, perhaps selfishly, I felt hostage to someone else's longings for fulfillment. Our affair had been intense yes, but long distance, mostly esoteric by any standards. A number of occasions when we dealt with each other as if we were destined to be united for the rest of our lives. But that was it. Nothing else. *"The miscarriage was the negative,"* my alter-ego insisted, *"but don't discard the positive. Alex, you're out of the loop. You never wanted to be part of Nati's pregnancy. Her decision caught us by surprise and created a situation not of our own making. It's over. Thank your stars. Imagine what it would have meant to have a child at this stage of the game. Maxine! How would she have felt? Now a few more difficult moments and that's it. It is only a matter of reassuring her, making her feel your pain and sympathy. How are we going to do that? I don't know yet, but I have ideas."*

That was my alter-ego talking again. It might sound harsh, perhaps cruel, but it was true. There was nothing we could do about it anyway. I'm not responsible. I didn't provoke it. It was chance, fate, whatever you want to call it. Nevertheless I felt Nati's pain. I also felt something strange inside me, I didn't know what, but it made me sad. After all, through her months of pregnancy — convinced there was nothing I could do — I toyed with the idea of having a baby girl. But it was crazy. And I knew it. Crazy!

I went directly to the hospital's seventh floor and a big anteroom outside Nati's suite. Zamora, Nati's mother and four or five other people were having an agitated conversation. Zamora saw and rushed to greet me. It was the first time I'd seen him in person since he sold the company. He was gracious and not saying anything, gave me what seemed, a heartfelt hug. A sign they all knew who the father was. I asked him when it all happened and he said, 'about 10, last night.' Her mother remained seated. I approached, knelt in front of her and tried to give her a hug. She stayed back and remained silent while I said a few words of consolation. But she didn't pay any attention. If anything she gave me what I considered a stern, vindictive look. I said a few more words and asked Zamora if he thought it was alright to see Nati. He said, "Yes, go ahead."

I pushed the door open and entered the room. A nurse was changing Nati's IV. She was pale, seemed weak, her eyes wet. I rushed to embrace her. She was shaking and cried inconsolably.

"I'm sorry," was the first thing she said. "It is my fault," Nati murmured.

"Try to rest," I said, kissing her lips firmly, trying to hide my deeply felt sadness. I moved her gently and climbed onto the bed next to her. Nati continued to sob. I kept quiet, holding her tightly. I couldn't talk, even if I wanted to.

"I knew it," she said, sinking her face in my chest.

"Stuff happens," I said. "It's a miracle to be alive," I said trying to disarm all her arguments with the simplest of them all. "We are a wonderful machine, but it is still imperfect. It needs tweaking and we know that."

"I prayed constantly my child would be healthy. I said, 'God, I'll do anything you want but give me a healthy baby.' I told him, I didn't mind if it was male, female, handsome, ugly, gay or straight. I just wanted a son."

"Why not a girl?" I asked.

"Hypocrite!" she said with an air of recrimination. "You didn't want a child or anything to do with it in the first place and don't deny it now!"

"How can you say that?" I demanded troubled by her vehemence.

"You didn't want him."

"Was it a boy?" I interjected, trying to deflect the onslaught.

"I don't know. They haven't told me. And I didn't want to know anyway. I didn't want to jinx his gestation. I wanted a child of my own, but He didn't want me to have one. The same way you didn't. I wonder what I did wrong. Perhaps knowing you. Falling in love with you; a married man. Having a child out of wedlock. It was too much to go unpunished."

"Will you stop talking like that? That's nonsense! Miscarriages happen every day. Thousands of them. You aren't the only one to suffer one and you won't be the last."

"I'm past my time and I won't be able to get pregnant again."

"Will you stop the nonsense? Today's women are having babies well into their forties; you're only thirty-six."

"You're a hypocrite. You always were. I can't believe I trusted you. To think of it; your wickedness made me happy! I can't believe it; the more lies you told me the more I wanted to hear them. I am such a fool, so stupid! Yes, stupid! I'm through with childbearing, I'm through with you and I don't know what to do with my life anymore. Those four months were the happiest of my life," Nati said, while she continued the dialog with herself.

I pretended to listen when in fact my mind had taken leave and I was watching the scene from a distance; as if I was having another out-of-body experience. Of course those were the happiest months of her life; a brief interlude. That's what happiness is. A few good memories in a sea of disappointments and frustrations. But to me happiness is a flawed concept; an everlasting one doesn't exist. The lucky ones among us can string a bunch of brief moments and build upon them as if we were building a castle with illusions for its walls. My poor Nati wanted it all and who could blame her for that? Perhaps her failure was to take me as her anchor. She needed one and I was her life raft. Haven't we all done that at one time or another in our lives?

I stayed with Natividad most of the afternoon. Finally, after another episode of tears and recriminations, I took advantage of a momentary lull and the arrival of two female friends, to excuse myself and go to my hotel. I helped them put their flowers in an empty vase and choreographed my exit, walking backwards all the way to the door.

I got to my hotel and quickly made it to my room. The rain hadn't stopped and the forecast was more of the same. I threw my jacket on the chair, took off my turtle neck and my pants, grabbed a convenient robe laying on the bed, went to the fridge and served myself a scotch. Walking instinctively to the glass doors to the terrace, I observed the dark, menacing clouds looming in front of me. Were they harbingers of things to come? It was true I had one less worry to be concerned about, but I felt for Nati and no one could predict how her future behavior was going to affect me.

Perplexed by my lack of amiable options, I dialed room service and asked for a small corned beef sandwich and a bottle of Rioja; I hated the wines at the mini-bar. I dropped on my bed and closed my eyes. My thoughts drifted to the new situation; it seems I didn't get out of one to enter another. My Paris forage was not very reassuring. I went to try to expedite signing a new agreement and found they not only weren't ready but were looking for other options for the North American market; a prospect I didn't dare to consider. By the same token, if it is true, I did some bonding with Sands, other than his friendly invitation to dinner, he offered no information or even a hint about signing a new contract. Now I come to Barcelona and found Nati in the hospital with a miscarriage. I wonder, what will I find when I return home?

After a brief nap and a recharging shower, I went back to the hospital. Nati's suite had new but fewer faces. I entered her room and found her sitting in an arm chair with an IV attached. She had a much better face and looked more animated than this morning. A couple of female visitors quickly excused themselves and exited as fast as they could. Nati pointed to a floral arrangement sent from The Alsace in Paris and seemed happy with their gesture. Unfortunately, as I moved closer to her, she began crying again.

"Things are getting better," I insisted. "You look stronger than this afternoon," I said trying to reassure her. "In a day or two you'd be home and — in a week's time — you'd be back working full time."

She ignored my assurances and demanded to know when I was returning to New York. "I'll wait until you're home," I told her.

"Could we spend a few days together?" she asked as if begging me to stay longer.

I said I'd stay three or four days, no more. No sooner had I finished my sentence, I was hit with a new salvo of recriminations. A tough evening, I somehow survived watching a shipwreck, an awful American movie, dubbed in Spanish, Nati decided to watch.

The following day we took Nati home. She had asked me to stay at her apartment and I said I would. Leaving the hospital became a traumatic experience. Many of the nurses and members of the staff came to say goodbye. There were tears and a great show of sympathy and support from everyone around. We left in two separate cars. Zamora and her mother in one and Nati and me in a limo reserved the day before. She continued to cry all the way home while I held her closely, not knowing what to say or do to change her mood.

Once at her building's entrance Nati asked her mother to go home. "I'll call you," she told her. Frustrated, the mother protested her willingness to help. But Nati firmly reminded her of Evangelina, her maid. After a brief, heated argument, the disappointed matriarch returned to Zamora's car and took off. I helped Nati to the elevator and together we went up to her apartment. Evangelina was waiting at the elevator door, with her face full of tears, hugged Nati lovingly and helped her walk directly into her bedroom. The exquisite room looked even better than it usually does. Delicate flowers on the dresser, reflected in a beautiful mirror, the soft lights of two table lamps and the bed dressed with the most exquisite Italian linen Nati possessed.

A warm bubble bath, fresh clothes, soft sandals and Nati was ready for the succulent lunch Evangelina had prepared for the two of us. Finishing lunch, Nati said she was tired, wanting to take a nap and excused herself behind her closed doors. Anxious to call home, I went downstairs and asked the porter for a quiet room with a telephone. It was three p.m. in Barcelona; nine a.m. in New York. I wanted to reassure Maxine of my brief delay and let her know I'd be home in two days' time. I dialed Ben, whom I figured was still home, and had a brief conversation with him. I mentioned my misgivings with the Alsace and a two day delay doing some private errands in Barcelona.

The calls over, I went up to the apartment again and told Evangelina I'd be back by eight. As I was driven to my hotel, I couldn't escape mulling over a number of gloomy scenarios ahead of me. Nati was despondent, seemed completely unpredictable and our relationship had cooled off considerably. True, we were living a traumatic experience. Nevertheless, I was certain our liaison was turning ugly and there was little I could do change it.

That night, at about eight, Nati asked Evangelina to order dinner from one of her favorite eateries. It wasn't the first time we had dinner home. The restaurants she favored usually accommodated her wishes and tonight wasn't going to be the exception. Then she said she wanted to watch a movie. I asked if she had any in mind and she mentioned Camille Claudel; a movie about Rodin's mistress, a role made famous by Isabel Adjani, a beautiful, talented French actress. Her selection immediately raised a number of red flags in my head. If anything, even if the subject was far from our present predicament, the movie is about a truncated love affair between the famous sculptor and his principal assistant, with the movie's title. Rumors had it, Camille was not only Rodin's model and inspiration, but the mastermind and perhaps the carver herself of some of his most admired works. In other words, she was used and abandoned once the sculptor had no more use for her talents or her favors. Sensing a long night of tears and recriminations, I told Nati I was against watching Camille. That something lighter and not depressing was the recipe for a relaxing evening. But contrary to my wishes Nati insisted and told me where to fetch it; and Camille it was.

We sat in her spacious living room in separate arm chairs, not as we usually did, me on the couch and she resting her back on my chest. There was only a soft light in the room and the mood was somber. An atmosphere more conducive to punishing ourselves than to easing her pain. Nati began to weep before Camille shed her first tear and cried more and longer than the unfortunate woman did during the whole picture.

The movie ended at about a quarter to one. Nati called Evangelina, who was still awake, and asked her to prepare 'churros con chocolate.' And we ate the churros at a small table in the kitchen under Evangelina watchful eyes, who kept anticipating Nati's most insignificant wishes. After the churros were gone, I asked Nati if she wanted me to stay. "You better go," she said. I asked her what time she would like me to come in the morning and she said not to hurry. Lunchtime would be okay. I moved to embrace and give her a kiss, but she pulled back and just waved me goodbye with a contrived smile. I blew her a kiss and headed for the door. I felt relieved. Had she been the one to leave, the agony of her departure would have been unbearable.

In my room I changed my mind and poured myself a cognac from the mini-bar. With my snifter in hand I walked to the terrace and sat on a lounge chair. It was a cool night in Barcelona. The city was quiet, as if anticipating a brewing storm. I gently swirled my cognac and sniffed its awakened aroma. I was worried. The situation with Nati seemed doomed and I wasn't sure my remaining day in Barcelona was enough to ease her pain or reduce her growing hostility toward me.

Next morning, after a very late breakfast I called Nati and ended up talking to Evangelina who said she had a message for me. First, she asked me if I was still leaving for NY tomorrow. When I responded in the affirmative, she promptly added, Nati preferred to skip lunch. Surprised, I asked her what was going on? She said that nothing was the matter and for me not to come until the evening; no later than seven, because Nati needed all the rest she could get. I asked Evangelina if those were Nati's words, and she said, yes!

That evening I took a cab with enough time to arrive at Nati's apartment right on time. The doorman didn't detain me, as he usually did, but asked me to go up unannounced. I knocked at her door and heard her say, "It is open."

I entered her spacious foyer and living room and found her resting in one of the arm chairs. The lights were dimmed, a piano concert on the stereo. Nati looked different, fully dressed, with black slacks and a colorful top. Her hair straight back, as she usually combs it, and a minimum amount of make-up, enough to accent even more her black eyes and high cheekbones. I took a few steps in her direction, but she lifted her hands as if creating a barrier between us.

"Serve yourself a drink," she commanded.

"You look great," I offered, and indeed she did. Much, much better than the previous day, but she didn't respond. I suggested a cocktail for her.

"No, I'll take wine with dinner," she responded.

I served myself a stiff shot of whisky, anticipating a difficult session and walked back and sat in the armchair next to her.

"Where is Evangelina," I asked her.

"She's off. I gave her the night off," she said curtly. "I asked her to fetch a simple dinner from 'Las Cuatro Estaciones,' since you raved about it."

"How thoughtful," I responded.

"Nothing fancy," she said. "I don't want you to go away with an empty stomach." She then asked me politely what I had been doing with my time and I said "nothing in particular." I mentioned going to the club for lunch and visiting a few boutiques around town. Nati said "Chloe had called earlier and mentioned your dinner at Sands'. That she picked you up at your hotel. She was all in rapture with you. 'Alex is great company, Chloe didn't stop saying. I couldn't get her off the subject. I wonder what you did to her, or was it your usual stuff? Did you fuck her?" Nati asked me point blank.

"No, I did not," I answered firmly and went through the event, from Sands' original invitation to my innocent goodbye kiss at my hotel's entrance.

Nati listened attentively and when I finished, looking me straight in the eye, said:

"You are a consummate liar," she said and walked straight to the dining room, turned off the lights and let the candelabra on the table create the mood and ambiance of the space. Unceremoniously, she directed me to sit at the other end of the table; an unheard of arrangement in all our time together. The piano music had ceased and now, Maria Callas was singing an aria from Tosca in which she laments harming no one, praying devotedly to her God and being abandoned by her lover when she needed him most.

Nati pointed to the salad and asked me to serve myself. I said, you first, but she insisted. I took some greens and tomato slices and passed the bowl on to her. She didn't say anything, just motioned to the pork loin on a center dish and said something about my taking some; I did. I took the wine and poured both glasses. That was how this emotionally charged dinner and my last night at Nati's began.

"So, you're leaving tomorrow, are you?" she asked me.

"Yes! I think the plane takes off at one."

"You must be happy..."

"Happy? I don't know why you'd say that? I hate to leave you in this condition," I responded a bit piqued.

"You're leaving nothing behind. No child, no Nati to deal with any more."

"Nati, I know you're depressed. Let's not flog ourselves. Sometimes we're victims of the whims of fate. You believe in that. There is little we can do; especially now and you know it."

"Yes, you want me to blame my God and not ourselves. You're evading any responsibility yourself. Putting as many miles between us as possible. I might not see you ever again."

"Don't say that. I know you're depressed, but don't make it worse. We don't want to end up in a game of recriminations, something we're going to regret for the rest of our lives."

"I know it. You used me; personally and in business. You abused me emotionally. I was only a fuck; that was all I meant to you; a fuck! You used me to get the upper hand with Zamora. He warned me. 'Your fellow is a pirate,' Zamora told me. 'An opportunist.' And I said no, no; he is not. He's honest. I believe in him. You broke my heart, Alejandro. You really did. You know how to hurt a person. I should have paid attention to Zamora. The old man was right!"

"Will you stop the nonsense?" I urged her in no uncertain terms. "You're hurting yourself and me too. Don't say things you'll regret tomorrow. Don't demolish in half hour what we have had for the last three years."

"What did we have? Tell me! I was the one that kept it going. I fooled myself. It is true I needed an anchor. Someone to share my life with and you made me believe we had it. You encouraged it. If you didn't really love me you should have stopped it then; be a man. You should have said! 'Natividad I don't love you and I don't want to father your son.' I'd have looked the other way. But you didn't. You're a coward."

Oh, she made it sound so simple. But, she was right! And I knew it. Sometimes it is better to live an unverifiable lie as long as it makes us happy. Why not take the risk, things as they come? Life is a crap game anyway. I for one, never cared about tomorrow. How long would it last was never a question I'd ask. If it lasted a lifetime, a week, an hour was good enough for me. Nati was an artist; a resourceful one. A female of the species after all. She wanted her son and she pursued it. A longtime companion would have been great. But presented with the choice, she took the practical road; a romance with a probable outcome. And I admired her for that. I loved to romance her too. We were great together. She was unpredictable. Full of pizzazz, energy, while feminine and graceful. A furry kitten you wanted to squeeze and never let go. She had it all and I devoured it all. Was I weak? Of course I was. Did I use her? The same as she used me. But I had no plan. She did. I was in for the ride. She wanted the ride and a prize. When she told me she wanted a child with me, crossing Como to Bellagio, I couldn't utter a word. My ego bolted, but my brain promptly brought caution to the equation. "Are you trying as we speak?" I remember asking her. She said, yes! Then reality set in. I retreated hoping the consummation hadn't been realized yet. But inexplicably, I also felt like God at that moment, granting her such an important wish not anticipating of course, what the enterprise would entail had it succeeded or failed, as it now did. I felt sad, unable to soothe her anguish. I loved her in my own way. But conflicted as I was, it was inconceivable to surrender my life, the years it took me to get to where I am, to help her realize her innate wishes. My eyes got wet. I felt impotent, unable to deliver a happy ending. What an irony; she was tough as nails. I looked at her and got up from my chair when she continued.

"Let's be frank with each other once and for all," she continued "Say it. 'Nati I don't love you. Never did and I don't need you anymore. Say it, I did it for the fun of it; to get my business going. It was a business decision. A pure and simple business decision. I have Chloe now and I don't need you. I never wanted to have a son with you. Blame me for being a fool," she insisted. "Say it! It's time to face the truth."

Those were the last words she said before asking me to get out of her sight. Never to come or call her again under any circumstances, whether business, illness or anything else. Nati wasn't crying anymore and there was nothing I could say to stop her madness. And I left, quietly. She didn't stop me or say another word.

THE ALSACE SHOWS ITS HAND

Three months passed since my return from Paris and Barcelona when I heard hard news about Natividad again. I had been in contact with Evangelina, her maid on a few occasions until she asked me not to call again. I wouldn't call, I told her, if she promised to contact me in the event of any new ailments or bouts with depression. Evangelina never promised anything, but the conversation ended in an amicable tone. Today I received a copy of a letter discussing Natividad's tour of the United States addressed to her, in Spain, signed by Sands. That was news to me. Bloomingdale had invited her — letting us out of the loop — to visit their flagship stores in five different states. Obviously the arrangements were conducted behind our backs although, it was true, Sands suggested in his memo that one of our executives accompany her during the tour.

In another sort of indirect way, I knew about Nati through Chloe with whom I had been talking since my Paris visit. I had sent letters to Sands and the Chairman thanking them for inviting me to Paris, but I also called Chloe at home, and revisited our afternoon and evening together. I recalled fondly our chat at the bar, the dinner at Sands and the trip back to the city. "It was an enchanted evening I was anxious to repeat," I told her. Chloe wasn't only grateful for my comments but coquettishly suggested she'd love to meet me too. We were so much at ease with each other we pledged to keep in contact and I did, every week or so.

Chairman Tessier finally arrived in New York after a number of postpone-ments. One morning I got a call from someone on his staff suggesting a meet-ing at the Oak Bar, at the Plaza hotel, at five p.m. sharp. An opportunity to chat, to get better acquainted I thought, but things didn't turn out the way I'd hoped. The meeting was a real disappointment. I arrived on time and had to wait for Tessier, to come down from his suite, for forty minutes or so. One of his men kept me company at the bar and stayed — by our side — during the Chairman's harangue. Ten minutes into our encounter, the fellow reminded the Chairman they were late for their next appointment. We shook hands casually while Tessier insisted he had great plans for the US; adding he "sincerely hoped I'd be part of them."

Confused, not knowing what to make of his remarks, I walked out of the Plaza convinced the relationship was in an unstoppable nosedive. Not a word was mentioned about our business, my contract nor my future participa-tion in his big plans. The more I met this fellow, the weaker my knees got.

Ten days before Nati's scheduled tour was to begin I called Sands in Paris. After a few niceties, I raised the issue of not being consulted about the tour, and he responded with a reasonable excuse; he had been left out and had only learned of it when Natividad called to refine the details. "That's when I learned the chairman had contacted her from LA and asked her to arrange the tour." Sands then asked me what kind of a role I'd play during Nati's visit. I suggested it should be Francine's role to escort her. "She's our general manager and the one in constant contact with each store in the tour," I told him. He said he'd pick up the tab for Francine's expenses and suggested that both women contact each other to review last minute's details.

If I believed Sands, chairman Tessier was a loose cannon who did things as he pleased regardless of pre-established business norms. If Sands lied to me, the situation was even worse. Ben had informed me early that morn-ing, he had received a fax from the Alsace's main office in Paris requesting an increase in our standing letter of credit. Our newest client — a mid-size chain store's — order had come up close to a half a million dollars and the French were asking for an additional two hundred thousand to deliver.

On the home front, our discounter was having problems of his own not approving deliveries to customers with sixty days and older balances.

We were also far behind paying our own fabric supplier and one of our manufacturers in Portugal. One was threatening a cut off before the winter collection came on line. The other demanding a payment at least half the outstanding balance. An ironic situation; the more we sold the deeper the hole we were in.

Flustered by the bad news in all fronts, I dialed Francine, who was visiting clients in Cleveland, and gave her the news of her next assignment. Francine was pleased I thought of her. Before we hung up she confided she had heard of Nati's trip a week ago, but had not raised the issue, thinking I had a different plan for it. "Honestly," I said, "it was news to me too" and asked her not to keep that kind of information to herself. "Gossip," I reminded her, "is an important tool in our industry."

Fortunately, home had been an oasis so far. My life with Maxine was a relaxed, serene kind of existence. It was my place to hide and create a world of my own. She provided me with the anchor I needed. Grief sometimes was inevitable; but peace and sincere understanding, she clearly afforded me no matter what.

That Tuesday I arrived at home rather early, served myself a scotch at the bar and went to our rooms where Maxine would usually be reading or watching the news. Maxine was sitting in bed watching the news. I kissed her forehead, walked across the room and sat in a comfortable armchair. We normally talked about her day at the college, her students, the news of the day, but seldom got into details of my business activities. It wasn't the case of Al Pacino in the Godfather, "don't ask me about my business," sort of thing. Today I mentioned Natividad's visit and she immediately demanded not to be part of it. I mentioned I was going to be out during those days myself, and that Francine would host Nati's visit and accompany her during her tour of the United States.

"Good! I don't want to see her!" she immediately said. "Where are you going this time?"

"Portugal, I need to visit our contractor," I responded.

"Any particular reason?" she asked me.

"Well, we have a bunch of new orders and he wants to revise the cost per unit. They're negotiating a new labor contract."

"That's logical," Maxine said. "Everybody deserves a share of the pie. How long are you going to be away?" she asked me.

"Don't know. Three, four, five days," I responded.

"Have a good trip," and she returned to the magazine she was reading.

I went to my study and closed the door behind me. My study consisted of another set of rooms. A library with my books, a comfortable couch, a stereo and my antique writing table. A small bedroom next to it, often served as a guest room, plus a bathroom. That setup was my own private world. There I store my memoirs, copies of private letters and my computer where I had encrypted several screenplays and the novel I hoped to leave for posterity.

Before I sat on my couch, I poured another shot of whiskey from my mini-bar. A few sips, a brief hesitation and I grabbed the telephone and dialed a number. I had been thinking about asking Chloe to meet me away from Paris for some time. We talked on the phone often. Sometimes late at night, she getting ready or in bed already. As time passed, we developed our own nebula and became used to each other's double entendre, a sort of intimacy, where we shared lots of trivia about ourselves, the arts and personal fantasies.

We would also talk business, but never about corporate secrets or her boss. Occasionally she'd flash tidbits that would multiply my concerns about the Frenchman's scheme for the North American market. So much depended on my dealings with the Alsace that I was determined to dare Chloe to meet me, not only to consummate our pillow-talk romance, but to pry into the Alsace's Chairman secret world.

"Oui," she answered.

"Hey, it's me! Is it too late?"

"I'm in bed already."

"Do you have space for one?"

Chloe laughed mischievously.

"Do you?" I insisted.

"Oui," she said.

"I'd give it all for a time machine," I said, frustrated by the distance.

"A plane ticket would do," she said coquettishly.

"Will you meet me in Portugal next week? I have some business in Porto but I have a few days we could enjoy. You said you liked Porto a lot."

"Are you serious?"

"Of course I am. Never been more serious."

"Are you trying to seduce me?"

"Seduce you? Love, I was seduced by your "Oui" concoction the first time you answered the phone. I was hooked! That "oui" still resonates in my brain. You know that."

"Oui, I know that. It goes both ways."

"I'm wet. You know ..." I whispered.

"Oui! Me too!"

"Will you meet me in Porto? Say yes, please!"

"I don't know if I can get off work. How long?"

"A life time!"

"A life time?" I'd bore you."

"That's my line. I said it to you first at my hotel."

"When and how many days?"

"Three, four, the weekend if that's all the time you have."

"Email me when, where and how and I'll call you tomorrow. I mean later on today. It is 1.30 already."

I flew to Lisbon Wednesday night, a day ahead of Chloe's arrival. There were no direct flights from Paris to Porto and Chloe insisted we stop briefly at the Fatima shrine on our drive to Porto. Portugal is a beautiful country with no long distances but difficult roads. I kept quiet about the Fatima suggestion although I had visited the shrine three times already; once with Maxine and twice with other friends. Chloe's suggestion was a surprise. Talking to her I surmised her being a non-practicing Catholic, not a devoted believer like my other catholic friends. But I didn't make a fuss. I am an anthropologist at heart and I loved to observe the peregrines' heartfelt displays, not to mention the church's choreographed ceremonies. Basically you watch the ill, with no ostensible cure, hope for a miracle. I had also visited Lourdes on two other occasions; a real irony for a nonbeliever. But Lourdes was an even more difficult experience to take. At Lourdes the sick are aligned and the prostrated ones wheeled in, in their own beds, to wait for the Holy sacrament's procession among them. A grotesque spectacle with high pitched hymns and prayers through loudspeakers with many of the sick raising their hands and crutches to heaven as if demanding a cure.

I used my Thursday in Lisbon to contact two fabric representatives. Even if their quality couldn't compare favorably with my Italian suppliers, their knock offs were decent enough at half price. Back at my hotel for a nap and a shower, Chloe called to remind me of her flight's details the following morning. A quick dinner followed. Coming back, from an all-you-can-eat Italian restaurant, I found the concierge waiting for me with a pair of urgent messages.

Ben was still at the office when I called. Intrigued, I asked him what the fuss was all about and he responded, "Francine heard in Chicago that the Alsace was buying a controlling interest in Federated. She said, the person who told her mentioned, there were negotiations going on in New York for more than a month now."

If the French controlled Federated I'm out of the picture. I'm gone! These people are forty percent of my business. I asked Ben "when Francine found out?" He said, "It was that same afternoon. She cut short the meeting with the buyer just to call me and let me know. She wants to talk to you personally and asked me for your hotel telephone and I gave it to her."

I called Francine once at midnight but she hadn't returned to her hotel. An hour and a half later my telephone rang and it was Francine. "Alex, I think I have bad news to report," she said really concerned. I know, I said and asked her to repeat verbatim her conversation with the buyer. "Her friend confided that while she was present when Rochenberg, Federated Chairman, placed two calls to Paris to discuss a few items with his Alsace's counterpart."

I was flabbergasted. It seemed as if all my setbacks and obstacles had been choreographed to pop-up one after the other. No let ups, no timeouts, but me watching — tied up by a lousy contract — based more on trust and a handshake than established business practices. Zamora, the prick, sold the store behind my back. It was Chinese torture. Nothing came as lightning and put you out of your misery. Could the Brujo be right and the curse be working?

I couldn't sleep. When the clock rang five, I took a shower and decided to go downstairs for breakfast. At the concessionaire, I bought a copy of The Guardian, a British newspaper, with more sobering views of the world. The electoral campaign was in full swing back in the US and I followed it closely. Once at the dining room, I ordered everything on the menu I had no intention to eat but devoured nevertheless.

CHLOE RENDEZVOUS

If my trip began with a mix of excitement, the previous evening's news had dampened my spirit thoroughly. Concerned also with the prevailing rain, I drove to the airport a full hour ahead of Chloe's arrival. Her flight landed at ten thirty, a half hour late. Coming through the gate her face lit up the moment she saw me. I also experienced a sense of relief and anticipation watching her walking, rushing toward me and folding amorously in my arms. Somehow her trusting demeanor reassured me. We kissed passionately while I held her tightly against me.

"Welcome to Portugal," I said.

"I'm dreaming," she said. "Don't wake me up!"

At that moment I felt as if we were a pair of lost souls in desperate need of each other's company. I didn't know what she could do for me or what I could offer her in return other than a few hours of relaxed bliss. But I knew if anyone, she could give me a peek --- perhaps a preview of her boss' intentions with Federated in the US --- and I desperately needed that.

I took her bag and pulling her behind me, rushed out of the airport to the car almost a full block away. We only had an hour and a half if we wanted to get to Fatima's noon services on time, but once inside the car — still drenched in water — we embraced and kissed for another five minutes. It was only when I reminded her of the time we had left to get to sanctuary that we got back to our senses and left the airport in a hurry.

It had been four months since our last meeting and — even if we had kept a continuous conversation ever since — we immediately began exchanging quips about each other while holding hands, when two weren't needed for driving.

"I think I'm dreaming," she said, resting her head on my shoulder.

"Does anyone know you're here, with me?" I asked her.

"No one knows!"

"Not even your boyfriend?"

"Not even him. No one. I went to Marseille for a wedding."

"I also dreamed of your coming," I told her, holding her hand firmly in mine. "Being together, sharing our time. I hope it will be as good for you, as I'm sure it will be for me."

"Come on, Alex, you're already justifying yourself," she said smiling. "These three days are going to be memorable, you'll see."

The rain continued unabated. The traffic was rather light but the road was narrow. Chloe reminded me she had a flight back early Monday. I told her she could take the very first commuter from Porto and make her flight with no sweat. Then, feeling at ease, we began talking about more mundane things.

"How is Paris?"

"The usual," she responded.

"I love Paris."

"And I love New York," she retorted.

"I know but Paris has something."

"I know what you mean. It is charming. We have a busy night life."

"How was your week? Any nights out?"

"Only Wednesday. I went to the Lyceum to a conference; a group of well-known eggheads. Eggheads?" She asked me, repeating the word.

"Yes, eggheads is correct."

"Discussing the future of literary criticism. Interesting but a little boring after a while."

"That's great. I do that every once in a while."

"We go for this kind of session at least once a month. The best part of those nights, if you ask me, is that a group of us end up having cocktails and dinner at Brasserie Lipp."

"A popular eggheads' nest," I said. "Are you also a writer?"

"No, I am a voyeur; a boring economy major; but Antoine loves literature. Me too in my own way."

"Antoine? Your shoe salesman?" I asked ironically, making fun of her boyfriend.

Laughing, she swatted my shoulder and said. "I told you Antoine is a very, what's the word? Cultivated?"

"Yes, that's the word."

"He is a writer himself and writes criticism for a small publication. A tiny one," she said separating only two fingers of the right hand. "I don't think he's that good, but it is readable," she said laughing. "We always end up having an argument."

"How about you?" I asked her.

"We have talked about it. I'm only a reader. But I have my own ideas. I prefer the theater, of course. You remember, we have discussed one or two plays that went directly from Paris to Broadway. Have you seen one lately?"

"Noo! I have been busy. One or two off-off Broadway…. Perhaps if I had someone like you close to me I'd do more."

"Ha!" she exclaimed. "That's a good one."

"But you know, I like movies, theater. Some literature, not too heavy though. What was the conference about?"

"Ah, boring. The future of criticism. I thought criticism was criticism but it happens that there are different kinds. At one time they claimed critics were ideologues, then it evolved?" she said, looking for my concurrence.

"Yes, evolved is the right word."

"…into new criticism. Something like artistic detail. But no matter what, the main concern has always been beauty."

"Speaking of beauty… You look great. Your haircut makes you very sexy. And I love your hands. I'm repeating myself, am I?"

"Yes you mentioned it in one of our pillow-talk conversations. 'I fancy female hands and feet.' Hands I could understand, but feet? Most women have ugly feet; out of shape by the wear and tear of high heels."

"I never said I loved all kinds of feet," I retorted laughing.

Half way to Fatima the rain let up a bit and the first sun rays came through the clouds. "Our first miracle," I said. We celebrated the break and wondered whose luck it was for the opening sky.

We arrived at the sanctuary some twenty minutes late. Fortunately, the rain had delayed the service enough to give us time to hear the last third of the mass and the rest of the ceremony. The sick and infirm were on display and the officiating priests in full regalia distributed communion. Chloe who had heard of the ceremony asked me if it was always like this. I responded if she hadn't heard? And she said she knew about it but not with all the details. I asked, "Aren't you Catholic?" She said, "No! I'm Jewish."

"Jewish? I thought you were a convent girl who had promised the Virgin Mary to bring me here if she granted your wish."

"What wish?" she demanded.

"Having a passionate rendezvous with me in Portugal."

"What? You're full of ….." she said, grabbing my neck, kissing my cheek. "You know what merde is?

"Are you accusing me of being full of shit? You have nerve!"

We were about thirty minutes out of Fatima when I reminded Chloe it was almost three and we should stop for a bite. We happened to be about ten miles west of an old castle I had visited once on a previous trip, and suggested we stop there for lunch. She readily agreed. The castle was also a hotel; and a very quaint one at that. A typical lunch of salad, sausage, cheese, a bottle of wine, a walk around the well-preserved gardens and we began to consider staying put, getting a room and postponing the trip to Porto.

"Why don't we forget Porto and stay here, I love it," Chloe said. "We don't have much time and I'm anxious to be with you."

"You want to?" I asked her. "This place is like taking a journey back in time. The rooms are very noisy."

"Can we go to a place you have never been before?" Chloe asked me a bit annoyed "I love it here but I'd obviously prefer a place that doesn't remind you of anybody else."

"Come on! I'm talking about listening to other people doing it. It is inevitable. The planks are as old as the castle is."

"Let's check in," she insisted.

Am I lucky? I've asked myself many times before. Well, whether I am or not, here I am with this enticing woman that I dreamed of devouring her entrails from the moment I set my eyes on her. I lusted for her body, but also fancied her brain; agile, intelligent, in control. I loved that.

The hotel was fully booked. The only space available was a mini-suite, at a stiff price, but we took it anyway. The moment we closed the door behind us, I opened my arms and Chloe folded in. We were finally together after a few months of late pillow-talk conversations in which we discussed many topics, including sex. I had found she was open about her sexuality to the point of confiding in me her sexual preferences and implying --- perhaps suggesting, differences with her present partner --- I surmised he resented, but I loved with no ill effects to my ego. So I remained passionately involved not impeding Chloe's anxious initiative as we kissed and caressed each other and she commenced a magical, if elaborate routine, kissing, tasting and biting every inch of my body --- from my neck, my chest, biceps, and belly --- finally taking it in her mouth. Thank God for assertive woman.

What started as a degustation menu for her quickly became a no holds barred, free for all. As I had predicted, in a few minutes we had orchestrated a symphony of sounds with a mix of old planks, aching bed frames and muffled guttural shouts that engulfed if not all, part of the old castle. If the sounds went beyond our walls, the scene inside resembled a kid's birthday party and the scramble for goodies after the breakup of a plentiful piñata. Exhausted, still relishing our shared ecstasy, we collapsed into each other's arms and succumbed to the restorative effects of a long nap only to be awakened by a knock at the door and a subtle voice announcing the closing of the restaurant in an hour's time.

The restaurant was a large room, resembling an assembly hall in size, with big stone walls decorated with flags, shields, coats of arms, swords, you name it. Had I not taken a good look at the people having dinner around us, I could have safely assumed being back in mediaeval times, sharing a leg of lamb with the king and his consorts. Seeing almost a full room of middle aged couples, some with kids, brought me back to reality as we were being taken to a table, right in the middle of the dining area.

The captain and a waiter approached us and, after a courteous greeting, recited his memorized menu in full order of appetizers and entrees. Chloe and I, trying perhaps to regain our lost energy, settled for a ragout of grilled octopus to start and a roast of veal with artichokes and mushrooms that sounded exquisite, for an entree. While discussing a hardy, young red wine the sommelier insisted we should try, the captain approached us with a bottle of wine in hand and presented Chloe with a business card. Intrigued, we both looked in the direction the captain was pointing at. Chloe smiled when she recognized the grinning fellow and — while waving at the man gently — told me with tight lips and a contrived smile.

"You are not Alex. Please think of another name."

"Don't worry. Roberto is the name."

"He is inviting us to an after dinner drink. What do you think?" Chloe asked me.

"I don't know. You decide," I responded. "Who is he?"

"A top banker; takeovers, multinationals, deal maker. You name it, he does it all."

"Is he your banker?"

"He helped us put together the Alsace."

"You mean, he finances your takeovers?"

"Yes. Sharp as an arrow. Listen," Chloe said with some urgency. "Let's have a drink with him, just one drink. If he says he's staying for the weekend we say we are only staying overnight. That we are returning to Lisbon tomorrow. Have you thought of a name and a different profession or line of business?"

"I told you; Roberto. Roberto Fernandez. I'll say I'm in advertising."

"No, no. He might be interested in using you!"

"In the US?"

"Yes, he's putting together a deal for us. But we can't talk about it. Not a word or I'd be in hot water."

Bingo, I said to myself. The takeover of Federated. If not that, what other US kind of deal could they be talking about? Christ, it is as if I were forced to be a witness to my own demise. Next I am going to be asked to build my own pyre and provide the matches. I can't believe my luck.

"Just say," Chloe continued, "that you're in transportation and don't give any more details. Alright?"

"A truck driver?" I said with a grin. Chloe ignored me.

Our dinner was ruined, I thought, perhaps our stay at the hotel too. I blamed myself for choosing this place knowing how popular it was. The wine the banker sent us was good, but not better at twice the price than the one I ordered. As we talked and dined we couldn't come up with a sensible excuse not to meet the group for drinks afterwards. But perhaps it wasn't such a bad idea after all. They might talk or say something of interest to me related to the takeover. Ironically, watching Chloe, I couldn't help but imagine the tempest in her head; here she was with me — the designated sacrificial lamb — introducing me to one of the ceremony's high priests.

Half way through our meal, the banker approached our table. He embraced Chloe and told her how happy he was to see her taking a holiday. Chloe introduced us: we exchanged a few pleasantries, and before returning to his group, the chap reminded us of his invitation. We thanked him for the wine and he graciously admitted it was tax deductible. As the fellow walked away, jocosely, Chloe and I congratulated each other for our luck. "We should be very cautious with this man. I work closely with him," she said, and continued eating her meal to the very end.

After our chocolate soufflé and an espresso shot, we walked to a room, built as a library, with a huge fireplace as its center piece. The fellow stood up and introduced us to everyone in his group; two bankers. One from Portugal and one from Spain. If I could understand why bankers meet, I couldn't figure out what they were doing there, in a rain forest, about sixty miles from Lisbon. After contagious laughter, a few quips and an inconsequential commentary or two, Chloe's friend asked me my line of business. I responded; "I lend money at thirty percent," and the group laughed, including Chloe. To my quip the man responded repeating his question but adding this time, I didn't have to answer if I didn't want to. Knowing I wouldn't get out of the situation without an answer, I said; "I'm an importer." And he predictably asked me what kind of merchandise. I said, "I have a couple of DC3s and fly flowers from Colombia." They all laughed again. Then, I quickly added I was in transportation back in the States; a trucking company and a freight forwarder. Having said that I went on the offensive and asked him "what were three bankers doing in a romantic castle hotel, a hundred miles from civilization?" The three laughed loudly. And our banker, looking at Chloe with a clever smile said, "Well we are putting our heads and pockets together for a big deal." I watched Chloe lower her head and then snap back; "well that's your job, isn't it?"

The conversation continued a while longer as we sipped our cognacs and discussed business in general. During a break I casually asked them how much longer they would be around. Chloe's banker said they were going home in the morning. Another cognac and shot of espresso and our men were ready for the sack and so were we. Roger, I think his name was, embraced Chloe and kissed her on both cheeks. I shook hands with the three of them and took their business cards excusing myself for not having one. Goodnight, we said once again and that was that.

Still stunned by the encounter Chloe and I walked back to our suite unable to compute the odds of meeting such a close acquaintance in a remote Portugal forest. While walking, concerned for Chloe's apparent absorption in the encounter, I tried to reassure her it was all the product of chance, but the closer we got to our room Chloe's easy, lighthearted personality had shifted to a taciturn demeanor, something reinforced by her tight grip on my hand. Once the door locked behind us, we engaged in a tentative, if passionate feast that lasted well longer than either of us probably anticipated.

Resting next to each other, she became somber again.

"What is it?" I asked Chloe seeing her perplexed demeanor.

"Nothing," she responded. "It is surreal; like an admonition. As if someone were telling me this is a mistake."

As I watched her talking to herself I became totally convinced her changing mood was a consequence of the Federated deal. I could see her really troubled, trying to make sense of the situation --- perhaps repentant of being here, with me --- while my demise was being planned by bankers in a remote Portuguese castle.

"Alex, I think I should go. I really do. I think this was a mistake. I should never have accepted your invitation."

"What are you talking about?" I demanded. "Why a mistake? We like each other, don't we? This is the most natural thing to happen; come together, get acquainted. Love each other," I said, desperate searching for more sensible arguments.

"That's not the way it works," she said with some vehemence, interrupting me. "We are involved in business and business is business. There is always a conflict of interest. It shouldn't be mixed with pleasure. It never works."

"Would you calm down?" I said to her holding her hand, preventing her getting off the bed. "Would you explain what this is all about? I don't understand how meeting this fellow can change your mood in such a way that, what began as a beautiful encounter, has turned into a mistake of enormous proportion?"

Chloe covered her face with a pillow. "I must go, Alex. I must!"

"It's two a.m. There are no planes from here to Paris. The next plane to Paris is at one this afternoon. Probably the same plane your friend is taking. I can ease your pain. I can tell you what it seems you're afraid of sharing with me. Should I do that?"

Chloe removed the pillow and asked me. "What do you know?"

"Federated," I responded.

"How do you know that? She said puzzled by my answer. "Is that why you're here with me?"

"No! No! Why are you immediately going to think that's the reason? I dreamed of being together the minute I met you... You're a lovely, sexy, cerebral woman. I love that."

"What do you know about Federated?" she demanded.

"Yesterday I got a call from Francine. She was in Chicago and a buyer, a close friend of hers, told her about Federated being sold...."

Chloe turned away from me and sank her face in the sheets covering her head with all the available pillows she could wrestle around her. Inadvertently perhaps, her sudden swirl had left most of her naked body in the open and her inviting, beefy tush sensually exposed, provoking a temptation impossible to resist. Bewitched I curled and pressed my body behind hers. If the encounter with the banker had dropped a heavy load on our libidos, just folding behind her, not only reassured her but fired up another round, if subdued, passionate sex.

"Did you sleep well?" I asked her, lifting her hair and kissing her neck amorously.

"Yes, I needed it," she responded, facing me.

"And we are still together, away from the world." I added trying to put her at ease.

"I wonder if they left?" she asked.

"I'm sure they did and we are free as birds to roam the forest around us. There is another beautiful old hotel about twenty miles north I want you to see," I said. "What do you think?"

It was a beautiful, sunny day as we drove up a narrow road going by a number of small villages, stopping here and there at an enticing fruit stand to buy grapes or — to inspect a ceramic shop — to purchase a plate or two for Chloe's apartment back in Paris. We managed to feel comfortable with each other, exchanging caresses, matching wits, notwithstanding the phantom of the Federated takeover we postponed for another moment.

Once at the hotel, I asked the concierge for a quick tour of the premises. The building was an extraordinary piece of eighteenth century architecture and the room I requested to inspect, spectacular. I had stayed there once before on my way to Porto and I knew Chloe would be hooked the minute she saw it. "Oh Alex, why didn't you insist on coming here?" she complained. We were at the room's terrace, facing a range of mountains that looked like a postcard from paradise.

The restaurant was a kind of rustic tavern kept intact from Don Quijote's times. It was built with exposed dark beams, wood paneling and large windows looking at the mountains. Ten minutes at the bar — sampling all kinds of delicious tapas — the captain led us to our table. After more Sherries, bites of delicious Manchego cheese and Serrano hams, we ordered a country style kind of meal we knew would carry us well into the night, perhaps even to the following morning.

"I love the place," Chloe said, once we sat at our table. "I wish there was a simple way to show you how I feel, how much I love this moment," she said grabbing my hand from across the table. "How much I'd like to postpone my departure. To stop what seems inevitable."

"I know. I feel it," I admitted trying to reassure her.

"But it seems it is a conspiracy of forces bent on smashing everything we have worked for so many years," she said in a meditative mood. "I swear, God help me if I'm wrong, it could be the end of this audacious ride to the top and perhaps the ruin of everyone swept in this risky venture."

Chloe's phrasing sounded apocalyptic. She had finally broken her silence and seemed hurting, tormented by what was going on. I felt tempted to inquire, to encourage her to talk freely. Instead, I tried to calm her down and delay the conversation for a more propitious moment.

"It troubles me to see you might become the first casualty of this affair," she said ostensibly anguished. "I pray you'll find the wisdom and strength to protect your interests and be ready for any eventuality."

"Chloe, please!" I said grabbing her arm. "I know you're hurting for my sake. But, don't, please! Let's get out of here and go somewhere where we can continue this conversation away from all these people."

Once in the car she continued. "I am very upset," she said. "I knew a conversation about Federated was inevitable. That's why I came; why I agreed to meet you. But I also wanted to be with you, believe me. You said you dreamed about this moment; so did I. And here I am."

"Oh Chloe," I said visibly moved. "If we could understand why these things happen? But we can't. For me the only explanation is chance; the luck of the dice. What some people call fate."

"But you see," Chloe continued, interrupting me, "meeting Roger here, with you, not at the airport, not with someone else, but here in Portugal, of all places and with you," she continued, "that's creepy. What's going on? Is this a sign? A premonition? I work closely with this man, almost daily. Perhaps I'm delusional. But, am I being reminded I'm betraying Francois, the man who helped me get to where I am today."

Moved and perplexed, I observed her dealing with her demons. I felt like a spectator helplessly watching his future un-spooling in front of him. Lost for words and unable to find a reasonable explanation for what was going on, I decided not to say anything, concerned not only about my fate but seeing her being drawn into my own spiral as another innocent victim of my curse. The damned Brujo said it; 'you and everyone around you.' And here we have it. Chloe, an innocent ally, personally concerned with my wellbeing is paying the price; puzzled by the events, punished with doubts, recriminating herself for betraying the people she owes the most.

ALSACE REVELATION

We drove up a steep road and stopped at a rocky lookout carved out of a dangerous mountain side. If anywhere, I thought the abyss in front of us as the ideal stage for my drama to unfold; allegorically perhaps, but remote and desolate, surrounded by the forest's beauty and interrupted only by the breeze and the bird's persistent quavers.

"What a magnificent place," Chloe said.

We got out of the car and walked to the mountain's edge. A beautiful landscape; a carpet of mountains and trees all around us. What a contrast; majestic and peaceful in all its beauty. We, worried and beleaguered; harassed by a chain of events we were unable to control.

"Isn't this fantastic?" I asked her. "I wouldn't trade this moment for anything in the world," I said resting my weight on Chloe's shoulders and embracing her tightly around her waist. "I'm happy Chloe; I'm happy to be alive and sharing this corner of the world with you,"

Chloe got herself loose of my bear hug and kissed me deeply. "Me too and I wouldn't trade it either."

We climbed a few rocks and got to a natural formation, a group of flat rocks shaped as an artist's bench. I rested my back on the rocks and let Chloe sat and rest her back against my chest.

"Chloe," I said, talking in her ear. "Now that we are as close as we will ever be, why don't we dispose of Federated so we can have whatever is left of the weekend for ourselves?"

"Actually, there isn't much to talk about. Just the fact that Federated approached us and offered a merge. Rochenberg, the Federated CEO, you heard of him."

"Yes! I know of him," I responded.

"Rochenberg asked his investment banker to contact ours and a meeting was arranged. Why he approached us in particular, we never knew. Francois had always been interested in retail operations. He believes in cash-flow and loved the twenty five percent your chain stores charge their credit card customers. He sees them as a cash cow; I myself think it is usury," she said vehemently, "but it is your system. So when this fellow called, he rushed to meet him. Rochenberg had a very appealing presentation and offered the store for about eight billion, cash, stocks and assuming their debt. Rochenberg has his own inside track; he'll get most of his money up front, two positions on the board and a golden parachute. It is obscene, but business nevertheless. Francois presented the deal to the board, which put up a stiff opposition at first, but a second meeting was arranged and he was able to convince half plus one."

"How?" I asked her.

"Francois's main argument was; a beachhead in America and here we are."

"Does he have the money for the acquisition or is he borrowing it," I asked her.

"The whole thing. Roger, the man we met, is the architect; Francois' medicine doctor. He's making a bundle himself, of course. That's why he's so happy here dealing in the boondocks with Spanish and Portuguese bankers."

"Fifteen billion in debt and no opposition from the board?

"He's a great talker and, if that wasn't enough, he had nominated the majority of them. I told him he was making a huge mistake. But he didn't want to hear."

"Doesn't he resent your comments?"

"Of course he does. But he trusts me, and he should; I have his best interest at heart. We have been together at this game for quite some time. But this is different. God forgive me, but I'm afraid Federated is the last drop."

"Have you talked to Sands or anybody else?" I wondered.

"No! I'm telling you because I need to unload. I feel like the president's psychiatrist who takes the load off his shoulders and can't handle it himself. There was a movie about that. Did you see it?"

"Yes, James Coburn was the psychiatrist, I think."

I was mesmerized. Being with her was like having one of those acid-induced trips. I felt so good I didn't want to wake up from my nightmare. As if I were running ahead of the bulls in Pamplona. I couldn't stop thinking, this egomaniac's pyramid might eventually collapse. What can I do? I briefly debated, while Chloe silently watched the sun setting on the horizon

"Shall we go?" I asked her.

"And let him set alone, all by himself?" she asked, holding me tightly. "Look at that fire ball, isn't he beautiful? What an enigma. At that distance he's our savior; closer, it'd consume us. A metaphor for mankind; he could sustain or consume us. Like people we know."

We took the car and I began our drive back to our castle. It was getting dark and I felt anxious about finishing the conversation. I came to romance and get a heads-up from her and I got double what I expected.

"Has my franchise been discussed?" I asked her quietly.

"Not in particular. But it is obvious you won't be needed anymore. We can do without you. Use your markup to reduce debt."

"It sounds so easy, doesn't it?"

"It is easy. Money has no face. It's a tough world Alex. A tough world."

"Chloe," I said, moved by her sincerity, "you have no idea how much I appreciate what you're doing."

"Don't thank me," she said. "I am a spectator like you are. Now, you might be asking yourself, why is Chloe telling me all this?" she said in a reflective mood. "It is very simple. I liked you since we met at the Rafael's bar. You said you were hooked with my Oui! I was fascinated watching you talk. I loved our pillow-talks… the more we talked, the more I wondered how you would be in the intimacy of a relationship. I wanted to know the person behind the facade."

"You flatter me," I said fascinated with the tone of the conversation.

"You also seem to be a decent person. Unfortunately your firm is miniscule lost in an ocean of huge corporations. What are your revenues? A hundred, a hundred and fifty million?" she interrupted herself.

"A bit more than a hundred," I responded.

"You ended up dealing with a twenty billion giant by accident. You mean nothing to us," she said with some anguish, perhaps trying to be gentle. "Don't get hurt by my frankness, please. But it is better you're fully aware of what's going on."

"Chloe, you're doing me a favor."

"Let me finish. Francois bought Nati in a lark. This is confidential, of course. For your ears only," she declared pointing to her ears. "They were lovers for more than two years. Francois' wife confronted him with a divorce and he chose to remain married. He was president at the time and in line to become CEO. A scandal was out of the question and he knew it. Nati was devastated. Zamora, the clever fox that he is, you must know him." Chloe said interrupting herself.

"Of course, I know the old man."

"Zamora showed up in Paris unannounced and demanded reparation. Perhaps not as crass as it sounds, but close enough. To make a long story short; Francois had been toying with the idea of getting into fashion a year or two before he met Nati at a Roman fashion show and became enchanted with her. They became an item overnight. At the time we were studying the possibility of acquiring her corporation that was also Zamora's all along. He owned the majority interest. After six or eight months the conversations cooled off. The consensus was her company wasn't a good fit for us. Not big enough to bring us into the fashion business and we started looking for an alternative; a bigger couture house. Francois gave Zamora a number of reasons for delaying the acquisition, but the relationship with Nati continued unabated to the point when Francois' wife confronted him. That was when Zamora showed up and combined Nati's heartbreak with her financial interest, demanding the completion of the buyout. Francois, having been made CEO a few months back, still concerned with his prestige, he pressured the board to buy Zamora out. Nati got a good lump of money, but the real beneficiary was the old man who made a bundle. We ended up with a company we didn't need paying perhaps twice as much as the company's real value. A costly breakup, no doubt."

I was mesmerized listening to her while focusing in the coming cars and the never ending curves on that narrow, hilly road.

"But all this is allegorical, gossip to the real purpose of my meeting you, of having this conversation," Chloe continued after a brief pause. "Frankly, my idea was to alert, warn you, if I could, of the storm on the horizon. I'm being selfish. My sympathy for your plight is rooted in my own personal experience. My father was a small entrepreneur. He owned three mid-size food stores and lost all his money thirty years ago with the introduction of the supermarket concept in France. Carrefour, the giant supermarket chain came to town and buried him alive. I was fifteen at the time and I remember, as if it was today, his long nights, his tortured phone conversations with his creditors, his fight with the bank and the final repossession of our home. My mother was devastated, not as much by the business failure as for my father's lost self-esteem. My sister and I were embarrassed, incapable of facing our friends in school. My father never recovered. Eventually he became manager of one of the new superstores; he had lost his independence, all he had worked all his life for. Unfortunately he never came to accept he had not failed but had been the victim of the times, conglomerates, forces beyond his control; the equivalent of a natural catastrophe."

I had watched and listened to Chloe spellbound by the story. What a mix of characters, histories, situations. Midway she had become really distraught with a torrent of tears running down her cheeks. I embraced and literally drank her tears with my lips. I felt for her... *Hold it, Hold it. Do not get carried away, my alter-ego interrupted. Chloe's nice; and lovely too. A great lay, no doubt. But, let's put the whole thing in perspective; under the same set of circumstances we'd probably have done the same. Her father's story was tough; she really moved me. Those were real tears and plenty, too. I'm convinced she really likes us. The way I project myself through you. Remember I am your brain talking. But let's leave that conversation for another day. Let's look at the problem ahead from the other angle. She's tying our hands, you know. That's what she is doing by telling us. I am almost convinced that's not her intention. But suppose we want to fight back. I can't think of any other way but going to court. I know it is the last recourse but we're being screwed; legally I know, but screwed nevertheless. What kind of argument could we adduce? Are we going to say she told us? Knowing ourselves, I doubt we will ever out her. Or are you changing your ways? I might find it difficult to believe, though.*

Ah, and before I forget, my ego continued. *Did you hear the story about little Nati? Our innocent girl had an affair with the chairman and cashed in with the breakup. I told you when she aborted; Good riddance, man. You thought I was a calculating son of a bitch. Well, here you have it. Who was right? But let's not get bogged down here. Let's finish the weekend, send Chloe home and let's go off to Porto to pacify those fuckers and get the hell out of Portugal. We got more than we bargained for.*

We were idling in our hotel's parking lot as she finished her story. I wanted to get to our rooms but I didn't dare to interrupt her. I had hit a soft spot and she needed time to decompress. What else I'd find tomorrow was a matter of conjecture. As much as I enjoyed her company, now I was anxious to go home. I felt like hiding and covering my head as if by doing that I could be spared the future she foretold. We walked into the hotel and directly to our suite. Once inside, she took a bath and I didn't even think of sharing the tub with her. I was mentally exhausted and so was she. Perhaps the dye had been cast and for us there was nothing else but to wait for our Monday morning departure; inevitably going our separated ways.

Monday morning came as if we had been waiting for it all our lives. We drove to the airport under a torrential rain; not a single word exchanged since we left the hotel. But silence has its voice and words I heard; Chloe was in pain. She believed my fantasies, perhaps crazy, but willing to share them. An understandable search for that extra something, the unknown a few of us crave and aren't afraid to look for. It had been a brief, if beautiful interlude, spiced with tears, fabulous sex, surprises, intrigue and a looming confrontation. An alchemist's idyllic — if mysterious — recipe for fulfillment if there ever was one. And as if it hadn't been enough, she also tried to do for me what she couldn't do for her father; save me from the catastrophe if she could. How was I feeling? Great! I had more tears in my eyes than all the rain drops on the windshield. What a mixture of emotions; enthralled and frightened. Feeling lucky for finding her; petrified at the specter of another long, protracted battle with no apparent solution. All in all, the dichotomy of my life; extremes, ups and downs but nothing in between. My struggle to be me, against all odds and life capricious dictates.

Once at the airport, we went directly to the Air France counter. The attendant issued her a boarding pass and told her the flight was already boarding. We walked to a corner and I embraced and kissed Chloe tenderly.

"Will I see you again? I asked her.

"I doubt it. Perhaps after the storm, if you still want me," she responded. "Will this ever be our secret?" she asked looking me deeply into my eyes.

"Yes! It will, regardless. Can I keep in contact?" I asked her back.

"I don't know. Why don't we let the storm pass? I won't ever speak about business again. Would you mind?"

"Trust me. It will never be mentioned again."

Her flight was called once again. We looked at each other resigned to the inevitable.

"It will be impossible to forget you, you know that."

"Oui," she said faking a smile. "It will impossible to forget you, too."

Tears were running down our cheeks.

"This is a better ending than Casablanca, isn't it?"

"We'll always have Portugal!" she responded sinking her face in my shoulder.

She pulled away from me and walked to the gate. She turned briefly and her fake smile had turned to tears. She waved once, turned again and disappeared.

I stayed around until her plane took off. I felt lost, my eyes wet. My flight to Porto wouldn't depart for another hour. I walked the airport as in a bubble, with no apparent aim, experiencing one of those low-highs, bittersweet states, as if enjoying a delicious torture, a sustained never-ending orgasm.

Chloe had been one of those rare escapades only a few lucky ones experience in their lives. I hated to see her go but I was also desperate to be alone — masochistically perhaps — to be able to concentrate and digest all the information she had revealed to me. I am a dead man walking, I concluded. If this takeover is completed, I'm toast and I'd better get ready to face the music. What I was living was like a diary, a book I read a long time ago, "Chronicle of a Death Foretold," Garcia Marquez famous story.

JULIE – MY LOVER

"Hey!" I said to Ben, as I entered his office closing the door behind me.

"How was it?" He asked me.

"Well, other than the news about Federated, things went as well as we could have expected. The Portuguese want us to pay the ninety days' balance. You know Vigny. He cried his heart out. I told him we'd send a check for a hundred. So, mail him a check in a week or two."

"Did you go anywhere else?"

"No, I spent more days in Lisbon than I intended and visited Porto to see Vigny."

"Alone?"

"Unfortunately," I responded with a chuckle. "How was Natividad's tour?"

"Let Francine tell you the story. We flew to Miami to welcome her; she looked great. What a piece of ass."

"Did she come alone?"

"I think she was meeting a friend here. But she was very gracious. We offered to drive her to her hotel but she said a limo had been arranged. She asked Francine to meet her at ten the next day. We spent less than five minutes with her. No word about nothing. I was surprised she didn't ask about you."

"Well, she knew I was going to be out of town. Did she give you any hints about Federated?"

"Not a word. We met her at lunch the next day and not a word about anything. She might be in the dark, for all I know. She spoke mostly to Francine about the trunk shows, the ready to wear pieces she is exhibiting and some personal business to attend including a long weekend in San Francisco. Natividad told Francine she was free to fly back to New York – that the Alsace would pick up the tab - and meet her again the following Tuesday in LA. She'll tell you all about it."

I loved to be back in the city. Manhattan, walking Fifth Ave, Fifty-seven street makes you feel you're in the center of the world and indeed you are. You feel the raw energy, short of the sophistication you experience walking Paris or London, but energy nevertheless. And nowhere is that energy more conspicuous than in a small group of restaurants in mid-town Manhattan. Eateries where groups of expense account wheeler-dealers congregate assiduously, to eat lunch; an ostentatious and exhibitionist routine financed by their corporate superiors. Today, by pure chance, my friend Julie — who happens to be a magazine executive — invited me to one of those top-flight restaurants; "The Four Seasons." Her boss is out of town and asked her to do lunch with an up-and-coming fashion designer. Fortunately, the fellow cancelled with such short notice she wasn't able to recycle their table and called me instead. And I, with a great sense of anticipation, couldn't resist the temptation.

The idea of meeting Julie, at such a lavish culinary cathedral, was enticing. But I was also looking for the opportunity to spend time with her and bounce off her my deteriorating financial situation. Not that she'd come up with a magical formula, but she was clever. An intelligent person, used to think out of the box that I could trust completely. Besides, I needed to talk.

Julie and I had known each other for more than ten years. We became lovers and kept an on-and-off romance for the first three, until she found the man of her life — Burt — and married him, three or four years ago. Even if we ceased being lovers then, we continued to see each other occasionally. We never ceased sharing some, if not all, of our most private secrets, never doubting our commitment to each other. Julie was ten years younger than I was, wore glasses and contacts intermittently, but was one of those rare women who not being a great beauty, people would feel irresistibly drawn to her. If I were to de-construct our relationship, perhaps the things that endeared me most to her were her intellect, sweet demeanor, cultivated style and common sense --- not to mention her sensuous body --- and our compatibility as sexual partners.

The restaurant was packed and I waited for the maître d' to lead me to Julie's table. I found her already seated, drinking a dry Martini.

"I love you," I told her kissing both cheeks.

"Hypocrite!" she said brushing my lips lightly and added. "I am a married woman."

"I'm not jealous," I retorted and we both laugh.

Julie and I were seated on one side of the room, facing a center aisle with several low cubicles dividing the space. On the other side were a number of tables against the wall and a loft-like structure, easily accessible by steps, where the bar and a few other tables were located. Before I sat, I took a bird's eye view of the place. What a sight; Darwinism at its best. A large sample of a new smart set fueled by corporate expense accounts, showmanship and charity work financed with corporate donations, never money of their own. A group new comers that has supplanted the old concept of class; the rapidly disappearing WASP elite. In other words, a new milieu, which had allowed these guys --- and this Cuban refugee --- to elbow in and share the fruits of our own successes, in a daring if different kind of style.

It didn't take long for Julie and me to get involved in a long, gossipy lunch talking about the people around us and the latest news in the magazine business. Almost two hours into it, Julie asked me if I were free for the rest of the afternoon. I said yes, and we settled for a run at the Met to check out the "Picasso Weeping Women" exhibition. No matter how many times Julie and I had come to blows, figuratively speaking, discussing his art and his alleged machismo, I insisted, the old man was a magnet for strong, independent women; her included. Having fired my opening salvo, she signed the check and we ran for the door.

The Metropolitan Museum was a short taxi ride from our restaurant and only Julie's media credentials permitted us to skip a long line waiting to enter the gallery. We mixed with the crowd and together walked the exhibition, stopping and sharing our thoughts at every painting. Picasso painted every woman in his life as he began the relationship and painted her again when the affair came to its end. Obviously, on his second attempt, the woman would be disgruntled, something that disgusted Julie the most. She'd claim that he took the time to ridicule them once the affair was over. My take was that he painted them in anguish because of the breakup, as if recording the affair for history, not to make fun or mock them in anyway. But she wouldn't listen.

We spent more than an hour skipping the multitude in front of each painting, elbowing our way to the front of each group. Finally when we got to the end of the exhibition she turned to me and said,

"Burt is away for two days. Why don't we go home for a drink?"

"I don't have much time," I responded. "Just got back from Portugal two days ago."

"You go when you want. I won't hold you."

The temptation was too great and I easily succumbed. We hailed a taxi to her apartment on River Side Drive. Julie had inherited a real penthouse on the roof, not the top floor, on the roof of a pre-war building overlooking the Hudson River. Just the idea of looking at the river — and The George Washington bridge in the distance — was more than enough to convince anyone to go with her. If that wasn't enough, my interest in bouncing off her my business concerns, topped with the pleasure of her company, was more than enough for me to say yes!

"This is an extraordinary vista," I said walking out to the terrace. "No matter the many times I've been here I always marvel at this view. You're so lucky."

"I'm so used to it I need other people to remind me," she said walking back into the apartment.

It was early evening and the sun was setting in the west across the river from us. Sunsets in Manhattan are spectacular. I don't know if the sun is or looks larger than it really is, but New York's sunsets are unique. Julie came back to the terrace with two drinks in hand and we toasted the sun and ourselves. I felt great; I love sunsets, full moons, everything that has to do with things beyond my reach. I wanted to close my eyes and forget everything that had no connection with the moment. Julie took a sip of her drink and kissed me. She turned her back to the sunset and rested on the roof's veranda edge.

"And what is bothering my poor Cuban refugee now?" she asked, rubbing her nose against mine.

"You know I can't talk seriously as long as I have you in this position."

"Would you prefer me lying on my back?"

"God is going to punish you for putting those thoughts in my head," I said, making fun of her Catholicism. "No wonder Lucifer, the serpent and all those devils were women."

"I always remember that Cuban song you translated for me. 'Blessed be God because if I have you in this life I don't need to go to heaven because, my dearest, the glory is you. What a night; Ocho Rios, our first trip together; nine years ago; wasn't it?"

"I don't know. You have a better memory than I do."

"Dinner at the Dream-walker. The guitar player, the horse driven carriage. What a night! I never wanted it to end."

"It hasn't!" I said.

"'I don't need to go to heaven because, my dearest, you're my glory,' beautiful words from a woman in love. You looked at me and said; isn't it? You're so vain," she said smiling, "that if I were singing Carly Simons' song, you'd really think the song was about you," she continued, pulling me inside the apartment.

We dropped on top of her thick rug, I embraced her tightly and kissed her passionately. I bit her neck and whispered in her ear; 'que me vas a hacer?' She went for my belt, I removed her blouse, together we lowered my pants, she bent and took it in her mouth sculpting it with her tongue all the way down. I pressed her flat on her back, tasted her swollen nipples and sucked her pear like breast, removing her panties, kissing her trembling belly, her ambrosian thighs, finally devouring her juicy entrails. She pushed me back quickly mounting me, having a wild ride to her own fulfilling orgasm.

The dark of the night came through the windows as we rested next to each other, covered with the throws, trying to protect ourselves from the cool breeze coming from the river. Julie laid almost on top of me, resting her head on my chest with her leg over my lap. We warmed each other as if we were two furnaces at full blast. And I loved it. I'm so lucky, I thought, I wasn't even thinking I wanted to see her to vent my frustration and speak about my problems. Nevertheless I kept quiet until her, sensing my mental unrest, asked me.

"What's nagging you now?"

I pulled her tightly against me and repeated the story of my last five months some of which she knew already. Julie would interrupt me at every step of my story asking a question or clarifying details about André and the Santeria job; how I met Chloe in Paris, Nati's miscarriage, my recent encounter with Chloe in Portugal and the news about the Federated take over.

"Could I use the news about Federated? It would be a first in the industry and would do me good; for my magazine and for me."

"I know, but the news would create uncertainty among my customers and might precipitate my demise, before the real thing comes to pass."

"I understand. Forget I said it," she said, kissing my lips.

"What do you think of what I just told you?" I asked her.

"I can't think of anything right off the bat. Perhaps we should talk to Burt. He's a corporate lawyer although I'd think you need a litigator, don't you?"

"Unfortunately."

"Why don't I prepare something on Saturday night and you and Maxine come. We'll have dinner and you can discuss the situation with Burt. Even if he can do nothing for you, he might have lawyers in his firm who could advise you."

"I haven't said a word about this to Maxine. She's a worrier and she'd be consumed by something she couldn't do anything about."

"Are you backing your line of credit with your properties?" Julie asked.

"Of course!"

"Well, if I were you, I'd try to reduce my exposure. Is La Finca part of the collateral?" she asked me.

"Yes!"

"How did you do that?" You always told me you'd never hawk your retreat, ever."

"You know bankers. They want your blood."

"If I were you I'd sift out as much cash as I could and get ready for any eventuality. I'll let you know about Saturday."

"I'm starving. Aren't you hungry," I said lifting myself and pulling her up from the rug.

ASTROLOGY

"Good morning," Francine said, marching into my office. "How was Portugal?"

"Nice, peaceful. Our people in Porto will begin to manufacture the winter collection in two weeks or so. Come mid-July or early August, we shall have eighty percent of the garments to begin shipping. Tell me about Nati's tour. I'm anxious to hear what you have to say."

"First, I know you aren't going to like what I'm going to say, but we don't have that many new sales. Even some of the standing orders were cut in half and two or three other clients postponed the automatic reorder. Ben probably told you already. Everybody is expecting a turn after the elections, but who knows?"

"But tell me about Nati and the tour."

"Personally it was quite an experience. She's a pro, a real diva. I was surprised how well she handled herself with the store personnel and the management. She massaged the important clients, generated a lot of good media attention everywhere we visit; had two interviews on TV, one in Cleveland and the other in San Francisco and I'd say she got at least, a newspaper article everywhere we went."

"Did she come alone?" I asked Francine.

"No, there were two other Spaniard seamstress with her. They handled the ironing, the packing. You know, everything related to displaying the garments."

"Good. Ben told me you had a long weekend off after San Francisco."

"Oh yeah! She met a guy and was driving "Route One" South to Los Angeles. Four days. We met in LA again."

"Did you meet the fellow?" I asked Francine.

"No, but she said he was quite handsome. Not to change the subject but, have you found out more about Federated?"

"I'll call Sands in a day or two. Anything new from your buyer friend in Chicago?

"Yes, she promised me to call the minute she heard anything else. What's going to happen to us if they buy Federated? Should I start looking for a job?" Francine asked me with obvious concern.

"Come on! We'll handle it. How long do you think will take us to replace Nati's line? I asked her.

"You don't replace seventy five million dollars overnight. Have you thought of any alternatives? Selling mangoes?" She said cracking up.

"That was good," I said sadly. "We might end up selling vegetables."

The following day I called Sands in Paris. He was out of his office but his secretary said he'd return my call and he did. After a few pleasantries, I mentioned the rumors about an impending Federated take over. He replied that it was true, but they were still finishing the transition details. You'd be the first one to know," he told me. Yeah! Thank you very much, I said to myself. Then I asked him about our negotiations to renew our contract. "As soon as things clear up," he repeated and they find time to focus on a clear strategy for the North American market he concluded. A new strategy? That didn't sound too encouraging to me.

With nothing else to discuss about the transition I asked Sands about Nati, if she was satisfied with her US tour. "She was ecstatic," he responded, "and to please thank Francine for her help. I dictated a letter," he said, "thanking you and Francine for the tour's success." He then apologized and excused himself with a meeting he had to attend. "Au revoir," he said and that was that!

On Friday, we sat down with our lawyer, who had postponed our original date twice. He apologized for the delay and said that he had done some preliminary research, something I considered untrue, and that he couldn't think of any grounds to file a lawsuit to stop the takeover; something I never thought of doing. We discussed the practice of passing on rebates directly to the customers instead of doing it through the representative, something I considered restraint of trade. He responded I had a point there, but that he'd have to do more research on that specific subject. I said not to bother. I didn't want a bill from him for learning his profession on my time. He finally concluded we needed a team of litigators. He offered to talk to some of his colleagues. "Only if it was free of charge," I said. And he readily agreed.

Julie went ahead and planned a dinner for that Saturday night as we had discussed. She knew Maxine well and once or twice a year spent an afternoon with her. She was much younger than Maxine but somehow developed a very close relationship with her. Julie's mother had died of cancer when she was in her early twenties and after meeting Maxine — during a chance encounter — five years ago, became a close friend. Julie found Maxine warm and accessible and, like many other people who came in contact with her, felt prey to her personal appeal. She was a ray of fresh air; honest, with not one fiber of ill will toward anyone, even when she felt uncomfortable and didn't like the person at first sight. The four of us would often go for dinner in the city, or spend a weekend together at La Finca, my Adirondacks retreat. Burt, Julie's husband, was about my age and a nature lover. At least twice a year we would use a long weekend to walk the woods or scale a small hill, something that would give us pleasure and make us feel proud of our achievement.

Julie set a beautiful table with her Limoges china, Czech crystal and a delicate floral centerpiece. The dimmed lights, a set of soft candles and some chamber music in the background completed the atmosphere. Julie claimed credit for cooking the fettuccine and felt reluctant to share her own private recipe. Burt made a toast to everyone's well-being and I added my usual, "for all the good things in live and that we have time to enjoy them." Everyone said amen, and we began our feast with a fresh salad of tomatoes and Mozzarella cheese, virgin olive oil, balsamic vinegar and lots of bread. Burt had a good selection of Italian wines and chose a nice 'Barolo' that I considered acceptable and drank with the fettuccine. Julie topped it all with cheeses, a basket of fruit, Junior's cheese cake and espresso, of course. We all remained at the table and began our après dinner conversation with a rare vintage port and a bottle of Burt's preferred aged cognac.

"Julie mentioned you are having difficulties with the French conglomerate already. Anything in particular?" Burt asked me.

"We haven't signed a contract. It is almost a year since they acquired Nati's outfit and they have been postponing the renewal from the very first day."

"What excuses are they giving you?"

"Organizational ones. You know the story; we aren't ready, we haven't decided how to proceed, give us some time. The usual stuff."

"Alex, I remember Zamora gave you a letter," Maxine interrupted, "an appendix to the contract, saying their corporation would recognize your effort introducing their products in this market. I remember listening to you talking about that kind of commitment. Do you still have that letter?"

I looked at Maxine and I saw the document right in front of me. Of course, I said to myself, we fought hard for a clause in the contract and all we got was a letter.

"That's a good point," Burt said. "I'd have to read the letter but it sounds as if they would recognize your efforts for establishing the beachhead."

"Yes! That's true. But it wasn't an appendix in anyway related to our original contract. It was a personal letter signed by the old man." I responded. "And in fact I have the letter."

"Women! You see," Julie interrupted. "Was it not for Maxine you would have overlooked a very important document. Behind every successful man there is a woman, watching, looking for the wellbeing of her man."

"Her man? This is a joint project; our project. We started this together," retorted Maxine. "But you know him. Instead of concentrating on one single thing and giving it his heart out, no! His head is somewhere else. Always dreaming, full of projects, ready to escape; becoming a Hollywood producer, one of them," Maxine said.

"Director," Julie interrupted.

"Yes, excuse me; a director, a writer, an author. He can't stay in one place for more than a few days. You see him here. I'm sure he's thinking of Key Biscayne or La Finca. He just returned from Portugal and in a week or two he will think of another trip. He gets bored. Needs new people. New blood. He is like a vampire. He feeds off other people's energy and moves on. I don't know how we've lasted all these years. I had always been expecting him to show up one day, after one of his trips, and tell me; 'Love, as he calls everyone, this is it.'"

"Come on Maxine, you're being rude with your poor husband. Remember he's a refugee," Julie said cracking up. "He hasn't grown up yet. Look at him. He wants everyone to love him. Look at his face, he's hurt."

"He's a nice man," Burt added. "He lets me beat him at tennis. You have to be nice to do that," he said, as we all started laughing.

"You know I'm kidding, but I'm serious at the same time. He has so many projects he can't concentrate on one," Maxine continued. "I don't pay attention to the horoscopes that much, but if there is a person who fits the description of a Gemini it's him. He's a real Gemini. You know, once he was negotiating to buy a radio station; did I tell you that story?"

"We knew he wanted to buy one but tell us the story anyway," Julie said.

"The owner became so involved with him, he changed his mind and wanted to become partners instead. The man believed in astrology and asked Alex to let a reader do his chart. You know him; it was like asking a blind man if he wanted to see. His curiosity will do him in. He immediately said of course! We were at La Finca and the woman called and asked to meet him. Imagine that? A woman asking to meet him. He said of course. And the woman came all the way from Poughkeepsie."

"Seventy five miles away," Julie interrupted, "just to meet him. I could see his ego."

"We shared the reading. 'Gemini with Scorpio rising,' the astrologer started. Imagine; the intellect sign of the Zodiac combined with the Erotic one. He was in heaven."

"That's when I realized the woman was an impostor," I interjected, laughing.

"He had begun the negotiations with a group of investors and, as the difficulties with financing started to pile up, he became disenchanted. You know him. Today! It has to be today; tomorrow is too late. And what was very promising — look at the value of radio stations today — became a burden for him. Obviously the financiers wanted a say on how to run the business. They were not lending him ten million dollars outright with no strings attached. He said no! He didn't want to work for anyone. He has always been like that."

"What else did the astrologer say?" Julie asked Maxine.

"A bunch of interesting things. I tell you; she was remarkable. She read him like an open book. I wouldn't have walked away for anything in the world. But there was a time when she asked to be alone with him."

"That's when she started talking about his Scorpio ascendant," Julie interrupted.

"Exactly. I moved away. I know him better than the astrologer or his mother; as if I had given birth to him. I went inside the house. It was cool anyway and I had to prepare dinner. We couldn't let that poor woman hit the road again with an empty stomach. "

I was fascinated. The three of them were looking at me with picaresque smiles on their faces. I said nothing, just listened and rested quietly in my chair amused by their spontaneous rejoicing. Maxine had been speaking nonstop since the subject surfaced and I saw Julie agreeing with everything she was saying, at every step of the way.

"I feel as if I am being de-constructed," I finally told them laughing. "I could add so many things to what you're saying, but I'm not going to give you the pleasure of knowing how I feel. If anything I feel like Gulliver listening to the Lilliputians."

"What did the astrologer tell you?" Julie insisted. "Come on Alex, tell us."

"Nonsense. It was flattering, though. But anyone who knows me really well, and I doubt any of you do, would know she was way off the mark."

"Alex, why don't we have a smoke?" Burt suggested. "I have two great Cuban cigars left from a bunch a client brought me from Europe. I've been smoking them nonstop and these two are the last ones; they're delicious."

Burt and I walked out to the terrace. It was a nice, cool evening. The view of the Hudson was spectacular. The tide was going out, a few barges were being towed up and down the river and the bridge was fully lighted in the distance. A magnificent spectacle. I had enjoyed that view and that terrace in quite a few different circumstances, but tonight was different; I felt lucky just being there. Watching the river flow, watching the few stars visible from this particular spot, having shared dinner with Maxine and Julie, perhaps the two people who knew me best.

"Julie mentioned the French are acquiring Federated."

"Yes, I found out last week."

"How does it affect you?" Burt asked me.

"If they complete the acquisition, they're going to own the largest and richest chain of stores in the country. I happen to service them with their own products, as we speak. I'll be redundant. They won't need me anymore."

"Hum... Julie told me they haven't renewed your contract yet."

"No, they haven't. They have given me a lot of excuses."

"What about the letter Maxine mentioned. Do you have it?"

"Yes I do! Maxine is incredible. She's so astute and has such a good memory. The letter states my interest would be recognized in case the Spaniard decided to sell their company. How it would be recognized is not defined, though."

"I'd have to read it to give you my opinion. But don't despair. Remember the Yogi Berra maxim, 'nothing is done until it's done.' Here we are worrying about something that might never happen."

MAXINE'S SUSPICIONS

As we walked out of the building, Maxine brought up the letter again. I mentioned I had the letter in mind, but that my intention always was to get an agreement with the French without recurring to threats or any other kind of pressures, if I could.

"Julie and Burt are extremely nice, aren't they?" Maxine asked me as I started the car and drove out of the garage.

"Yes, they are."

"You're very lucky. They treat you as family."

"They treat us, both of us, as family."

"But she seems to hold you in high regard, doesn't she?"

I looked at Maxine and with an air of surprise asked her. "What do you mean? She treats us, both of us, as family. Since I met and introduced her to you, she has displayed the same kind of affection for both of us regardless of who she met first, doesn't she?"

"But she treats you with some reverence; I don't know how to put it. She really likes you. She seemed to know about the astrologer and your chart. Did you discuss it with her?"

"No, not that I remember. But everyone who knows me knows I am Gemini."

"It is different. It is a special kind of look. Women notice that kind of thing. She looks at you as if you were her teacher, a guru. Like someone who doesn't need words to communicate; reverence, you know what I mean. I don't know how to put it."

"She talks to you about things she had never mentioned to me. I know because you've mentioned them on two or three different occasions. Not the subject of the conversation, but the seriousness of it. You have told me that yourself."

"Yes! We are good friends. We don't share intimacies, but we talk frankly to each other. In many ways she's a delight; friendly, cultured, elegant. No wonder Burt seems so happy with her. They are happy, aren't they?

"They seem to be. I don't know. You know how things are. People might seem happy at one level and be miserable at another. You know the saying; she's so happy she doesn't know she's having a bad time."

"It is true. How about us? Whenever I see other couples I think about us."

"I am happy. I hope you are too!" I said emphatically.

"You should be. You do whatever pleases you. God must be a man."

"Why not a woman?"

"Men have such freedom. You, yourself. You come and you go. I know what you're doing when I call your office."

"That's not true and you know it. I doubt there is another couple who keeps in contact as much as we do. I tell you everything that's going on."

"Everything?" Maxine asked me. "Come on Alex, you tell me the sanitized version of what you think I should know before somebody else tells me."

"You're in a reflective mood tonight, aren't you? What kind of insect bit you?"

"We talk Alex, but being in the car, you and I, is special. It's like being in a chamber."

"Yes! A torture chamber."

"You mean you consider it a torture talking about us?"

"Come on, Max. Don't put words in my mouth. We do talk a lot. We share a lot of things. I'm sure there are very few couples that talk as much as we do."

"What's going on with Natividad," Maxine asked me directly. "I haven't heard you mention her name for some time."

"Nothing! You know she had her tour. It was a personal success but it didn't translate into any kind of substantial sales. We haven't got many more orders."

"I was reading in a recent 'Hola' magazine; she had a miscarriage. Did you know anything about it?"

"Yes! I heard of it," I answered.

"How come you didn't mention anything to me?"

"I think it happened while I was in Europe."

"She isn't married, is she?"

"No. I think she had or has a boyfriend. I don't know if she has one now. Francine said, she met a fellow in San Francisco and drove south to LA, in a convertible with him."

"I never trusted her. It's one of those things. You know what I mean?"

"Yeah, I know. You never did and you told me several times."

"I know you like her. That aura of feminism, of career woman. Tough women... you seem to like."

"You're one yourself."

"Oh, come on. Don't give me that!"

"You're tough as nails. But you act differently. You don't grunt or pretend, but have a very effective tactic. You procrastinate, ignore, filibuster until you get your wish. You know that!"

THE CALM BEFORE THE STORM

A month passed with no news to speak of. No industry gossip. No word from France until I finally decided to call Sands. It had been five weeks since our last conversation and I was anxious to hear the latest about the takeover. Sands sounded apologetic. He excused himself for not being in contact, but at the same time reassured me I'd be the first one to know if anything happened. I asked him about Federated and he reluctantly said there had been a number of unexpected developments they didn't foresee, and that he doubted things could be settled in the near future. He excused himself again for not being forthcoming, but hoped I'd understand. We moved to other aspects of the business; the economy, the elections, etc. and concluded the conversation with his pledge to keep me informed of any developments, minuscule as they might be.

The telephone rang. "Have you heard?" Julie asked me.

"No! What?"

"There is a note in today's Women's Wear Daily talking about the arrival of the Alsace's chairman and secret conversations with Federated."

"Can you talk to the reporter and find out more?" I asked Julie.

"I have a call in to her. But she hasn't returned it yet."

"Let me know, will you?" I asked her.

That evening Julie called me at home.

"My friend wrote an article for tomorrow's edition about the negotiations between the Alsace and Federated and the possibility of a joint announcement before the weekend. She said they had secured ninety five percent of the financing with European banks and two large investment banks in the US."

Early in the morning my telephone rang. "Hello?"

"Did you read the Times? Front page. A big article about the acquisition. Five to eight billion dollars. Cash and stocks plus debt... Half of it deferred for five years. There will be a joint announcement late in the afternoon. We are fucked!" Ben said.

"There is nothing we can do but sit and wait," I responded.

"They talk about the Alsace's chairman as if he were the new enfant terrible of acquisitions in Europe. The variety of business under his umbrella with no synergy whatsoever. Ben added. "There is another article about the financing, his proclivity for borrowing money, the accumulation of debt. A very good article. If half of it is true, he won't last two years in the US market, believe me."

"We might not last two years," I responded. "Ok, let me go. I'm going to get the paper. I'll see you at the office at nine sharp."

I went downstairs and got the paper laying at my doorstep. I couldn't believe it. Two columns on the lower part of the front page. "French Conglomerate Acquires Federated," read the headline. I went inside and sat at the kitchen table. I anxiously read the front page and moved to the financial section where the article continued; "The "New Player Among Us," read the headline with a two column photograph of the happy warrior, holding a basket with a legend; "Fifteen billion Dollars." I'll be damned. Exactly as Chloe told me. I wondered for a moment if she was in New York with Tessier; but even if she came she wasn't going to risk meeting me. Perhaps I could call her at home tonight.

"*Ok, Ok, calm down. What's the rush? There is nothing we can do now,*" my alter-ego interrupted me. "*Take it easy. This is just the beginning. We knew this was coming. Let's take our espresso and finish reading the paper. Relax! Go to the art section. That's what we read first, don't we? We have time to regroup. There are no short cuts and we know there is a long battle ahead of us."*

"Let me see the headline," Maxine asked me, as she came into the kitchen.

I showed it to her.

"Have you talked to Sands, lately?

"No, I was thinking about calling him later on," I responded.

"There is nothing you can do but wait."

"I guess. Do you want some?" I asked her, holding the orange juice container in my hand.

"Yes, please. Any toast left?"

Maxine took the paper, sat at the table, drank her juice, ate her toast and read both articles avidly.

"You knew quite a few details already, didn't you? I heard you talking to Ben about the Alsace's accumulation of debt, the billions they are paying for Federated. Do you know who is doing what to whom in this deal?"

"I think they are doing it to each other."

"Didn't it occur to you to buy Federated stock? You'd have made a bundle with all the inside information you had."

Ben was waiting for me at the office. He wanted to know my opinion about the article and if I was going to try to contact Sands. I said, "let's call him right now," and I did. "Out of town," the secretary responded. When asked if he was in New York, she said, "Germany; visiting a division." She added she wouldn't hear from him until the next day, but she'd tell him I called and mention I wanted to be called back.

I contacted Julie. She'd read the Times' articles and made some calls to get the industry's reaction to the announcement. "The consensus was; Rochenberg had screwed the French." He got a great deal and an even better parachute. The opinion about Tessier was unanimous; flaky, that he wouldn't last in this market. I asked her how the Federated stock was doing. It had opened higher, she responded.

A week passed before I got a call from Sands. He was very apologetic, as usual. No doubt the man has good manners, nevertheless he isn't forthcoming with the information I want. He confirmed what we all knew and for the first time didn't reassure me about my franchise representation in the US. He was cagy, using words with no meaning. Listening to him made me realize how well he knew English. He explained he wasn't in charge of the new division because Rochenberg would continue as CEO answering directly to Tessier. He insisted there were no changes in our relationship and that we should continue as if nothing had happened for the time being.

Another six months went by before I had another contact with the Alsace administration. Sands had come briefly to New York, a week or so after the takeover was announced and I met him at the Palace for dinner. He excused himself again, but suggested they planned to continue working with me. And they did. For six more months.

Today, Ben got a call from a low level finance officer from Federated in Chicago who wanted to discuss our account. The man mentioned there was a small balance they wanted satisfied before they could discuss a new way of handling our account. The excuse; they were in the process of a huge reorganization to combine Federated and The Alsace's North American operations. In other words, me. We wouldn't answer or deal with Sands' International Division anymore, or so it looked.

Ben, surprised by the announcement, complained of not being formally informed. He asked the messenger if that directive shouldn't have come directly from the Alsace and be discussed with his boss, Mr. Faust. The messenger, with no particular diplomacy, informed him; "I'm your new Federated liaison, your contact at the Finance Division, and I am following instructions." "Will you put that in writing?" Ben asked him. He responded he'd pass it on to his immediate boss, a man he identified as Monsieur Barton. Monsieur Barton, he added, had been recently appointed VP Finance for the US Division.

That was the Alsace's first salvo. We were being downgraded in the best case scenario, or completely ignored or trampled on, in the worst. My first impulse was to call Sands, but decided against it. Ben concurred; we should wait for the letter and go from there. And we did. And the letter arrived three days later by express mail.

We had been made part of the US Division, the letter stated. From now on, we'd deal with Mr. Barton, VP Finance US Division, operating out of Chicago. The letter referred only to the economic aspects of the operation. It gave us the name of our new contact, Mr. Joseph. Adding to the intrigue, Barton's missive stated Joseph would be visiting us in the next ten days. He was authorized to discuss all the financial aspects between us.

Joseph came sooner than was announced and immediately demanded, in so many words, the over sixty days' balance. I didn't participate in the meeting, but Ben told him his request wasn't in the cards as long as we didn't discuss our future relationship. He explained we had overextended ourselves time and time again to comply with every request they had made in the past, but that they were also concerned about our future. Ben told Joseph that after several years of uncertainty, it was time to finalize the new contract and he suggested a meeting with the Alsace's higher-ups, in Europe or Chicago, to put an end to the uncertainty. Joseph didn't add much to the conversation and remained noncommittal until the end when he asked Ben for advice about a Broadway show to see before heading back to Chicago.

LA FINCA – MY REFUGE

Life is tough. The dreaded moment seemed to have arrived and I was running on empty. Literally, I had been thrown to the lions. No matter how much I had thought or looked for a way out of this mess I hadn't found a solution. I couldn't pray; I didn't believe in God. I had exhausted my credit line and even if I hadn't, it would have been a mistake to waste several millions with no future. What to do was the question and I had no answer.

I decided to escape to La Finca, my retreat in the Adirondack Mountains. I needed to hide. To be alone, by myself and called Julie.

"What are you doing this weekend?" I asked her.

"Why?"

"I'm going upstate. Will you join me?"

"Going by yourself?"

"So far."

"What about Maxine?"

"I didn't ask her, but I know she's busy. Jasmin, a friend from school is here. I don't want to drag them with me. I want to be alone."

"Burt is in Germany," Julie said.

"Better. Would you come?"

It was late Friday night. The New York Thruway was empty. The winter of my discontent was upon me. Any good news? No snow. A strange season; a rare, dry spell after Thanksgiving. I didn't feel like speaking. Julie, next to me, read a book with a pen light. The miles went by as quickly as my thoughts perked up and dissipated. Any solace? La Finca, another hour ahead of me. On the stereo; Flagstad, singing Liebestod. An old tape I listened to when troubled.

The sight of my retreat's entrance soothed my angst. Georgiana had left the gate open and I drove in, closed the gate behind me and went up my winding driveway. My place on the hill was lit up in all its splendor. My distress and worries seemed to evaporate; my retreat confines were soothing, so reassuring as if nothing wrong could ever happen to me there. I wanted to thank somebody for my luck and I did. On my own way.

The house was in perfect order. The lights in my pavilion on, the water running, the heat at sixty eight degrees and the fireplace with a fresh load of wood. What luck!

"Would you like hot chocolate?" Julie asked me.

"What a wonderful idea. I hope Georgiana left us some fresh bread. Are you hungry?"

"Yes! I didn't ask you to stop; I saw you deep in thought. I didn't want to interrupt whatever dialog you were having with yourself."

I looked at her and chuckled.

"It's fascinating to watch you escape your surroundings. For such a talkative man, you have that ability to abstract yourself from whatever is going on, and go away, by yourself, as if there was nothing else around you. Fascinating."

I didn't respond. I shrugged and gave her a little smile in return.

"Anything in particular you can share with me?" Julie asked, grabbing three thick chocolate bars from the kitchen counter and milk from the fridge Georgiana had conveniently fetched at the supermarket that afternoon.

"I was ruminating about something Bertrand Russell said, and I should add was one of the first things I read, back when I got interested in philosophy."

"I thought Camus was your guru," she prompted.

"Yes, but Bertrand was the first one I read. In a way he has more to do with my present predicament."

"Which one in particular? There are so many," she added ironically.

Julie poured the chocolate in two deep bowls; it was thick and hot with a great aroma. The toast was French bread, sliced in half and was hot and crunchy. We sat around the kitchen counter and devoured it.

"Bertrand said something like, I'm paraphrasing of course; To bear misfortune, a man should cultivate a number of different interests; You know, art, music, a hobby, that kind of thing. With zest, and I'd add passion, he should be able to surmount misfortune and not take one blow as fatal, as if our whole life were at the mercy of a single accident. And always keep in mind that we are at the mercy of death.'"

"That's your theme, isn't it? No wonder you like him. Did he die of old age or shoot himself?"

"Worse, old age."

"The quote sounds great and perhaps true, but I wonder how many people can abstract themselves from their tormenting problems. No one I know, but you."

"It's easier said than done, you know."

We finished our chocolate and walked to the pavilion. We sat on the couch; Julie dropped next to me, resting her back and head on my lap. I switched on the CD player and soft Satie sonatas we heard.

"I think old man Russell was into something," Julie said pensively. "If we go by what he said, you're a good practitioner of his philosophy. Look at us, or look at you. Here we are, away from the maddening crowd, even when the sky is collapsing around you."

"It is almost 2 already," I said.

"Yeah! Let's go up."

We walked up the spiral staircase and landed in bed fully dressed. Julie immediately rolled over me and we started our erotic routine taking off each piece of clothing, dropping them unceremoniously by the side and kissing thoroughly each and every part of our just exposed bodies.

Sex between us was like a liberating experience. We went at each other knowing our favorite weaknesses. Changing the order each time, as if not wanting to telegraph what we'd do next.

The morning light was glorious. The trees were naked. Only the pines looked great dressed green against the chill of the fall. I turned around and embraced Julie who was face down, fully covered to the neck with one of my old, wool pajamas. I kissed her cold feet and she jumped like a spring. We moved up in bed and rested our backs against the headboard. The view of the hills and the lake was sharp and crispy. I was lucky, I thought. Tomorrow be damned. We are here, now and nothing can take it away from us.

"Aren't you going to write your daily ration?" Julie asked me.

"Not today! I don't feel like doing anything; just rest, take it easy and soak up this gorgeous view as much as I can."

"Well, I'm glad you're in good spirits. You have this indomitable will to feel good no matter what. It scares the hell out of me. Sometimes I feel you just ignore the inevitable."

"Postpone is a better word."

"Most people would feel threatened by your present insecurity; lose sleep, stop eating."

"You remind me of my Maxine and her Cassandra's type predictions," I said in jest, perhaps wanting to deny my prevalent angst and feeling of impending doom.

The telephone rang; it was Ben.

"Sorry to bother you, but I came to the office and while I was here, the mailman delivered 'a certified, return receipt letter. I opened it; it was addressed to me."

"Cut the pre-ambles," I urged him.

"They are demanding the full account."

"You're kidding me."

"No, I'm not," Ben insisted. "They are giving us ten days to come up with the dough!"

"Who signed it? I asked him.

"Barton, Chief VP Finance North America."

"Just like that; pay up!"

"Just like that!"

"Anything else?"

"Nothing else."

"Ok. Go home and try to forget what you read, if you can. We can do nothing now. Monday, first thing in the morning. Alright?"

Julie was in suspense right beside me.

"Ben got a letter from the Alsace?" She asked me.

"No, Federated in Chicago."

"What do they want?"

"They are asking for the whole balance. They aren't talking about the over thirty day balance. They want the whole thing."

"That means...."

"We're fucked! They are in a hurry to terminate us."

I was downtrodden. I walked to and sat on my desk staring at the lake in the distance. Julie sat in one of the easy chairs next to me. I was deep in thought; she kept quiet with her face down. What an irony. It was a gorgeous, crispy afternoon in the Adirondacks; 40 degrees, no clouds, the sun almost at eye level. Once again, as so many times in the past, the bad news struck like lightning; at the most unexpected of times.

"We can go back to New York if you want to," Julie said.

"There is nothing I can do here or there. It is better if we stay. Do you mind?"

"Whatever you decide."

"Why don't we take a walk through the woods? I love the trail. It's so peaceful!"

We put on heavy boots and warmer jackets and walked in the direction of the forest. If you couldn't forget about your problems walking the Adirondacks, you couldn't anywhere in the world.

"La Finca" was a mile long and a mile wide, crisscrossed with ample trails, remnants of years of logging. That network connected with other wild properties and finally immersed itself in a hundred mile wide State Park. There were huge oaks, lots of other hard wood trees and plenty of pines. A small creek came down from the hilly elevation behind us dividing the property in two. As we entered the thickest part of the woods, Julie started to talk about fate, the way things work out in life and the necessity to reconcile ourselves with a higher power; to go back to our roots, what we learned as children.

"I just want you to hear me and say nothing. Are you going to keep quiet until I finish?" She insisted.

"Yes ma'am!"

"Since I've known you, what? Nine years or so?"

"About that."

"You've kept this almost mythological stance against God and all external forces. You deny God at every step of your life as if you were here by accident, as if there was no purpose or no direction in our lives. You grew up Catholic. Your family is Catholic and you still insist on denying the existence of a higher up." Julie stopped and addressed me directly. "And God is catching up with you. These are signs that things aren't working. Look at the number of setbacks that have afflicted you lately. Perhaps this is a way of telling you; stop, get down to earth and reassess your life, your values, the people you have around you."

"Don't take it personally, but you really sound like one of those evangelists on television," I responded. "Are you telling me God is teaching me a lesson?"

"Don't be cute with me. You know what I'm saying."

"Come on Julie, I can't believe you really believe that. Somehow you want to get back at me, I don't know why..."

"Are you mad?" she said, interrupting me. "Get back at you, why? You see, you just proved my point. You think everybody is against you! Even me, who has put up with you rain or shine. We want the best for you, silly. But none of us can understand the way you go about your life in this time of crisis. You need help and not only from lawyers, but you need peace; peace with yourself, peace with everyone around you. And it's getting late."

As Julie rebuked me, we had arrived at one of my treasured sections in the woods. An elongated span, like a cathedral nave, with dozens of dense high pine trees. I loved being there, surrounded by my trees. What an irony! Julie had begun to advocate a reconciliation with my religious past as we entered such a wondrous unique place. And I felt at peace with myself and nature all around me. I wanted to stop hiking and rest, sit there, quietly, not talking, arguing or explaining myself. And we did.

"Why don't we sit here for a few minutes?" "Don't you like it here?"

"I love it here, silly," Julie protested. "How many times have we made love under these trees? Have you forgotten already?"

"No, I have not. Just sit," I told her. "Let's stay here for a while, please," I said, as I held her hand and gently led her to a large, exposed root, shaped as a convenient resting place. Julie sat against the tree. I closed my eyes and laid next to her peacefully, with my head resting on her lap, saying nothing, just listening to the sounds of cracking branches and swaying trees, while apocalyptic thoughts raged in my head.

THE ALSACE – COUP DE GRACE!

Monday morning at 8.30 sharp I met Ben who had been at the office for a while already. We discussed the letter and decided we should give it a try, talking to France one more time. Anticipating Sands' answer we discussed a second step; contacting Federated and asking for a meeting before their schedule deadline. We knew it was an uphill fight, but one we were supposed to fight no matter what. After all, our lives and the wellbeing of all involved on this endeavor were on the line.

The call to Sands was short and sweet with a noncommittal outcome. He was completely out of the picture. The US division was on its own and the Chairman had given carte blanche to the division's President to do what was best. I inquired politely about Chloe and Sands said she was working nonstop. He wished me luck and politely offered his home if I ever decided to visit Paris again.

Out of options with Paris, I placed a call to Federated president. His secretary answered and mentioned he was in an all-day meeting; nevertheless, she said she'd tell him I called. That afternoon, monsieur Barton called. He said the president had asked him to return my call. I said, I'd like a face-to-face meeting with him and the president. He answered he was willing to meet me, but didn't know if his boss would have time to meet with us. He'd mention my request to him anyway. He also said he wouldn't be able to come to NY or Miami, but he wouldn't mind if we flew to meet him in Chicago; his secretary would call and give me a date if that was agreeable.

I looked at Ben, who had sat in front of me listening to the conversation and told him to get ready to fly to Chicago. It was probably a waste of time, but something we should do, no matter the outcome. We owed it to ourselves.

The reception in Chicago was cool but polite. We were ushered to a large conference room where Mr. Barton and Mr. Joseph, his assistant, were sitting waiting for us. The room was sparse; some old prints hung from the walls and a long table with old, worn-out leather chairs in its center. A real disappointment if we consider Federated was one of the trendiest store-chains in the US.

After shaking hands, Barton asked us politely what we had in mind. I began to recite a number of reasons why I thought it was improper and most unfair to demand the full balance in our kind of relationship and requested an explanation for their sudden change of policy. Barton cut to the chase and went directly to his prepared remarks. He said it was not the policy of Federated to discuss corporate decisions or business practices. He added it was important that before we discuss the situation further, we come up with the money owed. He restated their readiness to compromise and offered us another week to pay the full balance, if we so desired.

Frustrated as I was, I reminded Barton that our business moves in cycles. That we could understand their concern about the over ninety days' balance, but even the ninety days had a reason; we were in the middle of an election campaign.

Barton responded that the election shouldn't be used as an excuse for any payment delay. He said that's why The Alsace didn't deal directly with stores and have intermediaries like us; so they could isolate themselves from the ravaging of the retail markets. That we should have made provisions for a situation like this.

I shifted uncomfortably in my chair trying not to respond Barton's diatribe even if inside me, I felt like punching him. Ben couldn't hide his anger even if he tried. Barton had not given us any room and it was obvious, by his intransigence, the Alsace-Federated group had made the decision to terminate us. I asked Barton if this decision could be appealed and he firmly responded there was nothing to appeal. They had made their decision and it was a matter of carrying it out; that he'd appreciate we accept the situation for what it was and the sooner we could give him an answer the easier it would be for both sides.

Walk out of here and don't say another word, my alter ego interrupted. *We're fucked. This situation is a complete loss and there is no way you can recover or find an agreeable solution. Get your papers and walk out. Ya! Now!*

I stood up, collected my papers. Ben also rose and pushed his chair against the table.

"Thank you for your time," I said firmly.

"No problem," Barton responded. "When will you have an answer for us?"

"In due time. Like you, it is the policy of our corporation not to discuss internal matters or future plans. In the meantime, if you decide to share with us the future of our relationship, I will appreciate it. I'm sure it will speed up whatever decision we make about your request."

LAWYERS – LESSONS LEARNED

"You know what really bothers me," I said to Ben, flying back to New York. "The lawyers. The fucken lawyers are the only ones who benefit from this kind of drama. They end up in the middle and contrary to common wisdom, are only as good as the case is. In the end, you have to appeal to the empathy of the jury or play delicately with their ignorance. No matter how good the case is, we will ultimately be at the mercy of a jury."

"Did any of the lawyers you consulted gave you any idea, a reading of what they think of the case?"

"The prospect of a fat retainer is a powerful incentive for any lawyer. They all listened patiently and expressed their willingness to represent us, but so far, the word Federated hasn't been mentioned. The clinch will come when I disclose the name of the eight hundred pound gorilla. I wonder how they'll react when they hear the name."

Home again, I went directly to the bar and served myself a stiff Scotch. Maxine was in the living room and I joined her. "How was your meeting?" she asked me, putting down the book she was reading.

"They've decided to ax us once and for all."

"I don't believe you." Maxine incredulously stated.

"Well, we better get used to the idea we are facing a tough fight for survival. These guys take no prisoners."

"What's next... litigation?"

"Litigation!" I responded. "Lawyers, paperwork, witnesses. I hate it."

"I know you don't like to talk about money, but have you made provision for a war chest? I mean, put aside some money while this lasts?"

"Sort of...." was my guarded answer.

"Sort of, is not an answer. I'm talking about a regular flow of money. We can't maintain your far flung life style without the income generated by the business. Or can we?"

"You're right! Once we start on that road, no one knows where it'll end or how long it will take."

My first meeting was with a medium size law firm with a very big name, which Burt had recommended. One of the partners spent close to an hour with me and politely terminated the meeting minutes after Federated was mentioned. A conflict of interest. He confidentially stated.

My other two meetings with lawyers had a more or less kind of sobering, if disappointing effect. One excused himself saying they had a sort of ongoing relationship with Federated and it would be unethical to represent another client against them. The last one Burt had recommended, sounded ready to take the case, notwithstanding his assertion that, even if we had a good case, it would be difficult if not impossible to prove it to a jury. He said he'd prefer a trial by jury to a judge because the jury might be more sympathetic to a national fighting a foreign corporation. But he also mentioned that ideally it would be easier for a judge to understand the complexity of the case. One way or the other, he said, he could convince his partners to take it. Then I asked him if I decided to go with his firm, what kind of a retainer we could be talking about.

He pointed out that because of the Alsace's resources and the time he anticipated getting to trial, they would need a retainer of at least a hundred thousand dollars. He mentioned their fees were five hundred dollars an hour for him and three hundred for any of his associates. He mentioned that in the event he had to travel to Paris and Madrid for depositions, he'd use the Concord to save time and be alert at his arrival. Notwithstanding his fees and his conditions, he asserted he could not guarantee the success of our efforts and his best estimate was we had a fifty/fifty chance of winning the case. Our best bet, he continued, would be to get a settlement and if he could get us one, he'd take a third, obviously discounting our retainer fees and any other monies we had paid up to that moment.

While the search continued unabated, I was rapidly exhausting the list of prominent names Burt had put together for me. Another couple of unsuccessful interviews with firms of lesser name recognition had the same kind of disappointing results. Both complained of the size of the enemy, their unlimited resources and the difficulty of making a jury understand the intricacies of the case. However, they were certain we would prevail and requested a large retainer. Four weeks after having interviewed my first legal counsels, I still was in square one, trying to find who to retain.

With no other alternative but to find a lawyer, I finally met a smaller firm and a couple of self-assured partners who patiently heard me recite the intricacies of my case --- for close to two hours --- before concluding we had a good shot at beating the beast. Nevertheless, they cautioned me there was no sure outcome in a trial by jury, but after having heard the disclaimers of all the other groups, they sounded reassuring. They showed themselves ready to face the ordeal and requested a modest retainer, compared to what the other guys had demanded. I spoke to Ben and we mailed them a fifty thousand dollar check. We finally were ready to face the music, and we did. Almost a month after our initial meeting, my lawyers served the Alsace, Federated, Zamora's group and Zamora personally with papers. We sued them for restraint of trade, price manipulation and breach of contract.

While my search for a knight was going on, Federated had continued their harassment campaign. Just a week or ten days after our visit to Chicago, we received a letter from Barton thanking us for taking the time to fly to meet him reaffirming his interest in finding an amicable solution to our differences. He ended his letter reminding us again of the balance owed Federated and stating there wouldn't be any other contact until their conditions were met.

LUNCH ON MY BANKER'S TERMS

Our rupture with The Alsace, or Federated now, was well known in the industry, especially among our clients. We had stopped deliveries of the summer products and had not shopped the new line for the fall, something normally done around late February and March. We no longer offered Natividad's higher end line and consequently lost the prestigious names in the apparel retail sector, the Bloomies, Nordstrom, and Saks, who had also decided to stop buying our own popular labels. Once the rest of our customers got wind of our fall from grace, many decided to place smaller orders or no orders at all. Many others thought that by waiting it out, they might skip paying their owed balances altogether, and so they did.

Two more weeks passed before I heard from Francine in Chicago. She was concerned, she said, with the size of the few orders we had received and worried about our sales force. "Our guys are unhappy with their commissions" and "three of our eight regional reps are looking for jobs."

The tenor of Francine's conversation was the thrust of my meeting with Ben the following morning. He was concerned, he said, about the morale of the group in general. Ben also reminded me of the telephone conversation he had with Donald, The Institutional Bank VP who manages our account. The banker was very concerned," he said, "with a number of rumors floating around Miami about our future and suggested we have a luncheon in his private quarters next week; Monday, I think he said."

That Sunday Maxine dropped me at La Guardia on her way to hear mass. We didn't talk much about anything, something rare, once we found ourselves in the confines of a car. Fortunately my flight was on time and I arrived in Miami promptly at one thirty. I took a taxi at the airport and twenty eight dollars later, I got to my condo with plenty of time to walk the beach and enjoy the rest of a beautiful afternoon.

It had rained heavily all morning; the remains of a strong storm that had lashed the East Coast all week long. Fortunately it was clear and sunny again; the magic of Florida. The beach had paid its toll. The waves had carved the sand leaving a drop almost three feet high mid-beach, about a hundred feet from the ocean. I mourned for my beach. The walk from my condo to the lighthouse, at the end of the key, was a trek adorned with a luscious tropical forest on one side and the ocean on the other. An experience, if completely different, somehow comparable to a walk on my Finca trails back in the Adirondack Mountains. Up North I enjoyed the hard soil, birch, oak trees and the sun hiding behind a canapé of tall pines. Down here was the complete opposite; sand, palms, sea grapes and the blazing sun forcing me to run for cover. In other words, the dichotomy of my life; hard and soft extremes, either/or, nothing in between.

The sunset came early and I decided to stay put and order out. I called my default takeout joint which delivered tasty Cuban food and I ate it together with my house wine. A bit tired, my appetite quenched — unhappy with my present state of affairs — I took refuge in my VCR. "Les Amants," The Lovers, I had seen it at the impressionable age of fifteen, back in Cuba, and I switched on the machine and let the images of my beloved Jeanne Moreau fill the screen and my imagination once again.

"The Lovers," "The Mediocre Man," a book by Ingenieros, Dostoevsky's "Notes from the Underground" and "The Dream of a Ridiculous Man" had a seminal impact on my youthful evolving consciousness. The books instilled in me the fear of mediocrity and ridicule, but Malle's heroine leaving family and fortune behind, burning the ships and running away with her young lover — me, of course — was all I needed to stir my youthful imagination.

And here I am, some thirty years later, alone, by myself, with Moreau on the screen, confronting my demons, at another of my beautiful corners of the world.

The telephone rang. It was Ben. He had arrived late last night and hadn't slept well. We agreed to meet promptly at noon and drive together to meet our banker, another ten minutes away, in Coral Gables.

We arrived at the bank at midday. The receptionist made the obligatory call and asked us to wait. It was almost a half hour later when the secretary showed up, excused herself for the delay and asked us to follow her. The long walk through the hall to this fellow's office seemed interminable. Finally we entered his huge domain; "Sorry," the vice-president said, "I had to deal with something that couldn't be postponed," he added.

It was a cool reception, not like many others in the past. The stage was already set; a round table next to a garden window. *I wonder what he has in mind,* my alter ego interrupted. *Look around you. Six months ago, we weren't made to wait. The table was covered with a nice linen cloth, the china was elegant, real silverware, delicate crystal and two bottles of a good chateau wine already opened. Take a look. If this is a presage of things to come, we're in deep shit. A plain table, no table cloth, no silverware and a bottle of domestic wine. I wonder what we're in for. If I were you, I'd get ready for the worst.*

"I'm sorry I don't have a more elaborate lunch prepared for you," our VP said apologetically, as he lead us to the table, "I'm pressed for time. But I'm pretty sure you're going to like the roast beef sandwich; it's rare, almost red, something difficult to find in Miami."

We sat around the table and a female employee brought a cart with three plates, with half a sandwich each, a scoop or two of potato salad, and silverware wrapped in paper napkins. Our host took the bottle of wine and poured some in each of our glasses.

"It's an inexpensive wine from a client's cellar we foreclosed. You know, their business went belly up and we had no choice, but it's good. I like it with red meat."

"*You better eat your sandwich before they take it away,*" my alter ego interrupted me again. I couldn't help but laugh to myself and discreetly looked at Ben who perhaps thinking the same thing had already taken a good bite.

"Gentlemen, you might wonder why I asked you to lunch and there is a simple reason. We have been doing business now for close to five years and even if there have been rumors in the past, you have been able to keep your commitments to the bank. Your line of credit went from three million to five million, to twelve million and with it, the amounts of your deposits. You kept a substantial balance; not exactly what we originally planned, but I should say, acceptable."

This fellow is a pig; why don't you tell him to swallow the half sandwich he's got in his mouth and then speak, again my alter ego interrupted.

"I know," our man continued, "you had gone through a drastic upheaval with the Federated acquisition. Are you still doing business with them?" He asked me point blank.

"Actually no," I responded. "As a matter of fact, we're in conversations with a new European couture house to substitute Natividad's line. You remember Natividad."

"Of course," he interjected. "I don't know if I gave you the line of credit for your numbers or her figure," he said laughing. "You also sued Federated and The Alsace, didn't you?"

"Well, yes! We did. But it was more of a tactical move." And I went on giving him a number of tidbits, always excusing myself for not being more forthcoming with details because of the ongoing litigation. Altogether one of my best performances, trying to present an optimistic angle and showing a somewhat promising way out of the mess.

"Anyway," he finally said. "I would like to make you the following proposition. We're willing to go forward for another sixty days as long as you bring your deposits back to the level you maintained six months ago. Do we have a deal?"

"Sixty days is nothing in this kind of business. We talk about seasons a year in advance," I interrupted him.

"Ok, make it ninety days. I'll give you ninety days. Is that fair enough?"

Knowing that perhaps that was the best deal we could get, I swallowed hard and shook hands with him.

As we moved away from the table he stopped us and said, "You know André, your original manager has been visiting us. He's got a lot information."

"André was fired more than two years ago," I responded. "Everything he told you is hearsay," I said forcefully, shook hands and walked away.

Roberta came for lunch. "What's going on?" she asked me the minute she entered the apartment. I told her of our lunch with the banker and André feeding the VP malicious gossip about our collapsing financial situation.

"He's vicious." Roberta said. "I think it's time you stop denying the curse is working."

"No, I can't deny it, but by the same token we can also attribute it to chance doing its thing."

It was obvious since our visit to the old man two, three years ago, things had gone from bad to worse and there wasn't any hope for a quick upturn. Our suit was entangled in court with constant motions to dismiss, to delay depositions or produce records of any sort. They have also orchestrated a vicious campaign demanding all kinds of discovery about my private and family resources. A resolute push not only to obstruct and delay the proceedings, but to harass and break my will to survive.

"If I were you, I'd have gone to a Babalao a long time ago," Roberta insisted. "According to el Brujo, only another Brujo can do the trick. I'm dumbfounded listening to all the things that have happened to you, one after the other, and how passively you have taken it. As if you were a bystander. That's not the Alexander I met fifteen years ago."

There was no point in arguing with Roberta; she was right in many ways. But what she didn't understand was that my future was in the hands of the courts and not a Brujo. I didn't believe in God, for goodness sake, how I could believe in black magic or Santeria or anything of that sort.

Another perfunctory meeting with Francine and the remains of our workforce in Miami was held before my departure back to New York. I told the group we had sold the building --- when in fact I had surrendered it to the bank --- but had an option to lease. "Nevertheless," I said "I'd keep our commitments to them for two more months while hoping things could bounce back. But we wouldn't mind if they found other jobs that would ease the transition.

The meeting over, I turned to Francine and invited her and her husband for dinner tonight while walking the office and the atelier one last time. The walk over, Francine, with wet eyes, hugged and kissed me goodbye. As she drove away I went inside and looked around the office one more time. It was almost impossible to accept that a project that started with such good fortune and enthusiasm had come to this crashing end.

Disgruntled, I drove back to the key. It was about four, the sun was low on the horizon and I decided to walk the beach. It was beautiful! The ocean was calm, the tide low and the gulls and sandpipers were having a feast. Lost in my labyrinth, I began my usual walk to the lighthouse. I felt at ease, but my mind couldn't stop recycling numbers, facts and emotions. The building was sold, Francine got a substantial job, my designers repositioned themselves in the trade and the rest of my gang had two more paid months to find jobs; I felt good about that. Me? That's another story. I was fucked!

I got to the end of the key and sat on the rocks next to the lighthouse. There I was again, alone, with no one around. Where do I go from here? I asked myself. If I don't get to court soon, the apartment will go, perhaps La Finca too. Even if I win, I'd have lost everything in the process. Would that be a victory? Hardly. Is it possible the Brujo was right? I asked myself again. I couldn't believe it. Those curses are myths, fiction, legends based on obscurantism, ignorance, I repeated trying to convince myself. But it is happening. Everything he predicted is happening right before my eyes and here I am, watching, with my hands tied behind my back.

The sun was setting. Life is tough, Alejandro, I said to myself, starting my trek back to my apartment. But no matter what, we will win in the end. Of course we will, even if I lose everything in between.

MAXINE – LAWYERS – PROPERTIES

Maxine was at La Guardia waiting for me. Even if we kept in daily contact and I related to her a sanitized version of events, she would prod me for more information and details as we drove home.

"I think you should get rid of the Key Biscayne condo. You don't need it."

"You never liked it." I said to her. "That's why you want me to sell it."

"You're right. That's another of your hideouts; that and La Finca, when you're not traveling out of the country. I always preferred La Finca, although I haven't set a foot there since your performance artist, what's her name, Isadora got killed in the accident. Perhaps you should get rid of that too, before it is too late."

"I knew I should have insisted you waited for me at home."

"The torture chamber," say it."

"Look, I have enough problems as it is and I don't need to come back home and find I can't safely hide away from them. That's why I run to La Finca every time I have a chance. Let's get home in peace. I think you have said what you wanted to say and I need my time back. I'm meeting my lawyers tomorrow."

"What is it this time? It is more than a year that we filed suit and there is no progress. Are you sure these people are doing their job?"

"We'll know tomorrow," I told her firmly.

I grabbed a bite from a corner vendor before I entered a high building in mid-Manhattan. My lawyers' offices were half the entire twenty fifth floor and their conference room was as ostentatious as any other I have ever seen; and I have been to a few. I identified myself to a new receptionist and she ushered me directly to a corner office. Even if they were only two partners, they had a good number of associates and plenty of supporting personnel. I was mesmerized; it was a real beehive.

Rudy, my lead lawyer, came from behind his desk and shook hands with me.

"I have good and bad news. Which one do you want to hear first?" he asked me.

"The bad first."

"They flooded us with documents; half in French and half in Spanish. The bad news; we have to translate them."

"And the good?"

"They are willing to produce Sands and Zamora. We are still negotiating Natividad's deposition. We're lucky Zamora retains his position as vice-president with the Alsace, supposedly overlooking Natividad's atelier in Spain."

"How about the chairman?" I asked him. "He's the key to the whole thing."

"No dice. We would have to go through the ranks and tie him up to the decision to ax you. As it is, they want us to believe it was Barton, in Chicago, who made the decision. Can you give us any names at the Alsace? Who else did you meet from the Alsace organization? Do you remember ever having a contact or a conversation with anyone close to the chairman?"

I thought of Chloe. My value system was immediately challenged. Will it be my interest or the word I gave her? I remembered listening to my alter ego warning me; *don't commit ever not to use the information she's revealing to us. It would be a mistake. We might need it.* And it didn't take me long to realize that giving her my word was perhaps one of my biggest mistakes. Putting it crudely, I traded my well-being for a fuck. Chloe was the gatekeeper, the only one who could testify how the Alsace conspired to keep me out of the loop — while getting me all tangled up in their web — until they were ready to dump me. By the same token, she risked a lot by telling me the Alsace's future plans. To advise me to protect my interest while I could. And I will always be grateful to her for that.

"No, I don't know anybody else," I told Rudy.

"You better let me decide who is or who is not important in this case," Rudy said. "Sometimes we overlook the most obvious connections and we need all the weapons we can use. Anyway they're going to schedule two depositions, one with Ben and another one with Francine. Is there anything I should know before I prepare them? Your deposition will be next and I'll try to combine it with Natividad's. Is there anything special I should know about her?" my lawyer asked me.

"That could be tricky. We were lovers, you know."

"Aha! You had an affair with Natividad?"

"Yes, I did. She also had a miscarriage. She assured me it was mine." And I went ahead and told him the whole story. I also mentioned that, unbeknown to me, she had also been the Alsace chairman's lover.

"How do you know that? That's dynamite!" he said.

I said those were things I've heard, but I was pretty sure the breakup was one of the reasons — if not the main reason — why the Alsace bought Zamora's Natividad operations. It was a kind of payoff after the breakup.

"So actually your present problem is the result of someone else's love affair gone wrong?"

"You might say that. I was Nati's distributor, she broke up with her lover, he bought her business, he had ideas about the US market, bought Federated and I ended up in the middle. The turns life takes," I responded.

"I really don't know how I can bring that sequence of events up, but I'll find a way," Rudy said. "Obviously, all this is a little cheesy and not the kind of thing a business trial is all about, but it is great drama. It creates intrigue and suspicion in the jurors' minds."

Before we finished, Rudy asked me for another twenty thousand of my outstanding balance. We had not made such big progress in the last year and a half, but he recited the number of motions and his flights to Miami to represent me in court. I said I'd speak to Ben and he'll hear from us in a week or so.

Another twenty thousand was difficult to come up with. I had been financing the law suit with private funds. Now it was a matter of discussing it again with Maxine with whom I shared a checking account, stocks and a number of dwindling investments; nothing easy.

My meeting ended about 6.30 pm and I didn't feel like going back home to confront Maxine. Instead, I called her and let her know I was going to the Met for an opera I had never seen before; "A Ballo in Mascara." Not one of Verdi's best, but being sung by Pavarotti added a special dimension. Maxine didn't complain. Instead she encouraged me and said I needed a distraction.

Morning came and as I was getting dressed to go out Maxine woke up and asked me, "How was "il Ballo?"

"Nothing special. Pavarotti was alright."

"Did they boo him?"

"Our kind of audience will not dare to do that."

Maxine was referring to an incident we witnessed at La Scala during a Pavarotti concert. "Pavarotti e' finito," the gallery yelled. We were in Milan after a skiing trip to Cortina. We asked the hotel's concierge for tickets but he could get us two only in the top tier, where the real opera lovers sit. It wasn't one of Luciano's best nights and they booed him; but I loved it!

"What's the story with your lawyers," Maxine inquired.

"The same. Depositions are scheduled. A million documents to be translated. Another twenty thousand dollars."

"Why don't you sell Key Biscayne and La Finca?" Maxine demanded.

"I mentioned it to the banks already. Their response was predictable. 'If you do, we want the proceeds applied to your debt.' What's the point of selling them if we aren't going to benefit from it?"

"But they cost money to maintain especially La Finca."

"I'm pretty sure we can manage for a while."

"Have you explored the possibility of declaring bankruptcy?" Maxine asked me.

"That's not an option. It would pull us down too. We are personally tied to the business."

"How could all these dreams crumble like a house of cards? Have you asked yourself that question?" She demanded.

"Many times. But it was all the product of chance."

"You and your chance," Maxine said piqued. "Your favorite theory for everything in life. Why don't you write a book about it? You're going to have a lot of time on your hands."

"We're writing it as we speak."

"I should tell you the conversation I had with your parents last night. We had a cocktail before dinner and while drinking our screwdrivers, Mima mentioned a few things about the way you look, how restrained you are. She thinks you don't look or act as you normally do. She seems very worried."

"Parents!" I said. "No matter how old our children are we continue worrying about them. What a chain life is. There is no end."

"By the way, I have been wanting to ask you; how much have we left? I'd hate to write a check with no funds," Maxine said.

"Max, you get the statements every month. Everything about our finances you handle. I take care of the big items but I always mention them to you first."

"How much?" she insisted.

"About two hundred thousand plus your salary and benefits. Enough I hope to last up to the trial or a settlement if we negotiate one."

"It was a wise decision to keep my day job, wasn't it?" Maxine said mordantly.

The next two weeks were pretty hectic. My lawyers got the twenty they demanded. On the personal front, Maxine's reasoning prevailed; I succumbed to her insistence in getting rid of both properties. But always, as a firm practitioner of delaying the inevitable, I negotiated an agreement with the two banks to personally take care of both properties, a euphemism for keeping them for my own use, as long as they weren't sold. They consented gladly, obviously stipulating the proceeds would be applied to reduce the debt.

GEORGIANA, MY TRANSGENDER CARETAKER

As in many other difficult occasions, I felt the urgent need to be alone. Solitude was something I cherished. Arguments and criticisms have been a heavy load on my psyche for so long, I couldn't resist the temptation to escape. And to La Finca I went, perhaps one of the last times I would enjoy before the sale of the property becomes a reality. Georgina my caretaker was another concern. Even if she didn't depend entirely on the wages I paid her, they represented a substantial part of her monthly income. And I felt bad, that after almost twenty years, she would have to be looking for another employer.

I woke up early. It was a beautiful morning. For me they always are whether raining, snowing or sun shining. I prepared and drank my espresso, went outside to the deck and took a long look at what I was going to lose; my woods, the mountains, my marvelous view of the lake. It was written, the Brujo had predicted, "everything, including his beloved retreat would be lost, in stages, slowly, as if he were bleeding." Nevertheless, I felt lucky. Even at this late stage of the game, I was still full of hope and could enjoy my place a little longer.

I came back inside and sat at my desk. I was trying to write a screenplay, a 'ménage a' trois,' based on a thrilling adventure I had lived right there under that roof. As I wrote the first few lines I heard a car coming up the driveway. I looked through the back window and I saw an older man, Mandy, Georgiana's boyfriend. I went to the kitchen entrance and let him in.

Mandy seemed distressed and refused to sit and share a bit of espresso. He explained he had taken care of the house for the last three weeks because Georgiana had suffered a very bad fall and had broken a hip. She had refused to go to the hospital, he said and not being able to move, had developed pneumonia, with a high fever.

"I had no choice other than calling an ambulance, but she refused to be moved. Seeing her in pain, with a very high fever I decided to call the authorities. Only then was she taken to the hospital, still against her will."

"Why wasn't I informed?" I demanded. "I'd have come immediately!"

"She insisted on my not calling you. She was distressed and didn't want you seeing her in that condition. It was a very sad scene," he continued. "The town clerk, the hospital people, the police and quite a few neighbors were present when she was taken away. Imagine, if you see her today, she isn't Georgiana anymore. She's back being George, the six-two chauffeur of Mrs. Sanford. They removed her wig, her false tits, her padded butt and she has become a lanky, tall, seventy two year old man. She's even using her male voice again. But she's in dire condition; high fever and bad case of pneumonia. Nothing works, it seems."

I was overtaken by emotion. My mind rushed to Kazantzakis' Zorba, the moment when Bouboulina in Zorba's arms, laid on her bed dying. The old woman surrounded by a contingent of elderly female neighbors, dressed in black; a chorus of vultures perched around her bed waiting for her to die to run away with any remnants of her possessions. Bouboulina had no privacy and no dignity to expire in peace. And there was nothing Zorba could do. It was like a rite of passage in a Greek town. Georgiana's was a Sophocles tragedy, this time taking place in the Adirondack Mountains. She was stripped of her privacy. That carefully manufactured persona in which she had lived for so many years now forced to return to the one she abhorred, outed against her will. Nature, life, mankind, each and all of them are merciless. Why couldn't she pass away with dignity, peacefully as the woman she wanted to be?

Georgiana I met, dressed in drag, twenty years ago. I had been told he or she went as a woman. Nevertheless it was a bit startling to find a six-two man, wearing a dress, stockings and mid-size heels --- carrying a handbag, with a full curly wig, oversized false tits and butt --- speaking with a squeaky voice, telling me she could do everything I needed and more. I knew him or her, was strong. But somehow, in my mind, I thought I could be seen as taking advantage of her; whether a man or a woman, it didn't seem appropriate. Nevertheless, I couldn't care less as long as she could do the job; mind you, a job that besides simple chores included mowing sixteen acres of lawn with a tractor, cutting trees, branches, stocking several cords of firewood for the winter. Anyway, we did agree to a monthly sum for her services and decided right then and there, she should start the next day. And promptly the next day, she did.

I remember that morning as if it was today. She showed up with her wig, tits, butt, wearing large overall pants and a big hat. I was fascinated. We started talking and I mentioned a number of priorities. She said yes to everything and every once-in-while, during the course of the conversation, she coquettishly would re-arrange her breasts that inadvertently had moved under one of her arms, smile and continue the conversation. I admit, from that moment on, a special kind of relationship developed between us. We not only were employer and worker, but became friends in a peculiar sort of way. Sometimes she made me uncomfortable when sun tanning on my deck or swimming in my pool, but she always cherished seeing me with a female friend. That's the Georgiana I wanted to remember, not the one laying in a hospital bed.

"I ought to go," Mandy interrupted my thoughts. "I have to take care of a few things before I go to the hospital." We shook hands. I asked him to tell her "Hello" and to call me when the inevitable happened.

Back in New York, I returned a group of twelve relevant documents in Spanish I had taken with me to read and translate during the weekend. Rudy informed me he had a conversation with a French court translator who had agreed to review about fifty documents produced by the Alsace. He also mentioned both translators had been accepted by the Alsace's lawyers and that he expected the judge to okay them. Asked how much he thought the bulk of the translations would cost, he came back with a rough figure of about four to six thousand dollars, a number that made me cringe.

We had dinner at home that night about eight. Mother had prepared a chicken fricassee, salad and a bread pudding for dessert, out of this world. The conversation was the habitual one; what was going on in the world, the price of things and the latest news on TV. But mother had something else in her head. She cautiously asked how things were going. And I answered the only way I knew how; "good!" I said. "You know, we have complications, but I'm sure things will turn out well in the end; they usually do." Maxine looked at me with a stern look, as if reproaching my faked optimism. But both of them seemed relieved.

Mandy called; "Georgiana is dead!" That the county was going to cremate her and there would be a brief burial Friday at 11 am. I thanked him and said I'd do everything I could to be there; and I was!

Friday morning I dutifully showed up at the cemetery and found a small group of friends and a Protestant minister waiting to conduct the service. After embracing Mandy and shaking hands with the minister, we walked about a hundred yards to a section with ossuaries where we deposited the cardboard box, with Georgiana's ashes, on a prearranged table.

The minister lost no time. He made the sign of the cross, read a verse from the bible and asked God for mercy and a welcome reception for brother/sister Georgiana in the kingdom of heaven. Then he asked us to repeat after him a number of invocations. He concluded asking us to say a silent prayer of our own. He then proceeded to bless the box and all of us present; five in total.

He then closed his bible and said a few words:

"I don't know how to begin," he said. "I've officiated at many funerals since I was ordained, but this is an extraordinary occasion. We are giving a Christian send off to the remains of a person with two distinctive personas; George and Georgiana. Male and female in the space of one single life. Nature allowed George to appropriate the one gender chance had denied him at birth. And in the end, chance again denied her what he wanted most; to die as the woman she longed to be. Let's celebrate the person we knew and the character that lived for seventy two years among us. God have mercy on Georgiana. In the name of the Father, the Son and the Holy Ghost, Amen! Go in peace."

Very well said, I thought. I never expected a religious authority to recognize nature and not God as the giver of life and in the same sentence use chance in a supposedly preordained world created by the God he represented. I could see myself talking about nature and chance in those terms. I'm a firm believer in both, especially chance, but a pastor? Religion is changing faster than I thought. Happy perhaps, finding a pastor with such a progressive set of ideas, I approached and invited him to lunch. He excused himself, saying he had neglected another prescheduled appointment for this opportunity to send Georgiana off on her way to a new life. But if I give him a call some other day, he said, he would gladly accept.

LAWYERS – FINANCIAL WORRIES – HOLIDAYS

As time passed, my worries multiplied. If it wasn't my business, it was financial concerns or perhaps family worries. Back home in New York, unsettling news of another kind continued. My father had another bad night and, this morning suffered a fall managing the stairs. Maxine reminded me that those incidents usually happened when I wasn't around. Up to that moment the close-knit family glove was a welcome respite. Pipo's situation, if a natural progression, was destabilizing to our nucleus. My parents were my balancing act, company for Maxine while I was away. Without them, at this critical moment, all hell could break loose.

The litigation marched forward with obstacles galore and a new set of revelations. Yes, my lawyer said, among the documents the Alsace produced was a copy of the letter Zamora had given me with assurances about my investments. But there was also a follow up contract, he pointed out, which stated any previous agreement was overridden by the new one; something I had overlooked and didn't contest at the time. He said, "It could be a case of double dealing, but it might be difficult to make it stick."

Among the documents translated from the French, there was one between Zamora and the Alsace on how to handle the transition and my company in particular. The need to postpone the signing of a new distribution contract for as long as possible. "The only problem," my lawyer said, "these are long documents for a jury to understand and assimilate. First they will have to read them all and second, remember the sequence of events. A lot to ask from a diverse group of people rounded up — against their will — to do justice."

On the private side of my life, winter was around the corner and interest in my retreat in the Adirondacks dwindled down to nothing. But if there was good news up North, down South it was time for the snowbirds to escape the frigid Arctic winds of the Northeast. And two offers for my Key Biscayne apartment came simultaneously; a New Yorker, who fortunately wanted a rock bottom price and was rejected, but the second one unfortunately, was accepted. My nest on the ocean was gone; a South American afraid of his country's instabilities was willing to pay cash for it. Cash! I couldn't even fathom the possibility of lack of good credit or a mortgage rejection by their bank. More than seven hundred thousand dollars in cash; good Lord, how crude!

"I bet you're happy," I said to Maxine that evening sharing a cocktail at home. "The South-American returned the contract overnight and the closing is set thirty days from today."

"I'll be happier when the whole thing is over. You still have La Finca."

A week after receiving the signed contract, I flew to Key Biscayne to salvage some personal objects and prepare the apartment for the new owner. If the closing of our office building was hard, I figured the apartment would be even harder. Fortunately, the buyer had contracted to buy it fully furnished. I had also asked my broker to offer my car to his affluent client, but the fellow said no. He wanted to buy a brand new Cadillac, instead of taking my elegant, two year old, British Rover. So much for new money.

My flight was delayed for two hours in New York; stormy weather in Miami was the reason. It was close to eight and still raining when we landed in Miami. My loyal Roberta was steadfastly waiting for me at the terminal.

Next morning the sky hadn't cleared. The weather bureau had forecasted two more days of similar conditions and I took refuge in my writing. The same script I was writing for more than a year and had become a never ending project. It was about a triangle; I named it Triumvirate. It takes place in upstate New York and has all the details of a brief affair I treasured with a beautiful equestrian amazon, living close to Saratoga Springs. The makings of a movie with Beatty and a younger fellow disputing a damsel, with lots of intrigue, romance and the spectacular views my log home and the lake could provide.

"The rain became a light drizzle in the afternoon and I decided to defy nature one more time. I wore a windbreaker, a hat and walked the beach down to the lighthouse slowly, wanting to salvage whatever magic was left and had sustained me in so many other difficult times. That trek was also crowded with dear memories, romantic encounters, conversations with friends, birds and fish sightings. My everlasting affair with nature. The Adirondacks with my trees, birds, deer and an occasional black bear. Down here, with my turtles and their little offspring. The memories filled my brain. I didn't need any company today; I was content to be all alone with myself. What are memories if not a fountain of energy, I thought.

I got to the lighthouse and sat among the rocks. I turned to the impressive structure and whispered high enough for her to hear if she had ears. You haven't helped me much, have you? You and the moon have turned your backs on me. I thought we had a deal; one for all and all for one. But it hasn't worked, has it? I'm hitting bottom and can do nothing about it. I'm powerless. I've become a bystander like you are. Who is going to come to sit with you, offer you company and share this magnificent solitude when I'm gone? Others see you, but don't share with you. For them you're just an abandoned lighthouse. But you and I have shared time together. We know what solitude is; what to be left behind and powerless means. The moon is selfish. She flirts but flees. We could always come together anywhere we want, but you, you won't have me anymore. Yes I know, I'm the loser in this deal. I'll miss you.

The rain began to pour; I guess it was a way of telling me to shut up and come to my senses. I took a long, lasting look at the magnificent structure, turned my back, and retraced my footprints still indelible in the wet sand. I walked slowly, thinking about mine and my family's future; first the office building, now my apartment.... the meltdown is on. Will it ever stop?"

Thanksgiving and another holiday season arrived as well as important legal proceedings dates. Ben's deposition was finally scheduled for the coming Tuesday, to be followed by Zamora's on Thursday. As much as I hated the symbolism of each holiday season, on this occasion we had a good reason to celebrate; my lawsuit was finally moving again.

Friday morning, I picked up Ben at his home and together we drove to La Finca. My new caretaker had informed me we had six inches of new wet snow on the ground, but not to worry because everything would be okay by the time of my arrival. If the trip was only to coordinate a common legal strategy, I was also getting out of my normal environment and I needed it. There was nothing like La Finca to liberate me.

My retreat upstate was beautiful. The sun was shining, the snow brilliant and the house warm when we arrived around midday. I set Ben up in the guest side of the house and went to mine to take care of a few personal things. I placed a call to my district congressman and left a message to contact me, if he could. I also called the town clerk and discussed the possibility of getting together Saturday night for dinner and he readily accepted. He was happy at the prospect of meeting the congressman as well as drinking my scotch and — what he considered — my delicate wines; my Sherries and Ports, a long way from his habitual New York State burgundies. I also called Genevieve, my French neighbor, who cooked for me whenever I had visitors and she agreed to come and cook a meal for us. I also invited her to stay for dinner but she declined. She said, she would prepare everything and leave it ready for us to serve. And she did.

Ben and I had spent most of Friday afternoon going over business details, napped, and had a meal at one of my favorite restaurants and cognac back home before retiring for a peaceful, recharging sleep in the mountains. Saturday morning, the sun came through my glass enclosed pavilion and I was up and about in no time. I prepared myself an espresso and checked on the other side of the house for any sign of life. Ben seemed to be asleep still and I didn't bother him. I drank my shot of espresso in two short gulps while looking at the lake.

Genevieve came in early on Saturday afternoon and prepared dinner for six, counting the congressman, the town clerk and their two wives. I still had the remains of a good selection of wines in my cellar and, after a few cocktails, we all sat down to dine at about 7.30 pm.

Religion and politics were always a hot topic around my table and it didn't take long to ignite the conversation. The congressman was a Republican and the Town Clerk an independent-leaning Democrat. Bush had won the presidency in a close vote count in Florida and it was a burning topic for the Town Clerk who was up in arms blaming Al Gore for not contesting or demanding a full recount.

Close to 10 pm, the Bradfords, my across-the-road neighbors arrived. John Bradford was a law professor at the Albany Law School. He had been an activist and opponent of the Vietnam War, God knows when. After that, he had finished law at Columbia University in New York where he met Esther years after, while an assistant professor, helping undergraduates during a summer recess.

John loved the opportunity of seeing the congressman face to face. They had met several times in the past, more than once, at my place, and even if they disagreed vehemently about the country's last election, were civilized enough to maintain a dignified conversation about the future and especially the needs of our part of the state.

Esther didn't care for the conversation and asked me to prepare espresso before taking the shot of cognac she likes. We retired to the kitchen and, while I prepared another pot, she told me about a reporter recently digging for information about Isadora's accidental death, me, the kind of relationship I had with her and everything about the day of the accident. Esther had been on her porch when Isadora and I left La Finca that morning and was one of the first to arrive at the scene of the accident. Obviously I had passed out and didn't know it until several days later, when I recovered consciousness.

I told her I didn't understand this sudden interest in the affair. It had been more than nine years since the accident, but she reminded me Isadora's husband was gravely ill — supposedly dying of cancer — and a book about such a famous artist was in the making

As I poured the espressos, my mind retraced my affair with Isadora and all the other incidents that had happened in my life in the last ten years. There had been one catastrophe after another. My sweet Isadora's death was a devastating blow; I felt guilty for a long time; still do. Had I taken a safer road and tried not to save time on a secondary one, she might still be alive. The ramifications created havoc in my life. Maxine stood by me at the time, but from then on our relationship, extremely close, cooled and became that of roommates, and has continued like that up to this very day. Jessica, the other meaningful relationship in my life, broke off. She couldn't take it, as she ironically said, "A wife was enough, but another woman? Intolerable!"

"When the reporter approached me," Esther continued sipping her coffee, and began talking about the accident. "For a moment I thought we were talking about yesterday morning. I remembered saying goodbye from my porch and alerting you to the ice on the roads. Believe me, for me it was as if I was talking about yesterday! Memories and time are incredible, aren't they?"

I didn't add anything to the conversation and quietly listened Esther while she continued yapping about every detail related to the accident. Inexplicably my thoughts went back to another bittersweet, if troublesome story, my affair with her daughter, Sabrina.

"What do you think?" Esther asked me.

I came back to my senses not knowing what to say.

"You weren't listening to me," she said, disgusted.

"Of course I was listening, but in a most strange way I was also reliving Isadora's accident. Or our accident," I reflected, trying to justify myself.

John entered the kitchen and told Esther it was a quarter to one already. As always, he was disappointed with the congressman's views, but said he was a likeable guy, something that made me suspect the conversation among them had been a draw and they were tired and ready to go home. He said the other two couples were ready to go too and together we went back to the main salon and reunited with the group. They all thanked me for dinner and wanted to know when I'd be in town again. I said I didn't know, but we would keep in touch. Esther gave me a kiss and she and John left with the rest of the group. We said goodbye and the dinner was over.

Ben's deposition on Tuesday went without a hitch. He explained in meticulous detail, everything about our financial commitment to the success of Natividad's line. He also described the low profit margins we had accepted while waiting for un-kept promises of soon-to-be-made changes that never materialized. He explained in detail the extent of our indebtedness to several banks and the collateral pledged to secure our loans. He also spoke of the millions of dollars owed to us by retailers that in many ways were a form of subsidy to the Alsace. We ran the risk of extending credit to hundreds of small shops to carry Alsace's line of goods. They in turn took their time paying their bills. All in all it was a very powerful exposition of the Alsace's practices.

Zamora's deposition took place as scheduled, all day the following Thursday. I was present and sat quietly while he denied having committed to a permanent relationship; explained his need to sell their company to the Alsace, saying it was a matter of survival. Zamora asserted the letter he had given me was not a promise. Nevertheless, he continued, the signed contracts after that letter stated 'any previous documents or understandings were superseded by the signing of the new contract.'

That afternoon, when his deposition was over, Zamora approached me and said he was very sorry about what had happened, but it was business. He said he wished me and my family the best and would be agreeable to intercede, if he could, in the resolution of the case. I didn't shake hands, but asked him to say hello to Natividad, something he said he would do.

The following weeks saw a number of less important depositions on both sides. The Alsace also filed a "motion for summary judgment," based on Ben's deposition. A third one at that, having seen the first two denied yet another of a number of dilatory tactics to prolong the case and create havoc with my financial situation.

Christmas Eve came and we celebrated the festivities at home with a sit-down dinner for twenty family and friends. Our home was a large, old Georgian colonial, with an oversized living room, old bay windows overlooking both gardens, wood beams and a large fireplace. The house was all decorated with Christmas novelties, a seven foot high tree at one end of the living room and presents for everybody at its feet. Soft chamber music dominated the ambiance while a fire consumed dozens of heavy logs from La Finca.

Sometime around ten we sat down at a long dining table set in the living room. After a brief invocation by my nephew the priest, I stood up and facing Maxine, gave my regular toast:

"For all the good things in life and time to enjoy them."

While we toasted with a great Bordeaux, my mind took me far away from the scene. In a flash, I saw myself as a kid defying mother's and everyone else's strict rules. My schooling; thinking I only needed whatever I heard the teacher teach and a rigorous, last minute brush-up — fueled by amphetamines — before the exam. My dreams; like Sisyphus outwitting death by leaving something big behind, I didn't know what. Jessica one of my first sentimental attachments. College; the difficult times I faced as a non-conformist rebelling under Castro. My flight to the States; a new grand stage, the opportunity of a lifetime. My immersion in business. Ups and downs, risks and thrills, extremes, nothing in between and all in the course of a single life. And even now, here I am, in my mid-forties, celebrating another Christmas, still surrounded by dear people; Maxine at one end, Julie at arm's length, my parents, relatives and close friends. Feeling lucky if not knowing how the whole thing will end.

"Why don't you sit and eat your food? The beans are getting cold," Maxine yelled at me. "I hope that's all you had to say."

Back from my flash trip, I gulped my first glass of wine, looked around me and felt reassured being surrounded by friends. Yes, we were getting older, was the inevitable impression I got every year. Time is unforgiving; sagging cheeks, white hair, growing waist lines. There is no greater curse than time. But I loved Christmas, even if I didn't believe any of the stories attributed to it. The annual roasting of a seventy pound female-pig was also an event and the obligatory pilgrimage of my guests to the garden — to ascertain the pig's progress — a tradition of sorts. An annual routine that somehow contributed to the atmosphere and made everybody hungry for the evening feast.

Dinner ended close to midnight and we rapidly transformed the room into a chapel for the traditional Christmas Eve mass. Our nephew, a non-denominational priest, began the custom shortly after being ordained and in the space of a few years, it became a sort of annual affair. An opportunity for a dozen or so of our friends, to come and participate in what had become a very exceptional — and sought after — yearly event.

MY RETREAT GOES UP IN SMOKE

New Year's came and went. The cold and the snow made the short days in New York even harder to take. We went through several months of legal disputes, challenges to the translated documents, obstacles to Natividad's and the Alsace chairman's depositions, before a new judge or magistrate was appointed. His job to straighten out the mess. The new magistrate took two more months to call both sides to a conference and candidly admit he needed more time to familiarize himself with the case. If disappointed, we were relieved there would be someone supervising and speeding up the proceedings.

It took the magistrate another two months to come to the conclusion that our case belonged in State and not Federal court. A blow out of nowhere. Not even the Alsace, among their huge pile of legal maneuvers had requested a change of venue.

I was shocked while my lawyers professed to be up in arms. We had a long conference and discussed the decision in a three-way phone call; the result, a meeting was scheduled for the next day. That evening, in the privacy of our room, I informed Maxine of the latest setback. She looked at me disconcerted.

"What are you going to do?" she asked me.

"I don't know. This was completely unexpected. No one had filed a motion contesting our filing in Federal court or asking the case to be sent to

State court. His orders were to reshuffle the mess, period! I don't even know if he has authority to change venues."

That night the mood at the table was somber. Maxine had a few bites of a delicious red snapper mother had cooked and excused herself, promptly returning to her room. Mother looked worried, but asked no questions. I played cool and sat through the rest of the meal talking about everything but the business at hand.

After my habitual shot of espresso I went to my library, called Julie and told her of my latest setback. She was dismayed.

"I'm really sorry to hear that," was all she said.

"Shit happens, but there is no logical explanation for what is going on. Who would have thought this magistrate would send us to State court? It's weird, not even the Alsace had raised this issue. I'm flabbergasted."

"I'm not superstitious, but this is too much," Julie said. "I hate to be redundant, but if I were you, I'd seriously consider going to the Babalao in Miami. I know shit happens, granted, but this has been happening for more than two years. It has to stop."

Once again at my lawyer's palatial offices, I was led to the large conference room where Rudy was waiting. We shook hands and he said that Pete would join us shortly. Apologetically he added, he hadn't had time to go over the full decision, but he was almost certain there was no previous legal precedent for a magistrate to make that kind of decision under our particular set of circumstances. "Nevertheless, whether it was the right or wrong decision, we only had one avenue to appeal. A very costly and torturous proposition that would entail a lot of time and money," he concluded.

Pete entered the room and apologized for being late, but said he was sure Rudy had briefed me already. He added that even if he hadn't had time to read the full decision, among the ruins of our effort, there was something positive; the judge had not dismissed the case outright but sent it to a lower court. "That means that we either appeal or restart the case in State court. It would be very similar," he added, "although obviously the judges are not as well versed in this kind of case as federal ones. It means also a smaller jury; six instead of twelve people, that might translate into a more sympathetic group. Who knows?"

As I heard them talk my mind tried to make sense of their spin. I felt naked; abandoned to the arbitrariness of chance. Whether we appeal or start all over again in State court, it meant a new ball game. Two more years of my life wasted. Thousands of dollars more needed and they were already in short supply. How would Maxine take it?

"If you decide to appeal," Pete said, "if we succeed, we're only putting the case back on track in Federal court. I don't have to tell you, this means extra money, much more than the quantities we have discussed. But the same is true in State court. In both cases it is starting all over again. Obviously, an extra delay. But we still have a chance."

"Get back to us as soon as you can," Rudy said as he walked me back to the reception area. "We only have thirty days to appeal. But take three or four days off. It's not the end of the world, you know. Say hello to Maxine for me, will you?"

Once downstairs, I called Julie with my new cellphone and asked her if we could get together. She said yes, but not before three. She had a short meeting after lunch and we could have the whole afternoon after that.

Julie met me at the Pierre lounge. We sat at a corner table and ordered a Vodka and tonic for her and a cognac for me. I gave her a quick update of my lawyers' so-called strategy. She just looked at me quietly, as someone who shares your pain and couldn't believe what was going on.

"Burt and I had a long conversation about your predicament. As a matter of fact we continued talking about it even in bed."

"I hope I didn't spoil a romantic situation for you," I interrupted.

"Don't be sarcastic, ok? I'm serious. Burt also said you might end up with a more sympathetic jury in State Court. They're the same kind of people and they might be in favor of a small business man against such a big machine."

"Yes!" I responded, "but whether Federal or State Court what worries me are the documents; too many, too complicated. They have to read them all and remember each paragraph that showed their real intentions, what they did and didn't do to hurt me. There are close to fifty documents. Imagine what it is to ask a housewife to read a twenty-page document and remember a precise paragraph. Now that's one document, imagine fifty."

"I think I know what you're going through. But, it's time for you to get into one of those famous moves of yours and disengage for a while. Step aside and let the lawyers carry the ball. Let time take its course and something might happen you didn't even expect."

"Things are a bit different this time around," I tried interrupting her.

"I wish I had a magic wand to blow away all my darling Peter Pan's problems. But this is a serious drama; a Euripides tragedy. And all those malefic characters insist on dragging my Peter through the mud and so far, it seems they're succeeding. But if you need any money, you know you can count on me. It's my own money and Burt will never be involved."

A marathon of arguments, doubts and self-deprecating thoughts dominated my weekend. Finally Monday I called Rudy and set up another appointment to discuss my decision. I use the call to mention again I was strapped for cash and if they insisted on another retainer, I might have to search for another team. Rudy laughed and told me not to worry. That they would never leave me hanging and "we will find a formula and give it another try."

Right after lunch I got a call from my real estate agent who informed me he had shown La Finca to two prospective buyers and both were willing to bid on the property. I was traumatized. Two bids, not one. I couldn't believe it. My retreat was going up in smoke. The broker said tentatively he had mentioned a figure of nine hundred thousand and neither one had blinked. "Make them bid," I repeated. And he responded; "piece of cake."

I couldn't believe my ears. How many setbacks can you handle Alejandro? I asked myself. If it's true, I knew the time would come for someone to take a fancy to my place, I thought I'd have another year or at least a few more months. Enough time perhaps to let my case reach the courts. But no! My dreamy life, my enchanted world was inexorably crumbling all around me.

Wednesday morning Pete and Rudy were once again sitting across from me in their spacious conference room. We had coffee and pretzels delivered by one of their attendants and without much preamble, Rudy asked.

"What is it going to be? Are we appealing or going to State court? Have you decided?"

"Whether we appeal or go to State Court you're going to ask me for more money, or aren't you?"

"Alex, we are a vehicle," Rudy interrupted. "We use the law to the best of our abilities, but there is only so much we can do. We're talking to you honestly. We don't treat you like somebody coming off the street, not knowing his ass from his elbow."

"Alex, you're the only one who can make the decision," Pete intervened. "Whether we appeal or go straight to State court, for us it is as we are starting all over again. We have the State alternative and we should take the most expeditious route. And the State court is the appropriate one at this stage of the game."

"Suppose we decide for the State court, how do we go about it?" I asked them.

"In either case," Rudy intervened. "It is a new ball game. It's true, we have most of the claim already written. We could use the Federal one with some modifications, but it is work. We have a few depositions taken. We know what the Federal judge objected to, so we can work around that somehow. Still it's a new ball game."

"A new ball game meaning?" I asked Rudy.

"Well we need a new retainer to start."

"But why should you need a new retainer? It's the same case."

"In an ideal world we would do it pro bono but Alex, this is how we make a living, helping clients. We help you, but we need to get paid."

"Not only that," Pete interrupted. "Since we are starting all over again, we'd like you to clear the old balance," he said, reaching for the phone. "Rachel," he asked her. "What's Alexander's balance?"

"Alex we will work with you," Rudy continued. "We have your best interest at heart."

"Eighty two hundred and change," Pete interrupted. "It isn't much."

"What kind of a retainer are we talking about?" I asked them.

Rudy and Pete looked at each other like confused, looking for a number.

"Thirty thousand?" Rudy said while Pete nodded his concurrence.

"Another thirty thousand? You're out of your fucken mind! I don't have that kind of money," I said angrily. "We have paid you close to a hundred and fifty thousand and we have accomplished nothing. And now you want another fifty?"

"Well, don't rush to give us an answer now," Rudy prompted. "You have a lot to ponder. Go home and talk to Maxine about the prospects of the case. She should know. She is your partner. Talk to her. Don't give us an answer now and give us a call tomorrow, or the next day. We have time."

I walked away from that meeting not knowing what had hit me. I couldn't believe those vampires. We have accomplished nothing, nothing and here they are asking me for more money after all the cash they have collected already. If I was mad as hell, I was also dreading confronting Maxine. It was bad enough we had spent a lot of our reserves fighting the case. Now these suckers demand even more. Please.

The conversation with Maxine was long and painful. Her arguments were all framed on the idea of security, aging, and a safety net. She was concerned about our home, that I assured her was safe, and my propensity to flights of the imagination and risk taking. In other words, it was all my fault. She remembered minutely, all the advice she had given me, how much she complained about our association with Natividad and Zamora, and blamed me for living for the day and not taking steps to secure the future

I took it all quietly, sometimes thinking she was right, sometimes wanting to explain, all along knowing it would be impossible for her — in her present state of mind — to come to a sensible conclusion. Maxine had conveniently forgotten the fashion project was the product of her fancy. And for a while, it was a very good idea and later a complete success; obviously until the advent of the Alsace changed the equation.

In our private life, I had tried to adjust to Maxine's precepts about family, accepted her religious devotion and listened dutifully to her criticism. In many ways I had accepted living in a cage, a prisoner of her conventionalism. We were so different in so many ways and so similar in so many others. For me; life was a voyage of discovery, the day was not long enough, tomorrow was too late and death hovered around the corner. For her; life was preordained, the day had a time to wake up and go to rest, and death was the beginning of a better and eternal life. How did we last so long together? I didn't know. But in her own peculiar way, she gave me the space I needed. Something she always complained about, but because of her nature and my irrepressible drive, it never became a bone of contention.

Monday came and I placed a call to my legal team and conferred with Rudy. I said we were ready to go to State Court, something he agreed was a very intelligent decision. I also mentioned we didn't have the thirty thousand, something that seemed to disturb him, but, nevertheless, he said, we could try to work it out. He would talk to Pete and give me a call in a day or two and we would go from there. All in all, a very amicable conversation.

Used as I was to hear bad news, the new one about La Finca was one I dreaded to receive and above all so soon. The real estate agent left me a message; the two bidders went over nine hundred and fifty thousand. Finally, one of them offered a million. He said he had a ten percent deposit and wanted to arrange a propitious time to sign the contract. He added the couple had their financing in order and thought it would take about ten days to clear title and a few other things. We could close as early as two weeks or sooner, if we wanted to.

Damned! I said to myself. Why do these things go so fast and mine takes forever? Is there a logical explanation?

The sale and the speed of the transaction was a terrible blow. I couldn't believe my luck. My retreat, mi Finca going up in smoke. I'll have no place to hide. Now, if that wasn't enough, I'll have to clear the house. Move my art and some furniture in less than a month, a week before the scheduled closing. *Come on man,* my alter ego interrupted. *Of course Chance and, don't forget, El Brujo are hitting us hard, but look at it from the positive angle. You are going to get an extra thirty thousand or so from the furniture. The place is gone, finito. There is nothing we can do about it. But at least we'll get some dough for the furniture; pocket money, of course, but something.* What a consolation, you fool, I chastised myself.

Life is full of irony and, in the dichotomy of mine, what bad news is for a person could be good news to another. Knowing she would relish hearing the latest, I called Maxine at her office and told her about the sale. "Good riddance," she said and gladly admitted being relieved; and I believed her. She used the opportunity to remind me we bought La Finca full of hope and the illusion of a peaceful and cherished retreat. Then she went ahead and blamed me for destroying it all with my frequent escapades and eventually the tragedy of Isadora's death. The tirade could have been longer, but fortunately, we were on the phone and I didn't say a word. "I'd be happy to sign the papers," she repeated, and that was the last thing I heard.

On my way to the country I made a detour and stopped at my lawyers'. Pete was not available but I met with Rudy in his office. "I think we have found a solution to the retainer," he said, shaking hands. "I discussed your financial strain with Pete and we agreed we could cut the retainer to twenty five thousand and settle for a third of whatever we recover. That means we are risking all our time and expenses on the viability of the case."

"But that would be a lot of money. I mean, if I agreed to give you another twenty five thousand, we are talking about one hundred and seventy five. And now on top you want a third?"

"Ok, ok. Let me explain," Rudy interrupted. "Suppose if we win, we deduct the twenty five thousand."

"Why not the 150,000 thousand I have paid you so far?"

"I'll have to speak to Pete about that. We'll work it out. Where are you going to be later on this afternoon?"

I didn't say another word, went down to the street, got in my car and drove away as fast as I could. I was upset, sad, disappointed; I couldn't make sense of all the conflicting feelings in my head. I was tired of fighting. How much more could I endure? It was a struggle with no end. Up to now my relationship with my lawyers had been expensive, but pleasant, even if we had lost this important round. Now, I'm not only fighting the Alsace, the courts, time and financial ruin, but I have a new dispute with them too. It was my investment, my money, for God's sake, what we were trying to recover and these guys treat my settlement as if it were a found pot of gold, to be shared among lucky bounty hunters.

La Finca at last. The gate of my wonderful retreat had just materialized in front of me. I felt a bittersweet relief; a few days of peace and tranquility while I put in motion the dismantling of my cherished Shangri-La. I drove my uphill driveway the same way I did the day I visited the property for the very first time. The trees were flowering again; the pines growing another foot. I was so proud of my picturesque possession. I could understand why the new buyer was willing to upstage his competing rival. My retreat was out of this world.

The place was up and running. The heat was on, the fireplace in my pavilion had a few burning logs left. I felt good; it was pure luck finding a good caretaker after Georgiana died. I walked out on the deck and sat on my favorite lounge chair. The sun was shining, but it was a cool, glorious afternoon in the Adirondacks; it always was in early May. I took a long look around me. Hills, woods, trails and the lake in the distance. How many wonderful days had I had in this place? I dialed Julie at her office. I asked her if she could take a day or two to help me with the cleanup. She said she'd talk to Burt and let me know in twenty minutes.

The caretaker arrived and we shared a beer. He was sad when he heard there was a buyer. He had opened the place for the realtor to show the property to two different couples three weeks ago, and, although they felt enchanted with the place, he didn't get a feeling they would make an offer so soon.

"Both couples," he said, "knew about the affair and Isadora's accident, and wanted to know more about you and how you were doing. One of the ladies rested on your bed and marveled at the view."

"I hope you told her I was distraught?" I said to him.

"Of course," he responded. "I think for one of the women, the affair and the accident was one of the most alluring aspects about the place. It was as if she wanted to be part of such a legend. She remembered reading it in the New York Times; the wife of a famous artist dying in an accident while having an affair in the Adirondacks. She also referred to the photo spread in the New York Post. She was really intrigued."

Getting down to business, I mentioned the tractor was for sale and we quickly agreed on a price. He also asked me about the washer and dryer, but I said that would go with the house. He asked about some of the furniture and I told him we would have to wait for the auctioneer, but I was willing to sell him whatever he wanted at the upset price.

Julie called back. Yes! She talked to Burt and he had no objections. I told her to go to La Guardia, to the American Eagle ticket counter where a boarding pass would be waiting for her. That I'd be at the Albany airport waiting. Julie protested my largesse and said she could afford it. Nevertheless, I insisted and she assented.

My place had a few good pieces of art, valuable pieces of furniture, four oriental rugs and quite a few other collectibles; some were valuable, others had an emotional value difficult to ascertain. Maxine and I had owned the retreat for twenty years and every item was a remembrance of a time, a trip or a present from a dear friend or associate. Julie herself was familiar with everything around and knew what should be taken to New York City for auction, agreed with me about most of the things I should retain for my home in New York and changed my mind about quite a few pieces we could let the regional auctioneer handle.

The furniture was something else. It was obvious the dining room table and twelve Windsor chairs should go to New York for auction.

"You'll fetch twice as much selling them there than here," Julie said, and I obviously agreed. "The two living room consoles should go also," she insisted, "even if they are not originals, they're great reproductions, what? A hundred years old if I remember what you told me," Julie continued.

"Yes they are. I'm also taking my writing table!"

"Of course! It's a good piece, classy, masculine and took you years to find it. Where you're going to put them at home is another story," Julie added. "The same thing with your books. Where are you going to open space to put them? You have none in your library anymore."

"I'll make room even if I have to sleep on the floor. They are part of my life. Years of Maxine and I roaming every corner of the Adirondacks."

"You'll need a mid-size truck to haul all these pieces back," Julie said.

"I haven't decided what to do. We have to pack the china. Who the hell is going to pay five grand for a set for twelve here?"

"You can get double that amount in New York, I'm sure," she retorted. "Is Maxine coming?"

"No, she said she wouldn't step in here for anything in the world. But she's happy we're selling or getting rid of the place. She hates it since the Isadora incident."

"I don't blame her. I'd have hated you had I been your wife or your lover at that time. Well it created a problem with Jessica, didn't it? Or so you told me."

"Yes, she said she could accept my having a wife, but not a mistress on the side. You women are heartless."

LA FINCA & THE
HEMINGWAY MYSTIQUE

That evening we went to my favorite restaurant in town; the only one open until 9 pm. and had a very simple dinner; pork chops, French fries, a piece of apple pie and drank our bottle of wine. We returned home and went directly to make espresso. Julie, like me, liked espresso and we drank our shots and moved to the living room. The room looked empty; the paintings in one corner, the consoles next to them, there were boxes of small pieces on the sides, but the big, comfortable sofa was still set in front of the fireplace, with both end tables and lamps in place. Julie went to the stereo and got a tape of El Gato Barbieri and his sax filled the room in no time. She came back and sat next to me. I put my arm around her shoulders and just listened to "Europa" and all the classics he had made popular over the years.

"Do you want a cognac, or any other liquor?"

"Not now," she responded. "It's almost time to sleep."

"It's only 10.30. I won't be able to sleep so early no matter how tired I am!"

"What time is the auctioneer coming tomorrow?"

"Around ten.

"You know what I was thinking? Julie asked me. "The couple who bought the house needs furniture. Why not sell them the heavy pieces, like this sofa and the end tables? You will save the twenty five percent of the auction-eer's commission."

"Well, that's too late now, isn't it?"

"When is the closing?"

"In ten days. Ten more days and my Finca will be history."

An hour or so later, we went to the pavilion and climbed the staircase to the loft. It was cool and Julie went to the closet and got one of my old flannel pajamas. She dressed up warmly and watch me while I brushed my teeth in the bathroom. She then stood behind me while I peed.

"How simple, isn't it? Just open your fly, take it out and let gravity do the rest. I envied my brother when I was young. I had to undress, sit, do all the other things while you just shake it, and keep walking."

"Have a transplant," I told her.

"Will you give me some privacy?" she requested. "A transplant? And then what would I do with you? A role reversal?" she yelled, running out of the bathroom and landing on top of me in bed.

"You know I've never asked you this kind of question, but perhaps this might be the last time we are going to be together here. Has Burt ever asked where you sleep the times you have been here alone with me?"

"Never! He assumes you are a gentleman."

"And in a way I am, or I should say, I consider myself one."

"Perhaps he believes you're a eunuch," she responded and we both broke into laughter.

Julie arched herself and pushed her butt against my crotch. I hugged her, lifting her hair and kissing her neck. She was warm and inviting, but my brain was miles away thinking of my next move. The demise of my life as I knew it.

The lights came through the pavilion glass walls. I was up in no time while Julie remained in bed in the arms of revered Morpheus, god of dreams. I prepared myself an espresso and went out to the deck to enjoy the morn-ing mist. It was cool in the Adirondacks. The lake was barely visible in the distance, the birds were happily chirping and a woodpecker was busy drilling in one of the tallest trees. What an irony. The vibrant universe in front of me while my own world is inexorably shrinking. What would this be? The end of a chapter or the book's epilogue? I asked myself. Would I like to get my Finca back? I guess I would, although I think of myself as a bird; disturb his nest and he'll never return to it.

The auctioneer arrived at ten sharp. He came driving a huge truck with two other fellows. Just the sight of the truck convoluted me. Jesus, my furniture, my things, and all those amassed objects that have become part of my life are being taken away; dumped in that huge truck and offered to strangers just for money, regardless of what they have meant to me through the years.

Julie and I pointed out the pieces we are shipping back to the city and the auctioneer started making an inventory of the pieces he'd auction while telling his men to haul them to the truck. It took about two and a half hours to complete the removal of sixty percent of the house contents. Then he said we should get about eleven thousand after his twenty five percent is deducted. He said we should have a good auction because most of the pieces were good, but he would like me to sacrifice one or two of the excellent pieces that would bring in a wealthier class of bidders in the community. He referred to the Windsor chairs.

"Nothing doing," Julie interrupted him. "You will never get the price we would get in New York City."

"Eight hundred each," he responded.

"Less your commission," Julie added.

"Of course," he responded.

"Thank you. I think you have everything you're going to auction and that should be sufficient," Julie added, making our position absolutely clear.

The truck went down my driveway and disappeared behind the pine trees at the bottom of the hill. It was as if part of me was being taken away. Why does it have to be like this? I asked myself, but saying nothing, took Julie's hand and walked around the almost empty house.

"We better go," Julie said to me. "Staying here will only depress us both. I know you might get over it, but I can't. Even if it never belonged to me, I always considered it part of me. Don't ask me why?"

Sweet Julie, my alter ego interrupted, *that's why we love her so much, isn't it? Listen Alex, look at the positive side, man. We lived here twenty years; twenty! That's three life times for us. Lots of memories. Lots of people came and went and we had a ball. A few sad memories, Isadora of course, some disappointments; what the hell, we can't win them all. Always look at the balance, the bottom line. That's the only way to assess a life's success. Sometimes you ignore my advice. You remember when we bought it. What did I tell you? Do it man! Do it! This is us! Had you paid no attention to me and waited two days, as you wanted, we would have lost it. Fortunately Maxine loved it too and that helped us to make the decision instantly. What a ride, eh? What did I tell you? This is one for the books, man. Ok, just take a last look and let's get out of here. Don't get weepy on me, ok? You know I can't cry. I'm sure we have a lot still ahead of us. Hey! It is us, man; us! We won't stop until either we decide to go ourselves or time takes us out of this world. Come on, no tears now. And don't look back. Remember what happened to Lot's wife.*

Five days before the closing I got a call from the new buyer. The woman said she would like to buy the Windsor chairs, the dining table, the consoles and the fourteen foot Oriental rug. I told her I intended to remove them the morning of the closing, but she insisted she would match New York prices. I thought for a moment and asked her if she was familiar with their market value. She said she lived on the East Side of Manhattan. Twenty five thousand I mentioned and "twenty five thousand it would be," she said. Good! I won't have to remove and sell them in New York. I couldn't ask for more.

Five days later I met the couple at their lawyers' office and we signed the deed. The duo was very preppie, gracious and in their mid-forties. I knew about them through the real estate agent, but had not met them personally. She asked me what I did with the books, the paintings and a few other things.

"I took them home," I told her.

She said she had liked the way they looked behind my writing table and the rest of the room.

"Those books are part of my life," I told her.

Then with a cagey smile she mentioned she had read about Isadora's accident in the New York press. Her husband instantly cut in, saying something like, honey, this is not the time to talk about those things and she excused herself. I said nothing. They both insisted on meeting me and Maxine socially if it was alright with me.

"We live close by on the East Side," she insisted.

I said we might. Then she raved about La Finca. One of the things they most relished besides the beauty of the place was its coziness, its ambiance. They felt at home the moment they came in the first time. I said I had the same feeling the first time I saw it.

"We have decided to keep the name La Finca, in Spanish, the same way you did," she said. Then she added, she had read Hemingway called his estate in Havana, La Finca Vigia. He lived in that house twenty years."

"Yes, he did! And it is it's a memorable name," I said. "I also lived twenty years in my Finca," I added not able to contain a tear.

She stepped forward and tried to embrace me. I held her briefly and kissed both her cheeks.

"I only hope that you are at least half as happy as I was all the years I lived there."

Then she reminded me Maxine and I would be more than welcome should we decide to visit. In fact it would be an honor, she repeated, to have us as their guests. I smiled and wished them all the luck in the world.

I turned to her husband, shook his hand, turned my back and walked away. The chapter was closed!

MY WASP CONNECTION

Time passed with no movement on any front. The withdrawal effects of losing my cherished Sacandaga retreat were still raging inside me. Add to that the demand of my lawyers to agree to a new --- one sided --- retainer agreement, kept me awake at night with no viable alternative. I had also sent some feelers to friends and business acquaintances sharing my need to find a consultant job. A substantial income that would balance our budget and monetary needs.

Fortunately, Maxine continued working at her college. She was happy being head of her department and enjoyed the warmth and camaraderie of her colleagues. She would come home in the evenings about five, always going directly to our rooms until dinner, interrupted only with an occasional cocktail. I'd only talk about our personal affairs when I couldn't postpone it any longer. And she wouldn't ask too many questions unless there was something obvious going on. But we shared a great interest in many other subjects; the books she or I were reading, a commentary on NPR, a movie or a play we wanted to see. And gossip; but not the common ones; we both were interested in politics, the arts in general, that kind of stuff. She was exceptionally well read and the conversations were subdued, all-encompassing and never ending.

If those were the obvious good signs of our relationship, there were others; stress. Maxine would postpone everything that wasn't absolutely necessary. She would come out of our rooms only to go to work, dinner at night and mass on Sundays. --- For a person who had spent months and driven most of Europe and visited many countries in South America several times --- her present confinement was difficult to comprehend. I'd argue with her about staying out, sitting in our ample salon or in the garden to read her books, to no avail. Her reading light and the TV, with no audio, would be on with no end. Obvious signs of stress I had no way to ease.

On my side, I retained the same habits I had developed as a young man. I kept myself intellectually and physically fit and used an inherited capacity to compartmentalize almost, if not all my problems and, above all, delay the inevitable. The ability to concentrate only on what I must. For some time now, my worry had been the need to secure an income. It's said no news is good news and that could be true in many other situations, but not in mine. I needed a quick fix for my financial problems and, even though I kept my eyes wide open and all my contacts close at hand, nothing materialized around me. The silence was deafening.

But that Wednesday morning was different. Right after lunch, I got a call from Julie. She said Burt had a client interested in securing a coffee quota from a South American country and needed a consultant, someone who could travel and represent him with coffee growers down south. She said I should check it out. I'm interested, I responded. She asked me to call Burt. And I did.

A few minutes after twelve, I showed up at the Racquet and Tennis Club at Park and 53rd, in mid-Manhattan. Jack Cogswell, a WASP gentleman — member of the Four Hundred families in the United States Social Register — and my friend Burt were waiting for me. Cogswell was an interesting man, a member of an endangered species. A rapidly disappearing class of people in the U.S. but a gracious and affectionate fellow. He was about seventy, tall with a reddish complexion that I attributed to a combination of long exposures to a sun-lamp and large amounts of straight Bourbon, and indeed both were true.

As they ushered me to the second floor club dining room, I took my time to look around the building, a sort of old, stately British or other European kind of gentlemen's private club. A bit rundown, in need of a paint job and a bit of restoring here and there, but with the charm of an old lady facing the modern world under difficult circumstances. When we finally entered the restaurant, I took another detailed look at my surroundings; a sort of dignified, kind of graceful, if understated space full of Brook Brothers dressed fellows eating mostly hamburgers. Somehow I was sharing a piece of a disappearing world; a club with no women and strict membership restrictions. Altogether a strange but exhilarating experience.

We were taken directly to a table in the middle of the room. The captain was extremely courteous to Jack and helped him take his chair. Jack introduced me to the captain and he politely said it was his pleasure to meet me. Very civilized; I liked that. The captain asked us what we wanted to drink and a waiter brought back two whiskies and a very special kind of bourbon I had never heard of before. Once we had toasted each other and taken the first sips of our drinks, Jack immediately dug into my background and seemed to be pleased listening to my sanitized, short version of my uneventful life; Cuban refugee, mid-forties, college graduate, a masters-equivalent to business administration. His face lit up. "I have known a few Cubans," he said, and went on to recite a number of names I didn't recognize. "I'm middle class," I responded, trying to make him understand he wasn't dealing with the offspring of a rich Cuban family. "As an escapee, I left empty handed," I continued. "I lost nothing. My parents did; their home and personal belongings."

Nevertheless he seemed interested and listened attentively to everything I said. We finished our drinks and ordered another round. I excused myself and asked for a glass of wine instead. Then it was decided to order lunch; nothing fancy from a very simple menu. Jack wrote down each of our selections on an order pad, gave it to the waiter and after a brief toast, the conversation turned to the business at hand.

Cogswell's plan was simple, if extremely ambitious. The idea was to get a Central American government to surrender part of its coffee quota and let us convert it into instant coffee for the North American market. His investors would build a "freeze dry coffee" plant that would cost a few million dollars and employ fifty workers. Not much to offer for such a high risk decision,

I thought, but didn't say anything. After all, whether I took the job or not, the project would go on, with me or without me, so I kept my cool and went along with his presentation until he asked me for my opinion. I said frankly it would be a high risk proposition for any government to accept. He agreed with me. But said that's why they were looking for the appropriate person to do the job; in other words, to try. And he asked me if I'd be interested. Sure, I responded. And I asked him what kind of proposition he had in mind.

We agreed on a simple formula; a fixed amount per day, a per diem, plus expenses. If I was successful, I'd keep a half a percent point of the total investment. Not bad. Heck, what he proposed would bring in some money and keep me busy away from home. The country was Costa Rica, a country I had visited several times. They'd provide me with a number of names, including a couple of native investors who would facilitate my introduction to the coffee growers; an essential group if we were to change the government's better judgment.

Before we broke up, we decided to meet once again to conclude the details of our arrangement and schedule my first trip as a freeze dry coffee industrialist. And we did, a week after, this time at a lawyer's office in Mid-Manhattan. A sumptuous law office, at the Seagram building on Park Ave, directly across from the Racquet and Tennis Club. Three other fellows, Jack and their lawyer, Burt and I met in their elegant conference room. The president, VP and treasurer of the outfit were there. Nice guys. Everything was very pleasant and I signed a number of papers I had received and read a few days before. Nothing extraordinary, a secrecy clause, my remuneration, my take on the deal if I were successful. We shook hands and that was that.

COSTA RICA HERE I COME!

Costa Rica was a country I knew rather well. I was fairly familial with its people, the capital San Jose, its surroundings and its beaches in the Pacific coast. I arrived in San Jose late the following afternoon. A quick trip from the airport and I found myself in the fanciest hotel in the capital. I had reserved an executive suite, with an ample sitting room where I could conduct business, if I wanted to. Not to mention beautiful furniture in handsomely made leather, a fax plus internet service albeit slow, as well as a fully stocked bar; the works.

Used to our American ways of doing business and with an ample expense account, I quickly secured the services of a hotel supplied secretary to help me organize my calls, take notes and type memos. One hour later a young, good looking Costa Rican lady showed up and took over my scheduling dilemma. I gave her a list of names, some of which she knew or had heard off before and a few instructions on what and what not to say. Three hours later, Maria Elena, her name was, had scheduled my next five days; a series of lunches and dinners, at golf, equestrian clubs and four star restaurants. She left my late afternoons open for a game of tennis and a massage, if I wanted to, and recommended a night club or two for an after hour drink. Roberta could not have done better herself.

That evening I had dinner in one of the fanciest restaurants in the capital although its haute cuisine, was nothing to rave about. With time to kill before my bedtime curfew, I decided to try another of Maria Elena's suggestions. A classy if brand new club, patronized by the up and coming crowd. There were a number of couples at the bar and one of the fellows introduced himself and the rest of his group; his wife and another couple. They began asking me about my interest in Costa Rica and specially the purpose of my visit. I surmised they were bored with each other and needed a stranger to reinvigorate their exhausted chat. Close to midnight one of the couples said it was time to leave. The two men said they'd like to meet again and discuss the possibility of doing business in the US. We exchanged business cards. We said good bye and that was that.

Maria Elena showed up at midmorning. I gave her both business cards to read and she immediately recognized the name of the plant. "Productos Tropicales," she said. "They produce and distribute good quality products. She then went to the telephone, made an additional couple of calls, contacted my lunch guest and reconfirmed the reservation at an Equestrian Club, very popular among the power group in the country.

I arrived at the club around one and the porter took me directly to the bar. It was a covered terrace with a huge counter where, according to Maria Elena, la crème d' la crème of Costa Rican society get together for drinks and gossip before lunch. My contact had not arrived and I ordered a fino. My guest arrived twenty minutes late, prompt by Latin standards. We shook hands and moved directly to our table. Domingo Jimenez was about sixty five, balding, had a protruded tummy, but dressed sharply and had excellent manners. He owned one of the three largest coffee plantations in Costa Rica and showed a detailed knowledge of the industry.

Although courteous, Jimenez let me know right up front that his crop was sold to a single wholesaler; not a good augury, I thought. Nevertheless he followed my presentation carefully, asking the right kind of questions as I moved through the plant installation, the processing and the marketing in the US. No doubt the man knew his business well and was extremely frank with me. In fact, he recited all the flaws I had described to my partners in New York before I accepted the job, and more. He made it very simple, "why should I risk everything for something up in the air. A pie in the sky, as you say in the US." Brilliant! Nevertheless we continued our lunch talking about me, Costa Rica, women and everything else in a very free and spirited conversation. He even confessed he kept a mistress and she was also a member of the club. I smiled to myself and thought I was going to see her going by on her horse and she did, a few minutes later. And why not?

After almost three hours we departed but not before talking about getting together at his plantation the weekend, something that really interested me. A firsthand knowledge of the planting and collection of the grains was something I lacked and it could help me understand all aspects of the business better.

When I returned to my hotel, Maria Elena reminded me I had a tennis game at 5:30. I complained I needed a rest. After two bottles of a Chateau Plagnac I was ready for a nap. I wasn't used to big lunches back home anymore and today's lunch was an extravaganza. I asked her to give me a half hour to recharge and I'd be new and ready for tennis and the evening. She informed me my dinner guest had called and said he'd be a bit delayed, more like nine than the eight thirty we had scheduled. He also left word he was bringing his wife; an extra expense I hadn't considered.

The Tennis Club was another stately, refined venue. I don't know how many kinds of courts, but there were many; grass, clay, hard, you name it. I was met by my instructor Rosemarie Stark, a North American and ex circuit player, now living in Costa Rica. She had been the club instructor since she moved to the country, with her husband and two daughters, two years ago.

Rosemarie promptly, if delicately, showed her prowess at tennis. She made me run all over the court chasing balls clearly beyond my reach. She insisted on making it easier for me, something I resented; 'I'm a tough fellow,' I protested. After forty minutes, a life time in my condition, I begged for clemency and invited her for a cocktail. She accepted.

We moved to an open area, steps away from a tent covered bar with elegantly appointed tables and chairs. A very classy setting, something we miss back home.

"I could see why you decided to work here. This place has class written all over it," I said, as we ordered a couple of beers.

"This is a different culture altogether; very relaxed. The members are wealthy, educated and charming in many cases."

"How long ago did you leave the circuit? I asked her.

"Six years. I was thirty two and I didn't have a family and wanted one. The clock was ticking, you know. And she talked freely about her husband, her time on the circuit and members of the club. Once she stopped her bio, she quickly turned on me. "You're another corsair looking for a coffee or vegetable deal, I presume." I said nothing, just smiled.

I liked Rosemarie a lot. She reminded me of my Julie back home; I have to tell her that. She was about 5'8", slim, blond, with green eyes, with a quick and witty conversation. Not bad, not bad at all.

My dining companions arrived at 9:20 sharp, twenty minutes after our delayed scheduled reservation. Raul Ferrer, the owner of the second largest coffee plantation in the country. American educated, MBA from Penn State. The fellow was tall and handsome. Black hair combed back, and very well dressed. He seemed about fifty, a few years older than I was. His wife, Jasmin, tall and extremely good looking, in her early thirties; a trophy wife, I surmised if a wife at all. She might be his mistress for all I know.

El senor Ferrer said the dinner was his treat that I could probably benefit from saving the expense. "Thank you, very considered of you," I said not able to conceal a bit of sarcasm in my response. He proceeded to search the menu carefully and said he'd probably had suggested a better restaurant had I consulted him first. I said I understood this was the most prestigious one in San Jose. He said "prestigious, si. But there were better," and proceeded to name two or three, that remarkably enough, Maria Elena had chosen for my future contacts. I kept quiet and waited for him to suggest leaving the place. But he didn't and suggested a couple of entrees with a special kind of fish from the Pacific coast. I didn't object nor did I say anything about his selection of wine; a white Riesling from Germany that I didn't particularly care for. *Hey, if he wants to impress us it's alright as long as the tab is his. We're easy, my alter ego suggested.*

"So you represent a group in the US; what's the name of the group?

"At the present time it's just a group of investors with no name," I responded.

"What do they want?" He immediately interjected "Do you think I'm going to surrender my quota for their dreams?" Senor Ferrer said emphatically.

"I think you're going too far, too quickly..."

"Domingo and I are like brothers. Together, we control fifty percent of the coffee crop. That's why we get top dollar for our crops. We're no dummies. Look, I was educated in the US. I have an MBA from Penn State."

"Good for you. They should have taught you to listen before jumping to conclusions," I said, upset by the fellow's grandiloquence.

"Raul, why don't you let Mr.....?" Jasmin said looking at me for my name.

"Alex, please, call me Alex."

"Why don't you let the man talk," she said disgusted.

"He can talk, I'm all ears."

I went ahead and recited my presentation more or less in the same terms I had used with Domingo, his close friend. Senor Ferrer didn't interrupt me once and at the end of my talk he said;

"Look, my quota is out of the question. Ask me anything else. You want an audience with the president, you've got it. I like you," he said, jabbing my shoulder with a tight fist. "I think you're a man we can do business with. Perhaps there is something else we can do together. Do you have any other plans?"

In a way I liked the simplicity of this fellow. He was asking me if I had anything else to offer, as if I were a magician popping bunnies or deals out of a hat. Honestly, if it's true he started the night like a brawler, he quieted down considerably but not before his loving wife gently chastised and reminded him about good manners. Such was the change in his temper and demeanor we finished our dinner talking of a game of tennis, something he said he couldn't live without.

Maria Elena scheduling was like a time machine. The venues were fabulous, the food great and she gave me enough time in between to enjoy the ambiance and the people I was meeting. Still, there were some disappointments. The following day's lunch appointment with another grower, if gentler, had the same kind of response. He wasn't a risk taker, he said right off the bat, but I went through the notions thinking, while at it, of my afternoon game with Rosemarie. I shook hands, paid the tab and went to my hotel for a nap. Maria Elena was there and briefed me about my dinner appointment. I told her to write a letter thanking my last contact for his hospitality and dictated a few notes about another unsuccessful effort.

Wanting to meet my instructor again, I arrived at the club ten minutes before my scheduled appointment and found Rose battling a young woman with superb strokes. I sat at a distance not to distract her, but followed her closely. Rosemarie was very feminine, not like some other female athletes with masculine gestures and physique.

"She's pretty good," I said, offering her my hand when the game ended.

"I'm all wet," she said, leading me back to the court.

"I'm not in a hurry. Why don't you cool off a little?" I suggested.

"It's alright. I'll slow down playing you."

"Hey? Should I take that as a compliment?"

"I'm kidding. Her name is Rosa. She's the top female player in the country."

Rosemarie and I went ahead and played our game of tennis. After forty minutes or so, I couldn't hold the racket anymore. "I quit!" I yelled, and we shook hands at the net. "You're really good," I said. She only smiled. "You deserve a cold beer," I told her. "Only if you have one," she responded. And we sat at a table in an open area, surrounded by a wall of bougainvillea. We ordered beers and I requested two aspirins. Rosemarie eventually asked me what the reason for my visit was. I mentioned coffee, gave her an idea of the kind of contacts I was developing and a few names came up.

"Yes, Raul Ferrer has been taking lessons with me for over two years. He's a better player than you are."

"I don't believe you," I said, acting surprised and faking being upset.

Rosemarie smiled broadly. "No, I was kidding. He's much worse than you are."

We both laughed heartily.

I asked her about my three other prospects and she gave me a fairly accurate description of their character and standing in the business community.

"I think you could be an invaluable ally if I decide to establish a beachhead in the country." She smiled. "I surmise you have a better half, or another half or whatever. But I wish we could meet in a more relaxed kind of setting. I mean, dry and comfortably dressed. Is there any way you could squeeze in dinner?"

Rosemarie smiled. "Do I look that bad like this?"

"Oh dear, you're lovely as you are, in any condition."

"Perhaps next time you come to visit us again. Is that a deal?"

I got my wakeup call at 9:00 sharp. It seemed a beautiful day outside. I felt a bit of a hangover from the previous night's binge. I had spent the night with another of my contacts who was more interested in women, bars and clubs than talking about business. He gave me a tour of the most popular hangouts in San Jose until he deposited me back at my hotel around 3:00 am. I felt tired, took a turn in my bed, covered my head with another pillow and slept until the telephone rang. It was 10:20 a.m.

"Hello," I answered.

"Alex?"

"Rudy? How did you know where to find me?"

"I called your home and your wife told me about your trip. She said something about a coffee quota or something. I couldn't understand what your trip was all about. Coffee and quotas are a big deal. Are you making any money? I hope so."

"You only think of money. I'm helping a friend. What's up?"

"I wanted you to give us permission to have settlement conversations with the Alsace. A most interesting thing happened. Pete met one of their lawyers in court last week and he explored the possibility of a settlement with him. He didn't talk about numbers, alright? We aren't beginners. But according to Pete, the man was most agreeable. He said he'd entertain any ideas we might come up with. And there is nothing wrong with that. We do it all the time."

"You mean, us taking the first step?" I responded irritated.

"Well, if it is true we are, he said, they were willing to listen."

"That's not what you and I discussed and agreed on when we started the suit. They did screw me, alright? I'm not going to go crawling back to them to ask them for a handout.""

"Come on man, don't get upset," Rudy said sheepishly. "This is just preliminary talk. I called to ask you for permission. Do you want me to or not?"

"I told you we're not taking any first steps. If they want to talk, let them come to us. Not the other way around. Okay?"

"We will do what you want. You're the boss. But I think we should explore the opportunity. Let's face it, it's taking too long."

'Let's face it, it's taking too long,' resonated in my ears long after the conversation ended. It disturbed me because this might be a sign these fellows are reconsidering their prospects and not being a hundred percent committed to the case; perhaps they never were. It was also disturbing because now they were in a position to take a third of any kind of settlement; not wait for the trial and make a quick pot of money and run; mother fuckers.

If the coffee project wasn't as promising as my partners envisioned — only two of my minor contacts wanted to continue negotiations — I was getting acquainted with a good number of wheeler dealers in the country. Business men with experience and products that could be sold back in the US. By the end of the week, I had concluded I could become an agent back home. Costa Rican fruits and vegetables were of an exceptional quality and the food processing plants I had visited were rather modern, well-kept and efficiently managed. With a bit of luck, if not coffee, fruits and vegetables were another line of business I could pursue.

THE ROMANCE OF COFFEE

It was cool and sunny when we left San Jose that Saturday morning and drove up the hills with an endless number of coffee plants on both sides of the road. Sixty miles later, we arrived at El Cafetal, Jimenez' huge plantation; almost three thousand acres of coffee trees that made him one of the biggest, if not the biggest, plantation owner in the country. We entered a paved driveway and after a hill or two, we stopped in front of a fabulous colonial style house. A servant approached our Land Rover and la Senora Jimenez came down from the large porch with open arms.

"This is my wife Rosalia," Jimenez said kissing his wife's cheek.

"Senora, it is a real pleasure meeting you. I'm Alex," I said kissing both her cheeks.

"I've heard all about you. You want to steal our coffee quota against my husband's better judgment."

"Rosalia, it is the other way around. I only want to bring a new factory and jobs for the Costa-Ricenses and in the process, make your husband even richer than he is today!"

We laughed heartily and went directly to have lunch under a magnificent tree fifty yards or so away from their mansion. The table was adorned with an elegant white 'mantel de hilo,' a centerpiece of exotic flowers and a colorful Italian ceramic china. There were six bottles of French wine on a table next to us and a full bar with all kinds of liquors. Two male servants dressed in white stood by and helped each of us to sit comfortably in our arm chairs. A servant took our order and in no time I had a fino, a dry sherry, just opened for the occasion. Jimenez and his wife both ordered scotch and soda, a tough drink before lunch, I thought.

Most of the afternoon we spent driving around the plantation in an old model jeep Jimenez claimed was a Second World War kind of relic. We were high, about three thousand feet above sea level, and even with the radiant sun, it was cool and breezy. Jimenez showed me every step of the production; the plants, how to differentiate grains, when and how they were ready to be picked, and took me to a warehouse properly designed for drying before packing. As we made our way through the plantation, he introduced me to a number of farmhands he identified by name. He also asked some of them to give me an idea of what they do, and their place in the long chain of grain farming and collection. A first hand introduction to the world of coffee.

After our long tour we retired to our rooms for a well-deserved nap. Afterwards, we reconvened on the terrace for cocktails. Jimenez had invited a few other colleagues to dinner, including Ferrer and the Agricultural Minister, both overnight guests also. That night he assembled a table for twenty and we had a most enjoyable get together and a terrible meal of venison that I hated. Wine was served generously and after dinner drinks followed coffee.

Half way through dinner, Jimenez stood and addressed the group. He referred first to my proposal and pinpointed a number of reasons why he wouldn't participate in my project. He also introduced the notion of doing something in reverse; using me in the US as an emissary, or as a representative of their products. He mentioned a few of those present who either cultivated or processed a number of items in great demand in the United States market. After Jimenez finished, the Minister stood up and referred to my project in very positive terms. He referred to the agricultural potential of the country, but reminded everybody they needed jobs; manufacturing or processing jobs. That's why, looking to the future, he said the prospects of a plant to process coffee should be considered seriously and not be rejected out of hand.

Enthused by Jimenez' words and the Minister's clear indication of interest, seeing a clear path ahead of me, I addressed the group. I used the

Minister's encouraging words and did talk briefly about the freeze-dried coffee project, but in the end, dedicated most of my talk to the North-American market. The enormous potential of a vast and rich market and the closeness of Costa Rica to the United States. If the positive reaction of the group was an indication of my prospects as an emissary in the US, the reserved comments and requests for meetings by a few of those present were extremely positive and reassuring.

HOME SWEET HOME...OR IS IT?

What goes up must come down and vice-versa. I returned to the States late Sunday afternoon and as usual Maxine was waiting for me at Kennedy. Although I had made my usual calls every night and discussed with her the slow, sometimes disheartening progress of my meetings, she wanted to know more details. Driving home, I mentioned that even if the coffee project had no takers, I had explored the possibility of importing products from Costa Rica; something that reassured her. She was concerned at the slow progress of our case and referred briefly to Rudy's call. How surprised she was at his insistence in finding out the whole purpose of my Costa Rica visit.

I told Maxine I would have preferred her not to mention the coffee deal. I went over Rudy's disposition to see everything through the magic lens of money and my distress about their eagerness to settle or find an early way out of the case. I reassured her I wanted to finish the nightmare, but wasn't ready to surrender before we had the opportunity to recover part of our losses. She listened and didn't say anything.

A few blocks before home, Maxine asked me to park the car.

"I know you don't like to discuss these things and believe I use the car as a torture chamber, but there are things we can't ignore. Your father's health is deteriorating rapidly. He had two of the worst nights I've witnessed. Last Monday he fell in the bathroom and we couldn't make him stand for more than an hour. I was ready to call the paramedics but your mother insisted, and I didn't. She tried everything including praying, to no avail. She eventually made coffee and gave it to him. Believe it or not, don't ask me how these things work, but he drank the coffee and in about ten minutes he stood up on his own and walked back to their bedroom unassisted. The man was in bad shape. He had peed all over himself and your mother gave him a virtual bath. I really admire her. I don't know if I'd have the strength if you ever find yourself in that situation and we're still together."

I looked at Maxine and said nothing. Even when she was talking about the most serious things, she couldn't restrain herself and express her frustration. Mine was that in the long years we'd been together, I never thought of leaving her no matter what was going on in my life. She was my mate for life and my family was sacred, but she didn't understand it. My home was my home; the anchor I needed more than she and the rest of my family ever thought I did.

"Friday was a carbon copy of Monday," she continued. "He peed all over himself and fell on the floor again. Mima cried inconsolably; I wept with her. I know with all the problems we face this is the most painful. I don't mind losing everything, but the anguish of sickness is something I haven't learned to live with."

"Well," I said, "whenever you get to heaven don't forget to complain. Don't forget the people who stayed behind. If I do, and find that mysterious, merciful being everybody talks about, you can be sure I'll raise hell."

"Stop being silly, will you?" she said, as I started the car. "You know very well how angry you make me every time you use the occasion to deride my faith."

Father was in good spirits as we entered the house. I embraced him and kissed his forehead. Mother came after him with a smile on her face. Well, I thought, so far so good. We had a brief conversation and she said she'd have dinner ready in a half hour or so. I went to my rooms, took a shower and stopped at my studio to check the mail and a few saved messages on my private line; four of six were from Rudy asking me to call him; something important to discuss, obviously the settlement negotiations he wanted to begin.

Maxine and I went down to the living room and sat with my parents for a cocktail before dinner. I entertained them with a few stories; my visit to the plantation and the prospects of a new career representing one or more Costa Rican businesses in the US. Two vodkas and two scotches later, we sat down to have a wonderful arroz con pollo like no other in the world.

Cogswell and his group was anxious to hear the results of my Costa Rican adventure and I dutifully called him, went over briefly what I considered important and told him I would wait for his instructions. He recommended that we meet the group as soon as possible and asked me to put my impressions in writing, most important the Agricultural Minister's remarks. I said I would, and Friday afternoon one hour before lunch, I entertained the group with my stories, the prospects of the coffee plant and the reluctance of the big owners to sacrifice their easy life for a promise of a new industry, jobs for their countrymen and the risk of the unknown.

If Cogswell was my employer, Burt and Julie were my friends and, in many ways, my life raft so to speak. Having delivered a less than a positive report, I wondered if Burt knew how Cogswell's group felt about my efforts. That evening I arrived at Julie's penthouse and found her in the kitchen preparing a veal scaloppini out of this world.

Julie's apartment was exceptional, but her kitchen was a cooking cathedral. It was ample, with modern cabinetry and all the gadgets you have seen in home magazines. Julie was wearing a colorful apron and drinking a martini. "Get whatever makes you happy," she told me and I went to the bar and served myself a rare Scotch Burt keeps for special occasions. Julie took another look at the food in the oven and together we walked out to the terrace. The sun was setting, the Hudson was filling up with the rising tide coming from the ocean. The Washington Bridge lighted up like magic. What an enchanted life, I thought. What luck, a place like this. I wish I could hide here, cover my head and wait for all my problems to disappear. I took a sip of my whiskey, put my arm around Julie's shoulders and toasted the river, the Palisades, the bridge and everything and everybody else I had forgotten to include. If beleaguered by life, I was determined to survive and the river gave me peace and made me dream of beauty and a better day.

"What's the matter with Maxine?" Julie asked me.

"I'm really worried about a few changes I've noticed. She isn't reading as she used to. She complains it takes her longer to recognize written words. She's also having problems at the library handling the computer; that wouldn't be an important worry, who hasn't? Nevertheless she asked me to take care of our checking account, something she has done since we got married."

"Believe me, I didn't consider it opportune to talk about it before, but since you brought up the conversation: it's nothing new. I'm sorry to say," Julie responded. "I have mentioned it to Burt several times. He agreed."

"I didn't want to raise the issue either," I interrupted her. "You know how things are. The minute people realize you have a problem, they tend to shun you. Maxine would have been devastated."

"But she's a relatively young woman, although older than you are."

"Eleven years," I responded.

"Do not wait. Take her to a neurologist as soon as you can," Julie insisted.

Burt burst in and dropped his briefcase on the floor, kissed Julie, shook my hand, sat on the sofa and, with a pleading smile, asked Julie to prepare him a drink. And she did.

"I have been talking to Jack Cogswell and Julie about your progress in Costa Rica. I want you to take your time and tell me all about it."

I went over the whole week's incidents and described my experiences with "la crème de la crème" of Costa Rican society and business people. I described Jimenez's plantation and the ins and outs of cultivating coffee. I did gossip a little about the wives and mistresses of those fellows and Julie dug in at every step of the way trying to find out if I had scored, something that reluctantly admitted I had not.

We sat at the table and Burt asked me how I felt about going back to Costa Rica. I told him I'd do it as many times as they want me to go; very simple, I need the money. I added it was a great opportunity; important business people, good restaurants, nice hotel accommodations, an assistant; what else could I ask for? I thanked Burt again for his help. I also mentioned having explored the possibility of business in reverse. That I had left a number of contacts that I'd hoped to explore more on my next trip in three weeks. He said Jack Cogswell and his partners were impressed with my performance and even if I couldn't get anything concrete, were willing to continue the experiment until all the options were exhausted.

MAXINE - PRELUDE TO THE ABYSS

Waking up the following day I cornered Maxine and had a long conversation with her. I mentioned her failings, something she reluctantly admitted, and suggested seeing a neurologist. She excused herself saying we'd be going to Miami soon and she would use the opportunity for a check-up. She reminded me her brother — a celebrated children's heart specialist — knew a lot about medicine in general. He could advise her better and recommend a doctor. I thought that was reasonable. Why not? Family is family, I agreed.

Maxine quickly diverted the topic of conversation to Mima's taking my father to see the doctor and her disappointment to hear there was very little he could do. He recommended a flat apartment so Pipo didn't risk falling using the stairs. Mima admitted she couldn't handle him by herself and talked about finding an assisted living accommodation or something similar to obviate the problem and get us out of the equation. Brave woman my mother; she'd sink with her old companion like a captain would with his wounded ship.

Life, I said to myself. Now that there is a flicker of a light at the end of the tunnel, the health of those closest to me have taken a plummeting downturn. Neither Maxine nor father are in immediate danger, but their illnesses are long and debilitating. Mima is taking the brunt of dad's disease. But Maxine's impacts me and me alone. Ironically I'm alright; healthy, full of energy, looking to the future, but everything else sucks. I am Sisyphus incarnated. I roll the boulder up the mountain, but it rolls down again and again. I should pray to Zeus for release.

In the private world of my brain el Brujo had become a permanent fixture, a challenge to my sanity. At the beginning I dismissed him outright. Now I'm dealing with every facet he predicted. "Everything will crumble, while you watch; powerless, not able to stop it. That was the purpose of puncturing the goat's heart during the ceremony, to let him bleed slowly until its life ran out of its body. You're the goat Alex," el Brujo said, "and whether you believe these curses are possible or not, just watch; it will happen to you and those around you." And he was right! I'm bleeding, not figuratively speaking, but bleeding. A week and then another with no news from anyone. The telephone rang. Cogswell was calling to confirm another trip to Costa Rica, this time to explore the Agriculture Minister's intentions and do another round with the plantation owners in the country. I thanked him for the check I received two days earlier and asked him for a convenient time to meet his group. He said to wait for his call and I said I will.

That same afternoon when I returned home from shopping, I found two messages from Rudy asking me for lunch. I returned the call. He said he wanted to have lunch and an exchange of ideas. I asked him what the occasion was all about and he responded it was time to review the case and our present strategy. Rudy gave me two days choose. I said Monday, and Monday it would be at a small, quiet restaurant, he emphasized, east of Grand Central Station, in mid-Manhattan.

It was an eventful day after all. Julie also called. Burt had left for London again. She had the keys to a fabulous house --- right on the beach in Quogue, Long Island --- and if I needed a respite, we could take a day or two, if I could swing it. I said yes and hung up.

JULIE AT THE BEACH

A beautiful fall day ahead of us. Julie and I at ease, driving away from Manhattan, crossing bridges, looking for the expressway to the heart of The Hamptons. No conversation, just an occasional chit-chat, listening to classical music on the radio, never saying a word about my precarious situation.

A few miles short of our destination, we stopped at a great delicatessen and bought a few essentials; a huge pastrami sandwich for lunch and two steaks for dinner. I had taken three bottles of wine from my cellar and grabbed two loaves of bread from a Broadway bakery I usually frequented. Armed with everything we needed we arrived at a large modern residence, surrounded by an inordinate amount of land for a beach house. It had a tennis court and a winterized swimming pool. A large covered porch faced the ocean and a boardwalk cut through the sand dunes to the beach. Lovely! Julie procured some keys conveniently hidden in the garage and we walked through the main door as if we were just taking possession of our inherited magical kingdom.

"Who are these people?" I asked Julie.

"She's Paula Greenberg. I've known her since college. She's married to a Wall Street broker; very successful. His name is Harold. Twenty years and three children after, they are getting divorced. She had money of her own and inherited half this house from her parents. She bought the other half from her other sister living in California."

"You could see this is not a new money toy. The furniture is very stylish and comfortable. I love those wall windows; the way the house sets behind but above the dunes. Quite a feat. You can see the beach and the ocean from any corner. How many bedrooms upstairs?"

"Four and three full bathrooms. There is also a couch in the library. Take a look. You're going to love their books. As many as you have, and quite a lot of first editions," Julie continued. "We're lucky; we have plenty of food in the fridge. She had told me we didn't need to bring anything, but I wanted to make sure just in case."

I went around and raised all the blinds and rolled back the curtains. The sun invaded the lower level and I walked back to the kitchen to help Julie.

"They signed a prenuptial before they married, so everything she had or inherited before their marriage she keeps."

"Well, you also have a prenuptial with Burt, don't you?"

"Yes, I do. In this day and age you need one. Imagine had I married a man like you. We'd have nothing by now, no matter the prenuptial."

"It would have been worth it just for the experience."

Julie came from the kitchen and hugged me. "You're so conceited you really think you're hot shit."

We spent a few more minutes checking out every corner of the beautiful house and eventually devoured our gigantic sandwich looking at the ocean sitting on the porch. A quiet inviting atmosphere, pastrami and two cold beers; fully satisfied we got chummy and fell asleep in each other's arms on a corner comfortable couch.

"Hey, it is 4:00 already," I said in Julie's ear. "We napped more than an hour. Let's walk the beach. Another half hour and there will be no sun."

Long Island beaches are magnificent. There might be a bit of pollution here and there, but nothing beats the ocean breaking on its shores. The sun was low on the horizon, the temperature hovering in the mid-forties, no wind, a gentle surf, in other words, paradise.

"What are you thinking?" Julie asked me. "You seem to be far away, in another land, far from here."

"Nothing. I am watching this magnificent panorama."

"You have these most disconcerting lapses. You could be with a group, or with me; as you are now and whoever is next to you could think he or she is alone, as I feel now. You just seem to take leave of your senses, completely immerse yourself in your own thoughts, and forget you have company."

"Does it bother you?"

"Well, not necessarily. I know you better than you think. And in many ways, I'm happy just being here, the two of us; you and me alone. I wish I could say "you and me against the world." But I know better. That's what I always wanted; you know that."

I took Julie in my arms, held her tightly and kissed her cheek once and once again. I knew I could always count on her. Regardless, she'd be always be there for me. But my mind was wandering, as it often does, fighting other battles.

"I have settled for these moments; beautiful as they are," Julie continued. "I borrow you. I guess that's what everyone around you does; borrow you for a moment, live your fantasy and hope for the next time. But the fact that you always come back, silly as it might sound, makes me happy. I'm a fool, I've told myself dozens of times. But I'm happy here, with you, and that's something no one can take away from me."

Back in the house, we settled for steaks for dinner. "Once a cannibal, always a cannibal," she said, frustrated; reminding me of Sabrina's remarks once at Sacandaga. We had dinner in the kitchen, talked a bit about her job, Burt, and had espresso afterwards. It was 9:00 and something, and after washing the dishes and setting them out to dry, she took my hand and together we walked to the family-room. I know Paula has cable, Julie said. Now if we can find the remote we're in business; and this time I'm going to do the surfing.

I stretched out at one end of the huge sofa and Julie deposited herself next to me. I hugged her against my chest as she switched a few channels until, bothered by my indecision, she offered to surrender the control. "No, I won't surf, you do it," I responded, but took the remote from her anyway and quickly settled for 'Out of Africa,' being played on a local channel with a million interruptions.

"I hate that movie, it reminds me of you. What's his name, Redford's character, the one she claimed didn't belong to anyone, and she wanted to have all for herself. That's what we were talking about walking the beach."

"Denis Fink Hutton," I said pressing my lips — mocking Strip, with the strangest accent I could use — "Denis something, I think it is," I answered.

"He plays a guy like you. No one had a claim on him."

"Love is selfish; you're mine, you're part of me, that's why I love you." I said, holding Julie even tighter. And we watched Out of Africa to its end, cursing the local ads, weeping with the poor baroness and wishing we could be buried together and a pair of beautiful lions would visit our site every sunset to the end of the world.

I woke up early, put on a warm sweat suit and went downstairs to make espresso. It was cool and the furnace was cranking on. I took a shot of espresso and walked around the library; picked a book or two from the shelves; read a paragraph here and there, and made my way to the terrace. I felt cold, but the morning light was enticing and I wanted to be part of the sunrise; I wanted to witness it. A reddish, devilish kind of tint covered a portion of the horizon; it had a sort of foreboding message for me. Whether I imagined it or not, I take these signs seriously. If the sky wasn't enough, my sleep deprivation is also a harbinger of things to come; six hours is good enough. If I don't do five, I feel something looming in my immediate future.

"Good morning," Julie said, hugging me from behind. "Never heard you get out of bed. How long have you been up?"

"Not long, a half hour?"

"Anything wrong?"

"No, take a look," I said pointing to the horizon. "You know I loved to watch the sunrise."

"I know you do, but I sense that, behind that brave facade, there is something bothering you. I know you well enough and I've been dealing with a different person since you picked me up yesterday."

"Why do you say that?"

"For starters you fell asleep the moment you rested your head in your pillow. No matter how much I insinuated myself during the movie, after the movie, in bed, the fellow next to me wasn't Alex. Not that I pushed it, but I telegraphed I was ready."

"I know. I'm sorry."

"Please," Julie jumped. "I'm not talking about sex. You know what I mean. Your behavior was warm, but detached. Polite, but not the spark I know, always ready to react. I'm concerned about you. Share with me, I'm here to help. What is it?"

"I'm bogged down and it's nothing new. Look at all the problems that I have. Father's Parkinson, now Maxine, and on top of everything, my lawyers!"

"What about them?"

"They called me to have lunch on Tuesday. It's the first time they have invited me for anything outside their office; the two of them."

"Well, maybe they have good news to report. Perhaps they've found something and they want to review it with you, in person."

"In a restaurant, spending money? You don't know these guys. Do you remember what I told you about my conversation with Rudy?"

"Yes, that his partner had met a lawyer from the Alsace and had discussed settlement."

"Yes!"

"I wouldn't worry about that because they can't do anything without you. It is your suit. You're the one who decides. Come on, let's take a ride to East Hampton and do some shopping. I have a few things to buy."

MY BRAVE MOTHER

We returned to New York Friday midday. Burt was flying back from London and Julie wanted to be home when he arrived. After I dropped her at her apartment, I went home almost two hours before Maxine returned from work. Father was in the garden, mother doing something in her bedroom. I went up and found her organizing her drawers. I kissed her and sat on their bed.

"We're having problems, aren't we?" I asked her.

"Don't get old. That's the only advice I can give you."

"But you can't complain. You're having a rough patch. Not everything is roses, but up to now it hasn't been that bad."

"That's not enough. You never get ready for the rough patches, no matter how much you prepare yourself for them."

"Maxine told me, you mentioned again looking for an assisted living complex."

"I'm tired Alex. I must concentrate on your father. He needs all the help he can get. I'm also concerned about you two. I don't know what's going on with Maxine, but she isn't the same she was two years ago. I'm also worried about you. I know you well, better that anyone else. Perhaps you don't notice it, but your problems are taking their toll. You've changed a lot."

"How so?" I asked her.

"Your moods. You've always been full of energy, happy, always talking about new projects, travel. You're not a happy person anymore. No matter what you say. Your problems are taking their toll. Maxine is also unhappy. She spends the whole time in her bedroom when you aren't around. She seldom comes down. I'm very worried about her too."

"Don't worry about me, mom, I'll survive. Maxine is another story. But we'll handle that too. You'll see."

"You can stop being a wife, but you never stop being a mother, you know."

"I know!" I said, stepping forward and hugging her. "I know," and held her tightly for a while longer and then let go. But she continued.

"This house is too big for the four of us. Sell it. Move to a smaller place. It will be good for you two. We'll find a place, your father and I, and wait for the inevitable."

"It bothers me when you talk like that," I told her.

"I've been talking to Margarita. She has a friend in one of those places and she's taking me to visit her friend. I'll let you know if you're around."

Maxine returned from work and asked me point blank about my Washington excursion. I said I had met Jimenez and his partners and discovered two or three new and expensive restaurants. Then she asked me if I had plans to go back to Costa Rica soon. I said we'd fly together to Miami when she goes. "Would the end of next week be convenient?" she asked me. "Any time after my Tuesday lunch with my lawyers will be alright." Maxine agreed, and the trip was settled; the following Friday it was.

LAWYERS – THE GALL
OF A LIFETIME

I arrived at a small French restaurant on 51st, east of Second Ave. The place was full, but the maître d' took me to an empty table at the end of the salon, steps away from the kitchen's door. He said Rudy had called; he'd be late and wanted you to feel free to drink whatever kind of aperitif you wanted. I said alright. I asked for a dry sherry; a waiter promptly obliged.

Rudy entered the room and the maître d' ushered him in my direction. He excused himself for being late, too busy, he said and apologetically, tried to explain how difficult it had been to squeeze me into his busy schedule. He also apologized for Pete being delayed, suggesting we could start lunch any time we wanted. He then, getting private, insinuated Pete was facing a most painful and embarrassing situation. He pleaded for my sympathy and understanding.

"What kind of a problem?" I asked him.

"You have to promise you won't tell. Do you swear?" Rudy asked with a picaresque smile.

"Of course. It will be between you and me."

"His wife just hit him with divorce papers."

"That's very common," I said, discounting his secrecy.

"She left him for a black musician."

"Well that's more interesting. How did that come about?"

"He caught them having sex in his bed."

"What did he do?"

"He asked the fellow to leave. He told me he didn't talk to her for a week. I don't know the details but it seems they had a conversation and she sort of repented. But now he isn't sure anymore."

"Why?"

"She filed for divorce. She wants half of everything."

"Did he tell you all that?"

"No, but they served him the papers in the office and I signed for him. He wasn't in. I didn't know what the summons was all about and I read it. You know him; he might talk about it, but don't say anything. He's very sensitive."

"He always seemed a bit effeminate to me, is he? I asked Rudy.

"I don't know. I agree sometimes he acts like..."

"Maricon?"

"That's a strong word. But obviously lack of cojones. If you know what I mean."

As Rudy finished his sentence, Pete approached the table. He extended his hand and excused himself for being overburdened by a number of different problems and without any preambles he said to me:

"I don't know if Rudy told you, but my wife just hit me with divorce papers."

"Oh, I'm sorry to hear that," I said pretending to be surprised.

"She wants half of everything and alimony."

"Doesn't she work?"

"She quit three years ago. She claims she helped me finish law school and she wants half of everything."

"Well, if she did, she deserves her share."

"It isn't that simple," he said and went on to explain to me how and how much the law recognizes spouses' sacrifices, how he was humiliated by her demands and asked himself:

"I really don't know why she's leaving me...."

"*Maricon, she's fucking a man and not a maricon like you,* my alter ego interrupted. *I knew you were a queer the minute you opened your mouth the first time we spoke. You have no balls. I understand the poor woman, but can't understand why she married you in the first place."*

"Pete, since you asked the question, you yourself told me she refused to have sex with you for over a year now," Rudy said.

"Well, that's true but there are couples who seldom have sex and stay together. If you ask me, I really don't know why we didn't discuss it."

"Because you were sucking cock in a subway restroom, Maricon!" My alter ego interrupted again.

"I see you two started without me. I don't mind," Pete said, as the waiter stood next to him. He looked at both our plates and pointing to Rudy's said to the waiter. "Get me what he's having; and bring another bottle of wine, please."

"I began telling Alex about your encounter...." Rudy told Pete.

"Of course, let's not get distracted with my problems and let's review Alex's situation that seems very fluid and positive." Then addressing me, he said: "I know Rudy mentioned I met one of the Alsace's lawyers in court; different cases, of course. We used a break in his trial and discussed your case. Interestingly enough, we agreed it will take another eight to twelve months before we get our date in court. He insisted they won't produce the Alsace's Chairman unless the Judge forces them and he hasn't signed the order yet. I don't know why"

"You might not be doing your job," I interrupted him.

"That's not the case. We've been very diligent and kept them under pressure. Our problem is their firm has three hundred and fifty lawyers and we're two. They bombard us with paper, as if they were saturating Berlin during the Second World War. Well, to make a long story short, Rudy and I would like you to give us permission to settle the case."

"What the fuck is the cocksucker talking about? Permission? Permission to do what? Settle behind our back? Forget it. Don't do that! Over our dead bodies. Me entiendes?" My alter ego insisted.

"Pete, it seems your wife isn't the only person you are not talking to. I told Rudy not to approach the Alsace for settlement talks. To let them come to us."

"For all intents and purposes that's what happened; they approached us," he interrupted. "The possibility of a settlement came up and both of us said why not? It happens all the time. Lawyers keep talking to each other unless there is bad blood and our dealings with them have been rough at times, but very civilized in general. We could be in an adversarial position today and work together tomorrow on another case. Quite often we help our clients more talking to each other than talking to a jury."

"Son of a bitch. They're selling us out," my alter ego interrupted again. *"Tell the fuckers no dice and walk out. They want out; he said it in so many words. But better cool off. Let's take it easy and hear the scheme, but give them no answers if they want any."*

"Okay, Pete, cut the crap and tell me what you have in mind," I said, sensing the fuzziness of his argument.

"Alex, this is a David vs. Goliath kind of fight. We're going against a big firm with lots of influence at all levels. They have buried us in paper; motions of all sorts. The Judge told them to stop and cooperate, but they continue. They don't give a shit. They could appeal the verdict if it is against them. What we want is for you to be sensitive to our situation. We're partners in this case. We have a lot to lose if we lose the case."

"Partners? Did you hear that? These assholes have no shame. I'd walk away if we weren't in such deep shit, my alter ego interrupted. *Come on, man, answer him! Don't let that go by."*

"Wait a minute Pete. Did I understand you correctly; partners? You said we're partners? This is my case. My life. My wellbeing and that of my family," I said, raising my voice, almost yelling.

"Okay, okay," Rudy interrupted. "Cool it guys, cool it. Alex, be rational, put yourself in our place. We're two lawyers. They're three hundred and fifty. Their lawyers work out of their Miami office; we have to fly down there every time we represent you. At the present time we're working on contingency. If we don't win, we don't make any money. And this is how we make a living."

"You should have thought of that when I approached you," I said forcefully. "When I retained you two, none of those things were an obstacle. You persuaded me, you were convinced of the legitimacy of my case. That if it was true in this business nothing is written in stone, and nothing finished until the check clears, we had a good case a good jury of my peers could understand. That you could go to the end of the world to try the case; Miami was no problem. You didn't care how big their firm was. You told me it is a problem of quality and not of quantity. I have given you one hundred and seventy five thousand dollars. And now that you're going to take a third of whatever we win, you're telling me we're partners? No my friend. This is my case, my life and I make the decisions. I say when we talk and when we agree on a settlement."

"Alex," Rudy insisted. "This is a storm in a tea pot. Perhaps Pete rushed his words and didn't put the whole thing in the proper context. But I hope you take the main thrust of his argument and think about it. This has been almost four years and counting. We've been behind you every step of the way, but we are humans."

"Listen, say no more. I have lost almost twenty million dollars and I'm not going to settle for a pittance because you have more work now than when I retained you to fight these people. Keep in mind, this is my life, my case and I haven't waited this long to settle for the same amount of money I could have gotten with no lawyer. Enjoy your lunch."

I rushed out of the restaurant and walked the streets with no aim. New York was bustling in the early afternoon. The traffic was damning, the streets were full of people — everywhere you looked there were groups looking at the store windows — others coming in and out of the buildings. I stopped at the first hot dog stand I found. I ordered one and an orange soda more out of frustration than hunger. I was upset and I couldn't make sense of this turn of events. I called Julie and she was still at lunch. I left a message. Her secretary, who knew me well, said she wouldn't let her move. I took a cab and asked the driver to take me to the boat house at Central Park; one of my refuges now that I no longer have La Finca or Key Biscayne to hide and vent my anger.

Julie joined me an hour later and we sat at a table at the end of the terrace, close to the lake. She heard me patiently with no interruptions. At the end of my diatribe, she quietly suggested we start looking for new lawyers.

"It is obvious," she began, "your lawyers think it is their case as much as it is yours. Having made that decision, they feel a percentage of ten or twelve million now, is more appealing to them than a third of fifteen or twenty after a trial. That's the trick of the contingency fees. Use your head, your own philosophy; give yourself time. Tomorrow things might change again."

That night I went home, had cocktails and dinner with my parents and Maxine. We talked about everything but the conversation with my lawyers. Knowing Maxine, it'd have been a mistake to raise the issue. She'd have become troubled and anxious not having a solution to the problem, if indeed there was one. Instead, I concentrated on our trip to Florida and my jump to Costa Rica to continue my two-pronged negotiations. She'd stay with her brother and the rest of the family, something she had been doing every year for a long time. I discreetly raised the issue of a check-up, perhaps even seeing a neurologist. She looked at me a bit apprehensive, but I insisted, there will be no better or easier opportunity for a check-up than now that she was visiting her brother. And she assented.

Rudy called the following day. He wanted to reassure me of their commitment to my case and to please disregard Pete's vehemence. He asked me to remember Pete was confronting a painful personal crisis. It was all forgotten, I assured him and encouraged him to press ahead. He said of course and we hung up.

MIAMI – COSTA RICA

Time never stops. Friday came and Maxine and I flew to Miami. Her relatives picked us up at the airport and we spent the night at their home. After dinner, sitting in their garden, I discussed with my brother-in-law, a MD himself, Maxine's failing condition; a number of symptoms and many other signs easy to detect. Maxine herself complained of certain lapses, difficulty reading, and writing. Her brother wisely dismissed her concerns, assuring her the source of her problems would be found and she would continue working as before. Privately, he said that many of those symptoms were irreversible, but there were experimental drugs today that could alleviate if not reverse what she seemed to be suffering.

Jimenez and his chauffeur were waiting for me at the San Jose airport and took me to my hotel. Thirty minutes later we left for his home where a group of friends had assembled and were participating in a wonderful cookout. A pig roast, something more suitable to my taste, was being attended by two servants while a number of different dishes were being prepared by their head chef. Jimenez wife, Rosalia, introduced me to their guests, more than twenty all together, and especially to a thirty-something young woman.

"This is Anais," she said to me. "Anais, this is Alexander," she said to her. "Anais is American, a divorcee. She moved to Costa Rica with her ex-husband ten years ago. He worked for International Paper in the US and was in charge of all the Central America operations. They have a young boy, a beautiful child that looks like her."

"If she's the mold, I'm sure he's beautiful," I said, shaking hands with Anais.

"Well, now that you know each other well, I must go back to my other guests," Rosalia said with a wink and picaresque smile.

"Anais," I said as if spelling her name. "There is another famous Anais, you know. Anais Nin? Have you heard of her?"

"Of course. I was popular in my college because of her. Gore Vidal came to our school for a commencement speech once"

"What college was that? I interrupted her.

"Barnard, in New York. Vidal mentioned Nin, who very few of us knew, as a paradigm of women's lib. From then on everyone made fun of me. I was proud, though. He was related to her, he claimed. Overnight my name became an icon for my female liberated classmates."

"And," I said with a pause, "you're still one?" "Time forces you to see many other things that you don't when you're young."

"Are you a libber yet?"

"Of course!

"Me imagino que hablas Espanol? I asked her.

"Si, lo aprendi en college en Nueva York, tambien hablo Italiano. Mi familia es Italiana. Pero prefiero hablar Inglés siempre que puedo."

"You speak Spanish with a very seductive accent."

Anais didn't respond, but smiled sweetly.

"Do you work?" I asked her.

"Of course, at the American Embassy."

"A spy?"

"I wish," she said laughing. "I'm in charge of the archives. I'm the one to light the fire in case we have to evacuate. I'm kidding."

Anais and I spent most of the evening together. We went from one group to another, had champagne and sat together at dinner. She was delightful. She told me the story of her failed marriage and how proud she was of her young boy, Robert who was seven years old. I listened to her patiently and talked a bit about my job trying to change the outlook of coffee growers in

Costa Rica. We were interrupted a few times, especially after dinner, when we moved to the patio and a nice combo played a bunch of contagious tunes. I pitched my line with the freeze dry coffee and agreed to meet and discuss business during the week. At the end of the dinner I asked Anais if could see her again. And she said yes. She asked me how I was getting back to my hotel, and I told her Jimenez or his chauffeur was my designated driver.

"But I would love to see you again," I told her kissing her on both cheeks.

"It's possible."

"Tomorrow?"

"Isn't it too soon?"

"Perhaps for someone who lives here, but I have a scheduled departure. I might be history in four days."

Sunday evening I arrived at the restaurant she had suggested and the maître d' took me directly to the bar. Anais was having a cocktail and an unanimated conversation with an older man; I kissed her on both cheeks and she immediately turned around and introduced me to the fellow next to her.

"Alex, this is Robert Parker. Robert is the American Consul in Costa Rica."

Surprised I shook hands with the Consul. After a few pleasantries, he said Anais had mentioned my project and showed himself pessimistic about the prospects of diverting coffee from the export market. I concurred with his take, but insisted on talking to the Agricultural Minister, adding he had somehow opened a window of hope. Parker looked at me with a wary expression and suggested I shouldn't take the Minister at face value. "I tell you in confidence, not to be swayed by his by his positivism. There have been times in the past when he had led investors stray after consultation fees, etc."

Taking the first sip of my sherry, I invited the consul to join us for dinner. The three of us sat, dinned and enjoyed the most interesting conversation. He gave me a panoramic assessment of the political situation in Central America and I asked him strategic questions, some of which, he couldn't answer. A most interesting evening to say the least.

Having scheduled dinner with the Minister, I called Jimenez and met him for lunch at his country club. My job --- as their vegetable products representative for the US --- was discussed and I gladly accepted it. I made a number of recommendations and he thought my step-by-step approach was intelligent and renting an apartment in Miami would save us money; and rent we will.

As I was driven back to the capital, I couldn't stop mulling about chance and circumstances. Somehow I was being pulled back to Miami again. The frozen vegetables — if not the freeze dry coffee I originally peddled — had tended me a new lifeline, a new source of income. I felt reassured I'd have the resources I needed to continue fighting the Alsace and somehow maintain a similar kind of lifestyle to the one I enjoyed before the deluge began.

Things were moving at a rapid pace. The minister was next on my busy schedule and promptly at nine, I was having dinner with him. By the time our first course was consumed, it was obvious the American Consul had given me a fair description of my promoter's character; the Minister's readiness to get a piece of the action was obvious. I finished the dinner quickly with an improvised excuse and promised to go back to my investors and discuss his proposal thoroughly.

Free of my dinner engagement, I looked for a phone and called Anais. I told her I was free and wanted to meet her for an after dinner drink. She said it was late, but if I wanted I could stop at her home on my way back to the hotel. Twenty minutes later, Anais and I were sharing a great cognac she humbly professed to know nothing about but to me tasted heavenly great.

Anais lived in a comfortable, well-appointed house, right outside San Jose proper. When I arrived, she was playing a CD by some Spanish lady, with beautiful sad ballads; the ones that are dear to most Hispanic women; men asking for forgiveness, a second chance, or another opportunity to rekindle a truncated love affair. They were beautiful I admit, and I chided her for being an American and liking those sentimental songs. "Those are the kinds of words that would win any woman's heart," she said.

Anais demeanor was simple and unassuming, but she turned out to have a very complex personality. Well into my second cognac she began to delve into her breakup, going as far as to complain about her husband's immaturity and lack of self-respect. If the conversation wasn't of great interest to me, I listened attentively, something that seemed to open her up even more.

Half way a new CD, we were sitting on a love seat, our knees touching each other's, until I couldn't control my urge to kiss her and I gently did. She responded avidly; I tried to embrace and kiss her again, something she then rejected softly.

"I like you very much, but we shouldn't start something that isn't going to be finished," she said gently holding me back.

"I've been wanting to kiss you since Rosalia introduced us at the party."

"Perhaps on some other occasion. You will be coming back often, won't you?"

"I hope so, if everything works out as it should."

"Why don't you go now? She asked me gently. "Perhaps we could get together again before you go. Wouldn't you like that?"

Flying home was like flying into a battle zone. First thing was to visit Maxine at my in-laws. When I drove there, I found their front door wide open and Maxine, lights out, sitting in an arm chair watching TV in the living room. Had you been alone? I asked her. She didn't answer. I tried asking her if she knew the tests' results and she responded; "Why don't you find out? They might tell you what he won't tell me."

When my in-laws arrived, I ordered out for the four of us. Maxine spirits improved the minute her brother came back from work and kept talking, with impediments, during the whole dinner. I hadn't spoken to Bruno, my brother-in-law for a week or so, and suspected there were more bad news waiting to be heard, but I kept quiet until I found a propitious moment.

"It is incredible, Bruno said. "I saw the MRI and the number of bright spots, mostly on one side of her brain, are many. She has suffered a number of mini-strokes," he continued, "and she also suffers from a common disease, weakening of her cerebral arteries. The prognosis is serious; she could suffer a massive stroke or a hemorrhage at any moment. I told him I'd like to meet at least one of the neurologists and he said he would arrange as soon as one of them had an opening.

The following afternoon Bruno and I visited one of the doctors and were presented with the detailed results of Maxine's examination. The doctor confirmed most of what Bruno had stated and added that Ischemia, a sort of mini-stroke could be fought in most cases, with aspirin therapy, but unfortunately Maxine's MRI also showed tiny hemorrhages, like small drops of blood. So it was a rare combination of radically opposite symptoms, blockage and hemorrhaging. Both occurrences kill brain tissue, provoking troubles with vision, speech and motor coordination. "And most unfortunately," he went on to say, "ten to fifteen percent of people suffering these symptoms will suffer a stroke in the following ninety days."

The night before my flight back to New York, I asked Maxine if she wanted to go home. She demurred for a few moments and finally said she'd like to, but she preferred to stay in Florida, if she wasn't needed and I didn't mind. I didn't mind, I responded. I knew she was comfortable there and in good hands. I needed my own time to fight my battles and agreed with her. "I think it's the right thing to do," I told her, kissed her forehead and went to sleep in another room.

MY OLD ONES - DECLINE AND FALL

I flew north and arrived at home in the middle of a small crisis. Father had another relapse. Fortunately Juanita, the caretaker during my absence, was at hand and, together with mother, took father to his room where I found him resting comfortably.

"Would you be home for dinner?" mother asked me and I said yes. She had leftovers, she said, and we could share some picadillo, rice and plantains if I wanted. And we did. The two of us alone in the kitchen and drank a good bottle of Rioja while talking about the calamity around us.

"Is Maxine making progress now that she's with her brother?" Mima asked me.

"Not much. Her problem with words is one of the symptoms. Two different neurologists came up with the same diagnosis; she could suffer a stroke at any time soon."

"That bad?" mother asked me.

"That bad. We discussed her quitting her job."

"She loves her job. What is she going to do with herself? And you. How about you? How did it go? Did you find a job?" mother asked me.

"Well, sort of. I'm becoming a fruit vendor. I'm going to get a cart and sell fruits and vegetables in mid-Manhattan."

"You're kidding me. Come on!" mother said. And I went ahead and entertained her gossiping about the Costa Rican society and the oligarchs who ruled the country.

"I'm sure things are going to get better," she interrupted me. "Your luck is about to change. It has to change. But if there is any consolation, as I told you, I visited the assisted living facility we discussed and it is adequate. Nuns run it. I think your father and I are going to feel good there. It isn't home, but what can we do."

"You don't have to intern yourself for the sake of Pipo," I reminded her. "You're still a young person, have good health and your head is intact. You can function by yourself a lot longer."

"Where he goes, I go! That's the way it is. You won't have to worry about us. One less headache."

Tough woman, Mima. She knew things weren't going well for me and she was taking the initiative; clearing my path if there was any. I often wondered about a world without women. The answer was simple; there wouldn't be one. Mother was a good example; her home, my father, me. We were her world. Wife and mother, keeping house, raising me was her life. Worrying about my future, even now, sacrificing herself for my father, trying to ease my path. I was lucky and if I wasn't, she wanted me to be. Even if new problems kept creeping up on me, ironically, some were taking care of themselves. Maxine was going to be home and should mother stay, it'd have been another worry for her. The solution; mother and father moving on and my retaining the same caretaker to assist Maxine in my increasingly long absences Was I a calculating son of a bitch or was it life rearranging my future without me moving a finger?

"Oh, I forgot to tell you," mother said. "Rudy, I think his name is, your lawyer called. He said it was urgent. Did you know he speaks Spanish? He spoke to me in Spanish. Very charming man."

CONNIVING LAWYERS

Lawyers, lawyers. Rudy said he had good news, he always had, but wanted to discuss it personally, not on the phone. Ok, give me a preview, but he insisted; personally. And I went to his office that afternoon at two as we had agreed.

"Pete is with a client, but he'll join us as soon as he can," Rudy said, asking me to sit across from him on his office sofa. "Perhaps it is better that I begin. Pete will join us soon. The Alsace made a most interesting offer. They offered ten mil but I'm sure we can get a bit more if we insist."

"I think I told you I need at least sixteen million. Even sixteen won't be sixteen after you take your cut. Unless you sacrifice half your share. Otherwise, I'd have to declare bankruptcy. And you know it..."

"Come on Alex, be serious. You could take the nine or ten million, buy something in Florida and hide part of the money," Rudy said a bit agitated. "Obviously I'm not recommending that you do that. It would be unethical. But everybody does it. Your creditors will have to start a new action. The property, if it is your home, is beyond their reach."

"Will you be my lawyer?"

"Of course not," he said defensively. "You know that. We don't handle that kind of case. But you should be able to find another lawyer who could negotiate a good settlement for you," he insisted.

"Go back to the Alsace and try to get me at least sixteen. Not less and you have a deal."

I left Rudy's office and took an elevator down to the lobby, got my cellphone and called Julie.

"How did it go?" she asked me.

"Do you have time?"

"Come to my office and wait for me downstairs," she said.

I stopped briefly at a pizza parlor, had a slice and half a beer. Coming out of the joint, I noticed the sky changing. Dark clouds covered Manhattan, but I decided to take a leisurely walk to Julie's office anyway. I needed time to cool off. And I also wanted to surprise her coming out of the elevator. And I did; she was startled. Once in the street, we hailed a taxi.

"They're driving you nuts," Julie said. "I'm afraid you're going to end up in an insane asylum."

"The rats are ready to abandon ship."

"Human nature," Julie said. "The more I know man, the more I love my dog," who said that?

"I don't remember, but it is true. What a crowd these lawyers are."

"Not all are the same. Burt would never treat anyone like that."

"He's corporate. He deals at a different level."

"Why don't you stay tonight? Burt is in Washington and he won't be back before tomorrow night."

It was a stormy evening in Manhattan and we went directly to her apartment. I wanted to hide, stay quiet and lick my wounds. Julie prepared a tuna salad with eggs and, together with bread and a bottle of wine — a pecan pie for dessert — we had a feast. What a marvelous decision.

Right after dinner I called Ben. I briefly mentioned my growing conflicts with the lawyers and he said it was a pity. He read in today's Wall Street Journal that The Alsace was in complete disarray and the board was considering firing Messier. They suffered another substantial loss for the last quarter and it was all attributed to the lackluster Federated performance in the US. "It seems the Chairman is facing a stockholders revolt," Ben concluded. "Let's hope!" I said. "Perhaps that should help us settle the case."

Julie, who was listening to my conversation with Ben, mentioned Women's Wear Daily editor was also considering publishing a long expose of the Alsace and its flamboyant, bon vivant Chairman, in a future issue of their magazine.

The thunder and lightning was a spectacle from Julie's windows. The storm seemed to be right on top of the Washington Bridge in the distance and the lightning coming through the overcast sky seemed to be the work of a crazy pyrotechnic mad man. Still, it was a fascinating event and the whole scene reminded me of my stormy days back at my precious Sacandaga Lake retreat.

"When is Maxine coming back?" Julie asked me.

"Two or three weeks, if she doesn't decide to stay in Florida. Pipo and Mima will go to an assisted living facility in a month or two. There have been conversations with Medicaid to pay for their accommodations; their little pension, Medicaid, and I'll supplement the difference."

"Where will you get all that money?" Julie asked. "You have enough with your own expenses and Maxine's. If she quits her college position, even if she gets disability compensation, I'm sure you're going to face a shortfall."

"I don't know. But I'll handle it as well as I can. Is there any good movie on cable? I need to be distracted."

While doing my early morning routine with banks and customers' orders for our new line of vegetable products, Cogswell called and asked me to meet him for lunch at "21". The purpose I knew; the freeze dry coffee project was being terminated. I said great, and met him the next day at one. The "21" I liked and patronized it often. I had fond memories of it. I remember dearly the first time I was taken there; my first famous restaurant in New York and the first Chateau Lafitte Rothschild I ever drank in my life. If a bit apologetic, Jack confirmed the project's end although reassured me again, the group was grateful and proud of my efforts. Once the serious portion of the encounter was over, we forgot about business and enjoyed a relaxed and sweeping conversation that lasted the rest of the occasion talking a variety of subjects. The theater one of them.

ILLNESS VS. BUSINESS

My travels and my Miami routine were beginning to conflict. No matter the day or the hour I visited Maxine's at my in-laws, I always found her under similar conditions; no lights, watching television alone, non-responsive to anything around her. Her brother and his wife had asked her to go with them to a restaurant, but she preferred to stay home, but asked them to bring her a bite. A conversation about returning to her job ensued. After a long agonizing give and take, we agreed to call her boss the next day to discuss her resignation for health reasons. Having touched a number of sensible questions, I used the opportunity to mention Mima's decision to go to an assisted living facility. Maxine didn't like hearing that; her eyes became moist and asked me to stop talking nonsense. "You only bring me bad news," she complained. "If anything we should all move to Miami. We could find people here to help your parents in a small apartment." She went further and categorically said "I'll never accept to be confined to an institution. Period!"

Life if hectic was moving forward. On the business front I hired one of my old employees to handle cargo and all the warehousing activities. I had also asked Roberta to give me a hand with accounting and other office work. She said she'd help while I found another person. Roberta I trusted. She had been my right hand all along and I knew I could count on her with closed eyes.

On the personal front, to say things were settling down would have been an understatement. Maxine's resignation was accepted. My parents would be moving soon to the assisted living residence. My New York home had to go, although negotiating with the bank first was an imperative. If all that wasn't enough, finding residence in Miami will be a matter of contention. Maxine wished to live close to her immediate family in the suburbs; I opposed it. With all those worries in mind, I flew to Costa Rica.

One of Jimenez' employees was waiting for me at the airport and took me to an apartment in a modern section of San Jose. I was pleasantly surprised to find an ample flat, with beautiful views of the volcano in the distance, the most appealing furnishings and a maid at my service; was I lucky? No one could have asked for more.

It had been decided I'd work from Jimenez' office while in San Jose. The next morning, I was promptly driven, to a stylish old mansion very close to the city center. As I entered my new quarters, I was amused to find a group of young women sitting --- in modern steel desks --- directly facing two glass enclosed offices. Another young woman introduced herself as my temporary assistant and led me to a very comfortable office on the second floor, she informed me, was my own. She showed me her office next door and the button I should press to request her presence.

My first call in was from Jimenez, who asked me to meet him for lunch at his favorite hangout. A scotch, a sherry, a bottle of wine and a couple of lamb chops and he was ready for a nap. I excused myself, stayed behind at the club and called Anais at the Embassy. Luckily, she answered the telephone and after a pleasant surprise and a few gallantries, dinner was set. That night, at a restaurant of her choice, Anais and I met again.

Café d' Artistes was the venue's name, the same as the famous restaurant in New York. It wasn't big, but quaint and gracefully decorated, with painted walls reminiscent of paradise; a virtual copy, if with some variations, of the elegant eatery back home. Anais had not arrived, but had reserved a table in my name. I told the maître d' I'd prefer to wait at the bar and she took me to a corner, where the bar with a mid-size counter was located. There I sat among a group of guys, presumably business men and several young women having cocktails after a grueling day at the office. One of the fellows toasted me and introduced himself. Another North-American seeking fortunes in Central America. He inquired about my doings and I discreetly changed the conversation. Instead, I ended up learning about his family in Jersey, how much he missed them and his angst to return home.

Anais arrived and stood a few feet away from the end of the bar. She was a dark-haired beauty, about five seven, a size six perhaps, with sculptured legs and curvaceous hips; I loved her figure. She also had a kind of intimate speech, as if she was talking just to you and there was no one else in the world.

"Lovely to see you again," I said kissing both her cheeks.

She kissed my lips and together we walked to our table.

"I was expecting you to call and you never did," she said, as if mortified.

"I have problems," I said.

"Are they that bad you didn't have a minute to call and say hello?"

"Yes, they are, believe me," I said, as we sat at the table. Fortunately the captain approached us and suggested a million specials and the time each one would take to be completed.

We ordered what Anais suggested and drank a wine I selected. I'm fussy, if not difficult with wines and I don't want them to ruin the experience of a delicious dinner. And delicious it was. A quail fricassee with white rice and an avocado salad with palm chunks. If that wasn't enough, they served us a coconut flan with burned caramel sauce on top; extraordinary.

If the food was extraordinary, Anais demeanor was cool and detached most of the evening. Only toward the end did her mood warm up and gradually changed. At dinner's end, it was as if we hadn't stopped seeing each other all that time I was away.

Getting ready to order desserts, I asked Anais how good the espresso was and if we should try getting one somewhere else. Surprised, she asked me if I had any ideas of what to do next? I responded it was up to her. "Why don't we go home, then?" she suggested. "Alright," I retorted, "but not before the espresso."

Anais made me feel at ease. She was easy and unassuming. On the other hand, if her composure and demeanor were enough to make me like her a lot, her handling of the stick shift and her somewhat exposed tanned thighs, gave me a lot to fantasize about.

We arrived at her suburban home, enter her garage, got out of the car and immediately fell into each other's arms. She took my hand and led me inside her home. The beginning of a slow and pleasure-filled walk to her bedroom and a night that would last in our memories as long as we live. We didn't fuck. We made love tentatively as if we were discovering each other's fantasies, unencumbered by the problems we both knew existed and chose to ignore. Happy to be together, sharing time, her nest, giving pleasure to each other.

"You snore," she said as I opened my eyes. "You're smearing me," I responded. And we kissed, and kissed again until the telephone rang. It was the embassy, her assistant reminding her of a meeting in an hour's time. "When are you going back?" she asked me. "Tomorrow," I responded. "Tonight then?" she demanded. "Late," I insisted. She ran to the shower and I ran after her. We soaped each other, shampooed our hair, kissed and kissed again until time ran out. We dressed and she drove me to mid-town. I said "I'll see you tonight." She smiled, stepped on the gas and her car disappeared.

AN APOCALYPTIC THREAT!

Back at the office I called Maxine in Miami. She said, Mima had called, I had received a special delivery large envelope that seemed important. The return address is from your lawyers, she continued, but obviously she didn't open it. She wanted to know if she should mail it to us down here or wait for your return. I told Maxine I'd call my lawyers in New York and find out what the fuss was all about. And I did. Rudy answered the phone.

"Oh yes, Alex. Did you get our letter?" he asked me.

"No, I'm in Costa Rica, remember? I'm trying to make a living. What's so important you had to make an overnight delivery?"

"Alex, I think we got the best offer the Alsace is going to make. They had agreed to settle the damned thing for ten point five million and Pete and I believe you should take it."

"How many times do I have to tell you there is no way I'd settle for less than 16 million?"

"Well, good enough," Rudy responded. "Our letter says if you insist on trying to get more than ten, we are out of the case. You would have to release us or we would go to court and ask the Judge to release us from the case."

"What are you talking about? You're giving up? You can't leave me like this."

"Sorry Alex, but we can't continue. This suit is eating us alive. We have no time. We have many other things going on in New York and we can't continue just because you think you deserve a bigger settlement. If you insist, if that's your decision, we must part ways. You leave us no alternative."

"Wait a minute. I'm going back tomorrow and we can meet first thing Monday morning. Will you be at the office?"

"Make it Tuesday morning. I'm busy Monday. I have a couple of depositions and I have to prepare for another one on Tuesday afternoon. But if you want, we can meet Tuesday morning at ten sharp. Is that a date?"

"Tuesday then," I said, and I hung up disgusted.

Son of a bitch. I couldn't believe my luck. This is crazy. Crazy! What's going on? No lawyers and a trial in the not too distant future. How am I going to handle this? A new team of lawyers will demand a retainer. Money I don't have. What's going on?

I staggered around my office, stopped at a window, looked out, and couldn't see anything even if it was a bright beautiful day. I walked back and sat at my desk again. I repeated and repeated the same routine until my alter ego interrupted me briefly. *"Hey! Calm down. You're alive man. That's all we want out of life; to be alive and healthy. Everything else, we can handle. Remember our motto; we don't let anyone, anyone hurt us. Never! Did you listen good? Never! We might be forced to take some shit, but we don't take it from anyone just because they want to hurt us. We knew they weren't honest, didn't we? That's nothing new. What's new is that we have to face it now, rather than later. Let's concentrate. Where do we go from here? To begin, there is nothing we can do two thousand miles from home. Just sit down and take dictation. I'm going to tell you how we're going to go about it."*

New York looked gray and sad as my plane glided over Manhattan aiming at an empty runway at La Guardia. It was Saturday evening, a full flight of unhappy passengers making their way back home from the sun. Once inside the airport, walking the aisle I saw a familiar face in the distance; Julie was waiting for me. I rushed to the exit and embraced her. Together we went to retrieve my bag. I mentioned I wanted to go by my home first, to see my parents, and she said we'd do whatever I wanted. I asked her about Burt.

"He went to the opera. We had tickets for Turandot."

"What about you?" I inquired.

"Your problems are more important to me than Pavarotti singing Nessun Dorma."

Moved, I grabbed her hand, pulled her against me and kissed her tenderly.

She pulled back, looked at me and smiled. "I got you, didn't I?" She said, smiling, blowing me a kiss.

We stopped at my home to check my parents out and get the missive from my lawyers. Pipo and Mima were alright and in good spirits. I told mother I was going to stay overnight with Burt and Julie, but would be back by tomorrow afternoon. She said not to worry. She got Julie's number if anything happened. We kissed them both and Julie and I left.

Crossing Manhattan on our way to Riverside Drive, Julie interrupted a monologue I had begun the moment we got in the car and asked me a series of questions. A few were related to Maxine's health, her prognosis, what to expect and if she was aware of the full extent of her illness. Then she dealt with my plans to move to Miami, my future as a fruit vendor and finally my economic situation. If the first group of questions was relatively easy to answer, the ones related to my future were all full of ifs and nothing concrete. As I divagated trying to find answers a few blocks before her building, she found a vacant space on the road and parked the car.

"Where are you going to live in Miami?" she asked me point blank.

"I haven't decided. I have no money for a condo down payment, so I'll be forced to rent. Where? I don't know. Maxine is dead set against Key Biscayne and I wouldn't like to live anywhere else."

"I have been thinking," Julie said. "You know I am completely independent from Burt, financially I mean. Pretty soon, I'll be old like you..."

"Hey! Wait a minute, I'm forty seven," I said feigning anger.

"I have all this money making four percent at the bank, when I can make a lot more buying a property down there and renting it to you."

"Look," I said grabbing her by her shoulders. "I love you, period. But you don't have to do that. I love you. And in many ways I consider you my woman, my alter ego, I run to you every time something happens to me. But this is too much, and you know it. Look at my situation; I'm bad news. Nothing works. People lose their jobs or get sick and go to Santeros to contract curses against me. Do you want to end up sick? A pauper like me? No one can predict how this mess is going to end. I might end-up declaring bankruptcy for all I know."

"I don't care! The apartment would be in my name. You just pay rent and maintenance and that's it. You can declare bankruptcy if you want. It won't affect me. And if it does, I'll repossess all your shitty paintings, and all the Salvation Army stuff you call antiques. And if that isn't enough, I'll put a lien on your screenplays and confiscate your constipation pills. I'll be your nemesis, worse than Rudy and Pete. This is the only way I have to make sure you can't run away from me," she said, pulling me against her and giving me a kiss.

"You're crazy. Crazy! Completely crazy. Did you hear me? Crazy! I don't deserve you. I don't know what I did to deserve you. Really, I don't know who to thank."

"Go ahead and thank the universe, that's what you usually do. But think about guardian angels. That might be an easier answer than a galaxy influencing your life. It doesn't influence mine, for sure. You crazy, infantile Cuban refugee, you."

Tuesday morning, at eleven sharp, I was led to my lawyers' conference room. Rudy was waiting for me and came forward to shake hands.

"How are things in Costa Rica?" he asked me. "Any takers for the coffee plant?"

"Lots of conversations, but nothing positive yet. I guess it'll take another two or three visits before we get something concrete," I responded, trying to keep him in the dark about my prospects in South America.

"Did you read our letter?" Rudy asked me.

"Yes, I did."

"And?"

"You'll have to go to court to get the release. It is your decision to abandon ship, not mine."

"Why should we? It's obvious we have irreconcilable differences. You don't want to settle and we can't continue carrying on with a case that is driving us into the ground. You should be aware of that."

"I don't follow you. When we win, you will end up with close to three to four million dollars. That's money."

"If we win," he interrupted me. "The difference between a million now and two million at a trial is enormous. Full of ifs, hypothetical situations, a million things beyond our control. If you want to go that route, it is your choice. We want out!"

"You won't get any money!"

"We'll worry when the time comes. Now we need to get out!"

"Go to court then," I told him.

"The Judge will give you thirty days to find a new lawyer, if you don't have one. If you have a lawyer, it would be a good idea to ask him to be present. Otherwise you could participate by phone. You'll save the airline ticket."

LAWYERS NO MORE

It was Tuesday morning, I was home alone in New York, when the telephone rang; the assistant to the Court's Clerk in Miami was on the line. "Your lawyers' motion will be heard at eleven sharp," she said. "Please, be next to your telephone. We won't call a second time." She hung up.

My lawyers' motion to be let off the case had been hastily scheduled and Rudy had flown down to Miami to be heard personally. I had the option of staying put in New York and I had decided it would better if we didn't confront each other in court. There was no sense in fighting the inevitable.

At eleven sharp the telephone rang and I was informed I was in open court and would be heard on time. Rudy went ahead and said flat out: "Judge, we and Mr. Faust, have irreconcilable differences. We've gotten to a point when we should part company." And he went on and gave the Judge the same kind of reasoning they had tried with me; they were only two lawyers; the defendants, a 350 lawyer strong firm was running us into the ground. The case has lasted much longer than had been anticipated and it was a real burden for them and a disservice to their other clients to continue representing me. "And it's a disservice to Mr. Faust also," he hypocritically said. "We keep flying to Miami to represent him, sometimes with a very short time to prepare ourselves. We'd hate to be considered derelicts," he continued, "for not performing our legal duties for all our clients. It wouldn't be fair to Mr. Faust either," he concluded.

The Judge asked me if I had any objections to my lawyers' release and if I had new counsel in place. I told the Judge that I objected and had no counsel. I went ahead and gave the Judge a brief history of our last conversations and pointed out there was collusion between my team and the Alsace's representation. It was only now that the terms of our agreement had changed and they had the opportunity of making a quick million that they started conversations without my consent and insisted on my settling.

"Those are irreconcilable differences," the Judge said. "Of course, they are," I answered. "I just wanted to make sure there is a clear record, I added, that they were the ones who wanted out. "How long would you need to get new counsel?" the Judge asked me. "I don't know sir. I'm strapped for money. I have paid them close to two hundred thousand dollars. It is only when I ran out of money and agreed to a contingency that they decided I should settle."

"Well," the Judge said, "I see no point in forcing them to continue when you really have irreconcilable differences. Their motion is granted and you have thirty days to find new counsel." He hammered the end of the hearing and that was that. The Pete and Rudy team were out and I was standing naked once again against my adversaries.

I remained in my library stunned. It was as if for the first time I realized I was completely helpless. I was back to where I started, looking for lawyers. This was a low blow, a deep wound. If money was one of my biggest concerns, another delay was traumatic, a new load on my overburdened psyche. I turned to my tape player, and played Liebestod one more time. Wagner had the power to ease my angst and help me see things in a larger context. I felt harassed and beleaguered by things beyond my control, compelled to deal with never-ending situations empty handed, only with my will to prevail. But, as I rested in my chair, listened to Flagstad as Isolde rose to heaven — and looked at my paintings and my stacks of books around me — a new peace engulfed my brain, as my alter-ego would repeat again and again; *Hey! We're alive. Life goes on. Don't get off it now. This is just a bump in the road. There are more things to do, more adventures to live. They want to screw us? Ok let them try. They might win one, but there are more wars to fight, more worlds to conquer. Come on, man! Don't quit on me now.*

JULIE AGAIN!

Tuesday nights are a perfect day to enjoy Manhattan, the traffic is light, most restaurants are half empty; a great day to get discount Broadway tickets. Julie and Burt had asked me to meet them at a restaurant on Bleecker St. in the Village. Three times around the block was enough to find a parking space. I walked into the restaurant ten minutes late and found my couple having cocktails and hors d'oeuvres silently, staring at the entrance, waiting for my appearance.

The scene became animated the minute I sat down. The maître d' came quickly and secured our orders. Another bottle of wine was ordered and we toasted my good luck, or lack of it. Both Julie and Burt took turns asking questions and I gave them a full briefing. I have no lawyers and must look for new ones. Burt said not to have anyone in mind, but he'd ask his partners for a firm in Miami proper. Julie repeated again and again, she couldn't believe my luck and the conversation turned to "el Brujo" and the curse. Burt said he didn't buy any of it, but nevertheless admitted that it was obvious what the Brujo predicted was happening. Julie interrupted, "I agree with Roberta," she said, and suggested I shouldn't dismiss the idea of looking for help.

"We're atheist, or at least I am," Burt said. "Perhaps you could believe in curses because you're Catholic," he told Julie. "But for me it's absurd!"

"That's nonsense," Julie responded, "the fact that all these things are happening to him, is enough to consider everything, including Santeria. He was told, he heard it himself, for God's sake. Out of the blue."

As we went back and forth among ourselves, a couple sitting next to us became enthralled by our conversation. The woman, in her mid-fifties, couldn't resist the temptation and, after excusing herself for the intrusion, went on to relate a similar story concerning one of her friends. We listened to her politely while she told us about her husband's dalliance with an exotic dancer and the curse a gypsy posed on him that ruined the transgressor for life.

When the woman finished her anecdote, we changed subjects and Burt went on to talk about my Costa Rican adventure. He said Cogswell's group, if disappointed about the coffee project outcome, was very impressed with my work. Julie brought up the irony of my going in the pursuit of a coffee deal and coming back with a frozen vegetables deal instead. Chance, I retorted and the conversation turned into an animated philosophical argument.

Before returning to Miami, I spoke to Cogswell who had shown some sympathy for my situation. I told him I had no lawyers and was penniless. He said nothing about my penury, but mentioned a large firm in Miami he had done business with, but doubted they would be cheap. Nevertheless, he said he'd keep his eyes open and would get in contact if there was something to report.

Following Jimenez' instructions, I rented an apartment --- a sort of corporate hangout --- in Key Biscayne. Thinking of the logistics of my job, my private life and my search for lawyers, I decided to remain at the Key instead of using the family's home in the suburbs where Maxine was staying. The apartment was a large two-bedroom, with an ample terrace and a partial view of the ocean. True, it wasn't mine or comparable to the apartment I sold, but a good substitute I could use as my new private quarters while I decided to move or not to move to Miami permanently. Life goes on, Alex, I said to myself. I put on a pair of shorts, a polo-shirt and went to walk the beach.

Finding a new legal team I knew would be difficult. I dreamed of discovering a young lawyer, experienced enough to handle my mischievous opponents, wanting to make a name for himself, but reasonable enough that I could afford his fees. In other words, if my legal limbo was a nightmare, my quest for a lawyer was daydreaming. Nevertheless, I phoned a number of law firms in downtown Miami and, after a few conversations, I had three firms that had shown some kind of interest in my quagmire.

My first meeting was, if short, a very instructive one; a mid-size firm with four partners and eight associate lawyers. One of the partners invited me to his office and, after a brief exchange, asked me to give him an overview of my situation and what my expectations were in case they decided to get involved. I did, and mentioned the nature of our complaint and the present situation with my old counsel. He listened attentively until I took a breather, an opportunity he used to interrupt me. If apologetic, he politely advised me they wouldn't be able to help me. He gave no specific reasons, but the message was clear; "Federated is a big corporation. We represented them in the past and won't mess with them now. You're here today and gone tomorrow. They're here to stay," was his simple answer. Less than fifteen minutes after shaking hands, the meeting was over. I thanked him and moved on to the second interview of the afternoon.

Having an hour to kill before my next appointment, I sat in a café and drank two shots of espresso, watching people, trying to elude the steady drizzle we had all afternoon long. My thoughts drifted to my just concluded interview. It was obvious lawyers are susceptible to intimidation and, even when they pretend their job is to defend your interest, theirs is up there with yours and more often than not, above yours. Now the lawyer I just met is concerned with his future once my case runs its course. It was obvious he didn't want to bite the hand that fed him in the past; something I could respect and I thanked him for his sincerity.

The next firm was also mid-size by Florida standards, but considered a boutique, a term that defines their specialization in a certain kind of law. I had an interesting conversation with one of the partners who showed real sympathy for my case, but also pointed out the size of my adversary's legal staff. He said they'd need a very large retainer to make sure they wouldn't come out empty handed if we didn't succeed. "You'd be better off with another firm," he said. "We are not the proper one for your kind of case. Especially in the situation you find yourself in."

That was my second failure to find counsel although I have another scheduled interview for tomorrow. If that one also fails, I'm in trouble. Those three had been the ones I chose out of six I originally contacted by phone. Time was running out fast.

It was time to see Maxine and I drove to my in-laws in South Miami. I had visited Maxine every night since I arrived and kept her informed of my efforts to find counsel. She was mildly disappointed, but showed no particular interest in my search. Maxine's condition hadn't changed. No signs of improvement or any indication of coming out of the mild depression she was in. Dinner was ready, the maid informed us, and we all got together in the dining room where my brother-in-law and wife were already waiting.

We spoke of everything but the matter at hand. They were people who took their time to dine, something that made possible to entertain casually the most difficult kind of issues. One, my flight to New York to escort my parents to their new residence, something Maxine hated to listen to. The conversation turned then to the selling of the home in New York and my permanent move to Miami. Maxine showed a mild interest and expressed her wish to go back once again to select some pieces she wanted to bring down to Florida. After dessert and coffee, I excused myself, adducing the following day's heavy schedule. I took Maxine with me to the door and reassured her everything was going to be okay. That we'd prevail. I kissed her goodnight and drove back to the Key.

Jimenez was in town and we got together at ten for breakfast. He loved the restaurant at the Sonesta Beach Hotel and we usually got together there for eggs, bacon and café con leche; not to mention babe watching. Americanas — as he called them — with brief bikinis and oversized busts. Jimenez loved gossip and it was the first theme of the conversation. "Had you had any?" he'd ask me. He'd tell me about his mistress' latest demands, hiding her from his wife and other irrelevant issues. Once the subject was exhausted, we moved to the business at hand and my predictions for the future. We're doing great,

I informed him and explained how we were introducing our products at an incredible speed; three vegetable containers for Miami, while holding at two in New York. Fantastic, he said patting my back.

As we departed the restaurant, Jimenez inquired about my immediate plans. I shared with him the problem I was having finding counsel. He listened carefully and reminded me of the two lawyers we consulted here in Miami for our New York distribution deal. "I have used them for many other things. You never know," he suggested, and went on to discuss other topics.

My search for counsel continued. That afternoon, at four, I visited my third group of lawyers at an impressive building on Brickell. The partner I talked to made a number of observations very similar to what I've heard from the other firms. Nevertheless, he said they could do it for a combination of a large retainer, a somewhat adjusted hourly rate and a thirty percent contingency fee, in other words a holdup. I said I'd think about it and abandoned the premises before they could take me hostage.

It was obvious the latest esquire was a vampire. It was also obvious, the only answer to my quagmire was to keep looking for a more suitable group among the three or four firms I had originally discarded. Leaving the building, I called a friend and invited him to play tennis. I needed to vent my frustration and there was no better alternative than ripping balls as hard as I could.

A HOME FOR A NURSING HOME

Back in New York I found mother putting together the last boxes before her move. Margarita, her friend, was there, but father was downstairs sitting in the living room. The mood was somber. Mother was deeply moved and tears came to her eyes when I appeared at her bedroom door. She left what she was doing; I moved closer and embraced her.

"It's hard," she said, "leaving home knowing there is no coming back."

"Mima, don't be hard on yourself. This passage is unfortunate, but inevitable. Our home isn't what it used to be. Look around you; it's a huge empty house. It isn't what it used to be. The residence is very nice. You'll get used to it. I am sure you will."

Mother turned around and continued putting things in a box.

"Damned time," she said. "It doesn't forgive. I wish we had died in our sleep."

"You and dad might have another twenty wonderful years together. You never know."

"Twenty years? Don't kid yourself. I know the residence is nice," she said, "but it is a holding pen; like cattle kept alive till the slaughter."

"Mima," I said holding her tightly. "I know this is a bad time to be philosophical, but there is no intelligent explanation for all this; it's absurd. But to put it all in perspective, we all are on a queue. I'm behind you, you know that. It's a race to the abyss," I responded trying to alleviate her sorrow.

"Quite a mystery, isn't it?" she said with her eyes full of tears. "I look back and I can't find a legitimate reason for coming into this world other than to have you. What's the idea besides passing on the seed?"

"Well, if you ask me, I'm happy you two came before me. I'm here!" We both laughed heartily.

"It is like a social contract," she added. "A very expensive one indeed."

I left mother and went to my study; two dozen messages waiting to be answered. I quickly discarded most of them. Julie had left one asking me to call her the minute I got in. And I did.

"Hey! ... Two hours ago . . . Pipo y Mima are moving tomorrow . . . Are you coming all the way here? ... It would really make it easier than going by myself, just the three of us . . . Okay, thank you. Be here at eleven. How's that? ... What about tonight? ... Burt's partners? Not really. I have had enough of lawyers . . . I'll wait for you tomorrow.

The drive to the residence was made tolerable by Julie's entertaining flair. She joked with my parents about having a new nest, a new life all over again. Living by themselves, away from the watching eyes of their nosy, all controlling son. If the atmosphere during the ride was jovial, things became conspicuously quiet the moment we arrived at the residence. Fortunately the administrator had assigned us a porter to help with the boxes and in no time Julie and I were hanging my parents clothing in their bedroom closet, organizing the kitchen utensils and putting some cherished supplies in the kitchen cabinets.

Moments later, having tested their new bed, sat on the couch, turned on the TV and set their preferred Spanish channel, the four of us went downstairs to test the culinary expertise of the kitchen. It had been prearranged. We sat at the administrator's table; a no-nonsense forty-something woman who graciously had invited us to a welcome meal. If we were grateful for her invitation, we used the opportunity to explore the menu, taste as many entrees as possible and finally gave the joint a passing grade. Once the desserts were consumed, Julie and I walked my parents to the elevators. A tough moment, to say the least. I hugged and kissed them both and Julie did the same. The elevator door opened and they went in. We knew this was huge. Mother gave me a long, lasting look and I blew them a kiss as the doors closed shut.

"It wasn't too bad," Julie said as I drove away from the residence.

"Mother is tough."

"I admire her. I don't think I'd cage myself for Burt if something happens to him."

"What about me?" I asked her. Julie didn't answer.

LIFE IS A YO-YO

I returned to Miami the following afternoon. It was dark and windy. When we finally landed, I got my car at the parking garage and drove to see Maxine at her brother's home. A four car collision made twenty-five minute drive an hour and a half long. I blamed myself for not having gone directly to the Key, and paid dearly for my obstinacy.

Matilde, my in-law's maid, greeted and told me Maxine was in her room. "She has been rather quiet," she said. "Not getting out of the bedroom during the day, just at night, for dinner and to watch television with her brother in the family room."

Maxine was in bed watching TV. She looked at me, but didn't react. I approached and kissed her forehead.

"How have you been? Why are you watching television here and not in the family room?

"Don't start bugging me!" she retorted slowly, dragging the words one after the other. "You got here and already you're ordering me, telling me what to do," she continued with some difficulty.

"I took Mima y Pipo to the residence yesterday," I said trying to change the subject.

"You told me last night."

"Wouldn't you like to hear about the place? It's very nice."

"No, I don't. I think you... just got rid of them. They are no longer useful and you're storing them away. That's what you do with everyone around you when you can't use them anymore."

"You know that's not true," I chided her.

"This is why I don't want to move anywhere. I want to stay here. I don't want you to put me away as you did with them."

"What are you talking about? You knew very well Pipo's condition. You, yourself said it. That the house was too big for them."

"I never mentioned a residence. I said, bring them down here, where we could get a person to help them. Not to put them away as if they were a set of used furniture."

My in-laws arrived at about seven and found me in the backyard reading a glossy European magazine. Maxine's brother invited me to walk to the border of the canal at the end of the garden

"Are you staying for dinner?" he asked me.

"If you insist," I responded, and added. "What's your take of the situation?"

"It hasn't changed much. Still, she continues with her speech impediments. Looking for words, garbling many of them, but she manages to communicate all right."

"She got very upset when I mentioned Pipo and Mima's move to the residence. Is she still taking the antidepressants?"

"Of course. She seems more animated, but refuses to go out. We invite her to go with us to a restaurant, or visit a friend, but she insists on staying home. In the dark. Watching television. There is nothing we can do."

"I'm looking for a place to move permanently. I told her but she refuses even to consider leaving your home."

"She said that to me too and I told her she can live with us as long as she wants. Obviously, I reminded her, her place is with you, but she didn't want to hear. She can't accept that you put your parents away."

The sun was barely above the horizon when I decided to walk the beach. The new apartment wasn't on the water, but close enough to hit a trail to the park and across to the beach. The ocean was calm and the shore deserted. I only wanted to relax, take a walk with a blank mind, breathing the clean breeze from the ocean. Ten minutes, a bend in the shoreline and, as if by magic, the lighthouse presented itself in the distance. But even that wasn't sufficient to ease my angst. My mind had begun its habitual exercise, the constant duel of my positive nature versus the multitude of unfinished problems that weighted on me. No matter how hard I tried, I couldn't abstract myself from reality; after four years of futile litigation, I was back to where I started. An immensely complicated case, no lawyers and less than ten days to find new ones.

A fast walk back to my apartment, a shower, a light lunch, an espresso and I drove again to Brickell to visit the last firm of the original eight I had researched. The offices were smaller, but the result was very similar. "We were retained by Federated a year ago to defend a case.... it wouldn't be ethical for us to move against them now."

Ethical? I asked myself going down in the elevator. What the heck. They were all ambulance chasers no matter their real estate location.

I left for Costa Rica the following day but not before calling Jimenez and letting him know my frustration searching for new lawyers. He suggested I contact his legal firm and offered to initiate a call to introduce me. I asked him about their hourly rates and he said they'd accommodate me, if for nothing else, to keep him happy. His lawyers handle his coffee business and they were not going to jeopardize the account and not treat me fairly.

The flight to San Jose was full and noisy. Fortunately the company's chauffeur was waiting for me at the airport.

It was a cool evening in San Jose and I felt the urge to hit the town. I didn't have any friends to speak of, but I had made up my mind not to eat alone if I could help it, and it was about seven something when I decided to call Anais. Anais seemed detached on the phone. She asked me how long had I been in town and, not waiting for my reply, said she was going to be extremely busy for the next four days. I didn't ask why and she didn't offer an explanation. We didn't say another word and I hung up.

The morning light and the persistent crowing of a rooster rehearsing for the big event --- his daily mounting of every hen in the pen --- was a signal it was time to get up. Somehow the light and the cock made me feel in an expansive mood. I hailed a taxi and went to the tennis club for breakfast. I wanted to pamper myself after the pounding I was getting on all fronts. Breakfast over, I moved on to the warehouse where I gave the foreman the final instructions for an extra container of cassava I wanted for dumping in the Florida market.

I called the old man in Orlando for our daily chat --- who informed me he had talked to his lawyers --- and that they were expecting my call. "I gave them a bird's eye view of your situation," Jimenez said, "and they are willing to help as much as they can." Thanks, I told him and mentioned I was returning to Miami in two days. Perhaps I could see him before his trip back, but he explained he was taking two of his grandchildren to Disney and would fly directly to Costa Rica afterwards.

Back in Miami I went directly from the airport to visit Maxine at my in-laws. I found her watching a program about celebrities in Hollywood. She didn't react when she saw me. I asked her how she was, and she just gave me a sign she was doing so-so.

"Any pains, aches, anything?" I asked her.

"No," she simply said pointing to Sean Connery on the screen.

"Yeah, he is getting older. Where is everybody else?" I asked her.

"Coming soon," she said flatly.

My in-laws arrived and dinner was promptly served. The maid had cooked a delightful arroz con pollo and we devoured it as if we had been fasting for a week. After coffee, my brother-in-law and I retired to his office and discussed Maxine's condition.

"Nothing new," he said. "Her problem communicating is acute, although she manages to say what she wants. You saw her, she can't walk unassisted, but the maid takes good care of her and watches while she takes a bath. If you ask me, she's doing fine under the circumstances."

"I'm getting rid of New York once and for all," I told him. "My business is here, my court case and all my travels to Central America originate here. I have a place to stay with Julie in New York, if I want to. But before I close and sell the house, I'd like Maxine to come with me if she can and decide what she wants to keep."

"I doubt she can make the trip. Not in the condition she's in.

Before I left, I went back to the family room where Maxine was sitting — next to her sister-in-law — watching a soap on one of the local channels. I sat next to her and mentioned the flight to New York and the need for her decide what to bring down here or discard altogether.

"Where are you moving to?" she asked me with some effort.

"I don't know yet, but you can't live here the rest of your life."

"I won't move to the Key," she said referring to Key Biscayne.

"Nothing has been decided yet and we will have to move where we can and not where we want."

"A house for sale two blocks away," she said.

"This neighborhood is out of the question. I have to work. I'd spend more time in the car than at the office. But don't worry about those things now. I'm going back to NY in a week or so and I'll let you know what's going on."

NEW SEARCH; NEW BEGINNING

The previous evening's storm was history and the woods and foliage showed their gratitude for the generous downpour. A reddish belt girded the horizon as the sun lifted itself from the ocean. As I walked the deserted coast I couldn't abstract myself from my predicament. The blending of the ocean with my problems made me think of a red tide. No lawyers, a never ending case, Maxine's condition, the need to find a permanent home in Florida, no money for a down payment, the need to rent, another retainer for new lawyers, the disposition of the New York residence. In other words, a task made for a superman. But, as I walked, I kept looking at the ocean and the sun on my left, the sand, the forest on my right and the lighthouse in the distance and I felt happy; perhaps irresponsibly happy to be alive, surrounded by such beauty. If I could keep this, just this, what could go wrong? I asked myself and kept walking.

That afternoon I visited Jimenez' lawyers. I had spoken to one of the partners on two other occasions while we discussed the New York distribution contract, but this was different. Their office was humble by the other firms' standards. Nevertheless it was presentable; well-appointed might be a better word to describe it. A receptionist escorted me to the conference room. I sat with Bob Sherman, a partner, who asked me to relate in detail my situation. And I did.

Fifteen minutes later and after a few short interruptions, I concluded my presentation.

"It is a complicated case. I'd have to read the complaint to fully comprehend the legal approach the previous lawyers followed," he said and finished in a single gulp the rest of the coffee in his large metal cup. "Frankly, if it wasn't for Jimenez, who has been a customer for the last fifteen years, we wouldn't involve ourselves at this late stage. I won't offer anything yet, but let me read the complaint and we'll go from there," Sherman concluded.

"We only have three days left of the thirty the Judge gave me to find new counsel."

"We can always ask for an extension. How many years since you filed suit?"

"Almost five," I responded.

"Um, well anyway. I'll tell you what we require should we take the case. Jimenez told me you're strapped financially. We usually require a thirty thousand dollar retainer to take a new case. But since you're working for Jimenez and he asked us as a personal favor to help you, we will require twenty. Could you get that kind of money?"

"I don't know, but I'll try."

"Obviously, we will work it out as a contingency case since you can't afford our rates. We charge four hundred an hour."

I curled in my chair, but didn't say a word.

"I'll read the complaint," he continued, "talk to my partners and I'll be back to you before the weekend," Sherman concluded, as he stood up, shook my hand and led me to their office entrance.

That evening I placed a call to Julie. She was home alone and we had time to discuss my situation thoroughly. I described my contact with the lawyers and then went on to speak about a couple of apartments I had visited at the beach.

"First tell me about the apartments," she insisted.

"Two are at my old building. A very similar one to mine, one story up and another one on the side. It would be better if you come and see them yourself. It's your money."

"Which one do you like? She asked me.

"It isn't a matter of what I like. One is fifty thousand more than the other," I responded.

"Ok! We will decide it together. I won't be able to fly down until Friday evening. I'm not telling Burt what my visit is about. He won't be involved in the purchase. Could you pick me up?"

"What kind of question is that?"

"Let's talk about the new lawyers. How much do they want?"

"Twenty thousand. They're doing me a favor because of Jimenez."

"Did you explain your situation? In other words, ask for a reduction?"

"Yes Mom! That's the lean version of their retainer."

"Tell the realtor to meet us Saturday morning at The Towers. I'll see you Friday night. I'm sure we'll be talking before then. Are you happy?"

"Only when I walk the beach or talk to you."

Thursday, Roberta and I got together for lunch at her favorite hangout, the Beachcomber on Key Biscayne. I arrived ten minutes late on my bike and found her drinking an imported beer. As a routine, we discussed business first. She said I was going to need three people to replace her and I belittled her complaints with a kiss on her cheek and a promise I'd find four, not three, to do her work. But, she would have to supervise them, I insisted.

The waiter finally got to us and took our orders; "dos BLTs, and dos cervezas por favor," she said in her commanding Spanish.

"I love this place," Roberta said taking a deep breath, inhaling the cooling breeze of the ocean. How is the apartment you are in?" she asked me.

"It's nice when I'm alone. But every once in while I have people from Costa Rica, or Jimenez' friends who crash for a few days, a week now and then. I don't like that. I'm looking for a new place for Maxine and me."

"How is she doing?" Roberta asked me.

"The same. I don't want to talk about it."

"You haven't changed your mind about seeing the Brujo, have you?"

"No, I have not. What else could happen that hasn't happened already?"

"You never know. Your health, for one."

"The Brujo said you will be in good health, fully aware, so you can observe everything that happens to you and around you, but unable to do anything about it. Like a bystander. Wasn't that what he said? You were there."

"Yes, those were more or less the words he used. And you're living it. It gives me the creeps."

Back at home, the telephone rang, and it was Sherman's secretary. She asked me to hold the line and a minute after, my new lawyer got on the line.

"Alexander, I read the complaint and discussed it with my partners. They were not very enthusiastic about it, but I insisted. I reminded them Jimenez is a good client and they accepted it. I can see there are a number of outstanding issues, something I didn't consider when we talked about the retainer. But since I gave you a number, I'll keep my word. Having said that, the minute we get your check, we'll get rolling."

"I said it might take a few days, but I'll handle it." I added "thanks." I had new lawyers. Now it was a matter of putting the twenty thousand together.

The plane from New York came on time, for a change, and I was waiting for Julie with open arms. She was the first one to come out of the plane; the obvious convenience of flying first class. We embraced and went directly to get my car. After the regular talk about crowding, delays, etc. we settled in and began talking about other stuff. Where to go for dinner? La Choza, she immediately replied. And to The Hut we went.

La Choza I liked because of its convenience. Half a mile from home in Key Biscayne, continental and Cuban food, good wines, but above all, a pair of old Cuban troubadours who sang the songs of my high school days in Havana. There was a hitch, sometimes they would forget a word or two, but they would improvise a guttural sound, at times better than the word itself. After so many years frequenting the place, the pair knew me well and I'd tip them generously. Of course, I'd prep them beforehand, and they would sing the songs I liked most. Julie knew them well, but disliked the idea of them doing my dirty work. Nevertheless, the minute we sat, the troubadours moved away from the table they were entertaining, walked in our direction and began singing "Tu Me Acostumbraste," roughly "You Got Me Used to It". Julie immediately reacted.

"You told them to sing it, didn't you?"

"No! I did not."

"You know I love the song, how it sounds and what it implies, but I hate it because it is your hymn. I'd hate to count the number of women you have brought to this place and forced to hear it."

"Me, force anyone? Never!"

"Wasn't it here where the husband of an old tryst, listening to that song, ordered the Chateau d'Yquem?"

"A three hundred dollar bottle, I'll never forget."

"I'm going to order the wine myself," she said decidedly.

Morning came early. We rolled up in bed and engaged in another round of sex. Julie was passionate and I played a submissive role letting her take the initiative. And it was fun, as it always was when the two of us had nothing bigger on our minds than the pleasures we could give each other.

"It's ten," she said. "We have an appointment at eleven, don't we?

And at eleven sharp, we met the realtor in the lobby of my old building. I introduced the woman to Julie and the three of us went up to 7B, an apartment one floor above the one I used to own.

"The owner is anxious to sell. You know the story, a marital split. That's why the price is so reasonable," the realtor said.

"Seven hundred is not reasonable," Julie responded.

"Alexander sold his almost a year ago for six something, didn't he? The realtor rejoined.

"Is there any way of getting it down a hundred thousand?" Julie inquired.

"Everything is possible. Will she take it is a different story," the realtor added. "You haven't seen the other apartment on the north side of the building. It's cheaper."

"This is the one I want and that's my offer. I'll give you a ten percent deposit. But I won't pay a penny more than six hundred thousand. I'm not kidding. Tell your client we can close in three weeks. She won't have to wait two months to get her money."

Julie got her checkbook and wrote a check for sixty thousand and gave it to the realtor. I remained perplexed.

"I'm not promising she'll take it, but it's an offer and it's my job to pass it along," were the last words the realtor said as we parted and walked to our cars.

"You're a tough negotiator. I've never seen you make a deal before," I told Julie as I drove out of The Towers compound.

"I'm sorry for that woman. If the story the realtor told us is true, she needs every penny she can get. Almost sixty years old, thirty five year marriage and being abandoned for a younger woman. Gosh! That's terrible. I feel sorry for her."

"Why didn't you see the other apartment?"

"I always liked your apartment. I have good memories of this building, of an apartment like that. Owning it makes me feel part of the magic. Perhaps it's foolish of me. But that's the way I am. The last of the romantics. Or one of the last. You might be the other one if there are two."

That evening, going home after dinner, we stopped at Sundays at the end of the causeway just at the entrance to the Key. The music sounded great and the night was inviting. A Reggae band was playing and a multitude of blacks were dancing.

"Do you mind?" I asked her, in case she didn't want to feel in the minority.

"Me? Mind?" Don't you remember Ocho Rios? Follow that music, you told the driver and we ended up in a magical spot. People looked at us as if we were extraterrestrials. No one could surmise how we swayed and enjoyed their music as much as they did. Little did they know there was a Cuban ghost dancing among them."

Julie and I danced for an hour and as we left the venue, before we got to the car, spotted a group of people catching shrimp on a bridge ahead of us and stopped to share the experience. The tide was rising, the moon full and the temperature cool; why not? We approached the group and spent the next half hour chatting with the fishermen, inspecting the catch and making plans to eat "camarones al ajillo," garlic shrimp as Julie called it, the next day at home.

"What would it be, walk the beach or bike the trails?" I asked Julie as I prepared a pot of espresso the following morning.

"Biking will do. I haven't done it in a while. But before we do anything let's get business out of the way." Julie went to her pocketbook and took her checkbook out. "I want you to understand this is a loan, not charity. I don't want you to feel bad taking it. This is a temporary thing and I am convinced you'll succeed at the end. I know what I'm doing."

Julie got two checks and signed them. "Here, I'm giving you two blank checks in case you need to split the retainer or need money for something else. I don't care what. There is a limit. Thirty thousand. Your lawyers asked for twenty as a retainer. You have another ten, in case you need it. There is one condition; I don't want to talk about it."

I couldn't utter a sound. I embraced Julie; my eyes wet. I was grateful for her gesture, but felt terribly bad about myself. Where have I ended? What has happened to me that I needed to take money from others, when all my life, I've been a giver not a taker. Even in the direst circumstances, I had been able to fend for myself, with no help from anyone.

"We can stop at the Oasis and have some pastelitos or croquettes or something for breakfast. What do you think?" Julie asked me.

And we biked directly to the Oasis, ate pastelitos fresh out of the oven, drank another espresso and biked through the woods to the end of the Key. We walked our bikes to the lighthouse, sat on the boulders and watched a multitude of bathers bask their bodies under the burning sun. I felt whole, really good and I stretched out my hand and held Julie's. And as on so many other countless occasions, I didn't know who to thank for my Julie, my luck and for being alive and healthy. And I thanked the universe, my default benefactor, even if I stood submerged in this awful swamp my life seemed to be in.

A secretary ushered me to a conference room where Sherman was waiting. He rose gently and introduced me to a younger man, an associate, George, he said his name was, who'd help him in our case. I gave him my check for the retainer and told him he could deposit it the next day. He had started working that morning, he said, and his associate had a conference with the Judge's clerk. He related a number of outstanding issues and informed me he had a conversation with my old lawyers in New York. They were gracious, Sherman said, and offered to mail all the paper work related to our case. They asked me for a consideration in case we win, and I told them it'd be discussed at the appropriate time. I told Sherman, they didn't deserve anything, but it was a matter between them.

Sherman said the very first thing he would do is to talk to the lawyers from the other side and schedule the Alsace's chairman deposition. They'd like to take yours also; I assume you're ready, he said with a smile. From now on, George, he said, referring to his assistant, will call whenever we need information from you. The meeting was over; George accompanied me to the lobby; we shook hands and I left. I had lawyers; my fight would go on!

I drove back to my apartment and found two messages on my answering machine. The first one from the realtor; her client reluctantly accepted the offer and would like to close as soon as possible. Fantastic! I got my apartment. The second one was from Julie; any news from the realtor? I called her at home. Burt answered. We talked briefly and I asked him to put Julie on. She said she could talk freely. I told her, you've got an apartment in Key Biscayne. Good, she responded. I also told her I had deposited one of the checks for twenty thousand. She didn't react, but said she'd do the closing from New York. I thanked her again for all the things she was doing for me. She dismissed my gratitude with a chuckle and told me to get ready to move my things down to Florida. Yes mom! I said, and hung up.

A bit after eight and hungry, I went to the fridge, got a rib-eye steak, broiled it, an avocado salad, a baguette, my bottle of *vino de la casa*, and had the most delightful dinner on my terrace, with a most enchanting companion, myself. If alone, my solitude allowed me time to meditate and ponder about life and how chance and circumstance shape our responses to our most excruciating problems. I marveled at my luck, the way things happen, how everything conspires against you and how all of a sudden, the clouds dissipate, the chips fall into place and you have another go at it. The mystery of chance. Que sera, sera!

ON THE BEACH AGAIN

Sandals, shorts, a sweat shirt and back to the beach. My walk to the light-house, alone, with no one in sight was as peaceful and reassuring as the sun rising on the horizon. I had a new lift, but quite a few unsettled issues. The home in New York; sell it or give it back to the bank. Sell it was the best bet, I concluded. The bank won't give a damn about getting the best price. The other worry; the move to Florida. A fourteen room home full of everything you could think of. Just to vacate the house and move furniture and thou-sands of books would entail planning and a huge expense. I could sell some pieces to lessen the cost. But I hated the thought; some were dear to me. The biggest problem was my library; five thousand books weighed seven, eight tons, perhaps more.

I finally got to the lighthouse and stood in front of it. Hey! Do you see me now? Blink if you do. Yes, I spoke to the lighthouse as if she could listen. I'm back. I am as resourceful and stoic as you are; I think, or I hope, or I like to believe. I'll come around again and again. You know me; I can resist anything but temptation. Okay, I know it is Oscar's, but I couldn't resist.

I sat among the rocks, took a long look at the ocean and the fiery ball rising in the distance. We were alone again; me, the sun, the lighthouse and another continent out there, three thousand miles of water away. Close to shore, pelicans were having a feast. Me? My heart was in so many places; so many dreams waiting to be realized. Time is my obsession and my own quan-dary. I beg for it. Time and peace is all I always wanted; just to take a rest, to relax a little longer. But if time is my quandary, my curse is being conscious. Aware of life's nuances, of circumstances that shape my decisions against my wishes and often my better judgment. Fortunately, I am a dreamer, some might say a delusional dreamer. I knew what I wanted and I went for it regardless, always sure I'd rise, like that sun on the horizon; I'll rise.

My beach walks, my chats with my lighthouse, my trips to Costa Rica, the selling of my New York property, all that took time, and time passed. It was two months since I retained new lawyers and the house was sold; the closing to take place in a week or so. I sold some furniture, trucked some south, downsized my library, and brought down to Florida the remains of a once enchanted home. Maxine had refused to travel north, but insisted on certain pieces, and in some confused way, demanded I bring them down. And I did. My new apartment at the Key looked very much like the previous one, with some dear pieces of my original home and thousands of books I had refused to surrender.

I flew to New York and stayed at Julie's. She wasn't home, but had left me her keys with the concierge. Going up to her apartment was a treat. I'd use her key at the elevator and once at the penthouse, the door opened and I stepped straight into her apartment; a foyer first and the spacious living room next. I walked to the guest room, changed quickly and went jogging on Riverside. It was about five and the sun had begun its precipitous descent behind the Palisades, on the Jersey side of the river. A mile or two each way, I was ready for a cocktail and met Julie at the concessionaire overlooking the boat moorings. We sat and chatted until the last vestige of sunlight dissipated. The colorful bulbs lighted up. Julie then called Burt and he joined us for dinner and one of our never-ending conversations past midnight.

The next morning at eleven I went to my New York bank after my home closing. My banker was so happy getting some money back from a non-performing loan, he offered a preferential mortgage to my buyer. "Alex," he said, "you know I like you. Nevertheless it's my duty as the bank Vice-President to remind you, after this eight hundred thousand is credited to your balance, you still owe the bank, seven million. We haven't asked our lawyers to go after you, but I don't promise we won't. We have been patiently waiting for a prompt resolution to your case. How long now? Four, five years? God forbid you lose. I'll lose my job."

Poor thing! The trembling VP was afraid of losing his job; I had lost everything. I remembered our long lunches at fancy restaurants while my business grew and he shrewdly demanded all the collateral I could come up with. How his diligence changed once my prospects went south and it was obvious the problems with the Alsace were real and perhaps insurmountable. We went from a great restaurant in mid-Manhattan to a rushed sandwich in his office, demanding results. Life!

MAXINE & THE ALSACE

A good chunk — twenty five years of my life — went with the selling of my home. It was a period that encapsulated the beautiful years of my youth, the success of my early businesses and the end of my life as I knew it. I remembered fondly, never ending dinners with friends, Christmas celebrations with family, movies in the garden, and dunks in the pool after partying into the wee hours of the morning. But looking back, putting everything in perspective, the loss of each and every one of my properties had a different effect on my persona. I surrendered the Key Biscayne apartment without hesitation. It was a temporary stopgap, I thought; something needed to be done while waiting for my fight's success. The loss of La Finca, my magical retreat, was traumatic. I could not, in a million years, have thought I'd give up La Finca under any circumstances, but I did. Years of never ending litigation drained my resources dry and forced me to do the unthinkable. And I did. If I had to decide which had the biggest impact, I'd have to settle for La Finca. It was devastating. My home was different. My parents were sick and took refuge in an assisted living community. Maxine was damaged by her malady and her prospects were frightening to say the least. The house meant nothing anymore. I was the last one standing, going strong, watching the debacle that consumed me.

From the home closing, I went to visit my parents. Mother was at peace and Father's health had continued to deteriorate. We talked about my move to Florida and her eyes got moist. I reassured her I wasn't going to disappear, that I would always come to New York, at least once a month if not more. Mother began to weep and I followed her.

Later on, I had lunch with Julie at her office's restaurant hangout in mid-Manhattan. I told her about my visit to my parents and my banker's remark about his job prospects if I lost my case. "You owe the bank fifty thousand; you have a problem. You owe the bank ten million, the bank has a problem."

Julie and I split right after lunch and I hailed a cab to La Guardia. I felt melancholic; I no longer had a base in the city. Great memories. I arrived as a reluctant young refugee thinking it was a temporary adventure, a bend in the road, on my way to bigger and greater things. New York City fed my imagination and in many ways nurtured my never ending curiosity. Sinatra used to sing, "If you make it there, you can make it anywhere." Well, I made it in New York and I was still confident I could make it anywhere.

Back and forth, Miami to New York and back, I arrived at my in-law's home rather late. It was ten and Maxine was in pajamas, in her room, watching TV. We had a brief conversation; I told her about the closing; she wasn't interested. Are you reading your magazines? I asked her. Yes! She insisted. I knew she couldn't, she had lost the ability to read, but that was the way we depicted looking at the pictures, an exercise her neurologist had recommended. I reminded her we had a new home. But she ignored me. Thinking it was late, being tired, I told her I'd come for her tomorrow. But she didn't answer.

Fortunately, even if everything in my private life was in the dumps, my job seemed secured and the vegetable imports from Central America were flourishing. We had two large Anglo and one Hispanic supermarket chains and a great number of independent distributors that required a lot of attention. A secretary was added, and I begged Roberta to extend her supervisory role for another six months. And she did.

The telephone rang early in the morning. George, my new lawyer, was on the line. He told me about the tentative scheduling your deposition first and the Alsace Chairman's the following week. They insisted, George said, on taking your deposition first and we didn't object.

Time passes fast whether we want it to or not. A week and a day later, I was at the Alsace lawyer's office for my deposition together with my two lawyers. Sitting across the table from me, three of their lawyers and a paralegal. A court stenographer sat at the head of the table. The deposition lasted close to three hours with two fifteen minute interruptions. The Alsace's lawyer had a short conference with my team and renewed their offer of ten million. Nothing was decided. But it's something to consider, Sherman said. I answered with the same reasoning I had used with my previous lawyers. Ten million is eight million for me after you take yours. That won't cover my liabilities and I'd be forced to declare bankruptcy. I'd risk losing, if I can't get what I need.

The Alsace Chairman's deposition was scheduled for eleven, but didn't begin for another hour. He had flown from Brazil that morning and his plane was delayed two hours. He excused himself and blamed the airline. He was in a festive mood. He sort of offered to shake hands, but I didn't reciprocate. He repeated he regretted the present situation and assured me it was nothing personal. I asked him about Chloe. He answered she was as busy as ever and that she had asked him to say hello if he saw me.

The deposition was videotaped and went as we expected. The Chairman didn't remember half his actions, read the documents and the highlighted paragraphs we presented and claimed to have forgotten or not to be able to explain what most of them implied. He covered himself saying most of their actions were business decisions, driven more by business plans and economic projections than screwing me and forcing me out of the business. If anything, they wanted to help me.

I sat there seething, containing my ire and contempt for such a fellow and his callous remarks. When asked about Zamora, the Chairman said he had nothing to do with his previous decisions. The Alsace had followed the same practices Zamora had established conducting business with my corporation. They had continued the pricing practice they inherited at the time of the take-over. If Zamora had given me any assurances of compensation in case of a sale, those assurances were superseded by new agreements and contracts signed with the Alsace. They couldn't be responsible for previous commitments.

After the deposition we walked to the garage to get our cars. "The jury will see through his smokescreen," Sherman assured me. "This fellow is as sleek as a serpent. No wonder he's the chairman of a twenty five billion dollar conglomerate. But we'll lick him. You'll see."

Sometime at midday, three days after the deposition, I got a call from George.

"I think I have good news to report," he said.

"I'm dying to hear it."

"The Court Clerk just announced they're finally adding three new, retired judges, to ease the backlog. The good news is we might get the trial sooner than later."

"Is there any hidden risk in getting a judge who isn't familiar with the case?" I asked him.

"You never know. The courts are so overloaded with cases, these judges are like conveyor-belt operators in a meat packing plant. The idea is just to move the docket forward."

"Yes, I'm aware of that."

"We have a difficult case to prove because most of our evidence is in documents. You're aware of that!"

"Yes, I am."

"Some documents," George continued, "are more than ten pages long. You must show them the specific paragraphs, many of which you have unearthed and pinpointed very well. You did a good job."

The conversation with my lawyer lasted twenty minutes or so. All along I had been talking from my terrace, beyond the glass doors, that somehow gave me the privacy I needed to conduct business. I didn't want to give Maxine any reasons to worry. She had been in an amenable mood since I talked her into moving to our new apartment. I had also contracted Yolanda, a Guatemalan caretaker, to assist and keep her company well into the evening hours. But things had continued to deteriorate. Maxine wanted to stay in bed all day long, watching TV and her difficulty with words resulted in an embarrassing frustration that made her visibly unhappy.

Maxine's room was large enough and had a number of conveniences to make her feel comfortable. There was a small balcony she could use and never did, a good size closet and her own private bath. Besides her bed, night table and a large armoire, we added a comfortable armchair and a convertible love seat that could be used by a nurse or Yolanda in case of an overnight stay. A good number of family pictures and one or two of her religious icons were also hung on the walls. All together, with her TV on all day long, she seemed, if not happy, content in her present situation.

On my side, I kept the master bedroom for myself and made the second my study. My books filled up all the available walls and in many cases laid on the floor around my writing table. The room had a good direct view of the ocean — an open ended one — that often made me fantasize about the rest of my life.

The apartment's living room was long and spacious with glass doors that opened to a large terrace, with a majestic view of the Atlantic. A nice size dining area and modernly appointed kitchen — with a convenient break-fast nook — also with a good view of the ocean. A dream place for a man in distress, contemplating ruin in all aspects of his life.

This weekend, Maxine's daily monotony was broken. Mary Helen and Oswald — two of our closest friends from New York — came to visit and Maxine's mood changed favorably.

"Wow! Nice apartment," they said. "Did you win the lotto?" they asked me as they entered the spacious living room.

"You can say that," I responded and quickly turned the conversation to Maxine, coping with her situation and our friends' response to her illness. "I hope you won't press her for answers," I told Mary, "or expect Maxine to talk much. She gets frustrated when she can't articulate her thoughts, embarrassed especially among old friends."

"Not to worry," Mary responded, and the conversation turned to my predicament.

"What has baffled and perhaps frustrated me the most is," I continued, "since Maxine's first signs of her speech impediment, many, if not our very, very close friends, tended to stay away. As if they felt scared, powerless, perhaps embarrassed, by her condition. Now, you've heard me talk about these things before, but being a tireless observer of nature, I tend to compare human behavior in this kind of situation, with that of wild animals in the Serengeti."

"That's quite an extrapolation," Oswald said cautiously. "I see Maxine's condition and some of her friends' reactions and I compare it to a throng of scared zebras or gazelles in an African savanna, watching from a safe distance one of their own, captured, being devoured by a group of lions, in Maxine's case her illness. Boy, better her than me, kind of thought. A natural reaction, I'm sure. And some of her closest friends have kept their distance, inquiring yes, but denying her their presence when she expected them most."

"You know what? It makes sense. You're probably right. People will never admit it, but it is true. We stay away, or hide, perhaps ashamed of being powerless, unable to do anything," Oswald said.

Yolanda came to the terrace and, introducing herself, said Maxine was ready for Mary. I told Yolanda to let Maxine know I'd be ordering out and that we all could have dinner any time they felt hungry. Yolanda escorted Mary to Maxine's bedroom and I invited Oswald to walk to the beach.

The telephone rang and it was George, my lawyer. After a few amenities, he said we had a trial date in two months. A new judge had been assigned, my fourth, if I remembered correctly, and that should be it. The judge was a retiree from New York, moonlighting in Florida. I wonder if that would be good or bad, I asked him. "You never know," he said. "It could go either way".

I called Julie in New York. I mentioned my new trial date and my fourth judge. She said this might be the opportunity I was waiting for. Tricky, all these judges, I responded. "You never know... You're a man of luck," she added. "Things will turn your way, you'll see." She had been with my parents on Saturday, she mentioned, "and mother was complaining you hadn't called for three days, that you were forgetting already. I blamed your work, Maxine's health, the new apartment; you name it." New York is my next stop after Costa Rica, I told her. But Julie reassured me; "believe me, they're alright. Your father's weaker, but we knew it would happen."

Costa Rica was my new oasis, away from everything. I had mountains, a volcano for goodness sake, I didn't have to speak to anyone about my problems and — even if they were forever present in the back of my mind — at least I was distracted by a million other things. That same night, I got together with Jimenez for dinner. He uses any excuse he can find to skip dinner at home and entertain Margarita, his young lover, at his favorite, now mine also, restaurant.

Margarita was in her early thirties. Dark, sculpturally shaped and gracious. She started as a receptionist in Jimenez' office three years ago, quickly got attached to the old man and today is retired, has a beautiful apartment in a prestigious building and her own mini car. So much for upward mobility. Tonight she was in tow with Jimenez, and we all sat at the restaurant's veranda for a succulent paella and two fabulous bottles of vintage Bordeaux wine.

Jimenez and I discussed the distribution in New York briefly and the conversation then quickly moved to my personal problems. I admit I didn't want to discuss them, especially in front of strangers, but nevertheless, politely sometimes, defensively others, I skipped the first few questions and the chat turned to my new lawyers. I mentioned the coming trial and he offered whatever help I needed. I thanked him, had my espresso, a cognac, gave Margarita a bird's eye view --- kind of talk --- about Miami and New York and resisted her attempt to get me to convince Jimenez to let her visit one or both cities on her own. *We don't shit where we eat,* my alter ego quickly insisted. And I didn't.

Next on the agenda was to call the American Consul who was Anais' boss and one of my original contacts in the country. I had more than one reason to call him, but Anais was high in my mind. I wanted to know if she ever got over the marital situation she was in during my last visit.

I invited the Consul to lunch and we met at his club early that same afternoon. The diplomat was an avid tennis player but insisted on eating first and a game afterwards. We lunched a fresh tuna salad with delicious fresh tomatoes. We topped it all off with a bottle of Pinot Grigio. And of course, he graciously let me pick up the tab.

Wet and semi exhausted --- after two hours of tennis --- we sat at a table to drink lemonade and two piña-coladas. A silly conversation with a fellow from the Embassy went on for a few minutes when Anais showed up with a man at her side. She stopped briefly, surprised perhaps to find me there. The Consul shook hands with the fellow and said, "Long time no see." Anais, addressing me, said hello and just introduced her escort. "This is Robert," she said to me and "This is Alex," she said to him. I shook hands with Robert and they quickly continued on to the courts.

"That's Anais' husband," the Consul said. "They are trying a reconciliation. He left her for another woman, but she continues to be in love with him. He travels a lot, you know, a sailor with a woman in each port. Well, something like that."

"Handsome man," I added.

"Yes, he is. And a great talker. Give him five minutes, he'll have you in his pocket."

"I'm flying back to New York tomorrow," I said, "but I'll be coming back in three weeks or so. I hope you give me a heads up if you see any business opportunity worth pursuing. I won't divulge my source."

SHARING THE PAIN

My frequent trips to Costa Rica and New York had become a real nuisance; too frequent and troublesome to be enjoyable. This flight returning to Miami was no exception. Rushing to the airport, I got news that Julie had called from New York and wanted me to contact her as soon as I could. The airport was crowded. The telephone lines were long. What could have happened that couldn't wait another three hours? I asked myself. I checked in, took my seat on the plane --- got my book of Pirandello's plays --- ordered a scotch and had a most pleasant flight to South Florida that I could remember.

In Miami, I was one of the first to deplane, a long walk to a familiar customs officer, a stamp on the passport and I was back in familiar territory. I went to the American Airlines Sky Club and placed a call to Julie.

"Don't have good news to tell you," Julie said. "Mima had a stroke. She's paralyzed on the left side. But she'll survive. It happened this morning about eleven. The home took her to the hospital and called me. I saw her, she's doing fine. I arranged for your father to be transferred to another section of the facility for the time being."

"I just got back. Do you mind if I go tomorrow midday?"

"Take your time," she said reassuringly. "I'll handle it."

Alex, you better start believing in guardian angels, my alter ego insisted. *Our Julie is precious. Imagine this kind of situation without her in New York?*

I walked out of the terminal, in the direction of the parking lot, completely immersed in my thoughts. Cars stopped, drivers blew their horns, yelled at me for jaywalking. The realization that the deluge hadn't stopped overwhelmed me. Mother's stroke was another debilitating blow; not a clean outcome, but another lengthy, messy situation needing special attention. My parents in New York, Maxine in Florida, my Alsace suit languishing in court. Welcome back to Florida.

I entered Maxine's room and kissed her forehead. She looked good, with a nice dress, eating a peach yogurt. I didn't mention Mima's stroke and talked to her briefly about my time in Costa Rica. That I needed to fly to New York to do some business. I asked Yolanda to come outside and explained the urgency to go to New York. She said it was alright with her, but she needed a day to go home. I said okay, and my trip to the babel was postponed for another day.

Julie was at La Guardia waiting for me. We embraced and ran for the car.

"I'm sorry you're going through all this, but I'm sure you're used to it," Julie said with a resigned smile on her face.

"I thought Maxine would suffer it first, but not Mima. She looked so healthy."

"I took the liberty to transfer her to Mount Sinai. It is closer to my home. A walk or a bike ride through Central Park and I'm there. It will be easier for you too when you come to visit her. She will be at the hospital at least two weeks, perhaps three, and then moved to a rehab unit. Fortunately there is one at the hospital."

"How about dad?" I asked Julie.

"Well, they moved him to a full care unit in their complex. He was a bit lost, nervous, wondering about her, but okay. We'll go to visit him after we see Mima."

Mother wasn't very forthcoming when we entered her room at the hospital. She still was under stress; couldn't speak, but somehow she used her eyes to show she was happy to see me. I kissed her forehead and embraced her as well I could. I did talk about her positive prognosis, how lucky we were to have Julie with us, gave her news of father being in good hands and that I was going to bring him to visit her. All in all, an exercise in stoicism wearing thin as more and more problems piled up around me.

An attendant came with dinner; the usual bland stuff the sick are compelled to ingest. She said she would like to clean Mima up a bit. Having been there for a while, I used the opportunity to excuse ourselves for leaving. I told mother Julie and I were going directly to visit Pipo. Mother couldn't talk, but I could see in her eyes she understood and urged me to go; even in her dire state she couldn't stop worrying about her old mate. I kissed and reassured her once again that I'd be back and was on top of the situation. Then, with Julie in tow, I left the room to complete the second stage of my filial mission.

"It's a never-ending struggle, isn't it?" I asked Julie.

"Well, it ends, but not when we want it to end. Perhaps in the grave, with our own death," she responded.

"You mean there is no free will?"

"Only an ingrate, heartless fool, or an insane, sick person would abandon its dear ones."

"Did you watch Mima's reaction when I told her we were going to see Pipo? It was clear she wanted me to go. For her, he's more important than herself. For us, it is a chain. They do the early twenty years for us, now is our time to do the last twenty for them. It seems as if we're repaying a debt."

For the next few days I'd go to the residence, pick Father up and take him to the hospital to spend the afternoon with Mother. I'd leave him there for two or three hours, instruct the nurses about his condition, and go to do errands related to my business. Afterwards, I'd go to Julie's and go jogging or biking in Riverside Park. No doubt, even under tremendous pressure, I was lucky enough to escape, if briefly, from my calamitous life.

That night Burt and Julie had two couples for dinner. I didn't feel like entertaining anyone and wanted to excuse myself, but Julie insisted; they arrived promptly at seven. Anglos, I said to myself, no manners; why so punctual? Burt introduced me as a dear friend. One of the guys said he was a lawyer and his wife an account executive at Julie's magazine. The other couple were accountants, Burt said. 'Number crunchers,' I ad-libbed. And the woman introduced herself as Julie's friend from college, although younger, she promptly added. We all laughed and moved to the terrace for cocktails.

It was another gorgeous evening in New York. The sun on its way down, hiding behind the Palisades; a reddish tint colored the faintly blue sky and the tide was emptying the Hudson out into the ocean. I was present, but perhaps unconsciously, drifted to a corner of the terrace. My mind was on the beauty of my surroundings. I loved it. How many times had I found myself high on beauty with my feet nailed to the ground. High and low as if it was the same. A strange mood that helped me brush aside everything but the beauty of the moment.

"Alex," Jane, Julie's co-worker said coming closer to me. "I have heard a lot about you."

"Good things, I hope."

"Julie told me you write screenplays."

"Well, I dabble, perhaps is the word. I haven't been able to sell one."

"I'm a playwright."

"I know," I responded. "Julie has mentioned you quite often."

"Off, Off Broadway, but I had two plays produced in the last five years."

"That's fantastic! I envy you."

"I suffered a lot of rejections before I got the first one produced. I'm still waiting for someone to take one Off Broadway."

"Well, you have a track record established. I'm sure it won't be long."

"I know how difficult it is to have a movie produced," Jane continued. "Julie says she likes your stuff and it is only a matter of time before one is taken to the screen."

"She's very generous. I am from the old school, you know. I like things to develop. People seem to have lost their patience. Or perhaps I see things differently, have a different sensibility, or my scripts just suck."

"She says you don't like Hitchcock."

"Well, not exactly. I think he was a great director, but I think he has influenced cinema in the wrong way with his formula."

"Meaning?"

"This is what's going to happen. Now watch it, kind of thing. There is no movie today that you don't know its outcome in the first ten minutes. Perhaps I'm exaggerating a bit.

"We moved to the dining room and sat at the table; Burt at one end and Julie at the other. As usual I sat at Julie's right and Jane sat next to me. She seemed intent on continuing the conversation. Tomatoes with fresh mozzarella cheese was the aperitif, a large bowl of pasta, with a delicious Primavera topping, was circulated; next, bread, wine and Manhattan cheese cake — Julie knew I didn't favor Italian — completed the appetizing dinner. I complained I needed espresso and I was promptly assigned to operate the espresso machine. The rest of the group drank what was left of the American stale coffee prepared at the beginning of the evening.

The table was quickly divided in two different camps. Business, at Burt's end; arts and books at Julie's corner.

"Alex, I've told you about Jane not only being a playwright, but also being interested in literary criticism as well. She has or knows something about Darwinism… a new way of exploring writing, something like deconstruction."

And we became involved in a most original and perhaps ingenious conversation. Jane talked about a few small circles in academia that study the rudimentary elements of novels, of characters' personal behavior. The way the genders go about acquiring mates, if unconsciously, insuring the best genes for their offspring. In other words, the universality of human behavior. How writers in general, project themselves through characters and the way they structure their stories. She also discussed our need to write fiction and read it. The need to entertain. In other words, the study of those patterns or mechanisms is what is beginning to be known as literary Darwinism, she concluded.

"Something based on, or a derivative of, Derrida's deconstruction," I offered.

"Perhaps inspired by it," Jane retorted.

Being a crude observer of human nature, I always believed behavior is encoded in our genes. In writing a novel most writers tend to write about what they know best. Regardless of their effort to give characters different attributes, the writer's inner makeup transpires and leaves a detectable pattern, perhaps something like a finger print, in all they do. But there is a universal code. In other words, if we were to practice literary Darwinism, we could unearth similar patterns, like the ones she mentioned, in most of the novels we read.

While she continued her inspired dissertation, I was taken back to my stay in Portugal with Chloe, a memory I cherished and remembered as if it was today. A rainy morning, our drive from Lisbon to Fatima, our conversation, how she described her relationship with her boyfriend and their adventures in the Parisian world of literature. Her man was a writer, even if he sold shoes, or was the owner of several shoe stores. But he wrote literary criticism on the side and belonged to a group of writers which met frequently and Chloe entertained for a while. I was as fascinated with that conversation then, as I am with this one now. An exercise that, if nothing else, helped me put most of my worries away, even if for a brief time.

"You know, all that makes sense," I told Jane. "I once met a woman, in Paris of all places, and had a very similar discussion. Her boyfriend was a literary critic of some sort, and she introduced me to a new way of criticism, artistic detail or something. By what you're saying, even if it seems the art of writing fiction remains as it was a hundred years ago, criticism continues to evolve. Do you belong to a group? Meet playwrights often? What do you do other than writing?" I asked her and the conversation continued, unabated, I don't know for how long.

MIAMI – MAXINE - SANTERIA

Back in Miami I returned a call from my lawyers. "Alex," George say. "We got a call from the Alsace and they want to talk. We know exactly what you want, but I think it'd be a good idea to hear them out. We have nothing to lose. Do you give us permission to talk?" Sure, I said. "We will keep you informed," and he hung up.

Things seemed to be moving a bit again, but I was still disappointed; frustrated is a better word to describe my angst. I knew the Alsace's move was a maneuver. A move to show my lawyers they were willing to settle, that I was the intransigent one. But you never know. They might be able to accomplish what the previous group couldn't. As George said, there is nothing to lose.

Yolanda was roaming around my studio as if waiting for me to finish my conversation. I invited her to sit and asked her about Maxine. She's doing fine, she responded. "It is amazing," she said, all her bodily functions work like clockwork; has a good appetite. But she keeps the television on all day long. Sometimes she thumbs through magazines, trying to read the photo captions, quite often, unsuccessfully."

"The poor thing," Yolanda said. "In a way, although her speech impediment continues, it doesn't stop her from speaking her mind. Her brother came to visit, as he does often, and that made her very happy. A few of her friends called, but she ended up frustrated for not being able to speak her mind; you know it is easier to communicate in person than by phone. She spent most of her time watching TV. Today is an exception. I convinced her," Yolanda continued, "to sit on the balcony and she's been there for at least a half hour."

I entered Maxine's room and walked to the balcony. I kissed her forehead, but she didn't react. I sat next to her and mentioned what Yolanda had told me. I began talking about my trip to New York, but she didn't pay attention to what I was saying other than when I spoke of Pipo and Mima. She asked me, in her own way, how they were doing and why did I insist on keeping them in New York and not bringing them down here. I repeated the many reasons why they are better off there than here, including the economic one, to no avail. She was convinced my decision had some other mischievous reason.

Later that afternoon Ben called to say he had read an article about the Alsace and the problems with their banks. The article detailed a number of conditions the banks demanded in order to roll over five billion in notes due in two months. According to the article, they're complaining about Federated performance in the US and were asking for its CEO's head. All those problems might be a tempest in a tea pot, but they're symptomatic of something bigger going on.

It was about half past six the following morning when I prepared my espresso and drank it watching the sunrise on the horizon. It was cool and I decided to walk the beach. And I did. My round trip to the lighthouse usually took about an hour and today was no exception. Getting back to my apartment, the telephone rang. It was Roberta.

"Alex, just a short call to tell you, the Brujo we met died."

"When did that happen?" I asked her.

"Last night, my friend, the one who introduced me to him, called," Roberta said. "There is going to be a wake tonight with some kind of ceremony. The who's who of the Santeria world is going to be present. I won't miss it for anything. I'm going with my friend. Why don't you come along? I don't know what they'll do but, according to my friend, it's going to be a terrific sendoff with music and all kinds of dancing, you know, the kind they do with certain ceremonies."

I drove to the Little Havana section in Miami about nine that evening. The wake was at the Brujo's own home, the one I had been to, and the streets were jammed with double-parked cars. A policeman turned me away and said there was no parking space available for five or six blocks. Fortunately I met a neighbor peddling two garage spaces at ten dollars apiece. I took one.

The sound of the music was energizing. Bata drums, the ones used in African religious rituals, were rhythmically loud and a crowd of onlookers surrounded the house. I made my way through the worshipers to the living room where the casket laid open, with the Brujo almost in a sitting position, on his white wooden box.

I found Roberta and her friend in an animated conversation with a black woman decked out in white. Roberta's friend and I had never met, but I had heard a lot about her. This was a real coincidence. Because of her, Roberta had met the Brujo the first time. Without her, I'd have never heard of my curse. She introduced us and I thanked her for making possible Roberta's fortuitous encounter with el Brujo.

The rituals being performed by different groups were almost identical. The men banged their drums and several women danced around the casket. One fellow, supposedly a priest — probably another Brujo — circled the coffin with a sort of a wand, doing something similar to what a Catholic priest would do to a casket in a Catholic funeral mass. If alluring, the performances, if you can call it that, lasted far too long and seemed repetitious. I finally decided to cut it short.

After an hour or so, I excused myself with Roberta and friend, and left for home. I had satisfied my curiosity and, in many ways, I had witnessed something unique, at least for me. Not being a believer, I couldn't reckon if the death of the Brujo would affect me one way or another, so I tried to put it away and not let myself be influenced by this development. Believing more in chance than predestination, I decided to forget my foretold scourge and continue my life as I have done ever since I learned about it.

A HALLUCINATING WALK
TO THE LIGHTHOUSE

A new morning, another walk. The ocean was flat and the beach deserted. A few minutes into my walk a seventy-something, slender if energetic man with white hair and leather sandals, came out of the forest on my right and rushed decidedly toward me. If surprised — the park had just opened at seven — I didn't mind the opportunity of talking to or perhaps answering a question for a first time visitor to the park. We said hello and he asked me if he could walk with me to the lighthouse. Somewhat puzzled, I asked him how he knew my walk was to the lighthouse.

"I have watched you walk to the lighthouse often. I have never interrupted you because you seemed immersed in your own thoughts. I hope they are happy ones," he said. "Other people walk with one of those new gadgets, cellphones, listening to who knows what, talk-radio or music. I never see you using one. It seems you're contented being alone with yourself."

"I prefer the solitude of an empty beach," I responded.

"If you ask me, I'd do exactly as you do. This is an ideal stretch to meditate, deal with our inner thoughts."

As we walked, the conversation developed as any other usually does. He expressed interest in my habits, cultural taste and my ancestry having noted my remnant accent. Perhaps flattered by his curiosity, I told him superficially about my interest in the arts and my involvement in business in order to support a family, but above all, my interest in writing. The fellow talked about himself as if talking about a third person, vaguely mentioning his present idleness, a somewhat oblique reference about having been a professor or a preacher perhaps, something magisterial and writing plays. Curious, I inquired about his play-writing and he confidently talked about one or two having been produced Off-Broadway. I thought that was a great coincidence and mentioned the woman I met at Julie's dinner, who had two plays produced Off-Off Broadway. I told him her name but it didn't ring a bell.

"Could you make a living with your plays?" I asked him.

"No, no," he said. "It is more like an avocation. Wanting to say something, sharing an experience with a large audience. I've done that in the past and still love the interaction. What are you writing, a play or a novel?" He asked me.

"It is embarrassing to even mention it. Today everybody has a screenplay in pre-production or a novel in the works."

"Come on, don't be shy. A novel?" he asked.

"I really don't know.... I know it's some sort of theater; theater of the absurd, you might call it." I said laughing.

"A Pirandello like play," he interrupted.

"I wished," I responded, "Pirandello was a master. But I'm putting together characters, giving them feelings, but the dialog spells drama; there are beautiful images though; a ton of them."

"Is it autobiographical?

"Not precisely, no. But I'm using my experiences."

"We all do, if we aren't reluctant to talk honestly about our successes and failures. What is it about?"

"I don't really know. I know I'm writing about my life, the people in it. But it is basically about human relations. The way we interrelate, chance. How we now and then end up doing something completely different from what we had envisioned doing with our lives. What are your plays about?" I asked him.

"The same. There is not much else to write about, is there?" he asked me with a chuckle. "Tragedy was the first thing the Greeks dramatized. The drama written today is a distant echo of what they wrote then. Thank God for comedies, although many don't deserve the name."

"Sometimes we need a laugh, so we don't scream."

"Has it been rough for you?" he asked me.

"What?" I responded.

"The way you said it, it sounded as if you're writing about a tragedy."

A number of thoughts rushed through my mind when I heard him mention tragedy. I wondered about this fellow's intuition. Obviously we didn't know each other but, has he heard of me? Knows something I don't? Just the way he materialized out of nowhere and mentioned some of my beach routines made me suspicious. I've never seen the man before and even if I don't pay attention to other people, had he crossed my path, I'm sure I'd have caught a glimpse of him. Could he be an investigator working for the Alsace? He does sound like someone who could share or entertain more than a superficial conversation. I'm a sucker for an intelligent dilettante, always on the lookout for a tantalizing conversation, an alternative to the shallowness that surrounds us all. And he seemed to fit the profile of a dilettante.

We had arrived at the lighthouse and the man pointed to the rocks where I frequently sit. Instinctively we walked to the rocks and sat at talking distance from each other. As we continued our conversation, we seemed to share the same awe for the spectacle and beauty that surrounded us."

"I know you like to sit here. I'd do the same if I ever came this far," he said. "I know the ocean is soothing and this isolated corner invites retrospection. But other than its beauty, is there any other mystical or esoteric reason for you to sit at the feet of such a majestic structure?

"I talk to the lighthouse," I said timidly.

"Does she answer?" the fellow asked me.

"I don't know, but it makes me feel at ease. Do you know what I mean?"

"Yes, I do. Do you want her to answer?" he asked me.

"There are occasions when I feel helpless, like a leaf in the wind, blown by a maddening storm. But being here soothes my angst. I don't expect her to answer because I don't ask her questions. But she listens quietly. I can talk to her, as if talking to myself and not feel crazy."

"Blown by the wind, as if you couldn't master your life or control your destiny?" he asked me.

"Destiny," I said with a sigh. "Do you believe in destiny?"

"Things happen in certain ways and it is always for the best."

"That's Catholicism 101," I responded.

"Perhaps you yourself have a better idea."

"I'm not religious. I believe though, that if there is something that could cast, perhaps project our future, it is our brain."

"Well, haven't you found out that if you wish for something hard enough you eventually get it?"

"Not always, and not exactly as we wished. Tell me, do you believe in curses?" I asked the man.

"I have seen some work. How about you?"

"I think I might be living one."

"How so?" the fellow asked me.

"It will be a long conversation."

"I have time," he responded.

And not knowing why, I went ahead and described my conversation with el Brujo. My dealings with Natividad and Zamora, described André, my employee, whom I fired, who then turned around and instigated the curse. I mentioned my brief romance with the designer, her pregnancy and miscarriage. How her venture capital backer sold their company to the French, how, unbeknownst to me, Natividad had been the Alsace Chairman's lover. The Alsace bought Federated in the United States, my principal customer and source of revenue, and I became superfluous.

"Right there you have a sequence of events that looks as if it was planned. You even have a femme fatale, a necessary ingredient of any good drama." the fellow volunteered. "But tell me about the curse. What was the curse all about?"

"They sacrificed a goat, puncturing its heart, letting it lose all its blood, dripping slowly into a pan. The goat represented me. Its heart, mine. The idea, to make me suffer a humiliating defeat. My brain was to cook. My dear ones also to pay a high price, catastrophic, never-ending illnesses, while

I was physically healthy, watching helplessly the collapse of everything around me.

"That's vicious," the fellow said. "Did the Brujo tell you why they structured the curse in such a fashion?"

"He wanted it to be a slow process," the Brujo said, "with me lost in a labyrinth, helpless, fully aware of what was happening. An experience similar to the one he suffered watching his male lover die of Aids. It is really crazy."

"Oh, your man is also gay."

"Yes he is. I last saw him three years ago when we took his deposition. He had no reservations displaying his gayness. Not that we cared. I knew it when I hired him and I couldn't care less. For me homosexuals are a third sex."

"What you tell me is extraordinary. I have heard a lot of stories but the viciousness in yours is relentless. Nevertheless, after all is said and done, there is always something positive in what happens to people. Did you get any breaks throughout this ordeal?"

"Well not a break per se, but sympathy, a warning of things to come."

"I believe it," the fellow said.

"I met someone who accidentally disclosed a number of the conglomerate's juicy secrets. I couldn't ascertain the person's motives, but I avidly listened. I think I mentioned the chairman having an affair with my designer friend."

"Yes, you mentioned it."

"Well, there was a threat of a scandal during the breakup that could have cost the chairman his position. The designer's backer, her venture capitalist, astutely took advantage of that situation and demanded reparation; reparation being the buying of his corporation. Remember, he's an investment banker."

"Fascinating, blackmail at the point of a scandal. The stuff of great drama," the fellow said interrupting me. "Did you have a clue while you conducted your affair that the chairman was being blackmailed?"

"No. I didn't. It seems they were extorting the French while we were romancing each other in Lake Como, of all places."

"I hope your book is about this. Believe me, I'm not being fictitious, but so far your story has the ingredients of high drama. Your character is a tragic hero, with a femme fatale who rounds out your plot," the man added.

"The Chairman went ahead and bought my friend's outfit against his Board's better judgment for several hundred millions. After that, in a new expanding binge, the Chairman realized his dream of buying Federated, here in the US. You know, Bloomingdales, Macys, etc. A mega-chain that everybody knew had reached its maturity and had no place to grow. The French paid top dollar for another moribund business."

"The Chairman is a loser," he said.

"The only problem with the loser is that he bought Federated, my biggest customer; fifty percent of my business."

The sun was climbing feverishly as we talked and, mindful of my fair complexion, I invited the man to take refuge under the trees. The beach was still semi deserted and the only diversion was a flock of pelicans taking advantage of a school of fish close to shore. We sat under a canopy of trees and continue our long engrossing conversation.

"I was so engrossed in the conversation, I didn't realize it was close to eleven," I told the fellow.

"I don't mind. I have all the time in the world," he responded.

"You know, we've been talking for close to three hours and we haven't exchanged names. Alejandro Faust," I said extending my hand.

"Glad to have met you Alejandro," the fellow responded shaking mine.

"And you?" I asked him.

"You can call me Paul."

"Like the apostle."

"I wouldn't mind being him, really. He was the greatest PR guy of them all. He did for Jesus what Plato did for Socrates; even better."

"Are you an atheist?" I asked him trying to find where he was coming from.

"I have an open mind; anything is possible," he responded. Pascal was right," he said referring to his famous wager. "But I'm also aware of the transience of life. I think life is beautiful, but is it worth the trouble? Look at yourself with this sequence of traumatic experiences, no peace, not knowing what comes next. Is it worth it?"

"I agree," I said, glad to have found someone with a similar take on life as mine. "But once we find ourselves here, even if for a wink of an eye," I continued, "life is worth every moment, especially if we are conscious of its brevity."

"That's a lot. But tell me. If you have had a great life up to this unpleasant interruption, what's the problem? You will eventually overcome it."

"Well that's a different dimension. For me, since you asked and we are philosophizing, the problem isn't only my curse that is exhausting me morally and economically, but a philosophical and metaphysical one; time and death! For me, death is a wall and not a door as many people are taught to believe it is."

"We don't know that, do we?" Paul affirmed.

"But that's long a discussion and I'm really pressed for time."

"No, no, please," Paul interrupted me. "This is interesting. Talk to me."

"I'm talking about the absurdity of life, our brief stay in this world and our eventual return to the void, as if nothing had happened. It is absurd! Think about it. We open our eyes and here we are. Did you ask to come? Chance brought us here! Two strangers got together, followed their instinct and here we are!"

"It's true. It is a simplification but it is true. We are here because of other people," he interrupted me.

"Then the struggle for survival begins for each of us. Dependency, work, sacrifices, illnesses and eventual death. A waste…. There is no better metaphor for life than Sisyphus! You and I are Sisyphus. Our mountain; every day of our lives. Our boulder: the struggle to survive. Yes, some have it easier than others, but we all age, decay, get sick and eventually die. It is obvious the only purpose to come into this world is to die."

"You can say that," Paul added.

"If we were to believe we are the product of Intelligence Design or of an all-powerful creator, we would be the product of a merciless creature. Imagine letting your son be consumed by cancer or your parents lost in space because of Alzheimer's? Why create a world full illnesses, grief, miseries, injustices and some many other maladies. Why abandoned us here? For what? It would be absurd. If anything, we are the product of chance and evolution and nothing else."

"Fascinating," Paul said clapping briefly.

"But we touched something in passing and it was about curses. You said you've seen some work. Do you believe they're possible?"

"Of course. Life is a curse. You fall in love with life and before you know it, you're yanked away against your will. That fellow, your Iago... André? Was that his name?"

"Yes, André, my general manager."

"Perhaps he did you a favor. His curse made you aware of what life is all about. He forced you to live it."

"You know, I never mentioned André's name. How do you know that?" I asked him, intrigued.

"I don't know. I'm sure you did. Or it just came out of nowhere. I was thinking of beauty, music, a guitar player and perhaps André Segovia's name came to mind. Unconsciously, I baptized your Iago as André, some André, any André. Believe me."

"Perhaps you know my André and you're snooping, working for the French multinational."

"Look, you have revealed nothing to me. What you've told me is just a story, one of many. For all I know, it might be the plot of the novel you said you're writing, and you're probing me to see if your plot makes sense, when in fact it's pure fiction."

"No, you have to understand...."

"Just let me finish. Yes, your story is full of mystery, angst, drama, and chance plays the main role in the whole thing. But think about what I said; perhaps your Iago did you a favor. You said you're a thinker, a dilettante. He made you descend to the underworld, take a tour of hell, if there is one in this world. Whether he intended or not, he made you stronger, able to withstand what might be ahead of you. Perhaps you can peddle the story and become famous; who knows? Think about it!" he said extending his hand.

"Yes, I have to go too," I said, realizing it was getting late. "It has been intriguing meeting you. I hope we can do it again."

"I'm around," Paul said with a smile.

"Do you live in the Key?

"I'm always around. We'll meet again," he said walking away.

"Are you sure?" I yelled at him.

"You bet!" he responded.

He moved away rapidly and disappeared in the woods. I turned around and began my walk back home through the woods, trying to hide from the scorching sun.

MAXINE AND JULIE IN MY LABYRINTH

I got to my apartment and found Yolanda at the door, anxiously waiting for me.

"You better come to Maxine's room," she said. "I was giving her a bath and she complained of an excruciating headache."

I entered Maxine's room and she was resting in bed. She seemed disturbed, still trying to communicate, but completely out of focus.

"What happened?" I asked her.

"A shower, felt a pain here," she said with even more difficulty than before and pointing to part of her head."

"A scalpel," I said as she continued hitting her skull with her forefinger. I told her not to worry, that it was temporary.

I called her brother and told him what have happened. He said to take her directly to the hospital.

Maxine heard me, and angrily said no with her right hand.

I told him she refused. He put me on hold and called an ophthalmologist friend. After a minute or two, he got back on the line and asked me to take Maxine to see the ophthalmologist. "He is waiting," he said.

"She suffered a cerebral hemorrhage," the ophthalmologist said. And pulling me to a corner of the room, "a massive one. You could see it in the back of her eye. It's a miracle she's alive. I'll call the hospital to send an ambulance. I know an excellent neurologist, if you need one."

Maxine looked at me as if begging me not to leave her alone. I told her it wasn't that serious, although I knew it was. "But now we must go to the hospital for a checkup," I said, as confident and unperturbed as I could.

I felt terribly sad for Maxine. I had been told this could happen between three to six months from the original consultation. And it is six months to the date.

We got to the hospital and our neurologist friend was waiting. "I guess I prepared you months ago for this eventuality," he said somewhat apologetic.

"Your prognosis?" I asked him.

"I can tell you it isn't good, but I have to wait until I see the copies to tell you to what extent."

The technician came and gave us the copies, but not before telling us he should have waited for the hospital's resident doctor to see them first.

We walked toward a wall full of lit screens. The doctor hung the first six in order and immediately pointed to a white mass on the right side of the brain. "There you have it," he said. "It is massive stroke. I can't believe she's alive."

"What are we supposed to do?" I asked him.

"We could try to remove the blood, but I don't think she'll survive the surgery. There isn't much we can do other than observe her for two or three weeks, give her physical therapy so her limbs do not stiffen too much and obviously hope there is no new episode."

"Will she need a nursing facility?" I asked him.

"I'm afraid she will. Her cognitive and speech areas are affected heavily. The left side is weak, but she might regain some control in a week or two or she might not. She won't be able to walk, I'm afraid. Whether she stays at home or not, it will be up to you. Now we're going to try to make her comfortable. Time will tell."

The last five years have taught me to roll with the punches, while all these catastrophic things kept happening one after the other. I loved Maxine in my own personal way. I'd have never leave her for anyone else in any kind of circumstance. But this is different. At what price loyalty? Will I be condemned to bury myself for the rest of my life? I told her we'd be together until the end of time. Now it seems it's time to prove it.

LIFE AS IT COMES

Maxine spent two weeks under observation and was transferred to the physical therapy floor of the hospital for six weeks of intense rehab. Her left side continued to be weak. She couldn't take a step even with the assistance of two therapists. "She could be like this for the rest of her days," the head therapist told me. Ominous news I heard, but life continued unabated.

While my ever expanding drama continued to develop in Florida, on another related front, I spoke to the social worker in New York about my parents' situation; I sent her an email with all their financial information and made them full guests of the Empire State Medicaid apparatus.

Two successive calls from my lawyers announcing another setback. The trial had been postponed again for another month. Frustrated, but perhaps glad for the delay, I decided to ignore the situation. I felt threatened, wanting to escape. Refusing to accept that my problems kept expanding. And I ran away to Costa Rica, my oasis, to bury my frustration one more time.

Four days in San Jose were enough to take care of the business problems and afforded me a break from my hostile environment in New York and Miami. I also managed to play some tennis with the US consul, had a dinner or two with Jimenez and his erotic mistress and a cocktail with people from the office. I went scoreless with a couple of female friends, my tennis instructor one of them, but found talkative heads whenever I moved to the restaurant's bar before retiring for the night.

Fall was here and everyone was getting ready for another winter rapidly approaching. I loved the fall. I spent beautiful days at La Finca, my Adirondacks hide out, watching the leaves turn, the first snowflakes of the season and my neighbors getting ready for another crude winter, collecting wood and hooking snowplows to their pickups, dreading long nights and even shorter days. But it was also a very special time of the year to go away before the weather began to deteriorate.

With that mix of thoughts, I arrived in Miami once again and immediately called Julie. I told her I had a few days for my northern front and that I would be arriving in three days. She said Burt would be in London till the end of the week and she had an open calendar. She could take three days off if I could manage to get away. I said we would discuss it, took a shower and went to the hospital to see Maxine.

My arrival at the hospital was traumatic. Maxine was in bed, laying on her side, holding herself up with a firm grip, pulling incessantly at the restraining bar. Tears welled up in her eyes. She wanted to say something, but nothing but her sobs were audible. I came close and she looked into my eyes, as if asking for deliverance. I lowered the bar and got myself into the bed and held her tightly against me. She trembled, her pajamas wet with perspiration. I kissed her cheeks, her forehead and spoke softly in her ear.

"Okay, okay. Calm down. You'll see. Everything is going to be okay soon. This is just a temporary setback. We'll be home soon, but you need the therapy; two more weeks. I'm here to make sure you can return home soon; things will be like before, I'm telling you. No matter what, I'll always be with you."

I said everything that came to my mind. I wanted her to feel protected, safe. She was defenseless, like a gazelle in the African wilderness, caught by a cheetah or a voracious lioness. It took Maxine twenty minutes to calm down. It was hot in the room; the sun hit the glass with all the fury of its passionate setting. Maxine's sweat and mine wet my face, my shirt, my arms, but I didn't relent. Yolanda had called the nurse and she came and gave Maxine a pill. She was also being treated for depression and it was time for her second dosage of the day. I helped Maxine get comfortable and she surrendered to a placid sleep.

The nurse came back and brought me a towel. I was all wet with perspiration.

"She has been like this since yesterday," she said. "The pills are not working, or she might need a higher dose, perhaps a change in prescription. I wrote it in my report and the doctor might change the dosage when he comes again tonight. I'll make a point of talking to him, if I see him."

I thanked the nurse and wiped the sweat off my arms and face. My shirt was wet, in disarray and glued to my body.

"Sometimes this kind of situation is worse for the family than it is for the patient," the nurse said. They are away in their labyrinth while you're conscious and can do nothing. In most cases they fall deeper and deeper into the depression until we figure out the correct cocktail of antidepressants to stop it, if and when we do. How are you holding up?" She asked me.

"I feel powerless and the most profound sadness," I responded. "Even we, who pretend not to believe in anything, can't suppress the impulse to ask, why her? As if it was a punishment or something the person could have been spared. As if only her God wouldn't have permitted it; she's such a devout Catholic. Perhaps for someone like me, it's easy to understand that there is nothing sinister behind it all and that her condition is easily explained as a biological failure, even a product of chance. Our body is such an intricate machine; it is a miracle if it works."

"Don't lose hope," the nurse interrupted me. "I'd recommend you pray. We don't understand why these things happen, but God knows why and what is best for her, believe me. He's merciful."

"Merciful?" I asked her ironically while I marveled at the simplicity of her faith. She obviously didn't realize that if any of the things she said, only one was true, it would be the harshest indictment of her merciless God.

"Do you doubt he's merciful? There are things we don't understand, you know. Our minds are limited, not sufficiently developed to understand his wisdom. Remember we're simply mortals."

"I'm leaving," I told her. "When the doctor comes, please make sure you tell him what you saw. I don't want my wife to suffer. Please, tell the doctor I want to talk to him, no matter what hour of the night." I said, handing the nurse my business card.

Dinner was a concern. On my way home, I stopped at the Oasis, my refuge of last resort, and got some prepared food even though I wasn't really hungry. Twenty five minutes later, I was sitting on my terrace having dinner with myself. I couldn't have asked for more. After a brutal day at the hospital, I got a break; a peaceful and recharging evening, with the sound of lapping waves hitting the shore.

My dinner over, I settled for a movie. Not much to choose from and, after a prolonged session of channel surfing, I settled for Woody's Manhattan.

The telephone rang ten minutes into the movie; it was Julie at the other end of the line.

"Are you awake?" Julie asked me.

"You know if it's before one, I'm still up. How about you so late? Can't sleep?"

"I was thinking of you."

"What a coincidence, I was also thinking of you. I'm watching Manhattan once again, the part where Woody's trying to convince Mariel Hemingway he's not the man for her and that she should go to Paris and follow her dream."

"That was your speech a year after we began our affair. You insisted I needed a stable home, security and Burt was the only one who could give it to me."

"Wasn't I right? Look at the mess I'm in."

"I know your game. You love hearing me say I'd have gladly surrendered my security and peaceful life to share your angst, but I won't give you that pleasure. How is Maxine?"

"It was a tragic day at the hospital," and I went on telling her my experience, how Maxine was descending into a deep dark hole and there was no way of stopping her decline. "Her depression is eating her alive and we're all watching helplessly."

"You can say the same thing about your own situation. You're being consumed by your circumstances and there is very little or nothing any of us can do to rescue you. I definitely think it's a law of nature."

"Darwinism?" I asked her.

"Call it what you want, the poor zebra couldn't outrun the lions and it seems you can't outrun your devils either."

BEYOND THE VEIL

Another night of wicked dreams. Maxine in many, begging to be rescued from the malaise devouring her. Demanding that I perform a miracle, when miracles were only possible in her tortured head. Julie in others, helplessly watching me, her Sisyphus, rolling my boulder to the mountain top --- to see it roll down ---- again and again, with no foreseeable end. Exhausted, I got out of bed. It was still dark in Key Biscayne. I drifted to the kitchen, prepared my espresso and walked to the terrace to scrutinize the new day, the prospects of a new beginning.

Daylight. My attention drifted to the shoreline. The elderly couple walking the beach, one, perhaps two miles every morning and I marveled at their stamina. I've observed them time and time again and always wondered how long their relationship had survived. I couldn't see myself in a single liaison lasting that long. I have crossed their path during my usual trek to the lighthouse, but neither one ever initiated a conversation. 'Nice morning,' 'have a good walk,' we would tell each other, always polite, but nothing more than that. They seemed happy, just sharing a word or two with another living creature. Yet they were a fixed image in my brain and I missed them when they skipped a day and wondered what had happened when they skipped two. Seeing them reassured me and made me feel good. By the same token, the couple represented something missing in my life, a lasting, personal relationship. Come to think of it, Julie played that role since I met her, or at least that's what I wanted to believe. I never thought we would have to sign a contract to gain happiness, I did once and look where I find myself. I walked back to the kitchen and prepared another espresso, drank my shot, walked back to the terrace and watched my couple disappear around the bend.

I felt the need to stretch. To suffocate my anguish and no better way I thought than crushing balls, as if by crushing them I could defeat or at least outrun the wolf pack pursuing me. I went to the club to play tennis. After two hours with a gentle trainer who let me trounce the balls, never complaining about my disregard for the court lines, I returned home. I removed my wet shirt, shoes and socks, and walked barefoot to the kitchen, grabbed a beer, the telephone and walked to the terrace to call Yolanda at the hospital. "Maxine was rather quiet this morning," she told me, "with her eyes closed most of the time. The doctor changed the antidepressant dosage and she had a peaceful night." I thanked her for all she was doing and excused myself with my work and told her I'd come later. To please wait for me until I got there.

The telephone rang and it was one of my lawyers. "I'm sorry to sound like a broken record," he began saying, "but the trial has been postponed for another month. With good luck we are on for the beginning of November. I hope we are not delayed again because we might end up in the middle of the holiday season and another extension. A disaster, if that happens. Perhaps another postponement until after the beginning of the New Year."

Dumbfounded, I had nothing to add, but I thanked him for the call. I hung up and drifted through the room with no aim. An endless wait extended even longer. Listless, I called Julie.

"Hello?"

"Hey, I just wanted to connect," I said.

"What happened now?"

"The trial, another month."

"Don't say anymore. I'll call you tonight after eight. I'm very busy. When are you coming? It has been more than three weeks. Your mother is asking for you. I know you talk to her every day, but she complains you have forgotten them."

"I wish I could forget them. I wish I could walk away from everything, but I can't. Okay, call me. I really need to talk to you."

"I love you Alex. I know it is not much of a consolation, but you know I do."

I hung up and looked at the vast ocean in front of me. I was deep in thought, not knowing what to do next. I knew there were a number of things waiting to be done, but I didn't feel like doing any. Like a zombie, I went ahead and turned on a classical station. Fortunately, I hit Schubert, one of his quintets. I prepared myself a small lunch with some leftovers and, with his music in the background, I drank two glasses of wine, sitting on my terrace.

That night, about eight, Julie called. "How is my warrior doing?" she asked me.

"Not too well. I've decided to become a monk. Enter one of those remote monasteries where no one speaks to the other, and begin a quest for spiritual meaning. What do you think of that?

"You?" Julie asked me.

"Why not, I'm a spiritual man. It seems I have failed in this world. Everything is crumbling around me and perhaps meditation is what I need to recover my spiritual balance."

"Whether you accept it or not, you need people around you. Yes, you play the recluse type when it fits your purpose, but deep down you want people around you. When are you coming up?"

"A week, ten days, I don't know."

"I have a bit of good news; Burt is going to spend five days in London next week. We can go away, if you want, or we can stay here and do something, or nothing. Whatever you prefer."

Those were magical words to my ears. I wanted to escape; take a plane and disappear, I told Julie, and we talked for another hour before Burt got home and she had to sit to eat dinner with him.

The following morning I was back tackling a different kind of problem. Ben called me from New York.

"Did you see the Wall Street Journal?"

"No! What?"

"Are you sitting down?"

"They fired Tessier?" I asked him.

"Panagra is buying your competitor in Costa Rica."

"I don't believe you!"

"Page two. A two column article. They are quoting a Panagra executive, who wanted to remain anonymous. I guess that would jeopardize your operation, wouldn't it?"

"Of course. And my job."

Panagra is a big, perhaps the biggest North-American agricultural wholesaler. I had not heard any rumors about any acquisitions in Costa Rica. I wondered if the Consul knew. Son of a bitch. He didn't say anything when I bought him lunch. Now, if the report is true, and I have no reason not to believe it isn't, it will definitely have a profound effect on our business, not to mention my future.

Preoccupied with the news, I called Jimenez in San Jose and asked if he knew anything. He answered no. And we went on to discuss the implications and ramifications of a wholesaler of this magnitude taking over such a big packager, and the weaknesses of a small business like ours.

Jimenez was greatly alarmed. He was a shaky character, used to the easy selling of his coffee crops with no competition. He was also in love with the success of the vegetable distribution we created, something that gave him freedom to travel with his young mistress and the image of a maverick entrepreneur among his passive coffee grower friends.

"What do we do now?" he asked me.

"Keep on working. We have grown considerably since we started two years ago."

Two years, I repeated to myself, realizing again how fast time has gone by.

"Panagra was already in the US market when we started and we grew next to them."

"Can we compete?" Jimenez asked me.

"Of course we can. But it is going to be a cut-throat business from now on. Remember they also have US plants. It will be a tough fight, but we will survive."

"I don't know if I'm interested in a low margin operation, constantly struggling to keep our head above water. You made me see all the possibilities of this business, but we never talked about competition."

"*Maricon,*" my alter ego interjected. "*Fuck him. I knew it the very first day we met him. He's a mama's boy. Listen to me, we have to think about us starting now. You and I know Panagra is going to try to drive us out of business; they are famous for that, but I wouldn't tell Jimenez, not now! We need time to think what we're going to do next. He'll drive us crazy, crying like a baby. Remind him that with no distribution, he won't be able to justify so many escapades with his young chick to meet clients in Miami and New York... And let's tell her the first opportunity we have. She's going to be our best ally.*"

"Jimenez, there are no businesses without competition. Did you hear me?" I said forcefully. "To think this was going to be a successful, free ride, was and is, illogical. You're a business man. Competition is Business 101. It is the first thing that happens whenever something proves to be a success and I'm proud to tell you again, we've been a smashing success. We're selling thirty five million dollars in just two years of operations and we started from cero, nada!"

"Nevertheless, we stand to lose everything. I have invested more than four million in equipment. Perhaps we can sell our operation to Panagra, what do you think?"

"*Come Alex, what do you expect him to do, but piss in his pants,*" my alter ego interrupted me again. "*This is a mama's boy, a bean picker who has never worked a day in his life. You have to be strong with him. He only understands fear. Break his knees.*"

"These guys are not interested in buying us, they want us out of the way. They just bought a bigger outfit than ours. They don't need to buy us."

"Our clientele. We have a thirty, forty million dollar market. That's worth something," he retorted.

He's right, I thought. That's worth money right off the bat.

"I'm afraid to tell you, you're running scared with no reason," I told him. "They are not going to lose money just to get us out of the way."

"How about you?" Jimenez asked me. "What are you going to do if they come and offer you another twenty thou on top of what I'm paying you now?"

The son of bitch has a good point there. "That's very simple," I responded. "We are almost at the end of my contract and we're supposed to renew it for another two years. I have mentioned it several times, but you keep postponing it."

"Are you planning to come soon?" he asked me.

"I'm flying to New York at the end of the week. I had scheduled a number of meetings with several of our clients and now those meetings are more important than ever. But I'd really like to discuss and renew my contract once and for all."

"There is always time to do that," Jimenez retorted.

"But I don't want to hang up before reminding you all we've accomplished. You're not only a coffee grower, you're an industrialist. You now belong to a couple of North-American trade organizations and move among a number of international circles you never did before. You're lucky you can travel with Margarita. I'd think it would be a pity to lose all that, just because we're afraid of a little competition and perhaps a slightly smaller return on your investment."

Julie was waiting for me at La Guardia. It was eight thirty already and I decided to skip a visit to my parents. I suggested a restaurant, but she insisted she had food ready at home. And to her apartment we went.

During the twenty minute ride, we only talked about my conversation with Jimenez, Panagra's control of the vegetable business in the US and the prospects of losing the business and my job. Julie didn't utter a word but looked at me as my mood changed from absolute frustration, to anger and eventual resignation.

"I'm lost for words," Julie said, as we walked out of the garage two blocks away from her building. "What are you planning to do?" she asked me as we were entering the private elevator to her penthouse.

"I don't know. To tell you the truth, I haven't thought about it, really."

We entered her apartment and I walked directly to the guest room. I dropped my carryon bag, took off my leather jacket, went to the bathroom, washed my hands and came to the living room where Julie handed me a scotch.

We moved to the kitchen and Julie took a bottle of 1982 Chateau Pichon-Lalande, a present from one of Burt's corporate clients and handed it to me.

"This is a fantastic vintage," I told her. "Are you sure Burt isn't going to miss it?"

"He got three. We drank one with another couple and he'll have one left. Just drink it, if it is like the first one, you're going to be in your glory."

And I was; it was superb. We drank it with some lamb stew leftovers Julie had prepared the day before, sitting next to the large panoramic window, overlooking her terrace, the river and the Washington Bridge — all dressed up in lights — in the distance.

"I can't think of a better table in all New York," I said, holding Julie's hand tightly. "I'm so lucky. Thank you!"

"Don't thank me, thank the universe, as you usually do," she intimated with a smile.

"Remember Bernard Shaw's Major Barbara play?" I asked her. "When the Salvation Army's captain receives a check from Undershaft, I think his name is, and she says; 'Thank the Lord for this check.' Then Undershaft retorts, 'Why don't you thank me, I was the one who signed it,' or something to that effect."

We both laughed heartily, not as much for Shaw's wit as for being together, enjoying another of our interludes. And we went ahead and ate our dinner with gusto, drank a fantastic Bordeaux, had crème caramel for dessert and went to the terrace to enjoy our espresso.

"We have three days to go somewhere," Julie said.

I was overwhelmed with emotion and pulled Julie against me afraid of losing her. Then I kissed her eyes, her cheeks and finally her lips. I knew I didn't deserve her, but holding her tightly I whispered in her ear. "My castles are in ruin, I'm growing old, destitute, my quandary with life has no end and yet you want me. I thank the universe for making you possible. You're my only glimpse of a rosier world and all I can offer you is whatever is left of me and a hot-dog biking at Central Park. Where would I be without you?"

THE BEGINNING OF THE END

Two months passed, it was early December and Maxine was back at home, unable to speak, walk or feed herself unassisted. In a domestic arrangement, I had asked Yolanda to move in permanently. I hated to have people around me all the time, but she was an integral part of the household as it was anyway. She accepted gladly. We agreed to a day off every week and she suggested one of her relatives to cover for her. It was a complicated arrangement, but one that would allow me freedom to move freely. Thank God, some might say, for illegal immigrants willing to give that kind of service for a reasonable amount of money. The expense of a catastrophic illness at an institution would have cost a fortune I didn't have.

On the work front, Jimenez had postponed signing my contract renewal once again and Panagra was growing aggressively in our principal markets of New York/New Jersey and Florida. On the legal side, my trial was set to start Feb 1st and — for the first time in five years — it seemed it would.

On my side — trying to balance my filial responsibilities with my parents and Maxine's needs — I went to New York a few days before Christmas and had a celebration of sorts with my parents and Julie. We bought the traditional pork, two good bottles of wine and had dinner with them at their nursing home. We invited the head nurse, two of the female attendants and everyone willing to sit with us and enjoy our celebration. We ate, talked, joked and tried not to leave a moment free for contemplation. As we went through the motions, we all looked at each other as if we were having a great time, when in fact we knew it wouldn't get any better. Pipo seemed happy; Mima knew better; she always did. She looked deep into my eyes as if I had the answer to their quandary; as if I could still save them from oblivion.

Once dinner was over we opened presents; Julie had bought wool pajamas for my father and warm slippers for mother. We kissed and embraced as if exchanging gifts at midnight Christmas Eve. A tough scene; neither Pipo nor Mima would let our hugs go. My heart crumbled. I couldn't take their craving for human contact while fading into the dark. Julie fortunately was stronger. She wiped away a tear and demanded Pipo to put on weight so his pajamas could fit him properly. Then she struggled with Mima's feet trying to put on her slippers.

"I don't know if I'd been able to dine with them without you," I told Julie driving back to her apartment. She didn't answer, but I noticed a shining glitter off her eyes reflecting the oncoming lights.

Julie and Burt came for New Year's and stayed at the Sonesta, about a mile away from our condo. Midevening, Maxine became emotional when Burt and Julie arrived and shed a tear or two when Julie kissed and held her in her arms. The conversation was light. We had the TV on, with no voice, while playing love ballads by a Mexican trio and the usual songs by Sinatra and Nat King Cole. I had ordered out and the dinner was hot and promptly delivered at ten. We sat Maxine in a comfortable chair next to the dining table with Yolanda making sure she ate and got everything she needed. Max was quiet, but you could see her torment through her eyes. She didn't speak to anyone, only signaling Yolanda when she needed something or was uncomfortable in the position she was in.

We waited for the traditional ball to come down in Times Square. At midnight, when the countdown started, we got a large bucket full of water and dumped it over the balcony's rail. The tradition being to get rid of the bad spirits and everything rotten from the old year. Maxine's face lit up when we choreographed the action as if she was the one throwing the water together with the bad spirits. We knew it wouldn't do the trick, but what the heck. It felt good thinking we were leaving nothing behind from the old, tragic year.

THE COSTA RICA IMBROGLIO

Jimenez called me on the third of January. We exchanged good wishes for the New Year and he promptly asked me to fly down to Costa Rica. I said I could be there in a week and asked him what he had in mind. He gave me no clear answer other than to have one of our regular meetings. And we hung up.

A week to the day, I landed in Costa Rica and was taken directly to see Jimenez who was waiting for me in one of his regular hangouts. I found him at the end of the bar, in a darkened corner, away from the other customers. He was a bit drunk, having difficulty pronouncing his words, not to mention making sense. He immediately suggested having dinner. He needed to put something in his stomach, he said and I agreed. I didn't have any food on the plane and it was close to nine p.m. already. We moved to a table and ordered everything on the menu, from a bouillabaisse to a rack of lamb.

It took Jimenez half the meal to begin to make sense and complete his sentences.

"I wanted you to come," he said. "There are things I can't discuss freely with anyone. I hope you understand."

"Of course," I said, although I couldn't make out what the whole thing was all about.

"What I'm going to tell you is very personal," he told me resting his hand on my arm. "I don't want you to repeat it. Do I have your word?"

"Of course," I said.

"I broke up with Margarita."

"I'm sorry to hear that," I said relieved it was nothing that affected me directly. I knew it was a matter of time since the day I met her. She flirted openly. I wouldn't doubt she was screwing younger guys on the side.

"I threw her out of her apartment, got her car back and got one of my guys to recover whatever jewels she still had in her possession."

"Is it final?" I asked him discretely.

"Final! She put me in an unbearable situation. Gonzalez, you know, the foreman in the frozen plant, found her with another employee at the Mariposa hotel. La muy puta, didn't even try to hide. She said hello to him and his girlfriend and kept dancing cheek to cheek in the nightclub. I'd think she'd have, if not the decency, the common sense to go to a more remote place. But no, she had to go to the Mariposa of all places. That's where all my friends go; yes, with their concubines, but for us it is a serious place. And she knew it. She didn't even try to justify the unjustifiable. Not a word. She kept dancing."

"Hmm," was all I muttered, holding back my impulse to laugh.

"You know, in those circumstances I had to act." Jimenez continued. "Our name is all we have in this world. Mine belongs to an aristocratic family. It goes back to the origin of our country. How could I let this tramp trash my family name?"

"I understand. She is what, thirty?"

"No, twenty six," Jimenez said. "I made her what she is. Her orthography was horrendous, didn't type properly, but she's great in bed. I was always afraid of having a heart attack. Dying Rockefeller style, on top of her. You remember Rockefeller, don't you? What a way to go!"

"You said it. A wonderful way to go," I said and used the opportunity to laugh openly.

"I always suspected she might have had a younger fellow on the side, and that's understandable. As you have said many times," Jimenez said winking an eye, "it is better to eat chicken between two than no chicken at all."

We both laughed heartily.

My alter ego interrupted in the middle of my laughter: *Maricon, he has no cojones. I told him that while making fun, laughing at him. Knowing very well the dame was a tramp. You can't trust this guy for anything in the world. Look out!*

"Anyway, my wife is very happy," he continued. "My children are relieved, especially my daughter. She told me I should be ashamed of myself, going out with a woman who could be my granddaughter. Anyway, Margarita is history."

We had finished our second bottle of wine and he asked me if I wanted another or preferred a cordial. I settled for espresso and a cognac and we moved to a table at the bar. I was anxious to discuss my situation and thought the time was right. He was relaxed, a bit melancholic and perhaps in the right set of mind to open up about the future. And I pressed him.

"Panagra is hitting us hard," I said. "I've been thinking about ways to contain their expansion and I've come up with a new strategy. I also would like to finish our negotiations about my contract renewal."

"I also wanted to talk to you about that," Jimenez said sipping his martini and not looking at me. "Panagra approached me. I had a long conversation with its President, McCormack, his name is," he continued. "He offered to buy us out and asked me to give him a number. I gave it to him. I had been toying with the idea since things started to go south. It wasn't much; basically what I have invested plus time and effort. The fellow didn't blink. He said he would be back to me and he did. We should be closing in ten days."

"What do you mean we're closing in ten days? Did you agree to it?" I asked him upset.

"Yes, in ten days," he responded.

"Why did you keep me in the dark?" I demanded.

"It was Christmas. I didn't want you to feel bad. Anyway, I had made the decision and there is no way back. You knew I never liked the competition in the first place and it became even worse when they bought the other company here. It was written. Why torture ourselves when, had we stayed in the business, it would have been a never-ending fight we couldn't win?"

I was speechless. *"Hijo de puta. Maricon,"* my alter ego interrupted, *"the fucker is right. He did us in. Don't talk much and listen. We're in deep shit."*

"I didn't forget you," he continued. "I asked McCormack to give you a job. He wasn't very forthcoming, but he wouldn't be averse about you applying. He said he'd look after it himself. They have all the people they need. Sometimes more," he said. "But you never know. I gave you a good recommendation. You know I like and consider you a superb business man. Look what you did in two years."

I was speechless. I was seething and felt like breaking his neck. The bastard sold me out. 'I didn't forget you,' he said. 'I asked McCormack to give you a job.' Jesus, how callous can you be? Find me a job, as if he was recommending a clerk, not the person that had created a viable business out of nothing two years ago.

"Obviously you and I have an agreement and it will be executed," Jimenez continued. "We agreed on one year salary if we parted in two years or less and your two percent commission of our annual sales. I reviewed the contract with my accountant before I came tonight. I think everything is in order."

I was dumbfounded. I didn't know if I should walk out, remain patiently in my seat, yell; I didn't know what to do. The magnitude of the situation was rapidly sinking in. As I heard him talking, I was thinking about my future. Yes, I was getting about two hundred and fifty thousand all together, but I'd be out on the street having to reinvent myself once again.

"We have to pay our secretary and Roberta. We should give them at least three months," I said, looking for his consent.

"Why three months? In the States they fire you and pay your vacation if anything. They could apply for unemployment."

It was degrading talking to this man. I was afraid if he continued I wouldn't be able to contain my anger. I knew he was a callous son of bitch, but I never experienced it like today.

"Why don't we have dinner before you go back to Miami," he said casually. "When are you flying back?"

"In three days."

"What are you going to do?" he asked me.

"I don't know."

"Call the office. I'll tell them to have your check ready for tomorrow," was the last I heard him saying while I walked away.

It was late and I went directly to the apartment the company owns in San Jose. I took my clothes off and rested on top of the bed with my eyes wide open. Jimenez had outmaneuvered me, keeping me in the dark while discussing his deal with Panagra. There was nothing I could have done anyway. The truth is, I had no job. I could take the plane in the morning leaving nothing behind but two years of my life. My brain was on fire. I thought of calling Julie, but decided not to; I only delivered bad news.

The neighborhood rooster, I'd grown to hate, began its morning wake up calls and didn't stop for an hour or so. The garbage truck showed up at the other end of the street and didn't stop crunching trash for what seemed an eternity. It wasn't for another hour before I surrendered to the magic of Orpheus again to be rudely awakened by an incessant telephone ringing. The American Consul at the end of the line to inform me we had a court for that afternoon at two.

We met at the Consul's tennis club and after two well contested sets, sat for a cold beer. I chided the Consul for not disclosing Panagra's intentions to buy our competitor when we talked a few months ago. He gave me a long tortuous excuse and mentioned the irony of Panagra buying our own outfit now.

"I'm out of work and need to find a job soon," I said in one sentence.

"Not here," was all he said. He added, the Costa Rican economy was stalled, that it was driven by coffee and the price was at its lowest in four years. "This is a petit bourgeois society," he said, "plantation owners with lots of money, but not much imagination."

I left Costa Rica a day after my checks cleared. Never met Jimenez but had a brief telephone conversation; we agreed to postpone dinner until we met in Miami next time. Once at home in Florida, I called Julie and told her about my latest setback. She was shocked once again, but relieved Jimenez kept his word and made good on the settlement money. We commiserated some more and I mentioned my intention to travel to NY in four or five days. We kissed good night and hung up.

My lawyers were waiting. Sherman had left me a message to call him and I did. "Ten days to trial," Sherman said and asked me to come to his office for the final tune up. He reassured me they'd been working hard getting ready for the big occasion. I answered, a bit on the sardonic side, "I really hope you are."

I called Roberta and told her about my big fiasco and her having no work.

"I have two checks," I said; "one for you and one for Christine; a month severance, plus vacation time." She was happy for herself and disappointed for Christine. I asked Roberta to meet me at The Beachcomber for lunch, and she did.

It was winter and the 'Florida Opera' had four operas scheduled for the season. Tonight's performance was Norma that I had never seen live on the stage. I loved opera. As a young man I had dreamed of being a tenor, until the conservatory demanded that I read music and forced never-ending classes of sol-fa and other routines; another possible career truncated by my penchant for instant results. But today is different. I called an old flame, with whom I had shared a torrid affair years past, and she accepted.

'Norma' is a Druid priestess who betrays her clan for the love of a hand-some Roman invader, to be betrayed by the schmuck when he takes flight with a younger priestess. If not a carbon copy, our affair could have been construed the same way. Today, years later, perhaps unconsciously --- want-ing to pay for my misdeed or simply missing a companion --- I overlooked the implications and invited my dear friend. Another mistake. Even if the new Czech mezzo soprano's Norma was superb, the evening ended tragi-cally when all those hurtful feelings came back to haunt us. So much for my inveterate need for companionship.

The morning light grew stronger and I wrestled with my sheets trying to get up. My previous night's guilt had evaporated and another, nice and cool January morning made a walk on the beach inevitable. I bundled up a bit and trekked my way to the lighthouse watching the forest come alive and the sea-gulls dip into the ocean, returning with their catch to the beach. I felt good and at peace with myself; perhaps delusional, someone who knew my situation would have easily concluded.

I returned home about ten to eight and found Yolanda having breakfast in the kitchen. I said hello and prepared myself an espresso. Yolanda was about forty years old, slim, and had finished high school in her country before she came to the states five years ago and overstayed her tourist visa, surviving doing all kinds of jobs. She hadn't returned to her country since, afraid she wouldn't be able to reenter the US. She complained about missing her son, a twenty four year old postal worker, back in her country. We talked about her being young with such a mature son. She kidded about being knocked up at sixteen and forced to keep the creature because of traditions and family pressure.

It wasn't the first time I had heard about such tales, a teenager making an indiscretion, being burdened for the rest of her life with an unwanted pregnancy. I always thought nature was unfair with the female of the species, forcing her to pay a high price for an urge or emotion almost impossible to control. As she spoke, I came to visualize and understand her content with her new life with Maxine and me. After so many years in the wilderness, fending for herself, she had found shelter; "you are," she said, "my new family."

I left for New York two days later and met Julie, waiting for me, at La Guardia. It was cold in New York, twenty five degrees at eight o'clock at night. We didn't talk much: "I have food at home," she said and we drove straight to her apartment.

Burt was home and we sat down to dine. He had been gracious enough to wait for our arrival and had another wonderful claret uncorked to share with the meal. We discussed my new unemployment, my severance pay and my future search for a new job. I mentioned I wouldn't do anything until after the trial and he said he'd do another search among his clients to see if anyone needed a high power-consultant. We all laughed at his quip and moved to the living room after the espresso to drink cognac.

I felt at home with Burt and Julie; if Maxine and I had provided a family to Yolanda, Julie and Burt were my own. It was a strange relationship; the three of us. Nobody complained and I never raised the issue. Why rock the boat? I had some ideas about Burt, how well he tolerated my presence, our threesome, if you want. I always wondered about his travel to foreign countries, but never discussed it with Julie. I considered it part of his work, but I always had it in the back of my mind. I always kidded her about being Dona Flor with her two husbands, a reference to Jorge Amado's famous novel. I felt, or wanted to believe, I was Badiño, Dona Flor's deceased first husband, a rascal, that offered her the romance and exhilaration missing in her marriage, if you know what I mean.

"Have you made any progress with your play?" Burt asked me.

He was referring to a story I had been toying with and I wanted to convert into a play. I called it Final Judgment, about a man who commits suicide, finding to his surprise, there was an afterlife, and two characters --- a man and a woman --- playing God and the Devil.

"Yes, I decided I needed more than a play to say what I had in mind. Words haven't ceased percolating. It's like a stream of consciousness. First I thought of making it a short story. Eventually I settled for a novella."

"That is a much bigger project," Burt interrupted.

"You know what psychologists say about those who set themselves huge goals or a project so complex it's everlasting, impossible to complete," Julie said. "They don't have it in them to deliver a final product and want a perpetual excuse to hide their lack of resolve or perhaps incompetence. I'm not saying this is Alex's situation, but perhaps it's his excuse to procrastinate."

"You're right. I'm a procrastinator, I hate to admit."

"Well," Burt said, "one of my partners does legal work for a small publisher in Boston. I don't remember the name, but I can bounce it off him if you want."

A TRAGEDY HERE; A TRAGEDY THERE

It was crisp and relatively warm for a January morning in New York. I took Julie's car and drove to my parents' nursing home. The traffic at Queensboro Bridge was light. It was close to lunch time when I got the facility and walked directly to the restaurant. I felt a strange sensation looking at a multitude of residents, in wheelchairs, waiting for the restaurant's doors to open. They instinctively reminded me of cattle waiting to be squeezed into the slaughter house. I searched for my parents and found them in a corner, as anxious as the other residents to file in. They had nothing else to do but wait. Their lives were managed by a number of hired help wanting to deliver their cargo and move on to do other chores. What a life, I thought. I'd hate to find myself in this situation, completely depending on the charity of some and the need of others. By the same token, I was mesmerized by the dedication of the majority of the workers, many of them from the Caribbean Islands, perhaps happy they had a job, the same way Yolanda — in more auspicious circumstances — was of working and living with us.

After lunch I took my parents to the lounge and spent a half hour with them. There wasn't much we could talk about. Other than Mima's stroke and Pipo's deteriorating Parkinson, all their vital organs were working properly. Mentally it was a different story. Father didn't speak much, looked somber, although his face lit up when I addressed him directly. Mother was pensive, still looking at my eyes, as if waiting for something, I didn't know what.

I told them stories; Maxine was doing fine, the apartment in Florida was okay, I was busy traveling to South America. I talked about Yolanda, her twenty four year old son; how odd it was for such a relatively young woman to have a son that old. I don't know, whatever came to my mind to make time pass. Me, Alejandro Faust, killing time, an incongruity when I considered a week a lifetime and cherished minutes as if they were always in short supply.

The lunch hour was almost over and, before the rush to the elevators began, I took my parents to their room on the fourth floor. It was gloomy and depressing to walk among the residents sitting around the nurses' station. An older woman, strapped to a chair, insisted I take her to the toilet. Another one, immersed perhaps in her bewildered world, demanded to be taken back to Ireland. A sweet old lady complained she had been abandoned and wanted me to call her son; "he didn't know she was there." They all looked at me as a liberator, as if I could smuggle them out and take them somewhere, anywhere but there.

This was not my first exposure to this kind of environment. In fact, whenever I visited, I couldn't help but think of Marat/Sade, Peter Weiss' play about an insane asylum; or of Dante's Inferno, of his journey through his phantasmagorical forest of dead, moaning trees. What I experienced there resembled, perhaps in a different sort of way, the bard's vision of despair. An asylum in medieval times, perhaps prevalent at the time he wrote his Inferno. A dead forest as he described it, but in this case, a forest of living souls, if you may, waiting to be pruned by the inexorable ax of death.

My parent's room, away from the nurse's station, was or seemed as an oasis. We closed the door and became isolated, away from reality all together. I immediately turned on the TV; I needed it more than they did. I just wanted something different to look at. Another kind of noise, laughter, silliness of some sort. And I sat briefly next to them, talked nonsense a while longer, finally kissed them goodbye and promised to be back tomorrow on my way to the airport. There! I was off and I couldn't get away fast enough.

As I drove away, I felt guilty and relieved at the same time. I was out of there. I had done it one more time, and I had another twenty hours before I returned and said goodbye on my way home to Florida.

A straight landing, no rain, no clouds, no delays, nothing; not the Miami airport I'm used to. I drove to Key Biscayne and I felt recharged by the views from the bridge. Two keys in the distance, between the bay and the ocean; Biscayne the farther of the two, still eight miles away. I felt protected, back on my home ground. My apartment and my beach were waiting for me.

Maxine was in her room resting. Yolanda came to say hello and the three of us chit chatted about the last four days, if you could understand Maxine's limited participation, even though we had been in telephone contact all along.

"You're lucky, Alex," my alter ego interrupted. *"In the middle of all your vicissitudes, you have Yolanda taking care of Maxine. She's your escape hatch, someone you can trust. Now comes the hard part, the trial. Lots of questions waiting to be answered."*

I went to my lawyer's office for the final tune up before the trial. Sherman and George, were waiting together with Steve Fox, our damage expert, in a large conference room. Steve had prepared a number of charts he intended to use in his presentation and had an elaborate theory of the damages the Alsace had inflicted on me. The total was about twenty million plus, exactly what I considered my investment in the project was. He suggested a possible settlement should be around fourteen, fifteen million, the amount close to what I have asked for. He said the ten million the Alsace had offered would not cover my debts and I'd be left owing money to quite a lot of different people who would come after me no matter what.

George went over the overall strategy and his idea of an opening state-ment. He also brought up the sticky situation we had with André. The Alsace has him as a primary witness, a move we thought was a diversionary tactic. George mentioned André's deposition was three years old and that he had gone over it carefully. He also said that in his conversations with the Alsace's lawyer, they had mentioned André's ill health, but that the lawyer had not disclosed the cause of his ailment. Nevertheless he assured George, André was anxious to testify and would be one of their key witnesses.

I hadn't heard anything about André for the last three years. I knew he'd be the most embittered foe we'd face, but also knew we could demolish his arguments; if dangerous it was a problem we could handle. George then alluded to portions of videotaped depositions we had taken during discovery and our agreement not to insist on the Alsace top executives' presence during trial. We knew we had all the ammunition we were going to get from them and it wasn't worth the risk. We knew neither Tessier nor Sands would say more than what they had admitted already.

We went further and analyzed the testimony of our witnesses. Sherman came briefly when the session was almost over, as if somebody had told him we were ready to quit. He claimed to be ready for the big event. I had asked George that same question during a break and he said, "Yes that the old man was." Somehow I doubted, but didn't contradict him. Sherman also asked me how I felt a few days away from the impending trial. I said it was anti-climactic. That I had been waiting for such a long time; that I still doubted it was happening.

"Well, it's happening and pretty soon we will have an answer to your prayers," he said, smiling.

The drive home was peaceful and soothing as it always is. As always, I immersed myself on the beauty of the islands, the coral blue of the ocean, the surrounding woods and I felt at ease.

At home, Maxine was sitting on her lounge chair watching TV, Yolanda was in the kitchen preparing a chicken with vegetables, typical of her country. I told her to save me some, went to the bar, served myself a scotch and walked to my terrace to call Julie at the office.

"Can you talk?" I asked her.

"Let me lock my door," she said. "What did Sherman had to say? Are you excited?"

"Far from it," I responded. "I've been waiting for so long, it feels as if I could continue living without a trial or the millions I lost. It feels as if I've never had any."

"Wake up! It has been five years and change. Ten percent of your life; one of every ten years you've been on this earth has been consumed pursuing this trial. It's unbelievable."

"It's a waste! I know."

"What are you going to do from now until Monday morning?"

"Frankly, I wish I could walk away and leave everything behind. I've come to a point that I don't give a damn anymore. Perhaps it would be better to forget this nightmare ever happened."

"You will in time. Now you feel despondent, exhausted and humiliated. But you never know. Perhaps the whole thing is for the best." Julie said. "I wish I could be there with you," she said softly. "I don't know if it would help, but at least you wouldn't be alone. Call me tonight, will you? We're thirteen hundred miles apart, but I'm with you."

Sunday morning I went to the airport to pick up Francine. She was coming from Chicago where the winter was brutal and wanted at least a day at the beach. It had been almost four years since she went to work for Nordstrom and we only saw each other once when the Alsace's lawyers took her deposition. We started talking the minute she came down from the plane and we didn't stop until she checked in at The Sonesta, a mile away from home. I'd pick her up for dinner, I told her, and go again to the airport to wait for Ben, arriving on the last plane from New York.

Ben's plane arrived on time and on our way home from the airport, we reminisced about our times together. It was close to eleven when we left Francine at her hotel and continued to my apartment. Ben was staying with me and once at home, I served two cognacs and together we walked out to the terrace. It was cool in Miami, 56 degrees and clear; a perfect winter night. We sat sipping our drinks and chatting casually about family and business. The impending trial came up and we rehashed most of what we had experienced together. After a few minutes, he began closing his eyes, we decided it was time to quit. We said good night, he went to his room, I served myself another cognac and an hour later went to mine as well.

It was five in the morning and my eyes popped open as if I had been awakened by a huge explosion. It was a dark night still. I had slept for three hours and felt recharged, full of energy. I couldn't have stayed in bed because my brain was boiling with anticipation. I put on shorts, my beach sandals, a warm top and went down for a walk at dawn. The beach was empty, the ocean calm, with light waves lapping the shore and a gentle breeze coming from the woods.

I walked south to the lighthouse. It wasn't a matter of doing exercise, I needed the walk to slow my brain down. The time had come to face reality. In a few days everything would be history. Whether I won or lost, another chapter was at its end and a new one would beg to be written. Another reincarnation would be in order, but doing what? Writing, perhaps. My screenplays had gone nowhere. A novel. That's what that fellow Paul mentioned. I had thought about it many times, but I'm not Fitzgerald. Of course there are many other successful writers even if they don't compare with him or Hemingway. But I couldn't write pulp even if I wanted to.

The contours of the lighthouse were visible in the distance. It was a pity they had discontinued its use long ago. Still it was an imposing structure; a remembrance of things past. But I felt an affinity with it; she couldn't talk, but I thought she could listen; be my therapist. I thought about the Brujo's predictions; so far he had been right on the money. I had lost everything and the lives of everyone close to me were in shambles. There was only one thing left to be realized and that was my losing the trial. If I did, everything he predicted would be consummated.

I got to the end of the Key with the first signs of light on the horizon. I turned back and retraced my mile and a half walk as the lights grew stronger; a presage of the almighty sun's appearance. Ben and Yolanda were up, having coffee in the kitchen. I entered Maxine's room and kissed her forehead; she didn't react. Then I went into my room and called Julie. "How is my warrior holding up?" she asked me. "I'm at peace," I answered. "Que sera, sera," I said. "I love you," she responded. I blew her a kiss and that was that. I rushed to the shower and in no time was drinking my espresso and ready to depart. It was seven a.m. and the second stage of my day was about to begin.

We drove to my attorney's office in complete silence. The three of us went up to their office and found Sherman, George and two paralegal milling over a mountain of documents being stacked on legal boxes. After the brief amenities, George asked Ben and Francine if they had reread their depositions and they both assented. He turned to me and said, "Are you ready?" "Sure," I responded and he led the way out of the conference room to the elevators and to the garage to get to our cars.

If we exchanged no words coming to our attorney's office, we didn't exchange any as we followed George's car on our way to court. The trial was supposed to take place at a cavernous, tall building in downtown Miami, better known as 'Cielito Lindo,' Beautiful Heaven. The building had been baptized by Hispanic inmates because — besides having court rooms on the lower floors — it functioned as a detention center on the top floors and, from their cell windows, the inmates could see the clouds and open sky; hence, beautiful heaven. An irony, if you consider from there, many of them would be buried for years in the inferno of today's prison system in most parts of the country.

We went through the weapons' detectors in the Court building's lobby and up the elevators to the judge's chambers. Both, the Alsace's lead and their female corporate lawyer, with two other assistants, entered after us and promptly asked Sherman to join them for a brief conference. Both counsels wanting to see the judge to settle a number of procedural questions. Sherman came back to our side and told us they had agreed to expedite the jury selection and it was only for the Judge to okay their accord.

The atmosphere in the Judge's anti-chambers was charged. I sat in corner of the room reading my New York Times. Ben and Francine were talking to each other by a window, while the Alsace's group was in the other corner mulling over a bunch of documents. Twenty minutes later both counsels were called to a conference with the Judge. A half hour later Sherman came out and gave me a thumbs up. Moments later we were ushered into an old wood paneled, palatial courtroom, the likes of which we all have seen in movies and TV a million times.

THE TRIAL

"All rise," the clerk said, and the Judge entered the courtroom. He addressed the few of us present, gave us an idea of how he'd like to conduct the jury selection and ordered the process to begin. The first panel of potential jurors came in, the lawyers for both sides asked a series of questions and all were summarily dismissed. None of the panel members had any business experience or owned a small business, qualifications we desperately needed. Two more panels were summoned, both had a similar set of problems; no business experience, only a photo-shop owner, who begged to be excused claiming severe financial hardship if selected. It was close to mid-day when the Judge indicated we'd have to select some jurors or he'd have to declare a mistrial. Dismissing the last candidate from the last panel, the Judge's gaveled the end of the session; the jury selection to be continued in the afternoon.

Being in downtown Miami we quickly found a comfortable eatery with a quiet corner table. None of us was hungry and we agreed to divide a super Cuban sandwich in three. While at it, we discussed the jurors dismissed during the morning and the prospects of getting the proper ones in the afternoon session. If anything, we concluded, we were doomed to more of the same.

"All rise," the clerk said, and the afternoon session was underway. A new panel of jurors filed in, the perfunctory drilling of each candidate took place and it became evident none of them remotely met our elementary expectations. I watched anxiously as the Judge moved impatiently in his chair and after two other potential jurors were dismissed, he finally called both lawyers to the podium and — in a Solomonic kind of way — said, "either you select a jury now or a new date for a trial will be announced before we leave court today."

I became agitated. I couldn't delay the trial a day longer. It was a do or die kind of situation for me and I told my lawyer we should try to get someone with common sense if not expertise or experience. All along we wanted some small businessman or merchant — who could understand the situation I was in — as a member of the jury, but none volunteered or was available. It would have been catastrophic for their personal interest, they all claimed.

Before they returned to their seats, the Alsace lawyer called Sherman aside and sweetened their offer. Eleven million. Not a penny more. Sherman and I discussed it briefly but I finally rejected it. We were short five million of what my bottom line was. The offer was rejected.

Short of options, we picked four women and two men; an unnerving group to say the least. Three of the ladies never worked outside their homes. If anything, the composition of the jury had disaster written all over it.

Driving back to my lawyer's office, we revisited the conversations we had about the perfect jury. We thought of getting one or two businessmen who could understand — if not all — the sense of my business predicament, dealing and fighting an oversized corporation. We thought we could get more than one Hispanic and at least one career woman. No dice. The Judge forced us to settle with what we had at hand or the prospect of another postponement. There was no sense in postponing the inevitable, I thought. So, we took it!

Ben and I came home. I went into Maxine's room and found Yolanda feeding her. I stayed briefly, trying to make light conversation, but Yolanda pointed out Maxine's further weakening of her right side; another sign of her deteriorating condition. Ben went to the bar to prepare two scotches. I joined him on the terrace and together we toasted the awesome ocean in front of us. We didn't say much. Two more cocktails and a lengthy dinner at my favorite hangout and we were ready for a well-deserved evening rest.

It was late but I called Julie.

"How did it go?" she asked me.

"Terrible. If this is a presage of things to come, we're in a deep hole," I told her.

"How so?"

"The jury, we didn't have the right kind of people to choose from. I think the Judge is hostile. His comments, the fact that he forced us to pick from a shallow pool of jurors makes me wonder. I wish you could see him. He's an old retired judge from New York, moonlighting here, making some money while going to the beach. I don't know."

"Don't be so negative. You always see the other side of the coin. What makes you paint this doom's day scenario? Try to sleep. I know it will be impossible because you're strung up, ready to battle, but take a pill. Don't you have one? You should have one, you know."

"All rise," the Clerk announced, and the Judge came into the chambers. The Judge immediately said the jury selection had taken too long and that he intended to keep a quick and steady pace to reach a verdict before the weekend, if possible. And he saw no reason why we couldn't. That simple. Ominous!

The Clerk yelled "all rise," and the six jurors filed in. My long awaited trial was about to begin. I looked at the jurors long and mindful of their impact on the rest of my life; a scary thought. A group of individuals with no business experience, wanting to be fair perhaps, but with the limitations proper to their ignorance. Two men and four women, one a nurse, the rest had no higher education. No Cubans, no blacks or a Jew who could feel solidarity with an underdog. Two older, lovely grannies, one from Minnesota; Fargo, of all places. The other from Detroit, an auto worker's widow. These women had never worked outside of their homes and probably would associate my nemesis with Macy's or Filene's Basement and not a hungry multinational. The unemployed young receptionist had worked — on and off — for a temporary agency and had no clue as to what the whole thing was about. The elevator mechanic was a naturalized American from Poland, unemployed. The nurse, a sweet looking woman; a graduate of Albany, New York's, nursing school, now working for a small hospital in Miami. The student reminded me of a Woodstock sixties hippie, with the perfect excuse not to work, jury duty.

I lowered my head and a feeling of angst and frustration overtook me. "Estoy perdido," I'm lost, I said to myself in Spanish. My never-ending race to get to trial had finally come to this. I saw no way out, as if it had been written before the beginning of time. The Brujo said it. "You'll be wiped out."

The jurors, discreetly at first and openly later, glanced at me. They were probably as perplexed, as we all are, to be called to administer justice. Or a semblance of justice, as one of the discarded previous judges had admitted in a moment of reflection. Still, I was the guy who had hijacked them for a week or more of long statements, endless paperwork and recriminations galore. They were probably also asking themselves, who the hell is this lonely guy sitting across from us? What kind of a gall has he to sue such a big corporation? How could he be entangled with such a prestigious multinational? An opportunist, perhaps, I saw them thinking, looking for a windfall from a runaway jury.

Sherman rose and delivered a ten minute long opening statement. To begin, he misrepresented some of the Alsace's pledged commitments and I immediately knew we had to start correcting the record. It wasn't a matter of the sky falling, but it was embarrassing, especially for me. Right after Sherman's statement, the lawyer for the Alsace gave a lengthier opening. I had seen the fellow during the depositions and was never impressed with his wit, but I listened to him carefully, trying to understand the core of their defense. It was simple. It was not a matter of us being abused by the Alsace, but the weaknesses natural to small business trying to make it in the big leagues.

"What a hypocrite?" I said to myself. I had been working with Natividad and later with the Alsace, before they bought Federated in the US and we had been successful. What the hell is this guy talking about?

He finished his statement, the Judge gave us a bathroom break and the trial resumed with me on the witness stand.

Sherman began my direct examination by asking me to tell the jury how and when I started my fashion business. Under what circumstances I met Natividad and Zamora and negotiated a deal to distribute their private label in the United States. We introduced our first contract as evidence and we used the opportunity to explain to the jurors a number of clauses that demonstrated the complexity of our relationship. I went ahead and told the jury how I came to meet André and eventually hired him.

The Judge used the end of this portion of my testimony to break for lunch. He asked us to reconvene at 1:30 p.m. and we all ran for the elevators, tired, bored with the slow pace of the proceedings. As we shared a sandwich and an espresso, Sherman seemed to be happy with my testimony, but complained about the jurors disinterest in the evidence. Their cursory look at the documents, not bothering to read even the paragraphs highlighted. A bad sign, knowing we had thirty or forty more documents to introduce as evidence.

The afternoon session continued with Sherman posing questions about our meteoric growth, the successes of our own — ready-to-wear lines — the positioning of Natividad's haute couture line. The fact that the generous, extended terms given some of our customers, amounted to a clear subsidy to Natividad's line. A policy that had forced us to secure our own financing in order to be able to expand her line and sustain our clientele.

Another ten minute bathroom break and Sherman resumed my examination. My meetings with Sands — the Alsace VP for foreign sales — my eventual meeting with the Chairman, Francois Tessier and how I was reassured by both that, even without a contract, our relationship was solid and I was part of their North American strategy. Copies of a number of letters, and follow-up notes exchanged during those conversations were also introduced as evidence and distributed to the jury. To our chagrin, most of the documents were handled by the jurors in the same cursory manner they had exhibited before. An obvious sign we were going to have problems making the jurors follow the trail.

It was 4:30 in the afternoon when my direct examination was completed, the Judge's gaveled the end of the session and he ordered us to reconvene the following day at 9 a.m. Sherman, George and I spoke briefly while walking to the garage. We readily agreed we were running a great risk pouring out too much information to a jury that would likely grossly misinterpret or ignore it altogether. But we quickly concluded there was no alternative and would hope for the best.

BACK TO MY SHELTER

Key Biscayne in the distance. The causeway, the bridge, the ocean and the bay; the panoramic beauty was a reassuring sight. I had alerted Ben the session was over and I was on my way back. I told him I felt like cooking. I stopped at the supermarket and got a prepared salad and filet mignons for dinner. I drove to the Sonesta, Francine joined me and continued to my apartment. It was close to six and the three of us sat on my terrace, had cocktails, discussed the trial and the pomposity of the Alsace's lawyer. Ben, Francine and Roberta were scheduled to testify starting tomorrow and we went over their testimony again.

After a few more drinks we decided it was time to eat, went down to the beach and cooked the steaks we were all relishing about.

"This place is like paradise," Ben said, looking at the ocean while devouring his well-done piece of beef.

"It is paradise," Francine asserted. "If this were my place, I'd never go to work. Look at that beach." Then turning to me she asked. "Alex, what are you planning to do after the trial?"

"I haven't thought about it. Well, I suppose I have after all. I want to write, but I need an income. Perhaps I'll do some consulting. Who knows?"

"Wasn't that what you always wanted to do? Would you write in English or Spanish?" Francine asked me.

"English. I write poorly in both languages, so why not try English that is universal. Why take a detour?"

The night had fallen; a half moon had risen on the horizon and bathed our table with a delicate light. A delightful evening I didn't want to end. Francine had closed her eyes and enjoyed the sounds of the lapping waves. I suggested Ben and I go back to my apartment and drink our espressos, and we did. We came back down with cognacs and a sweet Porto for Francine. We toasted, talked for a while longer until Ben reminded us we had a busy day ahead of us. Ben took my car and drove Francine back to her hotel. I stayed behind and discarded the leftovers, tidied up the space and went up to my apartment.

"All rise," the court clerk announced, the Judge entered the courtroom and took his seat. He read a few announcements about his case load, had a short conference with both attorneys and asked that the jury be brought in.

Day three started with me back on the witness stand being cross-examined by our opponent. The Alsace lawyer was a pedantic fellow who talked as if he was delivering a funeral oration. He embalmed his questions with a rhetorical flair, always embedding his own answer to his question or what he wanted the jury to hear. He never mentioned my suit, but went on an elaborate fishing expedition, trying to show that our business wasn't sound, that if I had survived, it was because I lived beyond my means and my ever growing credit lines. He tried to show my delayed payments weren't normal in the industry and that they had tried to accommodate me up to a point, but their generosity had a limit.

Aware of his technique and his slanted spinning of the facts, I developed a system to answer his rhetorical questions denying his premise with a flat, no! Forcing him to rephrase his question in such a way, I could elaborate my answer and not assent to the premises already planted.

"Of course I needed the lines of credit," I asserted, "because I was subsidizing the Alsace's business. The delays in payments were the result of credits we gave our customers to carry Natividad's expensive line of clothing."

After the Alsace cross-examination ended, Sherman conducted the usual redirect and asked me to clarify some of the assertions made by their lawyer. He produced Zamora's letter and gave me ample time to read portions of it and to elaborate about Zamora's commitment. It was obvious, I asserted, that in the event of his corporation being acquired by another outfit, Zamora, committed himself to compensate me for whatever monies I had invested in introducing Natividad's line. "It was obvious," I said, lifting the letter for the jury to see. "It says so in the letter; clearly," I said again and again.

Another lunch break and the afternoon began with Ben's examination. All along, I kept an eye on each and every one of the jurors. It was obvious they were bored to death. I couldn't see how these people would understand my predicament. It wasn't a matter of simple sales transactions, but agreements, commitments, long documents with nuances in every paragraph, all together difficult for an untrained eye to assimilate.

Their lawyer came back and did not even mention the array of data and statistics Ben had explained for almost two hours. Instead he went over my tax returns, our quarterly salary withholdings statements. In general he wasn't trying to justify the Alsace's behavior, but used a sexier tactic; the spinning of a number of common occurrences in any small business as if they were only the product of my mismanagement and undercapitalization.

Sherman returned after the afternoon break and did a less than satisfactory redirect asking Ben to explain the reasons for the delays and how common these kinds of situations were in businesses our size. I was angry, troubled by Sherman's less than aggressive line of questioning. I felt like jumping in crying, yes, there were delays, but those withholdings were eventually paid, usually with the acquiescence of the correspondent agencies. But I couldn't and didn't.

From court I took Ben to the Miami airport. Once at the terminal, I embraced Ben and thanked him for his support. He went in, waved goodbye and I drove back to pick up Francine and go for dinner.

My frustrations in court didn't stop when I got home that night. The health of my dear ones was another worry and getting home forced me to confront them head on. Maxine continued to deteriorate.

"We had a very bad day," Yolanda told me. "She was agitated, couldn't stay quiet for more than two minutes."

"You did call the doctor, did you?" I asked her.

"He said to give her two pills of the antidepressant. I did and she slept for about two hours. When she woke up, she was calm for a while but became agitated again. I gave her another pill as the doctor suggested, and she has been sleeping for four hours or so."

"Well done," I said and she retired to her room.

I called Julie, as I had been doing every night since the beginning of the trial.

"How's my warrior doing?" she asked me.

"Not well." And I related the intricacies of our testimonies so far and the approach the Alsace's lawyer was developing.

"What did you expect? They can't justify what they did, so they try to destroy your credibility and discredit you personally. Did the Judge let them?"

"I'm afraid the Judge is on their side. I can't believe my luck. Even during cross, he let this fellow walk away from the testimony and develop theories galore about my financial situation, even me personally. He isn't even waiting to rebut and present his defense. He's all over the case already."

We spoke for another half hour and I finally let her go. She mentioned she had visited my parents at the nursing home and that they were doing fine. "Your mother is complaining about you not coming frequently enough," she said.

A new day. After the Judge's daily conference with both lawyers and the now familiar, "all rise," the jury was seated and a new session began. It was Francine's turn, as our General Sales Manager, to testify. Sherman began introducing a number of documents and charts explaining our company growth and the share of the Alsace's business in our revenues. The jurors sat impassively and gave the usual cursory look to another stack of documents as they were passed along. As soon as her testimony finished, the Alsace's lawyer jumped to the podium and began his cross examination. His strategy was simple; forget our claim, just hammer away at our economic shortcomings and financial difficulties. Francine battled him to a standstill with a number of quips; my paycheck always cleared, never heard any of my coworkers complain and on the contrary, our employees gave themselves fully to the task of making the company grow.

Sherman returned for a brief redirect. He clarified and added a number of issues he neglected to introduce before, complimented and thanked Francine for her testimony.

Roberta took the stand and responded every question Sherman asked her flawlessly. She pointed to crucial paragraphs in the documents, while struggling to beef up Sherman's dull questions that, ominously, had elicited a rash of yawns among the jurors.

The Alsace's lawyer didn't lose time pouncing on Roberta and began by reciting his own list of our economic shortcomings instead of cross examining Roberta's comprehensive testimony. No matter Sherman's frequent objections, the Judge lamely acquiesced to the Alsace's line of questioning, while asking their lawyer, to no avail, to concentrate on Roberta's testimony.

After the Judge announced a shorter than usual lunch break, we promptly reconvened at one. The afternoon had been set aside to play a number of videotaped depositions with Natividad, Zamora, Sands and Tessier. Being foreign nationals, the four were produced with the understanding we'd use their taped depositions so they wouldn't be forced to fly to Miami for the trial.

Natividad's deposition segment was short and sweet. She had been asked to relate how and when she and I met. Under which circumstances she introduced me to Zamora, and her positive endorsement of an agreement for the distribution of her label of 'pret-a-porte' in the United States. Nothing was mentioned about our romantic affair, but she corroborated the majority of my statements and corroborated, if regretfully, she had insisted I hire André.

The Alsace's lawyer carried on his redirect asking Natividad if she knew of my financial situation, my need for capital and other shortcomings they alleged were the real reason for my demise. She claimed complete ignorance to all his questions.

Zamora's testimony was played next and was contentious. The old man denied his letter's intention was to assure me of compensation in case Nati's atelier was sold or changed hands. He also denied asking us to take on riskier clients in order to expand our distribution beyond acceptable limits.

The Alsace's lawyer in his cross-examination asked Zamora if all the legal documents signed with my corporation stated, clearly, "This document supersedes or overrides any other legal document signed or agreed upon prior to this one." The old man said only, "absolutely." And that was his answer from then on to every question he was asked.

The jurors followed the playing of the depositions with interest. For them it was a welcome diversion from the boring routine. A large screen had been set up in front of their box. The videos were in color, with abundant close-ups and sometimes quick switching between lawyer and witness. Natividad looked radiant, with her dark tan and luscious black hair; Zamora had the look of an affable grandpa, who had only good intentions for the success of his grandson; me, of course. Incredible!

A short bathroom break and the VP Phillipe Sand's deposition was played. Sands was a handsome fellow; blond, with soft green eyes and a sexy French accent. It was obvious the jurors seemed enthralled with his screen personality. To Sherman's questions, he repeated their well-rehearsed answers. "They did their best to accommodate me; I was their smallest customer; they followed Zamora's practices until the Federated acquisition changed their way of doing business in the United States. That acquisition, he insisted, entailed new policies and it was obvious I couldn't keep up with those policies."

Right after Sands came Chairman Jan Francois Tessier's deposition play-back. There was no drama in watching what we knew already, but the jurors had the opportunity to observe another sleek Frenchman play dumb, being too busy to handle such a minor problem and blame — if any blame could be adjudicated — his subordinates for protecting the corporation's best interest. He restated that "he liked Alex very much, wanted to help him, but he, me, fell through the cracks." Falling through the cracks was an interesting observation to explore, but Sherman let it go unchallenged and that was all we could get from him.

The Alsace's lawyer followed up with his cross-examination and did apologize to Chairman Tessier for the inconvenience I had caused him. The same laundry list of questions ensued and Tessier played dumb once again and confessed complete ignorance and even surprise to the extent of my financial weaknesses. He added "had we known of his financial problems we'd probably have never done business with him." Hypocrite!

Tessier's video deposition was the end of the afternoon session. Sherman, George and I walked to the parking lot. We didn't talk much. I was mostly resigned to my fate and a possible negative outcome, even if I had great hope for my expert witness' presentation scheduled for tomorrow morning promptly at nine.

I drove back to my refuge at the Key. It was about six and the days were getting longer. My head was percolating with disparate thoughts, alternatives, trying to sort out the possibility of another debacle. I got to my apartment not knowing what I was going to find. Maxine's condition was susceptible to swift changes. Fortunately my apprehension was unfounded. Yolanda was preparing dinner for them and she was in a festive mood. We talked briefly, she offered to prepare something for me, but I declined, saying it was too early and I wanted to eat out. That, in fact was true. And later on that night, I biked to La Choza my dear Hut, just wanting to relax with no special expectation. The place was beginning to empty out and I sat at my corner table and ate more than I should have. But I felt good while listening to my pair of troubadours delight me with all those familiar songs that transported me back to the womb.

MY FINANCIAL RUIN - DAMAGES

The familiar "All rise," was heard, the Judge took his place, the jury filed in and the court was in session. Steve Fox, my financial damages expert, was sworn in and Sherman began his questioning.

The order and pace of Fox's testimony had been prearranged and we had agreed Sherman would ask about five relevant topics, Steve would elaborate on each and every one of them, present the economic history of our relationship with charts and a number of documents, present his conclusions and spell out the total damages estimate caused by the Alsace's actions. In other words, explain how the Alsace actions had caused my corporation — and me in particular — a twenty five to thirty million dollar loss.

Steve was about forty-five, lean, with a professorial look and exquisite attention to detail. He spoke softly, sometimes speaking to one juror or another, pointing out the main information on the charts and explaining every step of the way, the extent to which we had compromised our future to satisfy the Alsace's needs. How, on many occasions, we had paid dearly for doing things the Alsace insisted on, even if they were contrary to our interests.

It was perhaps the second time, after my testimony, that the jurors paid some attention to what was being said. Steve not only pointed out our sacrifice, but what could have been our future, had this interruption by the Alsace, not occurred. He projected a company growing by leaps and bounds, with an excellent administration, posed to become a player in the industry.

I felt somewhat at ease again for the first time since the beginning of the trial. Perhaps it wasn't too late to reverse the malaise Sherman, less than adequate performance, had instilled in the proceedings. I looked at each and every juror as Steve spoke and in an instance or two, I detected an expression of true interest in what he was saying. A welcome event, in a trial marred by the manifested detachment of its jurors.

After another quick break, the Alsace's lawyer began his cross-examination challenging Steve's expert credentials. Never short for answers, he quickly responded with six or seven other occasions in which his findings had been upheld, his clients prevailed and won the damages he claimed they had suffered. Worried about a confrontation that would rekindle the interest from the jury, the Alsace's lawyer quickly reverted to his formula of asking yes or no questions mostly about my financial situation. Steve somewhat defensively, but shrewdly, repeated the core of his presentation forcing the Alsace lawyer to quit before he could reverse his offensive and demolish his arguments.

Right after my expert witness finished his presentation Sherman announced we rested. The Judge called both lawyers to a conference and after a brief exchange announced we would resume the trial, as usual at nine, with the Alsace presenting their defense.

Sherman, George, Steve and I walked out of the court house. Once in the street, I told Steve he had done a great job and I was very pleased with his presentation. Sherman and George seconded me and said they felt confident the jury would see the case in a positive light. Steve was more cautious. "I've faced many juries," Steve said, "and it is very difficult for them to understand what you're telling them. This is not a criminal case in which you have a knife or a revolver. In this case, none of them have any idea what a business is all about. Yes, they see the numbers I threw at them and they might agree or disagree, but they are only numbers, whereas your case is buried in all those documents you introduced and they won't read. Think about it."

The evening came early, or so I thought. I took a steak from the fridge, a bottle of wine, bread and went down to the beach to barbeque my rib-eye. I needed time with myself to bask in my solitude and lick my wounds, to think of a way out if there was any. My thoughts drifted. I thought of myself with no prospect of winning the trial, alone, dispossessed, hoping for a clean break, an escape, another new beginning. I thought of death as my only way out; not mine, of course; my parents', even Maxim's; I needed a clean break. It was my luck. I thought they would die but miraculously they prevailed. They tricked death, like Sisyphus did before being condemned to roll the boulder. But it is me who ended up rolling the boulder, not them. Now their ailments seem chronic, everlasting, with no prospect of a quick end.

I finished my steak and drank the remains of the wine. It was a bluish evening and a few shining stars had shown up to keep me company. It had also cooled off and I pulled out a light blanket from my picnic basket, covered myself and let the breeze, the lapping waves and the chirping birds, sing me a magical lullaby. And I counted the stars and the gentle waves one by one as I sank into a sweet sleep, trying to escape, dreaming of a way out, and in a brief instant everything became dark.

THE ALSACE DEFENSE & ANDRÉ

"All rise," was heard again in the chambers and the trial continued with the Alsace's putting up their defense. Their legal team consisted of two lawyers with two other paralegals. Their lead counsel was a pompous asshole who loved to hear himself talk. He was prone to use his gadgets as props. He'd pull out a calculator and perform — to the amusement of the jury and the rest of the attendees — a simple addition, the result of which everybody knew in advance.

The second lawyer was the Alsace's corporate counsel. A stocky, early sixties woman, who relished a confrontation and argued with her co-counsel as if she was fighting for her life.

I looked at them both in disbelief. I felt sorry for them. I knew they were doing their jobs, but I found them lacking decorum; mercenaries justifying their loot. It must be hard to know your client did wrong and try to cover it up as if it was the adversary's fault and not their own.

The Alsace's first witness was a Federated Financial Officer. His testimony was brief. He was asked a number of questions related to their efforts to collect whatever moneys they claimed I owed them. The fellow delivered his well-rehearsed answers as if they were a monotonous chant. Sherman cross examined him and he claimed he knew nothing about our relationship with the Alsace. He claimed to know only the accounts receivables they inherited when the merge with the Alsace took place.

The Alsace first day of defense had been completed and their lawyer announced, at a conference with the Judge, their witness the following morning would be André. We were aware they had been threatening to use André — whose deposition we took almost four years ago — but doubted it because he could be a loose cannon; the man could go either way. We hadn't heard from him since and were sure the Alsace was bluffing when they included him in their witnesses list. But, to our surprise, André was back and we'd have to deal with him one more time.

Home again, I ate some leftovers from a previous meal Yolanda had prepared, drank my espresso and called Julie.

"You won't believe who is the Alsace's witness tomorrow?"

"You tell me," Julie responded.

"André!"

"André? You're kidding me."

"No, I'm not," and I went ahead and told her all about the day in court, the tapes played, a brief conference Sherman, George and I had about how to handle André and a few other tidbits to make the conversation pleasant.

After that we said goodnight but not before swearing I'd call her the minute André's court appearance ended.

Another day in court. "All rise," the Judge came in, the jury sat in their box and the clerk asked the Alsace's lawyer to call his witness. André's name resonated all over the empty chambers and everyone turned and focused on the chamber's entrance.

The door opened, and André, in a wheelchair was delivered to the witness stand by two strong, visibly gay, muscle guys. I looked at him, like everybody else in the room, attentively. He appeared extremely weak and very thin. He had lost weight and most of his hair. He was a cadaver. He had been rolled up from his tomb, just for the trial.

André held on tightly to both arms of the chair and looked ferociously at all of us, and me in particular, as he was deposited in the witness stand.

I had focused on the jury to weigh their reaction to such a scene, and at least two of the old women seemed emotionally affected. The rest were in shock. It was unusual to see people in his condition outside of a hospital, especially testifying in a trial that didn't involve them. I got close to Sherman and asked him if he knew André was in such condition. He pleaded ignorance and assured me it was the first time he saw him in his life.

The Alsace's lawyer walked to the witness stand and thanked André for his willingness to testify. André responded, with a trembling voice, it was his duty to set the record straight.

I was fascinated. If the Alsace's decision to put him in the witness stand didn't backfire, it would be a masterful stroke. We never entertained the idea of using his testimony, afraid of opening him up to the other side; the man was a loose cannon. But now he posed a real threat, and it would be our job to put him down. Unfortunately, I doubted Sherman, completely unfamiliar with him as a persona, would be able to do so.

The Alsace's lawyer set the stage, asking André to tell the jury when and how his employment with our corporation began. André began slowly, with a hesitant voice, to recount our first encounter in my place in Key Biscayne, the contract we signed, my offer to support him and give him carte blanche with the administration of the corporation.

A few key questions from the Alsace lawyer — to clarify a point or two — and then he asked André to tell the jury what happened next. André continued his story telling the jurors how I had decided to use Ben and my assistant, Roberta, to keep track of the finances. How humiliated he felt that his employees saw that — as a clear indication — he lacked my trust and the full control of the corporation. André kept on talking about a conspiracy to frustrate and make him quit. How I neglected to support him, especially during difficult moments when his partner was critically ill, and he needed my understanding and support.

As he spoke, I kept looking at the jury, especially at the two old ladies who had become visibly moved when they first saw him. Both, and most of the jury, seemed mesmerized with his tale. He spoke of his frustration and my disdain while he fought to regain his employees' respect. He ended up talking about the pain of losing his companion and my lack of interest in his personal wellbeing.

It didn't escape me that even if his story had nothing to do with my claim, André's account made me look like a heartless taskmaster who couldn't be trusted. Someone who conspired behind the scenes and finally dumped him when his knowledge and contacts were exhausted. André's disillusion was an ostensibly moving tale, no doubt, but only part of a two-pronged strategy the Alsace's lawyer had developed; Alex wasn't reliable as a person and his business was chronically underfunded. It wasn't what I claimed they did. It was my own doing. Clever.

After another short break, the questioning shifted from the personal to the cold subject of numbers. André began to answer questions related to my company's finances. He told stories about suppliers complaining about delayed payments, my original efforts to secure letters of credit to pay Zamora and my need to renew and increase my lines of credit with both banks. How he wanted to increase the salaries of two of his original designers and how I refused — for lack of funds — when at the same time I was traveling to Europe living an enchanting life. He finally confirmed with a rotund yes, each and every negative question the Alsace's lawyer had used to impugn my financial viability as a business.

For a person who had worked only a year for us, André claimed an unashamedly complete familiarity with my corporation's history, claiming knowledge of meetings, discussions with suppliers, bank negotiations, things that had taken place long after he had left our employ. A pack of lies and innuendos the Alsace's lawyer had been able to make the jury listen to, with the Judge's acquiescence, regardless of Sherman's constant objections of hearsay.

Two and a half hours on the witness stand, André seemed exhausted although his demeanor was strong. He had kept a steady pace even when at times he seemed to flounder over a detail or two. The Judge, perhaps sensing the witness needed a break, decided to cut short the morning session and asked the group to reconvene promptly at 1:30 giving André another half hour to relax.

Sherman, George and I went for lunch at a nearby restaurant. We needed to talk and we got involved in a spirited exchange while eating Chinese food in a dive, close to the courthouse. I was alarmed, I told Sherman, by the amount of unsubstantiated claims and hearsay the Judge had let the jury listen to. Sherman defended himself claiming he had objected to most of his testimony and it was mostly inadmissible; that the Judge will eventually instruct the jury, to disregard it. I wasn't so sure of it and emphatically told him he should have stopped André's testimony. He had worked for us for a year and he had claimed knowledge of things that took place three and four years after he was fired.

André was returned to the witness stand by his two friends. It was time to begin the cross examination and Sherman politely asked him about his condition to a chorus of objections from the Alsace's lawyer and a warning from the Judge.

"What does the witness condition have to do with the trial?" the Judge angrily demanded. "I won't allow that kind of question in my court or I will declare you in contempt. Understood?"

I couldn't believe it. I thought I was watching one of those staged courtroom dramas on TV, when the actor playing the judge, upset threatens to send the lawyer to the slammer if he doesn't behave. It was unreal.

Sherman sheepishly excused himself and made matters worse trying to explain his blunder, but finally began to impugn André's testimony making him reluctantly admit his employ with us lasted less than one year. That all the numbers and statistics he had claimed to know firsthand were the product of reading the discovery documents and not his own experience while working for us. Sherman also made André admit the mischievous campaign he conducted visiting our clients, claiming we were at the end of our rope, advising them not to pay money owed to us, asserting he knew we'd be out of business in no time.

André's testimony ended the session and the first week of the trial. The Judge asked counsel to approach. He demanded from each lawyer how much longer they needed to complete their legal arguments. Sherman said he only had his summation, but the Alsace's lawyer said he'd need still another day to tie up loose ends. Dismissing both counsels, the Judge promptly convened us for Tuesday claiming an ongoing case with two out of town legal firms. And that was that!

The first week of testimony had ended and we weren't any closer to a resolution than before. Regardless of Sherman's lackluster performance, our witnesses presented our case with aplomb, exhausting detail and plenty of evidence. Unfortunately we had watched the jury disregard the mountain of documents, the highlighted paragraphs that proved, beyond a shadow of a doubt, that the Alsace and the other companies they controlled had conspired among themselves to do us in.

I drove back to the Key with an empty mind. I stopped at the tennis club, found the professional available and signed up for an hour of uninterrupted bliss. Hitting balls and sweating my ass off felt good. A reinvigorating shower and I continued home where I expected quiet and tranquility to reign.

I found Yolanda in the kitchen preparing dinner for the night. She asked me if I wanted to stay and have dinner with them. I gave her a silly excuse. In fact I was planning to meet no one and had no plans other than a good meal.

I grabbed a scotch, went to my study and placed a call to Julie.

"How's my warrior doing? She asked.

"I really don't know. I think we're at the end of the trial and I'm in trouble. I guess everything rests now with Sherman's summation. The old man probably was brilliant thirty years ago, but quite often he sounds as if he doesn't know the facts and uses all kinds of gimmicks to try to prove a point with no aim. You get what I mean?"

"He doesn't know shit and pretends he knows it all."

"You said it. Ben, Francine and Roberta were great. It was like hearing myself speak. But André had a devastating effect on the jury. He's extremely weak, probably dying He's keeping himself alive just to testify against me. I can't believe it."

"What are you doing this weekend?"

"I don't know. My severance pay is running out fast and it has to last me until I get another job."

"Any prospects?" she asked me.

"I had an ugly vision of me selling café con leche, or latte as you call it, in Calle Ocho."

A WELCOMED DIVERSION

On Sunday afternoon I was invited to a barbeque at an old friend's home. A welcome diversion I also used to visit my in-laws in a close by neighborhood. We marveled about Maxine's condition, all the vital organs working like clockwork, although her paralysis and failing brain functions continued to accelerate.

"The time will come when you'll have no alternative but to put her in a nursing facility," her brother said.

"I've considered it many times," I mentioned, "but I'd be ruined economically, more than I am now. You know the state policies are draconian. We talked a while longer and I left for my friend's barbeque.

It was cool and pleasant, a perfect February afternoon in Florida. My host lived in one of those fancy, secluded neighborhoods and had invited a number of couples; I was the odd man out. The usual groups formed, the men talking about the past super-bowl and the Dolphins losing season. I felt out of place. I've never developed any interest in what we called football in the United States and drifted to the female group that welcomed my curiosity and funny disposition.

A few men followed me to the ladies side and the conversation eventually evolved and we began to discuss politics and the state of the economy. There was a doctor or two, an accountant and a few other professionals in the group. They were pouring their money into condo buildings at the beach and the stock market alike, and doing great. I kept quiet, but not for long.

After they all vented their luck and expertise, they asked for my investment preferences and portfolio acumen. I excused myself saying all my possessions were in my head and pockets and they had a great laugh. They thought I was being funny, little did they know I was telling the truth. Soon after that we began eating hamburgers and drinking a lousy pink wine, poured from a gallon jug; so much for class and new money.

Monday came and I felt somehow lost not having to go to court. Maxine's doctor had scheduled his monthly visit and he showed up promptly at nine. We'd been fortunate he was a close friend of the family and lived right on the Key. We discussed Maxine's medical condition as if we were talking about drinking coffee. We talked about the obvious; she had gained weight and become incontinent in the last few months, eating less of the good and more of the sweet stuff. Being friends, we discussed not keeping her on any strict diet — what the hell — there was no logical reason, within limits, for keeping her away from the only pleasure she had left in her life; chocolate within limits.

Yolanda showed up briefly and told the doctor more about Maxine's behavior and the peculiar ways she had developed communicating with her. They were an interesting set of observations rarely heard from an untrained person. When she left, the doctor said I was lucky to count on her services.

"It's a thankless job," the doctor said.

"I had a most revealing conversation with Yolanda," I said. "I told her I felt bad seeing her feeding Maxine, changing diapers, giving her sponge baths every morning. And she answered with the most disconcerting sincerity. 'I prefer doing this on my own time,' she said, 'living here with you two, to working in a factory and living in a substandard building or apartment. Besides I've grown used to her and now I see her, I mean you both, as relatives and her as someone from my own family who needs help.'"

That afternoon I had agreed to meet a friend for a snack at The Marriot of Coral Gables. I had not seen her for quite some time and I really wanted to renew the friendship. She was more than twenty minutes late. Afraid she had forgotten, I decided to call her. My cellphone battery was low and I looked for a telephone booth at the end of the lobby and dialed her. She was two blocks away and she'd be at the hotel in no time.

When I finished the call, I noticed a neatly folded piece of paper right under the telephone. As if someone had taken it out of his or her pocket and left it behind when the conversation ended. I opened and read it carefully and I couldn't believe my eyes. A strong tremor shook my body. I felt as if I were receiving a message, someone warning me, advising me to take things philosophically, if I could.

Life is like a
mystery.
There are things
you just can't
change.
Just when you thought
things were going
your way they make a
drastic change!
Why does it have
To be that way
I don't understand.
I wish everything will
be going my way, but
that's just a dream
escape!
I guess I'll have to
learn to live with it
everything upside
down, I guess it's
not all that bad
these mysterious ways!

F Y

The note had been written in long hand, with a black ballpoint pen. The letters were rounded, the t's were crossed at midway, the m's were not sharp edged, and it was written in a straight line, even if the paper was unlined. And what seemed a signature was a simple two letters, "F Y." Immediately I thought, "Fuck you," but it could also had been, "for you." Or the actual initials of a clever messenger.

A million thoughts came to my mind. I didn't know if the person had copied these musings from a book, someone else's ruminations on life, or if it was something he or she had thought about. As if making sense of a situation in life, something, that strangely enough, fitted perfectly with mine.

BACK TO TRIAL

Tuesday morning came and we reconvened in court promptly at nine. The window panes reflected no outside light. The huge chamber resembled a damp, empty cavern; just the Judge, a guard, two clerks, a stenographer, my two lawyers, the two from the Alsace and me.

The Judge asked counsel to approach and told them he sensed the end was near and asked how much longer they would need to complete their case. Surprisingly, the Alsace lawyer said they rested. The Judge, as if infused by lightning, said let's finish it. He called the jury and they entered their box looking tired, perhaps cursing me, for having interrupted their lives.

Sherman, George and I had a brief exchange. We couldn't figure out why the Alsace rested their case. They had two more witnesses scheduled for this morning. There was no obvious explanation and we concluded they wanted to end with André's image dying on the stand.

If I was concerned with André's impact on the jury, I was also concerned about Sherman's summation. I took him to a corner of the room and told him to plead surprise and ask the Judge for a brief delay for him to put his pitch together. But he said no that he had his notes with him and that would be sufficient. I quickly jotted down a number of ideas and concerns and gave them to him. He took my compilation of wisdom together with a bunch of other loose yellow pages and walked to confront the jury.

Sherman's summation was short, less than ten minutes — lacking the nuances demonstrated in more than forty documents we introduced as evidence — and with a complete absence of emotion. Missing that particular spark that might have made the jury stop and think they were dealing with another human being's life confronting an anonymous huge corporation handled by senseless bureaucrats. That it was not about money, as the Alsace claimed, but commitment, fairness, the double dealing of a huge corporation and its impact on a small business man that, very well, could have been one of them.

The Alsace's rebuttal was a bit longer, dispassionate and full of numbers. It was simple, their lawyer said, and he went on and concentrated on my lack of capital, my delays paying bills, the fact that even if they had agreed on one document, subsequent ones had overridden what they had agreed to before. That documents and not handshakes were the real thing in the business world. In other words, all their promises made during handshakes, when they needed my help, meant nothing once they had locked it in. "It was not their fault, it was mine," he claimed, not being ready to tackle the big leagues.

I sat quietly if seething inside me. The simplicity of the Alsace's lawyer argument was appalling. He reduced the complexity of a business relationship to those of regular people's suspension of their credit cards. From the get go, I questioned if this group could grasp the difference between their home economics and the business' world. And the way he went about it, made me wonder, if that was what was happening. Especially when the crux of my case was unfortunately buried in obscure paragraphs in the many documents we had introduced and none of them seemed to have paid attention to.

Sherman came back to give the counter rebuttal and repeated many of the same arguments he had exposed before. He mentioned the answer to the riddle was in the documents. He delivered his tepid counter rebuttal asking the jurors to be fair and not to be blinded by the size of the Alsace or the simplicity of their arguments, but to look at this confrontation as a battle between David and Goliath. A small business man fighting for his life being manhandled by a senseless, large, out-of-control corporation. Ironically, the last two sentences were the best rhetorical arguments he had mustered during the whole trial. Unfortunately it was too little, too late.

The cards had been dealt and I had no aces. It had been a long, stressful and tortuous road to get to this moment. A road full of twists and turns, betrayals, change of venues, judges, setbacks, economic ruin and — after all had been said and done — we were listening to the Judge's instructions to the jury of my, so-called, peers.

The Judge adjusted his glasses and read his instructions from a yellow pad. He instructed the jury to disregard hearsay, mentioned a number of objections made by each lawyer, told them to read the evidence, informed them that in the spirit of fairness, highlighted paragraphs had been eliminated. He insisted they should look at each particular document and consider it in the light of the whole evidence. He reminded them that the fact that one of the opposing parties was big, didn't necessarily mean, it was guilty or vice-versa. And he wished them God speed! In the end my fate was in someone else's hands; so much for free will.

It was exactly noon when Sherman, George and I left the chambers. Sherman said the court would alert him the moment the jury reached a verdict, that he had work to do and we would be in contact as soon as he heard something. He said that even in the worst circumstances, we had a good chance for an appeal. The Judge, he continued, had committed a number of mistakes and he was sure we would be able to reverse a negative decision if we wanted to. Obviously, he added, an appeal was an expensive proposition and he didn't know if I'd be prepared to spend another fifty grand pursuing it.

I didn't answer, turned my back on them and walked away with no particular direction in mind; just away. It was still cloudy. I stopped briefly under a canopy not knowing what to do next. Finally I turned around and went back to the garage where my car was parked. I sat inside my car quietly, turned on the radio and listened to some choral music. I thought of nothing, looked straight at the wall; my mind was blank. I stayed there thoughtless, just listening to the mournful chant the same way the garage's walls would, if they had ears.

I don't know when I finally got out of the car and went down to the street. I was hungry. I looked at a clock and it was 1:30. We had left the court at

12:30. I entered a cafeteria and ordered a sandwich; a salami sandwich was delivered; I thought I had asked for a Cuban. I ate it nevertheless. I paid, went back to the garage to retrieve my car and drove back to Key Biscayne, my refuge. I felt like walking the beach; I needed space, but it was pouring again. It would be silly, was the first sensible thought that came to my head.

And I went directly to my studio and laid on my couch quietly, listening to Flagstad sing Liebestod one more time. It wasn't long before I passed out, not to wake up again until Yolanda requested my attention. It was late, she said, six thirty, already. "Would you like anything to eat?" she asked me. She was preparing dinner for Maxine and herself and she could add to whatever it was she was cooking, a stew or something, she didn't say.

"Yes," I said, "but I wouldn't be hungry for another hour or so. Please go ahead. I'll have whatever you prepare when I can."

Yolanda sat in the armchair across from me and softly said. "You had a bad day, I think."

"Yes," I responded.

"How are things at the trial?"

"I don't know. We came to the end and now we're waiting for the jury to decide."

"What would happen if you lose?"

"Life will continue, I guess. It always does, no matter what."

"Would you need another job?"

"Of course. I need one now."

"If you lose, will you keep Maxine with you or would you put her away in an institution?"

"Nooo," I said trying to reassure her. "Maxine will stay with me to the end of days; or as long as you can help me. But the way things are, she might need more than one person pretty soon."

"No, no, I can handle her," she said. "You don't have to worry about her. I have my sister. She knows Maxine well, she's with her on my days off and she can help me, if I need help."

I had dinner about nine and called Julie.

"Haven't heard anything, have you? She asked me.

"No. I guess they'll have an answer tomorrow sometime."

"Did Sherman say anything about his own inklings?"

"Yes, that we could always appeal, if I had the money."

"That doesn't sound very reassuring, does it?"

"No, it doesn't."

"You're a resourceful man. You'll go on no matter what."

"Thank you! You sound like Sherman's appeal solution."

"It's the truth, isn't it?"

"Of course my love, of course. I was being fictitious. It is the truth."

It was a long night. I couldn't sleep and stayed out on my terrace watching the downpour with no end. I was anxious, dreading the approaching morning, as if something bad was going to hit me. The Brujo's prophesy would finally be consummated. He said it; "it was going to be painful, slow and agonizing." And painful, slow and agonizing it had been. I dreaded the thought, but I had no way of escaping it. My entire life paraded in front of me as if on TV and I wasn't able to stop the tape. It kept going forward, awfully fast with the good things and agonizingly slow with the dreadful ones, the last five dismaying years of my life.

Morning came earlier than ever, or so I felt; I hadn't slept. I had watched the rain end gradually, the sky became cloudless and the first lights colored the horizon. Another day was ready to begin. I felt like doing nothing, and nothing I did. Just prepared my espresso, drank it like a shot, and went back to my terrace. The old couple I had watched for years was walking the beach. I didn't know if they spoke to each other anymore and if they did, what about. I surmised they'd been together for so long, they didn't have much more to say. But their sight, I didn't know why, reassured me and I always watched them until they disappeared around the bend.

Yolanda was up early and offered to prepare breakfast for me. I didn't feel hungry, but exhausted. I took a hot shower and dressed up for the occasion. I had to wait for Sherman's call. I read my New York Times quietly, trying to forget the next few hours were momentous in my life. It was ten thirty when the telephone rang; Sherman was at the other end of the line.

"We have a verdict," he said. "Half hour in court."

And that was that. Another chapter of my accidental life seemed to have finally come to an end.

The drive to the courthouse was fast. The previous day's deluge probably discouraged most people from coming downtown today and, in fifteen minutes or less, I was parking my car and getting out of it, as Sherman and George parked theirs in another empty spot near mine.

Sherman approached me and we shook hands.

"I don't like it," he said. "Too quick for a positive outcome. But this is not the end of the world. We have a good case."

Yes, we have a good case, I said to myself, but it was carelessly mishandled.

"We'll see. This is not the end of the world," he repeated. "They might have a surprise for us," the old man said looking at George, who had kept quiet while walking behind us.

"Of course," George quickly assented. "That's the problem with juries. People are fickle" he said, trying to comfort me.

We entered the empty chambers before anybody else. We sat quietly in our corner of the room as if we had gotten to the wake before the corpse was exposed. The Alsace's lawyer and his lady co-counsel entered the room and went directly to their side, saying nothing. The Marshall came in, followed by the court's Clerk, the court's stenographer and — quickly after we heard the familiar: "All rise..." — the Judge entered the chambers, sat and immediately said.

"Will counsel approach the bench," he said. "We have a verdict. If you have nothing to add, I'll call the jury."

Sherman and the Alsace's lawyer looked at each, shook their heads, looked at the Judge and together said, "no, your honor."

The Judge signaled the Marshall, "Call the jury, please."

The jury filed in for the last time. All but one of them gave me a furtive look as if troubled by the pain they were to inflict me. The Judge asked if they had reached a verdict, and the woman foreman said, "Yes, your honor." The Judge asked her to read it out loud. The foreman said, "We the jury found the defendant, The Alsace Corporation, not guilty ...." and went on to say, "The Plaintiff claim was without merit." They found the Alsace not responsible for the plaintiff's claims and approved the Alsace's counterclaim for the moneys owed, but not the expenses for their defense.

Sherman turned to me and patted my back. "Well, at least we put up a good fight," he said. George shook hands with me, but said nothing.

The Judge thanked the jury for a job well done and as on television said, "The jury is dismissed." The jury took off quickly. Sherman and George crossed the aisle, thanked the Judge, and shook hands with the opposing counsel. Sherman congratulated the Alsace's lawyer and the Alsace's did likewise.

Hypocrites, I thought to myself and remained seated while their feast went on a few moments longer.

Sherman, George and I walked out of the building practically saying nothing. We got to our cars and Sherman, taking my hand, said;

"Take a week off. It has been tough, but life goes on. Let's get together a week from today, I'll make a note on my calendar, and let's review our options. There are some, you know. We aren't dead."

And indeed we weren't. We were walking empty handed.

I drove out of the parking lot not knowing what to do. It was the first time in a long while I had no hope. I knew I'd survive, but I also knew I'd have to reinvent myself once again. My hopes of being vindicated had collided with the innocence and benign indifference of a group of citizens not equipped to tackle the intricacies of the business world. So much for the fairness of the jury system. I had lost big, first trying to survive the Alsace's onslaught and now again — in an uneven fight — to recover what was mine; not only money, but my own self esteem.

CONSUMMATUM EST!

I went back to the Key like a stable horse returns instinctively to his barn. I wasn't paying attention to the surroundings, just driving forward. Chloe, came to mind. What happened to me was similar to what she said happened to her father. But in her father's case it was because of pure and simple competition, market forces, and not the manipulations of a small group of individuals. I got home and went directly to the telephone.

"Hey!"

"And?" Julie asked me.

"Kaput!"

"I was afraid of that. Listening to you through the trial, I got the impression things weren't going well. What was Sherman's reaction?"

"He scheduled a meeting a week from today to review our options."

"What are you doing now?" she asked me.

"Just got home."

"Why don't you come to New York for a few days? You haven't seen your parents in a while and mother always asks me. I know you talk to her almost every day, but you know old people. I think a change of scenery might also help you."

Irony of ironies, while I had experienced an excruciating setback in my life I hadn't lost my appetite. I put on some shorts, prepared myself a sandwich, grabbed a bottle of wine, walked downstairs and sat under the gazebo on the beach. I was alone and my mind was empty. I ate, drank half a bottle of wine and passed out on a lounge chair; I don't know for how long.

Thursday afternoon I was on a plane to New York. Everything had been quiet at the Key for the last few days and Maxine was in Yolanda's good hands. Before I left for the airport I called Sherman and cancelled my appointment. I wasn't leaving anything behind that would interfere with a few days of quiet relief.

The sight of Julie waiting for me at the baggage claim was reassuring. I was at my weakest ever. I've gotten used to certain markers, certain things I looked constantly for and I became apprehensive if one was missing. But just seeing her there made me think of my guardian angel. Seeing her was only comparable to my landing in Miami, being free from the nightmare Castro represented in my early life.

"Don't kiss me, remember I'm a married woman," she said throwing her arms around my neck.

"I'm not jealous," I retorted, while thinking to myself; oh, Julie, I'll never be able to make you understand what you represent in my life. If you knew how much I need you.

We left the terminal and the airport after a long wait for my bag.

"Do you want to do anything out of the ordinary?" Julie asked me as we were crossing the Triboro Bridge. "Burt can join us or we can pick him up on our way to a restaurant," she continued while sorting through the traffic. "I have nothing at home. How about Sushi?" Julie asked me.

Sushi it was and Burt joined us as we were entering the restaurant. We embraced. Burt was a warm, wonderful individual. I considered him a good friend. I had developed some kind of moral code that made it easy for me to be his friend and his wife's lover. Don't ask me how? It was natural. And Julie felt the same way. We were happy as a threesome.

Saturday morning I woke up early. Even if I was emotionally exhausted, I still couldn't sleep normal hours. I took my sweat suit from the closet, a pair of tennis shoes, prepared myself an espresso and faced the Hudson River's chill head on. It was 25▢ degrees in New York, but cloudless, and the sun was rising behind the buildings on the East. I jogged alongside Riverside Park and the piers to 34th St. and back with one or two other joggers ahead of me. Once in the neighborhood, I stopped at Zabar's, ate a croissant with my second espresso of the morning and continued on to Julie's.

Back at Julie's I met Burt preparing himself a pot of American coffee.

"You want some?" he asked me.

"No, I just had some."

"Julie mentioned you wanted to discuss bankruptcy. I can't now, but when I return."

"No, not this weekend. I'm going to be around four or five days, if you guys don't mind."

Burt smiled but said nothing. He left and I took a shower. When I came out Julie was standing outside the bathroom door in her robe. I walked over and tried to kiss her. She covered her mouth and said.

"I haven't brushed my teeth..."

"It wouldn't be the first time."

"What are your plans?" she asked me.

"My parents first, if I could use your car."

"Do you mind if I go with you?"

"Are you asking me?"

"I thought we might take a ride to Glen Cove, antiquing? It will distract you."

We arrived at the nursing home purposely at eleven thirty. The idea, to spend an hour with my parents, take them downstairs for lunch and split. I hated myself for shortchanging the only pleasure they had left; seeing their son. But I was emotionally exhausted and I needed some peace myself. In the end, time and circumstance bend your will and make you consider and do things you never thought you were being capable of doing.

But, my carefully thought out stratagem collapsed when we got to their floor and found they no longer were taken to the restaurant downstairs, but fed en masse, in a common dining area on their floor.

My parents' faces lit up the minute they saw me standing at the door. It was heartbreaking to fix eyes with them. It was so little what I offered them and so powerful their display of joy; it was unbearable. The thought that anyone could be happy with so little made tears come to my eyes. Six or seven attendants were feeding fifteen or twenty residents alternatively. All were in wheelchairs, with food running down their mouths, spilling half of what they took back on themselves. If there was a time to ask God where He was, right there and then was the time for those who believe there is one.

Julie entered the room ahead of me. We saluted the attendants, waved at the residents, who stopped eating to wave back, and approached the table where my parents were sitting with two other residents. We kissed Mother first and Father next and took the spoons from the beleaguered attendant's hands to continue feeding them both. And we did for the next twenty minutes, trying to be funny and encouraging them to eat faster. I didn't know how to thank the attendants for being such a devoted and charitable group while doing such slavish and unrewarding work. In our own small way we tried to help by reducing by two the number of mouths they needed to feed, even if for a single meal.

We finally took my parents back to their room and after another emotionally exhausting half hour, we excused ourselves with a merciful "we'll be back" and walked away. It was so difficult and traumatic to leave them behind knowing how desperately they wanted our company.

Julie and I got to the first antique shop. There was a beautiful 'empire' chest of drawers the broker said was circa 1803. A classic piece with a heavy black marble top, very similar to the one I sacrificed when my debacle began; the upset price was nine thousand with an estimated sale price of eleven thousand dollars.

"Brings back sad memories, does it?" Julie told me.

"I loved the piece. Maxine never liked it. She said it was one of my excesses. I rushed to sell it to pacify her, knowing perfectly well that it wouldn't stem the debacle. Are you interested in buying it?"

"Not at those prices. There might be another individual like you need-ing quick cash willing or needing to part with such a gorgeous piece for half this price."

Julie stopped for a second and, looking into my eyes, said:

"You looked extremely upset at the nursing home."

"It's unbearable, really. They're my parents and I'll never turn my back on them, but it's a fantastic emotional price to pay for our elderly. I don't know why they just don't die. It is so degrading for proud people to find themselves in those conditions. Begging for the attention of strangers, wetting their diapers, being rushed around as if they were cattle. It is sad the first time you put them away, because that's what we do, but then to see them after such a steep decline? Mother was relatively strong when she entered to keep Pipo's company. A sacrifice like that is difficult to understand. I advised her not to do it. But she did it for her old man. In a way, he didn't decline as much as she had. She's paralyzed, begging for attention, not able to speak, for God's sake. Why not just get it over with? There is no return. It is unbearable to see her like that."

We returned to Manhattan close to seven in the evening. Burt was already at home drinking one of his gin and tonics. "What are we going to eat tonight?" he demanded.

"If you don't invite us out, you're in trouble.

And we settled for an early dinner at eight and the late showing at the Quad, some mid-eastern movie one of his Arab clients had suggested him to see.

Sunday morning was dark and dreary, with light snow in New York. The three of us stayed in bed a little longer than usual, when at about eleven, Burt began banging pots and pans alerting us to come to the kitchen to eat break-fast. We sat around the kitchen counter, eating ham, bacon and eggs, with old left over French bread. We continued talking about the movie we saw the previous night and when the subject was exhausted, Burt suggested:

"Since we're prisoners of the weather, do you want to discuss your prob-lems now or read the Times first? I saw it already, so the choice is all yours."

I dreaded the idea of talking about my problems now, but I thought for a moment and said: "Yes, let's get it over with."

The three of us went to the living room. Julie and I sat at each end of the couch and Burt sat in his favorite armchair. I began by going over my financial situation, whatever money I had left in my bank account and a number of outstanding debts with at least two different banks, not to mention my ballooning credit card balances. I had lost all my properties, but some of the mortgages were still active, if unpaid, and the banks were waiting for their money. Or at least they waited until the trial was over. Now, having nothing to wait for anymore, they'd be determined to collect, hoping that they could.

"How much do you estimate you owe personally altogether?" Burt asked me.

"Roughly? Four, four and a half million. Not including some business loans I signed personally."

"You're lucky you live in Florida. You can protect your condo."

"I'm paying rent," I said, as Julie looked at me mindful of what I was going to say next. "A friend owns the apartment."

"How about Uncle Sam?" he asked me.

"About 250K."

"The IRS is tough to crack; they don't let go. But I'd clean the deck now if I were you; the sooner the better. There is no shame associated with bankruptcy any more. Your case is obvious; your business collapsed. Just clean it up and start again."

The light snow continued the entire afternoon and into the early part of the evening. We stayed home, reading, napping, watching TV and finally ordered Chinese. We had our dinner laying on the rug, with a great wine, brownies and espresso. Afterwards we decided to watch a movie. Anyone looking at us from a distance would confuse us with three college kids not knowing what to do with the rest of their lives.

After a brief argument, we settled for a movie, 'Lion in Winter' with Peter O'Toole; and why not? It was winter in New York, Henry II was a man at the end of his rope, frustrated with desertion in his ranks and a curse, historians claim, doomed his kingdom and legacy. If there was an apocryphal story that could loosely resemble mine, Lion in Winter came closest. And we enjoyed the plot, derided his children for forsaking their father and loved O'Toole's delivery of a wonderfully written dialog.

It was time to leave New York again. It was drizzling and cold, but I paid a last visit to my parents on my way to La Guardia. I was glad to leave town. Still it was a bitter sweet departure. I felt bad leaving Julie behind. She was the only meaningful thing I had left in my life. But somehow, instinctively, I always pulled away from her, something she couldn't understand and neither did I. The secret, perhaps afraid of not being able to deliver the magic she expected and I wasn't sure I could deliver. The perennial magic of what could have been but never was.

Two hours and twenty minutes later, as if by magic, I was back in Miami, happy to have left New York but worried about what I was going to find at home. The miracle of the jet age; leaving a tragedy in one place to immerse myself in another a thousand miles away.

HOPE IS IN THE AIR

The morning after my arrival it was a completely different ball game. The trial was over; I no longer had any expectations of a breakthrough, but in most aspects, my life remained the same. Maxine was in her delicate state, I owed money to the banks, had no job and my bank account was fading fast.

I called Jimenez who was in town and had left me two different messages. We agreed to have dinner at his favorite restaurant in Coral Gables, but not before a cocktail at the Sonesta, where he was staying.

I got a hold of Sherman who wanted to meet the minute I returned and went to his office the next day. The old man was very courteous, he took me to his corner office and we went over a number of what he called options; what he could do for me if we filed an appeal. His ideas were so foreign to my reality that I didn't bother to discuss them, but I thanked him nevertheless. Before we said goodbye, he mentioned Jimenez was in town and wanted to see me. I thanked him again and left his office as swiftly as I came in.

That evening I went to the Sonesta to get Jimenez and found Margarita with him. I couldn't hide my surprise to see him with his unfaithful mistress. But I played dumb, as if I didn't know what had happened between them. Jimenez hugged me as if consoling someone for the loss of a relative. He said he followed the trial through Sherman's snippets and was devastated to hear the outcome. But he reassured me, "if I needed any kind of recommendation, he'd be more than willing to write a letter." A letter, that's what I heard. And, with a straight face, I thanked him for his generous offer.

Having said that, he used a moment when Margarita disappeared for no apparent reason, to tell me there was no sense in keeping her away from him. Yes, he was upset with her indiscretion, but reminded me again of my own saying; "it's better to eat chicken between two than no chicken at all." He laughed and ordered another strawberry daiquiri. So much for a cavalier attitude.

It was morning again. I was tired, with a bit of a hangover, and I stayed in bed a little longer. It was about ten; I was in my kitchen talking with Yolanda when the telephone rang. Roberta was at the other end.

"You won't believe what happened? She said.

"Try me," I responded.

"You have no idea who died? André!"

"Come on, I don't believe you!" I said.

"He lived long enough to testify against you. I just heard about it. They had a big wake last night and he's being buried this afternoon at three. Do you want to go? I would."

"They would mob or lynch me if they found me there," I responded.

"I'm going. I'll let you know," Roberta concluded.

André is dead, I said to myself and drank my second espresso. I walked to my terrace and leaned on the railing. I remembered when I hired him. His enthusiasm was contagious. He pledged his unconditional support and offered to do his utmost, to get the company to all the corners of the market. Then came his management failings, his fallouts with the employees, his demands of absolute authority and finally the breakup. I knew he was a tough nut to crack, but never imagined the degree of bitterness and his obsession with my demise. Well, he probably felt vindicated when he heard the trial's outcome and my financial debacle. Vaya con Dios, André, I thought. Good riddance.

I went back to Maxine's room where Yolanda was having her breakfast. I told Maxine that André was dead, of Aids. But she didn't react, just looked at me briefly and continued eating her cereal as if I had said nothing. I turned around, went to my study and made a call to Ben.

"André is dead," I told him.

"So soon," Ben responded. "You said he was a cadaver at the trial. But I didn't realize it was that bad."

"Well, it was."

Concerned with my next move I dialed Julie and Burt. We talked briefly about André's death but promptly switched to my planned bankruptcy and two calls Burt had made to attorneys in Florida. Burt got off the phone and I continued talking with Julie who, although a devout Catholic, was glad the son of a bitch was gone. On a lighter side, I told her about Jimenez and Margarita, Sherman's offer and twenty other things. We ended the conversation talking about me finding a new job and my eventual cash transfer to her account in the event I declared bankruptcy.

Left with no other alternative but to declare bankruptcy, the next three weeks were taken mostly by meetings with the two lawyers Burt had recommended. I also spent some of my idle time preparing a lengthy resume to be circulated among a few corporations. Bored with so much research and typing, met Roberta for lunch at the Beachcomber. If the outcome of the trial dominated most of the conversation, André's burial and the large segment of the gay community that showed up for the affair, was the most entertaining part of the occasion.

Burt called that evening. He had met Cogswell and shared the news of me losing the trial and my need to find a job. Cogswell was very sympathetic, Burt said, and assured him he'd do his best to either find me a job or a commission that could make me some money.

April Fools Day arrived and coincidentally I got calls from two of my lending bank's Vice-Presidents. The first one said he heard from a reliable source I had lost my case. Politely he inquired about my financial situation and their prospects of getting some money from me. I mentioned I had no job or money to speak of. He said the bank lawyers were ready to file suit against me. I said, if that's what you have to do, there was nothing I could do to stop them. He was bitter and complained I had let him down. That I had told him I had a very solid case, and he had gone out on a limb not to force the situation. Now he had an eight and a half million dollar uncollectible loan that could cost him his job. I told him that I was very sorry and that I'd always be grateful for what he did, but not to overlook my own situation. At least he had a job; I had none. "How are you surviving?" He wanted to know. I told him it was a miracle. He said, "Next time you'll hear from our lawyers." And he hung up.

Later on, right after lunch, I entertained a very similar call from my other bank's Vice President. He didn't have any preambles. He quickly asked me if I could pay my debt to his bank and I quickly responded I couldn't. He said I had betrayed him after all he had done for me. I reminded him betrayal was a poor choice of words. He said they were filing suit if they didn't receive a commitment from me to pay my balance in twenty four hours. I said "sorry," and he hung up.

A WELCOME RESPITE

Fortunately, not all the calls were embarrassing. I just hung up with Charles Peretz, a fellow I had kept in contact with for years. He was an investment banker with a generous expense account. But he was also an avid reader and cultivated the friendship of several established writers. Today he called to invite me to a small dinner to entertain a publisher from New York, in Miami, negotiating I don't know what, with the directors of The Miami Book Fair. He said it would be fun and asked me to show up at his home, Saturday night at six and I did.

The gathering was a welcome change to my daily routine. It had been more than six months since I had a real mind expanding encounter with civilized, thinking people. Julie and Burt hosted a number of dinners a year, but this one was here in Miami. And it was a good opportunity to renew or refresh a circle of friends I had neglected for some time.

The group was a mixed bag. A very attractive woman with her husband, a University of Miami literature professor, a very engaging gay fellow who claimed to be a literary agent, a single woman who said she was a fiction writer, although she made her living writing romance novels, the fellow visiting from New York and Charles, his wife Janet and me.

Charles had organized a buffet type of dinner the group devoured after cocktails were exhausted. After coffee was served, a general conversation ensued about publishing and the fellow from New York talked about his dealings with the fair's organizers and a number of authors his publishing house was planning to send to the November affair. As the conversation continued, I ended up in a corner of the room with the gay agent, who happened to be enchanting, and the wife of the UM professor, who was both attractive and intriguing.

I wanted to know about the agent's doings, who he was representing and how successful he'd been getting his writers published. He mentioned he represented a few struggling or aspiring authors, and three or four others who were his real bread winners, although he admitted he had to do other things to supplement his income. The group was in a joyous mood and the conversation quickly turned into our initial aspirations in life and what had become of us after a few encounters with reality. The agent mentioned he wanted to be a ballet dancer, but ended up being a teacher in Florida. He used his major in English to shop a friend's book and got it published. The intriguing lady told us she became a drifter after college and — thanks to a generous father — worked in a few art galleries in New York and Rome. Then she met her professor — in Rome of all places — ten years ago, married him and moved down to Florida where he was offered a position at University of Miami. All of a sudden it was my time to talk and I gave them a sanitized version of my life. An aspiring tenor, a student activist, a revolutionary pamphleteer, a successful and then failed businessman, but all along, wanting to write for the movies and above all a novel, a big opus that would grant me immortality, I said, with grandiloquence.

"What about?" the agent quickly interrupted.

"Chance, human relations, suicide," I responded.

"Suicide?" the surprised lady asked. "Would you kill yourself?"

"Why not? Under certain conditions, of course. Sickness, no way out."

"You mentioned Camus before and he said suicide is absurd," she retorted.

"I agree! I think suicide without a reason would be absurd. I wouldn't like to leave this world ahead of time. Obviously at this stage of my life, it would be absurd, I have nowhere to go."

"I agree with you," the agent interrupted. "I'm Jewish and don't believe in anything. But I wouldn't kill myself. I'm an unabashed coward."

We all laughed.

"So tell me, what would you write about?" the agent insisted.

"Make me happy," I said. "That syndrome in human relations that denies our own responsibility in seeking or attaining happiness, but often blame others for our lack of it. It is a story about a man who longed for a 'final judgment,' so he could square accounts or settle scores with a number of relatives, romantic attachments and business individuals he had met during his life."

"Have you written any of the stuff?"

"I have several chapters already."

"Could I read the first one?" the agent asked me.

"Yes, I'd like to read it too," the lady added.

Charles, who was at a short distance from our group and looked more interested in our conversation than the one he was having, switched groups.

"I'm not ready to let a professional read it yet. I don't know if it's good enough," I said faking a bit of humility.

"Oh, it's good enough," Charles interrupted. "I'm one of his readers and I think Alex's take is a different approach to that kind of story. It needs tweaking, of course, it's only a first draft, but it could be a great book."

"I'd be delighted to be the first one to have a crack at your story," the agent said. "By what Charles says, you have a winner."

Charles' dinner was a welcome respite to my limited activities. But on Monday, I promptly went to the office of one of Burt's recommended lawyers. I had met many and was so used to the niceties of an eager lawyer, nothing they could say would move me. Nevertheless this new fellow was about my age, knew my story well, seemed really interested in my affairs and we discussed my prospects and the list of hungry creditors. I felt at ease with the esquire. Most lawyers make you believe they have your salvation at hand — even when they know they don't — and I was confident enough to tell him that, in a day or two, I'd have an answer.

I came home and found three letters from five of the companies I had sent my resume to. They were all well impressed with my qualifications, said they needed no one at the present time, but offered to keep my life story on file in the event they needed someone like me in the future.

Even if disappointed I looked at the positive side. It was a beautiful sunny afternoon, and although compelled to take advantage of it, intrigued by the agent's interest, I sat at my computer and reread my opus first chapter. Something was missing, I concluded. It needed more work and this wasn't the proper time for that. Why not finish the first draft and come back for a rewrite? And I put it aside.

A week went by, my bankruptcy papers were ready to file and I told my lawyer to go ahead and file. The other two companies I had sent my resume to responded negatively, leaving me with no possible job in that segment of the industry where I thought I could find one.

Ben called me a little later this morning.

"Did you hear?"

"What?" I answered.

"The Alsace. They fired Tessier. There was an urgent meeting of the Board of Directors and they fired him. They named the same CEO he had staged his coup against, six years ago, to replace him."

"Where did you hear that?"

"The cable channel. Just five minutes ago. A spokesman for the Alsace, speaking off the record, said the directors decided to fire him in anticipation of a shareholders' revolt prior to their annual meeting in two weeks. The Directors were probably afraid of losing their own jobs." It is fascinating, Ben continued. "There was a slate of new candidates headed by the fellow they named CEO. Very clever, they took the leader of the opposing slate, made him CEO and squelched the revolt."

"I wish they'd have done it sooner though" I told Ben. "Three months ago it'd have meant a world of difference. Now it is too late, I'm filing bankruptcy papers as we speak."

A month passed. Having filed for bankruptcy and disposed of all my creditors' claims, I felt at ease although concerned with my future. Maxine's condition had not changed much, her vital signs continued to be strong although she remained paralyzed. Fortunately, Yolanda was still at her job and determined to keep at it. On my other flank, my parents were also going strong, although with the same degenerating ailments. I had no job offers, my bank account was getting thinner. I felt frustrated, but fortunately healthy with a good sense of humor and determined to survive.

If my prospects of coming out of my slump seemed distant, this morning I felt — for the first time in quite a while — the winds of change blowing at my doors. I had hung up the telephone with Cogswell who had gotten me a new contact with real estate investors in Costa Rica and had scheduled a meeting in New York for next Tuesday. If that new prospect wasn't enough, on the mischievous side, I had also been savoring the Alsace's crumbling debacle and Tessier's demise. He hadn't been only summarily dismissed, but made to look like a clown in the press, both in France and the United States.

Thinking of Tessier's demise, the info I was looking for I couldn't find anywhere. I wanted to know about Natividad's status after the blow out. Frustrated, I called an old contact in Madrid who knew "nothing," but talked about her absence from the social and trade circles the last few months. Nevertheless, my colleague promised to inform me in the event she heard.

Reading about the Alsace's reorganization, I kept searching for news about Chloe. I surmised she had gone down with Tessier and I worried about her well-being. I had never forgotten our brief encounter in Portugal and her revelation about the Alsace and Tessier's intentions to buy Federated. I also felt badly for Sands, whom I didn't consider a bad person but a peon, following his boss' dictates.

As I finished reading the story, I tried to contact Chloe in Paris again. Her telephone number had been changed and the new one was unlisted.

A LA RECHERCHE DU TEMPS PERDU

Although burdened by the last cycle of events, the prospect of a commission — going to Costa Rica again — somehow worked wonders for my psyche. True, the cloud of my bank account was ever present, as money continued to be a missing part of my life's equation. Yet, my will to survive remained intact. I maintained my daily routines making sure I kept fit and my brain wasn't bursting with unnecessary trash. I worked out, walked the beach, continued to visit my parents in New York while, all along, being nurtured and reassured by Julie's unflinching devotion.

The early lights painted the horizon. I struggled to open my eyes and get out of bed, but fell back and had another of my labyrinthine dreams. My subconscious active emptying the dustbin of my mind. But it was morning and I forced my eyes open and stumbled out of bed. I looked out and marveled at my mornings feast; the sunrise, the Atlantic Ocean, the surf, my stoic woods, birds galore and the elderly couple walking the beach; paradise.

It was also a new chapter, I concluded. I drank my espresso and went down to the beach for another walk to "El Farito." The beach was deserted; a few gulls kept me company as I began my walk with no aim. Inevitably, the wide screen of my imagination illuminated and, in quick succession, I had a cinemascope review of my present day's saga. My thoughts overwhelmed me but, as I walked, the film changed, the past was erased, and my thoughts and sights evolved into my future. My mind, as if by magic, fast forwarded six months and I pictured myself finishing my novel, finding an editor who'd love it, would hand me a check to do a rewrite and I would fly to Rome, away from my regular surroundings, with the peace of mind necessary to put my opus to rest.

"Alex, Alex!" I heard.

I saw what looked like a familiar figure approaching me from the forest, a hundred feet away. I was surprised. The beach was deserted ten seconds ago and now I saw this man rushing across the sand calling my name. It was Paul, I surmised, the same fellow I had met months ago walking the beach. There was no doubt. He was tall and thin, with long white hair. Anyone familiar with the scriptures could visualize him as one of those prophets of doom announcing the end of the world in our lifetime. And I stopped and waited for him to join me.

"Man, I haven't seen you in ages. Where have you been?" I asked him.

"I'm always around," he said casually.

"I haven't seen you."

"Because you haven't taken the time to look around you," he complained.

"Me? I know every branch of each and every tree in that forest."

"It seems you're missing something. Anyway, it would be difficult to explain, I know, but tell me, how have you been?"

"Good! I can't complain," I said putting my best foot forward.

"I'm glad to see you again. You look good and relaxed. But, you won't believe this, I have been thinking about you lately."

"Hmm!" I uttered while looking at him closely.

"I was wondering, how did your drama end, if it did?"

"How do you know it ended?"

"It's a figure of speech. Nothing ends. You know that..."

"Yes, I do!"

Somehow I was intrigued to find this fellow again. The fact we had met before, having not seen him for quite a while and now finding him again, in a very similar circumstance, intrigued me even more. His take on life, his faith in the designs of destiny was a challenging proposition that made me think --- even though --- I had come to my own conclusions long ago.

Nevertheless, I enjoyed his kind of mind game — that stimulating give and take that I relish — and is rarely found in a rushed world with little time for reflection.

Together, as we spoke, we continued our walk by the side of the ocean, skirting the lapping surf, as we watched the sun making its way up in the horizon.

"Tell me. I'm anxious to know. Are you happy? Unhappy?" he asked me.

"Resigned, perhaps."

"Oh, that's a great choice of words. Accepting things as they are and not trying to force fate."

"Fate? The last time we met, I remember, you talked about destiny. Do you really believe in predestination, that fate decides everything about our lives?

"Do you have a better explanation?" he asked me, stopping for a moment to address me directly.

"You are accepting fate by default, the same way mankind has surmised the existence of a God by default; for lack of a better explanation."

"Perhaps. Wasn't it Beckett who said, 'God doesn't exist, the bastard?'"

"I wish there would be a God even if he was a bastard," I said. "If one exists, another life would be remote, but possible. An alternative to the void we all go into for sure."

"That's a lot for an atheist to say," Paul added with some irony.

"You know I'm being fictitious. But there is so much absurdity, despair and evil to complain about in this life, we would have a good reason to organize a rebellion. A slave revolt against our master if there were one."

"There you have it. A wish for another life. 'The Revolt of the Masses,' Ortega's masterpiece."

"I have thought of that but in a different fashion. Dreaming of another life, if confronted by a higher up, I would challenge him to an in depth dialog-duel to include Luci, who I'm sure has her own gripes to bitch about."

"That's original. Lucifer, Luci as a woman," Paul added.

"Why not? Paradise Lost. I'm sure if we ask her she would have a lot of arguments about who was right and who was wrong then. I would add a similar kind of gathering with my dear ones, friends and enemies. So many situations go unresolved in real life. A great opportunity for an all-out clash to set the record straight. Could you imagine? A Final Judgment!"

"It sounds great. Still no one has ever offered a theory about how things happen or why they happen. As long as there is none, fate is as good as anyone else. It might not be scientific, but..."

"How about chance?"

"Chance? Yes, chance of course. But I don't think chance alone could explain what happened to you."

"I haven't said a word about what happened."

"You said you were resigned. I'd assume resigned with an outcome you didn't expect. Believe me, the story you told me was so engrossing, I have been thinking about you ever since we met months ago. I wish you'd tell me what happened if you don't mind. Tell me."

And perhaps eager to find an explanation to my mayhem other than the curse, if there was one, I thought of sharing my saga with this fellow who seems to be wise and have no particular reason not to give me anything other than his honest take on my quandary.

"I lost."

"Are you sure?"

"Everything came to an abrupt end with the trial. Years of hope and anticipation collapsed and new worries emerged; financial ruin, sicknesses, a malaise all around me."

"Perhaps it is too soon to understand the real outcome of your drama."

"I doubt it. It's history and continues to develop as we speak!"

"Ah history... History according to whom? You mean fate?"

"I lost everything."

"I'm sorry to hear that! I vaguely remember our conversation. Time is corrosive, you know. Why don't you tell me again?"

And I went ahead and told him the sequence of events. The myriad of incidents that, together, made possible the debacle.

"There you have it," he said when I finished. "One after the other.... Fate!"

We were walking the beach taking turns speaking, challenging each other's ideas. A mano a mano, you might say, trying to make sense of the unthinkable. It would have been a perfect scene for a movie, I thought. Like the last shot of Bergman's Seventh Seal. Death leading a chain-gang of characters in the picture.

"I have to confess," I continued. "I feel embarrassed rehashing these events."

"We all need to talk and attempt to make sense of what pains us. Talking to me, you're really talking to yourself and you know that. You can regurgitate your story one more time, not afraid of ridicule. But that's another story. Let's talk about your femme fatale... Natividad? What ever happened to her?"

"It's remarkable you remember her name."

"You mentioned it, I'm sure. Besides, it's a beautiful name; it has to do with Nativity, Christmas. It is the same in Spanish, isn't it?"

"You also speak Spanish?

"Un poquito. I've been around Alex, you should surmise that. But tell me about Nati."

"Coincidentally, I just heard about her and her partner."

"Good news?" Paul asked me.

"You won't believe this.... to start, the old man..."

"Zamora?" he interrupted.

"The old man had a heart attack when he heard the Alsace's new board of directors wasn't going to make good on the two hundred million they owed him. He was counting on the balance to complete a new acquisition."

"What a turn of events. If you ask me, he's probably in Hell. I read about The Alsace CEO losing his job. What's his name?

"Tessier," I responded.

"And your friend, his lady assistant... Chloe?"

"I wish I know something about her... she probably went down with Tessier. The whole group got fired. But I heard about Natividad..."

"The femme fatale," Paul interjected.

"Natividad took a sabbatical, married a fellow designer, found him in bed with another man, divorced him and fled Barcelona ahead of the paparazzi."

"I told you that lady was bad news. What ever happened to your South American plantation owner? What role did he play in all this?"

"You won't believe this. He took Margarita, his mistress, back. Did I also mention her? Well, he forgave her."

"Chicken between two," Paul said with a quip. "Why not? He followed your advice."

"The list of casualties is unbelievable," I continued. "André died of Aids, Zamora had a heart attack, Natividad lost her business, Tessier was fired, and Federated was sold back to its American original owners. I declared bankruptcy; my bankers lost their jobs. It's a horror show, isn't it?"

"The valley of the fallen," Paul interrupted. "Whatever happened to your crooked lawyers?"

"You mean, Pete and Rudy?

"I don't remember their names."

"They broke up. Pete remarried his ex-wife. Eight months later, she ran away again, with another guy, and Pete went into a deep depression. Their practice nosedived. Rudy tricked Pete into surrendering his half and they ended up in court suing each other, while facing a number of malpractice suits."

"Their own greed came to haunt them."

"It's a Greek tragedy alright. I had a comfortable life. All those characters and situations materialized as if by magic, one after the other, then the alchemist exercised his magic and — after the damage was thoroughly inflicted — all those characters vanished, the same way they originally materialized. As if they just got together just to screw me."

"And you claim to be the one with the curse?" Paul asked ironically. "Perhaps one of those characters was the one with the curse and you played a role in his or hers perfect storm."

I cracked up. It is true. What if what he said is true? I was collateral damage and not the main character in the drama. I immediately thought of Bergman and Woody filming my life, each at one end of my heroic tale.

"You must feel morally devastated…?" Paul asked me.

"Crushed, is a better word. I saw it coming and I couldn't stop it."

"And now?"

"I don't know. I am an amateur philosopher… a dilettante if you wish. I lost six, perhaps seven years of my life that I will never recover. Early on in my youth I became aware of the passing of time. Since then it has been a race against time, death if you wish. I knew I'll eventually lose it, but I wanted to live as fully as I could and confront death on my terms, as Sisyphus did, if I could."

"You and your Sisyphus metaphor. Sisyphus tried to outwit fate and look what happened to him. Zeus doomed him to roll the boulder forever," he added.

"I know. I'm also rolling a heavy one myself. Life is absurd. The struggle is such a waste. Whether we win or lose, nothing matters at the end. We will be gone, kaput, finito. Does it make sense?"

"I see your point," Paul interjected.

"We are an accident, Paul. A product of nature like a plant, a fly, bacteria. And like them we pop up, enjoy a brief stay and disappear as if we haven't ever existed.

"There is no alternative to that," Paul said.

"Suicide; exiting on our own terms."

"Come on Alex. Dante's seventh circle is crowded already. He doesn't need another suicide. Look, if you ask me, you might be hit with a heart attack and have no time to load your gun."

"Of course. Chances are, we'd leave this world not realizing we are already gone, dead. That's why suicide is the ideal way. You would be conscious to the last moment, listening to Wagner's 'Liebestod' or Sinatra's 'My Way' while observing our life's trail; to see if it all made sense."

We had walked a slow mile and a half to the lighthouse in an hour and some. Instinctively we looked at each other and without saying a word, walked to the rocks, sat and the conversation continued unabated. The lighthouse was behind us, silent, but reassuring. The surroundings were inviting; the woods framed the tower with a green radiance and the gulls, circling for fish, gave it a sort of magical realism. An inviting scenario for reminiscing and dreaming of better things to come.

"Has the storm abated?" Paul asked.

"The storm has left me in a swamp. Obviously we all get ill sooner or later; it's natural, but it isn't the ailment in itself, but its corrosive effects on everyone close to the ill-fated victim."

"You're referring to your parents' and your wife's situations," Paul interrupted me.

"My elderly parents in New York, my wife here in Florida, a short walk away from us. In both cases the impact of their particular events would have been enough to end with a short outcome. But in both situations — after overcoming insurmountable odds — their maladies have acquired lives of their own. They survived and they could go on, unabated, for years to come; short of a miracle, of course."

"The miracle being?" Paul asked.

"Death! I can't believe I said that," I added.

"Walk away. Just forget it. You've had enough. Walk away!"

I looked at Paul and my alter ego interrupted. *Is he crazy? He makes it sound so easy. Of course we wished we could walk away. Escape is even better. But how? Ask him.*

"Are you serious?"

"Yes!" Paul answered. "Walk away, you have free will."

"Free will is such hogwash," I said. "Did you decide to come to this world? Aren't we all forced to deal with constantly changing situations? All we can do is to choose between a poor choice and a worse one. But we wouldn't be who we are if we walk away, as you suggested, and leave our own stranded."

"I understand," Paul said. "I'm talking about the sacrifice."

"No doubt. A high price to pay for duty," I said. "To think the precious years we have left are going to be consumed worrying and taking care of a love one with no chance of making it on its own; it's maddening."

"It seems André and his curse had you all tied down, or is it fate?" Paul asked me.

"Perhaps. I only know everything I was told would happen, happened."

"Do you believe that kind of cult could exist?"

"It's bizarre, I admit. But how could I believe in witchcraft if I belief all it's the product of chance. That there is no God. We are alone, Paul. Alone!"

"How do you explain it then?" Paul asked me.

"I don't know. Chance? Chance is a game of sorts with no rules and an unknown end. You can say it is absurd. It really is."

"My guess is, you'll have to wait to the end of days, as you say, to find out. But keep in mind, whether you attain that eureka moment or not, it doesn't prove or disprove the adventure wasn't preordained." Paul responded.

"You sound like my friend Julie. I only know we showed up here by chance, as if coming from a void and we will return to an eternal one when we die."

"You're a pessimist," Paul said. "Think of the Pascal's wager."

"Do you believe in heaven?" I asked him.

"Why not? I'd preach it if I were an evangelist. People can't live without hope. I'm not talking about a religion in particular, but hope in general. Hope is hope. The feeling that somebody is ready to give you a hand."

"Santa Claus!"

"Think of it. You close your eyes and say, please help me! And immediately you surmise help is on its way.... It relieves the pressure, even if nothing happens. Most people other than you believe that," Paul argued.

"If I tell you," I said taking a philosophical stance. "It's tough to be under siege and not feel tempted. I once visited the Reims Cathedral with its impressive high gothic arches reaching for heaven, magnificent rose-windows, huge carvings and art in each and every altar. It was dark and empty but there was a chorus rehearsing chants that late afternoon. At that moment, I felt, if there was a God he must have been there somewhere, and if he was, why didn't he talk to us. The ancient architects tricked mankind. They built those huge cathedrals, Bach composed heavenly music, artists painted masterpieces, altogether architectural gems, places where --- if people wished --- they could find Him. I never asked for help, but I was grateful for the idea of a God that inspired so many treasures. If you ask me, when you put it all together, God was the only one missing."

"Now that we've explored all those esoteric themes, does your experience make you believe that kind of thing could be real?" Paul asked me.

"I don't know. I only know, everything I was told would happen, happened."

"How do you explain Julie?" Paul asked me.

"I have no explanation for her. Perhaps, if guardian angels exist, she is my guardian angel alright! Other than that, she's my other yo. An indispensable part of my life. I don't know how I'd have come this far without her."

"What's ahead for you?" Paul asked me.

"Are you asking me? For me tomorrow is too late. It always was. The future? I'd give anything to know. Wouldn't you?"

"Would you really want to know? Or would you rather follow the dream? You're a dreamer Alejandro. That's a gift. Whether it goes far, or doesn't go far at all, it doesn't matter, it won't last anyway; everything is fleeting. Concentrate on your dream. As long as you're able to dream - and abstract yourself from reality - you'll always be young, rich and probably happy, no matter what happens. After all it's foolish to fight the tide. Just dream! Your dreams will take you to the end of time, regardless."

I don't know how or why, but that was the last I heard Paul say. At that moment there was a commotion on the beach and I turned around to watch a group of gypsies getting into the water. When I got back to Paul, or whatever his name is, he had disappeared. He said no good bye, I'll see you around, nothing. He disappeared among a group of bathers and I think, the last I saw of him, he was going through the woods.

Frustrated, I began to walk back to my building with the sun one third up in the sky and getting hotter. The beach was still half empty and, other than a blue heron searching for crab, I had no company. As I walked away from the lighthouse, I felt somewhat disappointed. My conversation with Paul lasted, I don't know, one and a half two hours, but I didn't want it to end; I thought it had been inconclusive. He went away before I could ask him for another round, another opportunity to get together again and continue what we started. Nevertheless, I felt at ease. As if I had a concluded a séance where I revisited my life, reencountered all those characters that somehow had a role shaping it and concluded, if mistakes were made, most of the things I had done, — at one time or another — made sense, and I'd do them again if confronted with the same set of circumstances. If anything, I was more certain than ever that chance and circumstance were the main architects of our lives. There was a weird moment though, when Paul talked about quitting, forsaking our own. It struck me as insensitive coming from such an insightful, good natured man who conducted himself like an evangelist, with his white beard and long hair and acted professorially with his challenging discourse. But the more I thought about it, I saw Paul as Socrates, challenging a disciple to come up with an answer, eliciting a philosophical discourse about my life in particular and helping me define my response to one of its enduring challenges; dependency and commitment. It was obviously a conversation to be continued, but when, who knows.

As I put more distance between me and the lighthouse, my thoughts returned to the mundane chores and obligations that permeated my life. It was almost eleven and I had to get back home and check out Maxine's condition, pacify mother with a telephone call, put some checks in the mail before my creditors resorted to new threats and spend the afternoon preparing some numbers for my meeting with Cogswell's new contacts.

Once at home, I thought of Julie and decided to call her first.

"Hey!"

"How is my Sisyphus doing?" she asked me.

"I don't know! As my saying goes, 'no matter what happens, nothing happens!' I was walking the beach and --- out of nowhere again --- Paul reappeared. Remember, the gospel type of guy I met eight or nine months ago? Well, we walked the beach again and had another long, exhausting conversation --- something like Proust's "In Search of Lost Time." That kind of regurgitation. Then, you aren't going to believe this, but when the conversation ended, while I turned around to watch a group of gypsies going into the water fully clothed, Paul disappeared. No goodbye, I'll see you around; no nothing. I was shocked. Had I not spent almost two hours talking to this man, listening to him pontificate about the power of dreaming, I could swear the whole time I had been talking to myself."

"If you ask me," Julie said, "it is as if you had dreamed the whole thing. This man Paul, could be the product of your imagination. Somebody you needed to sort out your thoughts and your life — as when you were a kid and had an imaginary friend — whom no one but you could see. You're so lucky Alejandro Faust... It is so wonderful to be able to dream."

ROME .... of all places.

ACKNOWLEDGMENTS

This book would not have been possible without the help of a few friends. One in particular did the most; Sonya Strikowski who read and reread my rewrites, edited and argued for certain passages in the book and was frustrated the occasions when I disagreed with her. Thanks to her encouragement and dedication this book is seeing the light of day. To her, my eternal gratitude.

I'm grateful to my friend Lillian Castaneda, who read assiduously portions of the original manuscript, before it was finally divided into shorter and more concise chapters --- We had long reading sessions topped by dinners at different restaurants in Miami. Lillian offered different suggestions.

I'm also grateful to Ursula Schiftan, my Argentinian "philosopher" friend --- who I baptized as "Nietzsche's great-great granddaughter," --- who read the whole manuscript avidly, made different suggestions and considered "briefly" to translate a chapter or two, to the German language.

My thanks to Levent Tugrul who also read each of the chapters, --- in its original, disorganized format --- and made some clever and important observations. To Gary Fischer who helped me identify and organize, briefly, all the characters in the story. And last but not least, my thanks to Marilyn Pollio, my psychologist friend, who also read the first draft and likewise made some appropriate observations.

And finally --- In Memoriam to Robert (Bob) Rothman --- who was the first person who read the very first things that I ever wrote and patiently sat and suggested long and detailed changes to my writings. Unfortunately Bob passed-away before I finished the first draft of the novel. "Thank you Bob." Rest in peace.